D1190947

WHEN DARKNESS FALLS

WHEN DARKNESS FALLS

a Violet Darger novel

L.T. VARGUS & TIM MCBAIN

WHEN
DARKNESS
FALLS

PROLOGUE

The music blared, generic hard rock pumping out of the boombox speakers and echoing funny in the cavernous hall of the logging cabin. The reverb on the snare fluttered like 1986 was alive and well, if only on the stereo.

John Ellinger adjusted his baseball cap and staggered over the plank flooring. Wove his way through the rows of bunk beds. A few of the mattresses were occupied despite the blasting music, the blankets bulging with the shapes of the bodies beneath them, but most lay empty.

Home sweet home.

Some three dozen lumberjacks, nearly all of them men, bedded down here every night for weeks at a time — an isolated camp, way out in the Alaskan wilderness. Chopping down trees by day. Sleeping in a rack of bunk beds by night. Just another way to make a living.

It was late, closing in on 2 A.M. The whole crew had the day off tomorrow. A few had made the hour-long drive into the nearest town. Most, out of sheer exhaustion, had stayed in and capped their long workday with drinks. And drinks. And more drinks.

Ellinger lifted his cap again, smoothed his hair and brought the hat back down. Then he blinked and focused on the dark rectangle in the distance. The door wavered there, its blurred state leaving it more a concept than a full-blown reality for the moment, at least to Ellinger's perception. Still, he was getting there — a little slower than he'd like, but he was getting there.

Jake Jordan was currently puking his guts out in the

1

restroom. He was a loud vomiter. A screamer. One of those people who heaved from the gut — put their whole body into it — and somehow used the toilet bowl as a kind of acoustic amplifier. Projecting the retching sounds like a porcelain megaphone.

That rendered the bathroom a no-go, at least in Ellinger's mind. Even if there were free urinals and stalls to be had, he wasn't traipsing in there for a piss while Jordan bellowed into the next toilet over like a goddamn opera singer. No thanks. Even as drunk as he was, he maintained enough self-respect to avail himself of that cringe-fest.

He would go outside and whiz on a tree trunk instead. Not a problem.

He shuffled toward the fluctuating door. Blinked again like that might help the damn thing hold steady. Leaned an elbow on one of the bunk frames when his balance wobbled. Kept going.

Another tortured howl shot out of the bathroom and echoed around the cabin. Deep-throated werewolf screams ricocheting off the walls and pinging out of the corners.

"He's fightin' it," a voice next to Ellinger said.

"Huh?"

Cyrus Haywood sat up. His face rising from the shadows on one of the bunks nearby, moving into the light. His hound dog eyes blinked once within the paunch of his haggard face, those dark eyes looking wet and somehow wise to Ellinger. Reddish hair hung down toward his chin in strands, a little greasy as always.

A hand-rolled cigarette dangled from Haywood's mouth, bobbed up and down when he spoke.

"Jordan." He tilted his head toward the restroom. "He's fightin' the urge to hurl. That's his problem. You've gotta, you know, let it out. Go with the flow and whatever."

Ellinger squinted. Struggled to process the words.

"Uh, yeah. I guess."

"Like my nephew, he does that. Fights it when he needs to puke. Spends all day with his belly achin' rather than lettin' it out. And then the second he starts to fall asleep — BAM! Pukes all over hisself. But he's six. Jake Jordan is a full-grown man, *supposedly*, and he hasn't learned this shit. You puke, you feel better. It's how the digestive system works. That's a scientific fact."

Ellinger didn't know how to respond, so he bobbed his head once. Kept sort of climbing his way along the bunk frames, working hand over hand.

"You got a boy of your own back in Maryland, don't you?" Haywood said. "Zach or Zane or something like 'at, right?"

The image of his son flashed in Ellinger's head before he answered. Dark hair and eyes. Freckles on his cheeks.

"Zeke."

"Zeke. That's right. How old is he?"

"Eight. His birthday was last week."

And he hated again that he was here, thirty-four hundred miles away on the opposite coast, while his boy was growing up, becoming himself. Each day that he missed was one that he'd never get back. Birthday parties. Ball games. Sand sifting through the hourglass, the time ticking down to zero.

Ellinger did it for the pay. He could make more out here logging for three months than a whole year at any job back home. Save up to make sure Zeke could go to whatever college he wanted. That was the dream, right? Do this backbreaking work so the kid would never have to. Set him up on a better path and let him go, like teaching him how to ride a bike and watching him roll away.

But was it the right move? He didn't know.

He'd found the line between happiness and suffering almost comically thin in his life, the two never as far apart as he'd imagined they would be. Likewise, he'd learned that the path forward was perpetually murky, unknowable. He never knew if the moves he chose were the right ones.

When he was young, he'd thought that the *right move* would look clearer with age, experience granting wisdom or perception. Now? He was pretty sure nobody knew what they were doing.

Haywood hit his cigarette. The cherry flared bright red and sizzled a second. Then he plucked the smoke from his lips and pointed it and the two fingers around it at Ellinger.

"Where you off to?"

Ellinger nodded toward that door, which still shimmered like a mirage in his bleary eyes.

"Gotta take a leak."

Haywood nodded and stood.

"I'll go with ya."

Ellinger blinked.

"Um. OK. But you're going to need to, uh, get your own tree."

Haywood tilted his head back and laughed. Then he nodded.

Ellinger licked his lips. A little confused. Drunken thoughts plodded through his head.

Guess he thought it was a joke.

Whatever, dude.

Bottom line: I ain't sharing a tree. Not with him or anyone else.

Haywood led the way now. Opened the door. Then he looked back and raised his eyebrows as Ellinger struggled to walk the few paces to get outside.

"Not much of a drinker, huh, Ellinger?"

"What?"

"Tequila really got to you guys. Between you and Jordan, I mean. Jesus Christ."

Ellinger staggered through the doorway. Stepped out under the yellow porch light. Some part of his mind saw the bulb's tint and thought: *Caution.*

He careened over the wooden deck. Death-gripped the handrail as he stumbled down the steps.

And then he spilled out into the gravel below. Stepped out from under the awning all at once.

The sky opened overhead, heavens yawning just beyond the bill of his ball cap. That vast black nothingness reaching out to eternity, dotted with the brightness of the moon and stars.

He took a deep breath. Felt the crisp mountain atmosphere as it coated his throat and lungs. It took a second for the chill swirl in the air to get through to Ellinger's nerves, but at last his skin felt the sting of it. Cold as a beer out of the way back of the refrigerator.

They tromped over the dirt and rock of the lot. Advanced toward the darker line where the towering spruce and hemlock trees took over the land.

Ellinger found another tangle of confused words leaving his mouth. He pointed off to the left.

"OK. I'm, uh, headed this way. Right in here. By myself."

Haywood laughed again. A rich belly laugh this time, like a toddler or maybe Santa Claus.

"Holy hell, Ellinger. I know you're awful worried that I'm hankering to whiz in close quarters with ya, but I'll give you a wide berth, man. Jesus, dude. It's gonna be alright."

Ellinger stared at the dark blur of Haywood's face for a

second.

"OK."

Then he crossed into the gloom.

☾

His eyes bloom in the darkness. Wet stones peering out of his skull.

He waits.

And he watches the cabin through a patchwork of greenery. Leaves bobbing in the breeze in the foreground.

He stands just inside the cover of the woods. Creeper wrapped around his feet. Boughs nestled about his shoulders.

Still and quiet, he waits. Grits his teeth. His hand flexes on the grip of his weapon. Ready.

The cold surrounds him. Envelops him. An ever deeper chill coiling everywhere as the night grows more and more frigid.

But heat radiates from his chest, from his arms. Rolls off the top of his head like steam.

The cold can't touch him. Never could. Never will.

Muffled music booms inside the logging cabin. Song after song leaking past. Sounding muddy through the walls, through the wooden siding. Each track cutting or fading out, the stereo taking a breath before it switches to the next. Counting down the minutes.

Through it all, he waits.

Waits.

Eyes and ears sharp. Focus never drifting.

At last the door swings open. A slice of the cabin's interior is laid bare.

He hears the tinny sound of the music funneling through

the open doorway. And then it cuts back to that deadened hum as the door closes.

Two figures drift through the pool of yellow light on the porch. Morph into silhouettes as they pass under the bulb.

His field of vision seems to zoom in on them. Pushing through the strands of plumage dangling from the branches around him.

They stumble down the steps. Start across the lot. Feet stabbing the gravel with sharp crunches.

One of them walks funny. Wobbling. Drunk.

And they're loud. Practically yelling about tequila and pissing and wide berths.

When they near the edge of the woods, just a few feet shy of his position, he crouches. Allows the foliage to cover him up to the shoulders.

So close now. So close.

He waits.

☾

Haywood had just zipped up when he heard it.

A high-pitched whimper emitted from Ellinger's area. Sounded like a kitten or puppy or something, but he knew it wasn't. Knew it by the way the goosebumps rippled over his skin, all the follicles drawing taut in a wave that traveled over his body.

He wheeled his head around. Stared into that dark section of the woods. Didn't see much more than the outlines of the tree trunks jutting up out of the dirt, even the branches and leaves somehow impossible to discern in the charcoal smears there.

"Ellinger?"

His voice came out smaller than he liked. Made him feel dumb. Preemptively embarrassed.

He thought about all the times in life he'd been a little spooked, frozen like a rabbit in the quiet, in the dark, and it had always turned out to be nothing.

This time would be the same. Exactly the same. It had to.

Probably tripped. Fell down or got tangled up in some deadfall and snapped his ankle.

He could picture Ellinger. The dark blue baseball cap on his head. The slumped posture. The glazed-over look in his eyes.

Jesus. First, this asshole thinks I want to watch him take a piss. Now he goes and pulls this shit.

This time his voice came out confident, solid.

"Ellinger. Whatsamatter, buddy? You end up needing to drop a deuce or what? 'Cause I can go get toilet paper. Not a problem."

He took a few choppy steps that way. And the fear returned quickly. Crept up his spine again like a cold spider.

He slowed. Took more care with his stride. Quieter.

He reached the area where he was pretty sure Ellinger had been, but he couldn't see anything. He scanned the darkness. Tense. Quiet. If the drunken idiot was there, either standing or sprawled in the weeds, Haywood could detect no trace of him.

His fingers fished into his jacket pocket. Pried out his lighter. Flicked it.

The tiny flame beat back a small sphere of darkness. He lifted it. Swept his arm around. Wielded his minuscule torch to and fro.

The orange light glinted on the undergrowth. Leaves and fronds and stems and stalks. Their shadows twitching around them as the glow moved.

The flame guttered out, and the darkness swelled again.

Stronger than before.

He swore under his breath and relit the Zippo. An orange peak jumping from the lighter's mouth.

There.

A glistening spot on a birch trunk. Dark and wet. Ellinger had been here alright.

But he wasn't now.

Haywood instinctively took a step back. Licked his lips and felt the frigid air assail the wet flesh right away. Violently cold the way only an Alaskan night could be.

He wanted to call out again. Wanted to yell for Ellinger, for anyone.

But his throat wouldn't budge. The valve at the back of his mouth clamped tight.

He turned around. Ready to scoot back to the cabin.

A dark spot on the ground caught the corner of his eye. He wrenched his head down. Stared.

Ellinger's hat lay at his feet. The dome of the ball cap crushed flat into the dirt where someone had stepped on it.

☾

At the first gray of predawn light, Haywood bustled out the cabin door. Most of the other lumberjacks fell in behind him, some thirty-two total pounding down the wooden steps.

The search began. Many men and a handful of women splaying into the woods. A disorganized manhunt.

Haywood beat his way through the thicket. Swinging arms. Kicking legs. The brush swishing out of his way in little green explosions.

After looking around the best he could in the black of night, he'd huddled with the others in the cabin for the last two hours of darkness. No one had slept. On edge. Unsure how to proceed.

Ellinger was still out there in the woods. Somewhere.

Maybe he'd passed out in the weeds. Sleeping off his drunk, facedown in a sprawling bed of creeper or some such. That seemed the most likely explanation, the only thing that had kept them from calling the cops.

But Haywood's gut told him otherwise, especially now that he was out here, stomping through the roughage.

Something had gone wrong. It was no dark flicker of his imagination this time, no mistaking mere shadows for monsters. This was real darkness, real life.

And even before the final revelation came, a bereft feeling settled over his being. A heaviness in the belly. A floating feeling inside his head. His mind, his being, disconnected from his body. Disconnected from the others.

All alone in a dark, dark wood.

The gloom under the canopy still clung to the last of the night, the shadows deeper here. Weak light trickled through the translucent leaves. Made the green wedges look like they were glowing above — organic Christmas lights.

He stepped through a tightly knitted stand of firs into an open place, the land clear and flat here. And then his feet stopped beneath him.

It was there.

The bloody stump hovered in the distance. Skewered on a pole. Dead center in the open area as though put on display. *Impaled.*

All naked flesh. A milk-white sheet of skin. Bled pale.

The arms, legs, and head had been removed. Leaving the bare torso there on the stick.

Yawing wounds where the limbs and skull used to be.

Something ragged in the way the pieces had come off. Tattered meat.

Haywood's middle flexed and then went still. Whole body gone rigid. Upright. Frozen.

He could only stand and stare. Breathless. In awe.

He didn't blink. Didn't move.

Footsteps crunched toward him. Sets of shoulders soon occupying both sides of him.

Then more footfalls. And more again. A bunch of the others clustering there to behold the image.

Ellinger's limbless and headless body. A man reduced to a wounded block suspended upright. A trunk on a stick.

What was left of his anatomy had been crafted into a spectacle here, some kind of brutal showmanship at play. Astonishing. Audacious. Striking and profane.

None of them could look away.

No words were spoken. A few gasps, and then quiet.

They held still and gaped. Shocked and hollow. Some awful kind of wonder shuddering through the ranks.

Haywood could feel it like a cold ripple in the air.

That wave of silent revulsion touching all of them.

CHAPTER 1

The jet engines throbbed, doing their best to lull Special Agent Violet Darger back to sleep. The flight from Seattle to Ketchikan, Alaska, was just under two hours long, and Darger had slept for most of it, only waking now as they made their final descent. She peered out the window, hoping for a glimpse of the forested scenery, but a haze of white clouds blotted out the view for now.

She turned to Loshak and found him gazing into his bag of complimentary pretzels. The corners of his mouth were turned down in what she took to be concern or perhaps disgust.

"What's wrong? You find a cockroach in your Rold Golds or something?"

"No," Loshak said, pressing his lips into a hard line. "I was just kicking myself for not grabbing a Cinnabon when we were at Sea-Tac."

Darger snorted, then realized he was serious.

They landed a few minutes later, and Darger scrunched down in her seat to better see out the window.

The concrete walls of the Ketchikan International Airport lay almost flat to the land — an architectural pancake, tiny by airport standards. The building sprawled in front of a rolling green hill, the structure somehow looking all the more deflated situated next to the natural peak.

"Well, this might officially be the dinkiest airport I've ever encountered," she said, studying the building. "It's smaller than my high school."

Loshak leaned over to catch a glimpse.

"I flew into Great Falls once. Montana. Airport there might have been smaller. Hard to say."

"I wouldn't hold out much hope for a Cinnabon," Darger teased.

There was a bulky knee brace on Loshak's left knee which he rubbed absently.

"Yeah. You're probably right," he said, his face grave.

The plane came to a stop, and an electronic ping sounded as the *fasten seat belts* light turned off. Darger clambered out of her seat and pulled the cane from the overhead compartment, handing it to Loshak so he'd have an easier time getting up. He'd had knee surgery a few weeks ago and was still on the mend.

"When did you become such a Cinnabon freak?" she asked as he groaned and pushed himself to his feet.

"It doesn't have to be a Cinnabon. I'd settle for a Danish. Or an apple fritter."

They shuffled down the aisle, and Darger chuckled to herself.

"Does Jan have you on some sort of sugar-free diet or something? Got you craving the hard stuff now that you're out on your own?"

"No. Why?" His eyes went wide. "Oh! You know what else sounds good? Banana bread!"

In lieu of a jet bridge, a set of metal steps was connected to the side of the plane, allowing them to disembark straight out onto the tarmac.

Being asleep most of the flight, Darger had missed the in-flight views, and she was now getting her first look at the Alexander Archipelago. The airport was situated across a small channel from the actual town of Ketchikan, which huddled right on the edge of the water. Docks crisscrossed in front of the buildings, and a small harbor housed clusters of fishing boats and yachts.

The terrain behind the town rose steeply. Nearly every direction Darger turned featured a backdrop of mountains, green with spruce and hemlock.

Loshak paused on the tarmac. He set his suitcase down and unzipped it, pulling out a coat so puffy that his arms stuck out a little bit.

"What's that for?" Darger asked.

"What do you mean? It's Alaska."

"Yeah, but we're headed into the Tongass. A temperate rainforest. The average temperature is still in the 40s and sometimes 50s this time of year."

"But it drops to near-freezing at night."

Darger shrugged.

"I'm more worried about rain than cold. I read that this area gets twice as much rainfall as Seattle."

They followed the other thirty-or-so passengers up a covered stairway and into the airport. As predicted, there was no Cinnabon. No Starbucks or Applebee's either. She spotted a tiny lounge and an even tinier gift shop.

A large bulletin board on one wall featured brochures and fliers for a variety of local activities and attractions. Whitewater rafting. Improv Night at the community playhouse. Sea kayak adventures. An American Indian Arts and Crafts show. Seaplane "flight-seeing" tours. Dinner theater at Dolly's. Eco hiking. A fundraising spaghetti dinner for the Alaska Raptor Center.

Loshak paused in front of the sign for the spaghetti dinner.

"Oh man," he said, licking his lips. "Spaghetti."

Darger started to laugh and then stopped. She grabbed Loshak's arm and turned him so she could stare into his eyes.

As she suspected, his pupils were two tiny pinpoints of black.

"Oh my God. You're high?"

Loshak scoffed.

"No." There was a brief pause, and then he added, "I mean, I'm on painkillers for my knee. But it's a legitimate medication."

"So you're *legitimately* high." She dragged him away from the bulletin board. "Come on. Our guy said he'd be waiting in the lobby."

Their local contact wasn't hard to spot, dressed in his park ranger getup. But as he approached, Darger noted that in addition to the standard tan uniform with Forest Service patches on the sleeves, he also wore a gun belt with a full array of law enforcement accoutrement.

"Are you the folks from the FBI?" he asked.

He was absurdly handsome, almost cartoonishly so. Between the chiseled jaw and dimpled chin, Darger couldn't help but picture Dudley Do-Right. Technically, Do-Right was a Mountie and not a ranger, but close enough.

"That's us," Loshak said. "I'm Agent Loshak. This is my partner, Agent Darger."

Dudley Do-Right extended his hand.

"Officer Henry Bohanon. Forest Service Law Enforcement." He glanced at their suitcases. "You folks all set to go?"

"Lead the way," Loshak said.

They followed Dudley Do-Right outside, across a parking lot, and over to a sheltered path that led down to the water. Darger had to stop thinking of him as Do-Right, or she was liable to accidentally call him the wrong name at some point.

His name is Bohanon, she thought. *Officer Bohanon.*

It was almost 50 degrees outside, but a brisk wind whistled over the water. Darger zipped up her parka and then noticed

Loshak smirking at her.

"Shut it."

It was a three-hour ferry ride to their destination on Prince of Wales Island, but as they stepped onto the wharf, Darger didn't see the ferry. She wondered how long they'd have to wait for it.

Bohanon marched down to the end of the concrete pier, where a yellow floatplane was docked. A pilot bustled around the craft, clearly getting it ready for takeoff, and they were heading straight toward it.

Darger froze. Loshak stopped beside her.

"What's wrong?"

She was still gawking at the seaplane.

"I… assumed we were taking a ferry to the other island."

Loshak followed her gaze and cocked his head to one side.

"Apparently Officer Bohanon arranged for alternate transport."

Darger's nose wrinkled, as if smelling something foul. She hated small planes.

Loshak chuckled and clapped her on the shoulder.

"Welcome to Alaska, Darger."

CHAPTER 2

Darger had expected the plane to rock like a boat, but it was surprisingly stable on the water. Even as they climbed aboard, she only sensed a gentle swaying motion.

It reminded her a little of being on Owen's sailboat. *He'd love this*, she thought.

Still, she was uneasy. She didn't particularly care for flying in general, but at least the big planes were fairly reliable and safe. When a plane did go down, it was almost always one of these little puddle jumpers.

As they stowed their luggage and buckled into their seats, she tried not to think about it. At least they had plenty of room. The plane could seat at least ten people, but it was only the three of them and the pilot.

Fewer lives lost when we crash, Darger thought, then immediately regretted it.

OK. No more of that. Focus on the scenery.

The plane's engines sputtered and built to a roar. The pilot flicked some knobs and switches, and the aircraft lurched into motion.

Darger gripped the armrest, anticipating a bumpy takeoff. Turbulence. Choppiness.

Instead, the plane skimmed over the surface of the water for a few seconds before lifting smoothly into the air. It was, perhaps, the most fluid takeoff she'd ever experienced.

Things only improved once they were in the air. The views were awe-inspiring. Mountains and trees and rugged coastline. She suddenly understood why, despite the remoteness and the

17

extreme weather, people chose to live here. Every angle out the window looked like a painting.

Darger spotted a massive ocean liner on the water below. Headed toward Ketchikan, if she wasn't mistaken.

"Is that a cruise ship?" she asked, craning her neck to see it better.

"Oh, sure. We get them regular on both islands," Bohanon said. "That's one of the main industries here at this point. Tourism. Used to be logging until the USDA adopted the Roadless Rule in 2001."

"The Roadless Rule?"

"Basically said that if there aren't roads already in a national forest, you can't build 'em. And without roads, it's pretty much impossible to cut or transport timber. Kinda killed the logging industry here in the Tongass. The state as a whole went from about 4,000 jobs in saw and pulp mills to less than 400."

"But there are still some logging outfits, clearly."

"A few small ones, here and there. In Klawock, where we're headed, there's one of the last sizable mills in Alaska." Bohanon nodded his head toward the boat still visible out the window. "Anyway, those cruise ships can have 13,000 people on board. When it lands in Ketchikan, it'll essentially double the entire population of the town for a few hours."

"And you said the ships dock on Prince of Wales Island, too?"

"Oh sure," Bohanon said. "Whole population of P.O.W. is under 6,000, so it's a flood of tourists."

Because of his looks, Darger had assumed Bohanon would be kind of macho and cocky, but he had an unexpectedly genial demeanor. Maybe that made sense. A gentle park ranger. Was that a thing?

"So, Forest Service Law Enforcement… does that make you

a ranger or a cop?"

Bohanon's glacier-blue eyes crinkled at the corners.

"Well, I suppose I'm a bit of both."

"And you work alone?".

"I don't have a partner, if that's what you mean, but I do a lot of cooperative work with the various local jurisdictions and the rangers themselves."

"What kind of crimes do you usually investigate?"

"Well, nothing like what we're dealing with right now, I'll tell you that." His brow furrowed. "Mostly we oversee National Forest lands. Make sure any hunting, fishing, and logging are being done legally, with the proper permits and whatnot. Poaching and illegal deforestation are a real concern out here. But there are public safety issues as well. It's rugged country, and sometimes people get into trouble. And it's never what you expect.

"Had a fisherman reported missing by his wife last year. They'd come out every fall to fish the silver salmon run. He'd gone out at the crack of dawn to do his daily fishing. Usually hiked back to their rental cabin for lunch and to drop off his morning catch before heading back out. But he hadn't come in. She waited around a while, but once it got into the late afternoon, she started to worry. That's when I got called in. I had her stay at the cabin with an extra radio in case he showed, and then I headed out to his regular fishing spot a few miles into the bush. Found him halfway down a gully with two broken legs. He'd gone to answer nature's call sometime that morning, tripped on a tree root, and tumbled all the way to the bottom. He'd managed to crawl part of the way out, but it was rough terrain. Steep and rocky. It had rained, too, so he was soaked to the bone. I called it in on the sat phone, but it was going to be several hours to get a chopper in, and I was worried he'd go hypothermic before then. He was already shivering uncontrollably and was only half-conscious. So I strapped him onto my portable evac sled, dragged him up the slope, and hauled him back to camp."

Darger raised her eyebrows.

"By yourself?"

Bohanon shrugged.

"It's not as dramatic as it sounds. I rigged a pulley system in some of the trees at the top of the ravine, so once I had him up there and on level ground, it wasn't too difficult to tow him back to his camp."

"Did you hear that, Darger?" Loshak said, elbowing her. "Sure, he single-handedly dragged a man out of a ravine and back to safety, thereby saving his life. But he used a *pulley*, so… no big whoop."

Officer Bohanon smiled sheepishly.

"My point is, we have our share of misadventures out here. Accidents. Casualties. Had a camper get mauled by a bear maybe ten years back…"

Bohanon's eyes went distant and haunted for a moment. When he spoke again, his voice had dropped into a lower register.

"But even the worst tragedies I've dealt with were nothing like these… these murders."

CHAPTER 3

As a quiet settled over the plane, the grisly photos from the case file flashed in Darger's mind. Three people murdered on the remote island, their mutilated bodies put on display like some sort of homage to Vlad the Impaler.

The first victim had been Alice Carr. A 42-year-old woman on a fly-fishing trip went out one morning and never returned. A few days later, her naked torso was found near a popular local hiking trail.

The second victim was Nicole Baird, a 25-year-old survivalist who made a living teaching wilderness skills. According to friends and family, it wasn't unusual for Nicole to hike into the bush for weeks at a time, so no one even knew she was in trouble until her dismembered corpse was discovered on display near the isolated worksite of a group of lumber workers.

John Ellinger was the most recent victim, and so far the only male in the bunch. A 28-year-old lumber worker with Valhalla Timber Corporation, John left the bunkhouse one night to answer nature's call and was attacked and abducted by an unknown assailant while a coworker stood only yards away. A search ensued, but in the pitch blackness of the Alaska wilderness at night, they could find no sign of him. It wasn't until the next morning, when the search reconvened, that they came upon Ellinger's mangled torso in a nearby clearing.

The missing limbs and heads of all three victims had yet to be found.

Despite the remote locale, the story had eventually hit the mainstream media, popping up first on 24-hour news broadcasts as more and more gruesome details of the crimes came to light. One of the cable anchors had dubbed the killer "The Tongass Butcher," and the name stuck. The branding seemed to dump gasoline on the publicity fire, trending on Twitter and pushing the story onto more and more front pages overnight. If another body turned up, it'd hit the networks. Darger was sure of it.

Bohanon's voice broke through her thoughts, scattering the gruesome images and media snippets.

"If you look out your window, there, Agent Darger, you can see one of the lumber camps," he said with a tick of his stony jaw.

Darger spotted a few buildings and some machinery among the wedge of cleared land and fallen timber. But she saw nothing else for miles around other than the spiky green tops of the uncut trees surrounding the camp.

"How far from town?"

"Oh, about 30… 35 miles from Klawock, which is where most of the lumber outfits here are actually headquartered. And roughly half that distance is a rugged logging road that is all but impassible if you're not in the right kind of vehicle. When the road conditions are dicey, it can take over an hour to drive from the camp to the main road."

Darger blinked.

"I knew the camps were remote, but… I don't think I truly realized what 'remote' meant, in this context."

Bohanon nodded.

"I spend a lot of my days in areas like that. The difference is, I get to go home at the end of the day. Most of the logging crew stays on-site while they work an area. It's just more efficient that way. There's no good way to commute, I guess you could say."

"Looks like most of the buildings are the prefab types," Loshak said. "I assume that's because they're portable?"

Bohanon nodded.

"That's right. Once they finish working one site, they load it up and drop it at the next. Out of the four buildings down there, two are probably bunkhouses, one's a sort of improvised mess hall-slash-recreation room, and the other is administrative. Everyone calls them cabins, but the majority of them are nothing more than a standard double-wide."

"Can the workers leave on the weekends?" Loshak asked. "Go into town? Go home to visit family?"

"Depends on the job site. Sometimes they're close enough to an access road that trips into town aren't too inconvenient. But like I said, you generally need the proper vehicle to get into a camp like this one, and the workers aren't driving in on their own. They limit traffic on these roads to keep maintenance to a minimum. So for the more remote camps, they mostly stay on-site for the duration."

Loshak scratched his chin.

"Reminds me of the guys that earn their entire salary on a crab boat for a few months a year."

"It's exactly like that," Bohanon said, staring out of the window. "A lot of these guys, they come in from all over the country to work their contract, however long it might be. Three months. Six months. And there's no McDonald's out here. No Costco. No movie theater. These guys come to work, and that's about it."

"Doesn't look like anything's happening down there at the moment," Darger said, noting that none of the vehicles were moving.

"Both Valhalla Timber and Tongass Lumber halted all camp work as of the latest... uh... tragedy. So most of the lumber crews are staying in town until it gets sorted out."

A few minutes later, Darger got her first glimpse of Craig, Alaska. The town was a fraction of the size of Ketchikan, occupying a small fjord on the west side of Prince of Wales Island.

The water landing was nearly as smooth as takeoff, skimming down onto the lake and slowing. Then they puttered over to one of the many docks jutting into the bay to deplane. Bohanon thanked their pilot for the ride and led them to a white Ford Bronco marked with the Forest Service insignia parked in the dockside lot.

"Rentals are limited here on the island, so the earliest I could get you your own vehicle is tomorrow morning. In the meantime, I'm happy to chauffeur you around as necessary." Bohanon removed the campaign hat and ruffled his hair. "I hope that's not too much of an inconvenience for you."

"Not at all," Darger said. "I think we can manage one day without our own ride."

"Great. Well, I booked rooms for you at the Driftwood. One of the fishing lodges. It's not exactly the Ritz, but it's got fantastic views of the water. Plus, some of the guys who were present at the most recent crime scene are staying there while the camps are closed."

Loshak raised his eyebrows.

"You think we could squeeze in a quick interview with them before the task force meeting?"

"Should be plenty of time for that."

Loshak opened the passenger door of the vehicle and tapped his cane into the ground.

"Well then, let's get to it."

CHAPTER 4

The Driftwood Lodge was a handsome structure clad in cedar siding and a red metal roof. Inside, a bank of floor-to-ceiling windows in the common room looked out on the choppy blue sea.

After checking in and trudging down a long hallway, Darger let herself into her room using a key with a carved wooden keychain shaped like a salmon. She found something quaint, even charming, about the old-school setup after years of using digital locks and swipe cards.

She tossed her suitcase on the bed and stepped to the window. A pair of birds paddled on the water just beyond the dock, bobbing in the wake of a fishing boat that had trolled past a few seconds earlier. In the distance, she could see another island, the top of which was concealed in a vaporous white cloud.

She met back up with Loshak in the hallway, and they proceeded to the common room, a massive space with a central river rock fireplace that stretched all the way to the peak of the cathedral ceiling. Ornate antler chandeliers illuminated the room with a warm amber glow, and the walls were bedecked with various taxidermied fish and game animals.

Officer Bohanon stood with one shoulder propped against the nearest face of the four-sided fireplace, talking to a pair of men seated in overstuffed leather chairs. The big park ranger turned his head and waved them over.

"Meet Cyrus Haywood and Donnie Struthers," Bohanon said. "Gentlemen, these are the folks from the FBI I was telling you about."

He met Darger's eyes and gave a subtle nod, which she interpreted as an indication that he was handing things off from here.

"You mind if we ask you a few questions?" Darger asked.

"I reckon that's the whole point of you folks comin' all the way out to this godforsaken island," Haywood said, lifting a bottle of Miller High Life to his lips and taking a long pull.

He was a burly man with reddish hair and stubble so thick it looked like if he wasn't careful, it would grow up over his cheeks and into his eyes like ivy. His response wasn't exactly in the affirmative, but Darger forged ahead anyway.

"You two work for Valhalla Timber, is that right?" Darger asked. "And you were at the camp when John Ellinger was killed?"

Donnie aimed a thumb at Haywood.

"Shit, Cy here was out taking a piss with him when he got took. Or taken. Or whatever. Witnessed the whole thing."

He smiled nervously, revealing a gap between his top front teeth. Donnie was thinner than Haywood, but in that ropey way that suggested hidden strength and stamina. Wiry. He also appeared younger, but Darger wasn't sure if that was just because of the perpetually wide-eyed expression he wore.

Haywood adjusted the sweaty beer bottle in his hand.

"It's a shame what happened to Ellinger. He was a goofy kid. Kind of a dingus, if I'm honest. But he didn't deserve that. No one does."

"And what did you see that night?"

"That's the thing, I didn't see or hear anything. One second he was there. The next…" He shook his head. "Just vanished. Whoever took him didn't make a goddamn sound."

Donnie muttered something that Darger thought sounded

like, "whoever or *whatever*," but Haywood only glared at him and went on.

"I thought it was some kind of prank at first. Some of the guys in the camps are into that. Saran-wrapping the toilet seat or putting Icy Hot in each other's drawers. Ellinger was a big-time prankster, but… once he didn't come back, well…"

Haywood's already somber face went grim.

"There's a tradition in Michigan, where I'm from. The buck pole," he said, staring into the fire. "The first week of deer hunting season, everyone who nabs one brings it into town. And all the gutted carcasses get hung up on a big scaffold. Slit down the middle and gutted. That was the first thing I thought of when I saw the kid in that clearing."

Darger wondered if Haywood wasn't onto something with that. Perhaps the killer saw his victims as prey, their dismembered corpses as trophies. Why else the blatant display? The killer might not think of himself as a murderer at all, but as a hunter.

"Can you think of any reason someone might have wanted Ellinger dead?" Loshak asked.

Haywood paused and scratched his chin.

"Crossed my mind at first that maybe it was one of the tree huggers. But they don't have the backbone for this kind of thing. They'll skulk about, spiking trees and fucking with our machinery, but this? This is too direct. The tree huggers are chickenshit at heart."

"What about someone else with a grudge against the lumber company? A disgruntled former worker?"

Haywood squinted his eyes.

"Most guys who quit this job do it 'cause they can't hack it out in the bush. The remoteness gets to 'em. When they bail, they can't wait to get the hell out of camp. Can't imagine one of

27

them stickin' around to wreak this kind of havoc.

"Had a guy once, and this was years ago, who wanted out of Dodge so bad that he walked the whole twelve miles down to the main road because the thought of being stuck in camp for another two days until the transport truck came in was too much for him."

He took another slug off his Miller. Then he shrugged.

"Besides, even if I could think of someone who had it out for Ellinger, it wouldn't explain why they killed them two ladies. Probably not what you want to hear, but that just seems the shape of it to me."

"No, I think you're right," Darger said. "I don't think we're going to find an ordinary explanation for this."

Donnie's eyes somehow managed to stretch even wider than they already were. An excited gasp slipped out of his mouth.

"See? Now what did I tell you, Cy?" He slapped his knee, and then fixed his intense gaze on Darger. "This is exactly what I've been saying all along."

"Jesus wept. Don't start with all that happy horseshit again," Haywood said through gritted teeth.

"But you heard the lady. No *ordinary* explanation? What does that leave but the *extra*ordinary?" Donnie again turned his focus on Darger, head bouncing up and down like a bobblehead. "I just want you to know, that me and you, we're on the same wavelength."

Darger glanced at Loshak, who frowned in such a way that said he was as lost as she was.

She cleared her throat and addressed Donnie.

"And uh… what wavelength is that?"

Donnie hunched his shoulders and leaned in, lowering his voice.

"Look. I know you probably can't tell me. Not directly, anyway. I get it. This is some of that Area 51-type stuff, right? Classified and shit. Super hush-hush," Donnie said, grinning.

Darger raised an eyebrow.

"What is?"

A laugh hissed out between Donnie's teeth.

"I love it! That's exactly what I'm talking about." His face went slightly more serious. "I'm just saying, I know you have to conduct your investigation as if this is a cut-and-dry homicide. For appearances and all. Like, the official record. But I'm just putting it out there that I… you know… get what's *really* going on."

He gave her an exaggerated wink.

"And what's really going on?" Darger asked, even more lost than before.

Donnie scooted a little closer and now his voice was barely above a whisper.

"The Old Man of the Mountain."

Darger blinked.

"The what?"

"You know… Bigfoot. The Sasquatch or skunk ape. The Yeti, as folks call it in Asia."

A slow smile spread over Darger's face. She narrowed her eyes.

"Oh, I get it. You must be one of the pranksters Haywood here was talking about," she said.

Haywood grunted.

"I wish."

"A prank. Right," Donnie said, winking again. "Of course. I'm just *joking.*"

He put exaggerated air quotes around the last word. His head bobbled again for a couple of seconds. Then he went on.

"And if I were to tell you that I myself have felt something out there in the woods — something preternatural, let's say — that would also be 'a joke.'"

Darger stared at him.

"You're being serious."

"No! We're *joking*, remember?" Now Donnie winked twice. "Cy here might think I'm some kind of simpleton for believing in this stuff, but it's a perfectly legitimate theory. If there's no such thing as Sasquatch, why have so many cultures had similar mythology? Coincidence? Oh, I think not."

Darger brushed her fingers over her lips, not sure how to respond. But Donnie apparently didn't need a response. He kept right on going.

"The same legend has persisted for thousands of years, all across the globe. Long before the *Weekly World News* or the *National Enquirer*. The tabloids merely picked up where the oral histories of ancient civilizations left off. The skeptics love to say that if Bigfoot were real, then we'd have found proof by now. But they just found a fossil of a whole new species of dinosaur here a few years back. That just proves we don't know half of what's out there, even still."

"You'll have to excuse Donnie," Haywood said. "He watches too much damn TV."

Donnie rolled his eyes and smirked at Darger.

"That's exactly what they want you to think." He sighed and shook his head. "I mean, I'm sure you all have seen the photos of what happened to Ellinger. But being there, seeing the wounds in person… the limbs ripped off. And I mean *ripped.* Like ragged and shit. No human could do that."

"And that's where you're wrong," Haywood said, his voice louder now, gruffer. "What your little pea brain fails to understand is that the most horrific perpetrator of violence on this planet has always been man himself. Not aliens or lizard people or Sasquatch."

Haywood paused and gazed into the fire.

"Human history is just people killing people."

CHAPTER 5

After the interview, they headed back out to Bohanon's Bronco. The evening's chill bit at Darger's cheeks.

"Sorry about that," Bohanon said. "Folks around here can be kind of... superstitious."

"No need to apologize." Darger chuckled. "I can assure you, that was far from the most bizarre interview we've had."

"No, that distinction would go to the guy who thought Darger here was going to try to force him to give a sperm sample." Loshak made his eyes go wide and did an impression of the man. "'Ohhhhh no you don't! You're not gettin' *my* sperm!'"

Bohanon stopped walking, his brow wrinkled.

"Why'd he think you wanted his, uh, sperm?"

Darger sighed.

"I have no idea. I said something about DNA, and I think his mind just kind of latched onto that and ran with it. It took several minutes to convince him that I genuinely did *not* want any of his sperm. Like I really, *really* didn't want it. But by then we were pretty far off track, and the interview just kind of spiraled. He kept balancing this Dixie cup on the arm of his chair and yelling, 'sperm whale!'"

There was a sudden wheezing noise, and Darger realized it was the sound of Loshak laughing.

"Settle down over there, or I'll tell Bohanon about the witness who slipped a pair of her panties into your jacket pocket."

Loshak's smile died. His face went serious, and he jabbed a

finger in Darger's direction.

"You promised we'd never discuss that again."

Darger unlatched the rear door of the vehicle and climbed in.

"You're the one that brought up Sperm Whale. Tit for tat."

After buckling himself into the passenger seat, Loshak folded his hands in his lap.

"Well, I think he made an interesting point."

"Sperm Whale?" Darger asked.

"No. Donnie Struthers. His point about how this type of legend has persisted for literally centuries. And in more than one place. Even Tibet has the Yeti, like he said."

Darger leaned into the space between the front seats.

"Victor Loshak. Are you trying to tell me you believe in Sasquatch?"

His lips flattened into an annoyed expression.

"Did I ever tell you that when I first joined the Bureau, I worked with a guy who'd investigated the Silver Bridge collapse?"

An incredulous laugh burst out of Darger's mouth.

"Oh my god. Are we talking about the Mothman?" She closed her eyes. "Even better."

"What's the Mothman?" Bohanon asked.

Darger gasped.

"You've never heard of the Mothman?"

Bohanon put the key in the ignition.

"Can't say I have."

"Go on," Darger said, gesturing that Loshak should continue. "Enlighten the man."

"It's a part of West Virginia folklore. Sightings of a large creature with wings and glowing red eyes have been reported all around the Point Pleasant area over the years. Some people believe the Mothman was a harbinger of sorts. An omen foretelling the collapse of the Silver Bridge in 1967. There were also UFO sightings around the same time."

Darger shook her head.

"You've been spending too much time with Spinks."

"I'm not saying I believe in any of it. But from a sociological perspective, I think it's pretty intriguing. The notion that time after time, various groups and cultures have sought out these supernatural explanations."

Bohanon put the Bronco in gear, and Loshak reached up and took hold of the grab handle on the ceiling.

"Of course, it made more sense in the earlier periods of civilization. Before they had the means to explain certain phenomena scientifically. But even now, these myths persist. Why?"

"Because the scientific explanations are too mundane," Darger said. "Forty-six people died in the Silver Bridge disaster. And the explanation was that the bridge was old and overused and poorly maintained. There was a crack in one of the bridge supports, and on December 15th, 1967, that support broke. But I think it's hard for people to swallow that. The idea that all those people died because of a hairline crack in one little structural component of the bridge? It's underwhelming. No one wants to die because of some stupid, trivial mistake. They want a Reason with a capital 'R.' They want something or someone to blame. So they tell themselves stories. It was because of the Mothman. It was because we built this town on an ancient burial ground."

She took in a breath and watched the trees whiz by in a blur as they turned onto the road to town.

"Anyway, I think Cyrus Haywood was more right than he knew. Because even when it isn't man's inhumanity toward man, it's man's apathy toward man. We let bridges collapse. We let people starve to death and die of curable diseases. People die every day because no one cared enough to do something about it."

The silence stretched out for several long seconds before Loshak turned and fixed his eyes on Officer Bohanon.

"You're gonna find that my partner's unbridled optimism can be contagious. So watch out for that."

CHAPTER 6

Bohanon's Bronco carted them back into the guts of Craig, Alaska — what little guts the town possessed, anyway. A few mom-and-pop shops and a couple of gas stations cluttered the street sides, the main stretch featuring not so much as a single traffic light.

Wet brickwork shone on the buildings, the ruddy masonry turned shiny like glass. It must have sprinkled while they were interviewing the lumberjacks.

Loshak had Bohanon stop at the closest bakery with fresh donuts — a café kitty-corner from the station. He wanted to get a couple dozen and ample coffee for the meeting. He even asked the girl behind the pastry case about banana bread, once again let down to find none available, his shoulders drooping.

Darger shook her head. *Enough with the banana bread already.* She wondered when the hell this fixation with baked goods would end.

She didn't remember ever getting the munchies when she was on painkillers. They tended to have the opposite effect on her, in fact.

Loaded up with donuts and an urn of coffee, they proceeded across the street toward the Craig Police Department. The stench of fish was on the air, pungent and strong. Darger realized it was probably coming from the cannery a few hundred yards to the west.

Gotta love that fresh sea air, she thought.

The front door of the station opened onto a cramped reception area blocked off from the rest of the office with freestanding cubicle partitions. Behind the half-walls, there was a second desk and a small meeting area.

Darger saw four doors with placards at the back of the room. The first said, "Dispatch." Through the partially open door, she spied an array of screens and a woman wearing a headset. The next door was labeled, "Records/Storage." The third room was the office for the chief of police. The last door had a high-tech electronic lock and said, "Holding."

She was impressed that they'd managed to cram a police station, the dispatch center, and the jail all in maybe 1,200 square feet of space.

She stepped closer to Loshak, keeping her voice low.

"Another record for 'smallest ever' to put down in the books."

They waded past the partitions to the meeting area, and introductions were made all around, a process which usually wouldn't happen given the size of most task forces they were involved in. But this wasn't most task forces. Despite including the entire police force of both Craig and nearby Klawock, their group totaled nine people, including Darger, Loshak, and Bohanon.

After Loshak divvied up the coffee and donuts, the group settled around the table. There were only six chairs, so extras were wheeled in from the office area.

Claudia Rhodes, chief of police in Klawock, was up first. She looked to be in her mid-forties, with dark hair cropped short and swept to one side.

Rhodes had been acting as the liaison between the task force and the State Medical Examiner stationed in Anchorage and would present the autopsy findings on the most recent victim.

She stood at the head of the table and peeled open a manila

folder.

"OK. The autopsy report on Jonathon Liam Ellinger came in from Dr. Wauneka this morning, and I had a chance to go over the findings with him about an hour ago. Just to cover the basics, Ellinger was a Caucasian male, 28 years of age. Abducted October 21st at approximately 0200 hours from Valhalla Work Site Number Four. Found deceased at approximately 0800 hours."

She licked her thumb and flicked to the next page in the report.

"Obviously a visual ID was impossible. And without hands, we weren't able to secure fingerprints either. However, Dr. Wauneka was able to confirm the decedent's identity by the tattoo on his chest."

Rhodes held up two photos. The first showed the torso laid out on the autopsy table. The naked trunk had looked wrong in the crime scene photos, but Darger thought it looked even more incongruous in the stark environment of the morgue. Too small and so incomplete on the stainless steel table. The skin looked plasticky and reminded Darger of an enlarged version of a Ken doll missing its head and limbs.

The second photo was a close-up of the aforementioned tattoo, a set of Roman numerals below Ellinger's left collar bone.

"His family informed us that the tattoo represented the birth date of his son."

One of the officers blew out a breath.

Rhodes flicked through the file and pulled out another set of pictures from the autopsy.

"Now, you'll recall that our first victim, Alice Carr, had a gunshot wound from a 7.62 mm caliber rifle."

The photo Rhodes slid to the center of the table featured a

metal ruler lined up with the wound on Carr's chest to show the scale. She nudged a second photo beside that, this one from Baird's file.

"You may also remember that Dr. Wauneka discovered a distinct lack of tissue damage and subcutaneous hemorrhaging around the penetrating chest wound with Nicole Baird, victim number two, leading him to believe that Baird was not shot with a gun, but with some kind of projectile, like an arrow."

She added a third photo to the spread.

"The same lack of tissue damage was noted with John Ellinger, and after more in-depth analysis, Dr. Wauneka believes that both Baird and Ellinger were shot with crossbow bolts with a broadhead measuring approximately one inch, which is a fairly common size used in deer hunting."

Darger scooted forward in her seat to get a better look.

"Why would he switch from a gun to a crossbow?" Bohanon asked.

"Could be for stealth," Darger said. "A crossbow would be nearly silent."

"There's also no muzzle flash with a crossbow," Loshak added. "He killed Ellinger at night, with witnesses in the vicinity, so the crossbow would have kept his position concealed. But that doesn't explain why he used it on Nicole Baird, considering we're pretty sure she was attacked during the day with no witnesses within miles."

Darger chewed her lip, thinking.

"Maybe it's an ego thing. A crossbow requires more skill, right?" She glanced at Bohanon, who nodded. "So maybe it makes him feel more… cunning to use a weapon like that. More proficient. Like he's proving his expertise, his dominance."

One of the uniformed officers swallowed audibly.

"Lord almighty. Is that really how a killer thinks?"

"Some of them," Darger said.

"Well, that's not the only notable finding from Dr. Wauneka," Rhodes said, slapping down a new photo on top of the rest.

A swath of grayish skin filled the frame. Ellinger's shoulders and the stump of neck that remained from his beheading. A second wound, smaller, slit a line in the skin just below his Adam's apple.

"See this wound here, on the neck? Dr. Wauneka theorized that though Ellinger would have likely bled out from the wound from the crossbow bolt over time, the killer slit his throat before that could happen. And there's something else," Rhodes said, holding up a finger. "This is a close-up of the perimortem wound on Ellinger's neck. Note the cross-section showing that the wound is quite narrow and V-shaped. Wauneka tells me that means it was made by some kind of knife. Something long, thin, and sharp, like a fillet or boning knife."

Craig's chief of police was Bill Whipple. His head was clean-shaven, and he rubbed a hand over the gleaming dome.

"I thought he said the killer used an axe on the previous victims."

"For the dismemberment, yes." Rhodes shuffled the pages in her hand and selected several more photographs. "These close-ups show the various wounds from the dismemberment. Again, there is a V-shaped cross-section, but the cuts here are much wider than those found on his neck. The wider cross-section coupled with the tool marks evident on the bones is what led Dr. Wauneka to surmise our perpetrator is using an axe to remove the limbs, and he remains confident on that point."

The table was now covered with autopsy photos. A collage of bone-white flesh interrupted by slashes of pink and red.

"So he shoots Ellinger with the crossbow... to immobilize him, I suppose. Then slits his throat to finish the deed and commences with the postmortem dismemberment," Whipple said. "Do we think he did the same with Carr and Baird?"

Rhodes selected another pile of photographs from the folder.

"Well, after the discovery of the inconsistent wound on Ellinger's neck, Dr. Wauneka went back over the photographs from Carr and Baird. Here and here, he thinks he noted the more narrow V-shaped wounds consistent with a knife. It's difficult to see since the axe wounds overlap with the alleged knife wounds, but Dr. Wauneka has suggested this may be evidence that Carr and Baird also had their throats slit with the same type of long, narrow knife prior to being dismembered with the axe."

"It's like a bow hunter taking a deer down with an arrow and then slitting its throat to finish it off," Bohanon said, his expression grim. "He's acting like they're just game animals to him."

Rhodes brushed a strand of dark hair from her forehead and shrugged.

"Yeah well, I figure that kind of speculation is the domain of our two profilers here, so just give me a moment to tidy up this mess I've made, and then I'll hand things over to Agent Loshak and Agent Darger."

CHAPTER 7

While Chief Rhodes gathered up her photos and resettled them in the file folder, Darger glanced over at her partner. He was furiously scribbling something in his notes, lips pursed in concentration.

She thought of his drug-induced obsession with sweets and imagined that he was writing, "BANANA BREAD BANANA BREAD BANANA BREAD," over and over in some kind of feverish frenzy.

She breathed out a nearly silent laugh, but apparently it wasn't silent enough. Loshak's head snapped up.

"What?"

She shook her head.

"Nothing. Just a little tickle in my throat." She made an exaggerated *ahem* sound. "You ready for this? I mean, you're feeling OK and everything?"

She hoped he wasn't too doped up to handle his half of the profile, though she could do it on her own if she had to.

Loshak flipped the topmost pages of his notes down and tucked his pen behind his ear.

"Wish I had time to scarf another donut, but I'll live."

Darger had been taking a drink of coffee and nearly choked.

Loshak stared at her. Brows knitting together.

"You know, you keep saying I'm being weird, but from where I'm sitting, you're the one acting kooky. It's like you're on wacky pills or something."

That only made Darger whisper-laugh harder. The turn of phrase replayed in her head, the camera in her imagination zooming in on his lips.

Wacky pills.

Loshak's frown deepened. He reminded Darger of her 9th-grade gym teacher who wore a permanent scowl of disapproval and was always poised to yell at someone to "quit playin' grab-ass over there!"

"You think you can pull yourself together for twenty minutes so we can do this thing? Or should I do the profile alone?"

"No, no," Darger said, starting to stand. "I'm good, I swear."

The group had fallen into muted conversation during the transition, but as soon as Loshak stepped to the head of the table, the voices fell silent, one by one.

"I'd like to begin by acknowledging that the dismemberment aspect is obviously a very gruesome element of this case, one I'm sure we'd rather dwell on as little as possible. Unfortunately, it's something we have to focus on a great deal in terms of the profile, because such an act often hints at something symbolic, both for the perpetrator and for us."

There was a laptop on a stand set up at the head of the table, and Loshak tapped at the keyboard, flipping through an array of horror movie posters.

"Pop culture has used the taboo nature of dismemberment as a tool to shock and stimulate audiences for decades. It says something about how primal our feelings are about it. Now, this makes sense for cultures who believe the body remains sacred, living or dead. And yet we find that even societies who believe there is no life after death — or those who believe that once a person is dead, their corpse is merely a hollow shell of who they once were — even those people will have a visceral reaction to images or descriptions of a mutilated corpse.

"It is illegal pretty much everywhere in the world to desecrate a human corpse. There was a woman in Oklahoma recently who went to the funeral of her lover's ex-girlfriend and cut off both of the corpse's breasts and one of her toes. She was sentenced to sixteen years. The maximum sentence for assault with a dangerous weapon in Oklahoma is ten years, so let that sink in. The punishment for injuring a dead body is, in certain circumstances, more than that for injuring a live one. That's how powerful the taboo is."

Loshak drew a nearby whiteboard closer and uncapped one of the markers.

"Thankfully for us, dismemberment is quite rare. It only occurs in about 1-2% of all homicides. The relative scarcity makes it a particular challenge to research, though that doesn't mean we haven't tried. Numerous studies over the years have allowed us to come up with a categorization based on the particular motive behind each dismemberment."

Loshak scribbled the categories on the board and underlined the first category.

"Most of the literature suggests that the defensive type is the most common. In these cases, the main motive for the dismemberment is to cover up the crime and thus reduce the chances of being caught. For lack of a better word, it's purely practical. Moving an entire human body in one piece is difficult and not just because of the weight. If you break it into smaller pieces, suddenly you have options. You can put it in suitcases, garbage bags, a duffel. There was a Scottish serial killer named Dennis Nilsen who literally flushed pieces of his victims down the toilet."

Several of the task force members grimaced in disgust, but all eyes remained firmly fixed on Loshak.

"Defensive dismemberment can also be used as a method to conceal the identity of the victim, or at the very least, make identification that much more difficult. In these cases, we usually see only the hands and head removed. Without fingerprints, teeth, or a physical description, it can often be nearly impossible to make a preliminary ID on the victim."

Loshak paced back and forth in front of the whiteboard as he went on.

"When I started, I mentioned the notion of symbolism. With defensive dismemberment, there's little to no symbolism. It's merely a means to an end, a way to make it easier to move and dispose of the body or to muddy the forensic waters, so to speak. In these cases, the victim is usually known to the perpetrator, a prime reason they'd want to monkey with the identification. The murder is usually unplanned, and the body is usually found in or near the perpetrator's home."

The dry erase marker squeaked faintly as Loshak scrawled "unplanned, body found in or near perp's home" on the board.

"Next, we'll address the aggressive type. This is most often seen in cases of acute rage. The dismemberment is a result of what we call 'overkill.' The perpetrator is going far beyond what's necessary to end the victim's life. One study referred to this as 'gratuitous brutality.' In some cases, the dismemberment is the cause of death, as with aggressive decapitation. This group also includes psychotic dismemberment, in which the perpetrator is in a delusional state while committing the crime. Again, the perpetrators usually know the victims and are motivated by anger, jealousy, or revenge."

Loshak swiveled to face the small audience more squarely.

"There was a case in Chicago not too long ago where a 59-year-old man was living with his mother. He claims they had a dispute over him playing music too loud. A violent struggle

45

ensued, and she ended up butchered in the bathtub. Now, if that's not the very definition of overkill, I don't know what is. Guy could have just turned the music down."

Turning back to the whiteboard, Loshak jotted down the defining characteristics of aggressive dismemberment.

"Decapitation in these cases is a way to depersonalize the victim. The crime is usually not planned, and the severed parts are often left where they fall with no attempt to dispose or conceal. It's as if the perpetrator is in such a blackout rage, they barely realize what they've done. There are often dozens of other wounds, and they tend to target the face and genitals in particular."

Loshak capped the marker and tapped it against the third category he'd written on the board.

"Moving on to offensive dismemberments. This group includes lust killers and necrosadists. People who get off on the physical act of killing and torture. The mutilation of the body itself is part of what excites and arouses the killer. It gives them a sense of power and gratification. The dismemberment in such cases is often considered an extreme form of piquerism, which in its less severe form includes biting, stabbing, and cutting. Piquerism often serves as a sort of pseudo-penetration for perpetrators who are unable to commit sexual assault but want to. This is another case where we often see dozens or even hundreds of wounds. The victims are sometimes, but not always, dismembered while still alive."

The next slideshow Loshak clicked through was a lineup of serial killer mugshots.

"The dismemberment may be the entire point of the killing in these cases, and the perpetrators can be divided into two types. You have your Jeffrey Dahmers, who kill and dismember to fulfill their necrophilic urges, and then you have your full-bore necrosadists, like Andrei Chikatilo, who needed to inflict pain and suffering to achieve an erection, let alone gratification. Mutilation may occur before death and progress into dismemberment afterward, as in the case of Armin Meiwes, who cut off his victim's penis while he was still alive and only fully dismembered him after death. But it is more common that the mutilation and dismemberment occur only postmortem, as with Ted Bundy and Ed Kemper."

Chief Whipple raised a tentative finger in the air, and Loshak pointed at him with the marker.

"I don't mean to interrupt…"

"No, no," Loshak said. "The more questions, the better. Go ahead."

"Well, it's just… wouldn't the fact that the victim is already dead kind of make the whole mutilation thing pointless? I mean, I'm trying to think like a sicko here, and it just seems like torturing a corpse is like, well, beating a dead horse."

Loshak clapped his hands together.

"Ah! I'm glad you asked that. I've found that we non-sickos often struggle to understand this. A profound lack of empathy is a hard thing to intuit, I think. So I'll explain it like this: these types of offenders tend to see their victims as mere props, objects, to fulfill their fantasy, and it follows that this type of perpetrator wouldn't make that much distinction between whether their victim is alive or dead."

Loshak tilted his head a little as he went on.

"If anything, they may feel even more complete ownership over a victim who is dead by their hand. A dead body becomes a pure prop, not unlike a doll. It can offer no argument, no fight, no rejection, and the mutilation or dismemberment serve to prolong the sense of complete control and power they have over the victim. In one case, the perpetrator stated that the act of dismemberment proved that his victim was not only 'nothing,' but 'little pieces of nothing.' It's not enough for this type of perpetrator to merely kill. They are driven to act out fantasies of complete domination with the victim's body. Does that make sense?"

Chief Whipple screwed up his face.

"In the most twisted and perverted way, yeah. I suppose it does."

CHAPTER 8

Loshak glanced around to see if there were any other questions before continuing.

"Next up, necromanic dismemberments," he said, knocking his knuckles next to the fourth item on the list. "This group includes those who dismember for the purposes of keeping a trophy, serving a fetish, or engaging in cannibalism. Despite what we see in the movies, this type is quite rare, though they do exist in the wild."

Here, Loshak showed a photo of a pudgy, middle-aged man in a baseball cap.

"Matej Čurko, also known as the Slovak Cannibal, is a prime example. He's known for trolling suicide forums on the internet where he would find victims who 'volunteered' to be killed. He'd take them into the forest, drug them, stab them in the heart, and then butcher the bodies. He stored the flesh in his refrigerator, which he would then cook and eat at a ceremonial altar he'd constructed in the woods. He had two official victims, but there is evidence suggesting he may have killed as many as twenty-eight more. Among other things, investigators found body parts in the fridge that did not belong to either known victim. But as Čurko was killed during his apprehension, we may never know how many he killed."

"Jesus," Whipple muttered, shifting in his seat.

The marker squealed and squeaked again as Loshak paused to write out a few more notes before continuing.

"The final type is sometimes called the communication type, but one might also call it the organized crime type. In these cases, the dismemberment is used to send a message. The overly gruesome method of killing is meant as a warning or a threat, essentially. *This is what happens if you talk or disobey or come onto our turf.* This type is most commonly seen in relation to drug cartels and terrorist groups."

Loshak waved the marker in front of the list he'd made.

"Now, it can be difficult to properly categorize a dismemberment without knowing the perpetrator or their motives. But by studying the crime scenes and the victims, we can use patterns to guess at the most likely motive behind a dismemberment. For example, if you're dealing with a singular victim who's been decapitated, you can learn a lot just by determining what the killer has done with the head. If it's not found with the rest of the body, we would lean toward defensive, in the assumption that the head was removed and hidden to prevent identification. If the victim is decapitated and the head is found with the body, we would be more likely to consider aggressive, in the assumption that the head was removed in an act of rage or psychosis with no plan for what to do with it afterward.

"Likewise, any time you're dealing with multiple victims, it's more likely to be the offensive or necromanic types. If there is dismemberment with wounding to the genitalia, we would look for evidence of sexual activity. If there are signs, we lean toward offensive or necromanic. If not, offensive or aggressive."

Loshak handed Darger a stack of papers, and she began distributing them to each of the task force members.

"Agent Darger is handing out a quick cheat sheet on everything I've covered, but there's one important thing to note about these classifications. And that is that none of these characteristics are hard and fast. I mentioned Dennis Nilsen before. He dismembered primarily for defensive purposes, which is considered rare for serial killers. So there's one example of an outlier for you.

"Now might also be a good time to note the distinction between the motive behind the murder and the motive behind the dismemberment. We've established that lust killers generally fall into the offensive dismemberment category. However, Jerry Brudos is an example of someone who was a lust killer but dismembered for necromanic purposes. Brudos had a lifelong shoe fetish and cut off the left foot of his first victim. He kept it in his freezer for about ten months, during which time he would take it out and dress it in various high-heeled shoes he had in his collection."

A hand went up. This time it was Chief Rhodes.

"Is it possible for a killer to fit into multiple categories?"

Loshak's eyes lit up, pleased at the question.

"Absolutely. Jeffrey Dahmer, for example, admitted to being aroused while he dismembered the bodies of his victims, which might lead one to categorize him as the offensive type. On the other hand, he also engaged in cannibalism, kept body parts for fetish purposes, and planned to construct an elaborate altar with the skulls and bones of his victims. A complete trifecta of the necromanic category. Kemper and Bundy kept trophies as well. I would consider all three primarily the offensive type with a secondary necromanic motive. Dahmer and possibly Kemper also dismembered to make it easier to dispose of the bodies, so there's also a potential tertiary defensive motive. These are not necessarily black and white classifications. Nothing in profiling ever is."

Rhodes nodded and then bent her head over the sheet Loshak had passed around, writing a note in one of the margins.

"Now before I pass things off to my partner, I want to address one important thing about the type of offender who dismembers a body," Loshak said. "If you were to try to envision what emotions would be running through a person in the midst of severing the limbs of another human being, you'd probably imagine some mix of horror, fear, guilt, anxiety, revulsion, shame. And that's because these are part of the spectrum of normal human emotions.

"We talk about lack of empathy with many types of serial killers, but the type of perpetrator who routinely dismembers bodies like this might display the most profound lack of emotion of all. An absolute coldness. There's a fundamental disconnect in which the killer does not see their victim as a person. I know of one case in which the killer had engaged in cannibalism after dismembering his victim. He explained he did it because he wanted to 'feel something.' When asked *what* he'd felt when he'd eaten his victim, he shrugged and said it felt the same as everything else in his life. So it would be a mistake to assume that we're dealing with someone capable of remorse. And a perpetrator without remorse is the most dangerous of all. Because he will not stop. He will not surrender."

Loshak gazed out over the rest of the task force, his face grim.

"And he will not hesitate to kill anyone who gets in his way."

CHAPTER 9

The room was already quiet, but a weighty stillness seemed to hang over the group after Loshak's pronouncement. Darger could hear the faint *tick, tick, tick* sound of the clock on the wall and the sharp *click-clack* from the dispatcher's keyboard in the next room.

She uncapped a dry erase marker and cleared her throat.

"So let's take a look at our scenes and consider what we have. Three victims. One local, one seasonal worker, and one visitor. No real pattern in terms of the age, race, and sex of the victims. We have a 25-year-old White female, a 42-year-old Black female, and a 28-year-old White male."

Darger stepped to the whiteboard and gestured at the first item on Loshak's list.

"I think we can easily rule out defensive dismemberment, by the sheer fact that this is a repeated act and that the torsos were left on display. Defensive dismemberment, again, is all about practicality. This type wants to hide the body, not put it out there for all the world to see."

She drew a line through "defensive."

"Likewise, the fact that only one of the victims was local suggests that most, if not all, of the victims were unknown to the perpetrator. That would seem to rule out the aggressive type. I think we can also rule out communication type, unless Prince of Wales island is a secret hotbed for cartel activity."

There was a mild chuckle as she crossed out "aggressive" and "communication."

"Given that we haven't seen evidence of obvious sexual

activity at the crime scenes, one might be tempted to rule out the offensive type. However, the fact that the bodies have been posed is something that can't be overlooked.

"Posing and staging are quite rare, only seen in about 1% of homicides, by one estimate. They are, similar to the types of dismemberment, separated by motive. We use the term 'staging' to refer to instances where the perpetrator has moved the body and altered the scene in an effort to confuse or mislead investigators. An example would be attempting to make a homicide appear to be a suicide. Or a perpetrator might remove the clothing of the victim to make it appear that it was a sexually motivated crime when it was not."

Darger paused to write a summarized definition of "staging" on the board before turning back to the group.

"Posing, on the other hand, is done to serve some fantasy of the perpetrator and is thus part of his signature," she continued. "Posing is far more likely to be seen in serial cases versus staging. Sometimes it's motivated by anger at the victim. There was a serial killer in Detroit a few years back who murdered three sex workers and posed them after death on their knees, in a kneeling position. The theory is that he was making a religious statement. That because they were prostitutes, they had sinned and needed to ask God's forgiveness.

"Other times, there's a sexual motivation. Going back to Dennis Nilsen, he very carefully posed his victims after death to satisfy a specific sexual fantasy. He'd take photographs and arrange multiple mirrors around the body so that he could enjoy the tableau from various angles."

Chief Whipple cupped his chin in one hand.

"I said it before, and I'll say it again," he said. "*Je*-sus."

"One important thing to note is that Nilsen did not leave

54

the bodies for anyone to find," Darger went on. "That fits with the fact that he wasn't a sadist. Because the type of killer who poses a body with the intent that it will be discovered by the public is motivated by extreme rage. It's a giant 'fuck you' to investigators, to society.

"Jack the Ripper is a prime example of a killer who not only mutilated his victims but posed them as well. He very much wanted the gruesome scenes he left behind to be seen. He wanted to shock and horrify, and he was flaunting the fact that he believed he wouldn't be caught. He was also likely sending the message that his victims, as sex workers, were disposable. And that highlights the fact that posing is also an effort to further degrade and humiliate the victim."

"So it's sort of like the cases of offensive dismemberment, where the killer is doing all this stuff with the body to prove how much power and control they have?" Chief Rhodes asked.

"It's exactly like that," Darger answered. "Furthermore, posing often serves a specific sexual fantasy in the perpetrator, especially in cases that included mutilation and evisceration. And that is one of the key reasons I'm not willing to write off offensive dismemberment at this point."

Darger pointed at the remaining category on Loshak's list.

"So that leaves us with necromanic. And given the meticulous nature of the dismemberment and the fact that the torsos are displayed in an almost ritualistic fashion, we could very well be dealing with some kind of necromanic motive. I'll also point out that, as of yet, we have no idea what he's doing with the heads or limbs of the victims. Is he keeping them as trophies? Taking them somewhere and engaging in cannibalism or some sort of fetishistic activity? We just don't know the answer to that yet."

"Christ," Chief Whipple muttered. "And here I thought this

case couldn't possibly get any more sickening."

"Well, let's focus on what we do know and what we can make reasonable assumptions on. We can say with cautious certainty that he's not preselecting his victims or targeting a specific type, but rather he's finding situations that give him access to vulnerable individuals. We call this 'premeditated opportunism.' Serial killers who use premeditated opportunism often target sex workers, people in bars, drug addicts. In this case, our guy is using the isolated locations to his benefit. And the fact that he brings multiple weapons with him tells us that he goes out with the specific intent to kill.

"He's using long-range weapons — a rifle and a crossbow — to immobilize the victims in a blitz attack, which says he prefers to take his victims by surprise. This suggests our killer is socially incompetent, which is common among disorganized killers."

Darger's throat was starting to feel dry, so she took a sip of her coffee. It had gone lukewarm, and she had to fight the urge to spit it back in the cup. She forced herself to swallow and carried on.

"Now let's talk about some of the common characteristics among dismemberment killers specifically. In the past, there have been theories that this type of killer was more likely to have worked in places like slaughterhouses, mortuaries, butcher shops. Places where the killing or dissection of bodies — animal or human — wouldn't have been so out of the ordinary. However, there have been various studies on this, and I'm only aware of one incident where a perpetrator was found to have such a history, that of Katherine Knight. Knight worked in a local slaughterhouse beginning at the age of sixteen. In February 2000, she murdered her boyfriend, John Price, by stabbing him at least 37 times. Once he was dead, Knight meticulously skinned his entire body, cut off his head, and then posed his body. She also cooked some of his flesh with the intention of feeding it to his children."

One of the Craig PD officers, a gangly kid with a red-blond crew cut, shuddered involuntarily.

"In my opinion, this idea of a dismemberment killer having a history of handling dead bodies or cutting up animals is one of those things that sounds like it makes sense, but it's just not something reflected by reality. Even if it was, I imagine hunting is a common hobby out here in Alaska?"

There were nods around the table, and Darger shrugged.

"So I doubt knowing how to field dress and butcher a game animal would be an unusual skill to have."

The group murmured their agreement with this assessment.

"That being said, studies have shown that dismemberment killers are two times as likely to have a history of being violent in school compared to other types of killers, and they are very likely to have been referred to mental health services in the past. The most common diagnoses are psychotic disorders and personality disorders. In other words, they are less likely to be the 'he seemed like such a normal, nice guy' types. These are angry, compulsive, unstable people, often with lengthy criminal records.

"So, given what we know about the crime scenes, the victimology, and the potential dismemberment type, I believe we're looking for a White man between the ages of 25 and 45. Usually we'd go with 25 to 35, but perpetrators who pose their victims tend to skew older for some reason."

Darger uncapped the marker and began to write out the demographics of the profile on the board.

"He likely did not finish high school and has a history of

drug and alcohol abuse in addition to some kind of psychiatric disorder. He very likely came from a dysfunctional and overtly abusive family and has a lot of hostility toward his parents. Both his relationships with women and his employment history will be rocky at best. I wouldn't expect him to have a stable job. If he's ever been married, he will be either divorced or separated now. The fact that he seems to kill in these very isolated locations, far from any roads, might mean he doesn't have reliable transportation. Likewise, he is most definitely local and knows the area well, spending a great deal of time outdoors."

She paused to consult her notes before continuing.

"There was probably some sort of precipitating stressor prior to the first murder. A fight with a romantic partner, the loss of yet another job, eviction, financial trouble, etcetera.

"Given the meticulous posing at the scenes, I can say with relative certainty that this is a man who compulsively seeks attention and stimulation. He likely fantasizes about the reactions of those left to discover the body. In fact, he may even stay in the area to witness the discovery firsthand."

"Wouldn't that be a big risk for him?" Chief Rhodes asked.

"Yes, but we're dealing with grandiose narcissism here. He might even believe himself invincible, on some level. And like Jack the Ripper, he is probably certain that he'll never get caught."

Recapping the marker, Darger angled herself back to face the table.

"I'd also like to point out the escalation we've seen with the most recent murder. In the first two, the women were taken when they were utterly alone. They were killed, dismembered, and brought to a specific area to display. But in the third, the killer approached an area much less isolated than the first two

58

abduction scenes. Not only that, he returned to that scene specifically to display the torso. This is a clear escalation in boldness and in aggression."

Darger tapped the marker against her palm.

"And while I'm sure we're all sick of the references to Vlad the Impaler in the media, I do think it's an apt comparison. In ancient times, impalement was a tool employed by warlords and tyrants to terrify their enemies and subjects into obedience. The victims of this particular punishment were often left on display as a message to others. I think we're seeing something similar here. When he placed John Ellinger's corpse in that clearing, he wanted to strike fear in everyone in that camp. Likewise with the placement of Alice Carr and Nicole Baird. There's something almost territorial about it."

"You think it could be someone with a tie to one of the camps?" Bohanon asked. "Maybe a disgruntled former employee of the logging company? Something like that?"

Darger and Loshak exchanged a look. She knew they were thinking the same thing, even before he spoke.

"It's possible, but that kind of motive is almost too… clean, if you will." Loshak said. "Too logical."

"OK. You said it feels territorial, right?" Chief Whipple said. "So maybe it's one of those bleeding heart eco-nuts who got his panties in a twist over the logging happening in a National Forest."

Darger shook her head.

"We call that type of killer 'mission-oriented.' They are motivated by a perceived 'sense of duty' to kill, usually a specific type of person. Ted Kaczynski, for example, targeted anyone he felt was contributing to the destruction of the environment or the advancement of technology. His attacks were extremely organized and also carried out from a distance.

That's common for mission-oriented killers. Their kills tend to be quick and efficient. Bombs. Shootings. They take out the target and move on. They don't spend time dismembering and posing the bodies."

Darger thought again of the crime scene photos. The angry red wound where John Ellinger's head used to be. Nicole Baird's naked torso propped up on a spike and looking more like a mangled mannequin than anything human.

"The level of gratuitous savagery here feels more personally motivated," she said, shaking her head. "Something more primordial than a political cause. Aggressive. Animalistic. There is something deep within this killer that compels him to act with a level of violence that goes far beyond what's necessary to simply kill."

Darger imagined him stalking the woods with his crossbow. Taking careful, practiced steps. Slipping through the trees unnoticed.

"And what's more, I think he enjoys it."

CHAPTER 10

Loshak came to stand beside Darger at the head of the table.

"So now we know what makes this guy tick. The question now is how do we use that to our advantage? We'd like to circulate a modified version of the profile to the press. Like my partner pointed out, given his history, this isn't the type of perpetrator who fools his neighbors into thinking he's a normal, amiable guy. And given the small population of the island, I think we have a real chance of finding him through tips from the public. I imagine this is the kind of place where everyone knows everyone. And that means someone knows something. Or at least has a suspicion."

He turned his focus on Chief Whipple.

"Were you able to get the tip line up and running like we discussed yesterday on the phone?"

Whipple nodded.

"Affirmative. We tested it out this morning, and it's ready to go."

"Excellent," Loshak rubbed his hands together. "We've got a press release written up. I'd suggest we get it out there immediately. The big question is whether or not we'll be able to get this in the hands of the local media outlets before the evening news. It'd be great to have some tips to work on first thing tomorrow morning."

All eyes went to the clock on the wall.

"It's gonna be tight," Chief Rhodes said, shaking her head.

"Let me call the Press Officer with the Forest Service," Bohanon said. "She's a bulldog. If anyone can get this out tonight, it'll be her."

Bohanon stepped into Whipple's office to make the call, and one of the Craig PD uniforms went to upload the press release to the department Facebook page as well as a local online news bulletin.

Whipple stood and hitched up his gun belt.

"Not that I don't trust your expertise, but you really think this will work? I have a hard time believing that Joe or Jane Public is gonna call us up to implicate a family member."

"Oh, it's not always family members. Could be a neighbor. A coworker. But I think you'll be surprised just how many people will report a boyfriend, an ex-husband, a brother, and so on." Loshak crossed his arms. "And sure, most of them will be pure bullshit, but someone out there has seen glimpses of this guy's anger. His capacity for violence."

He paused and glanced over at Darger, a sly smile spreading across his face.

"But if nothing pans out from the tips, we do have a Plan B."

"Yeah? What's that?" Whipple asked.

"I think we might be able to draw this guy out by engaging with him through the press. With the attention-seeking behavior and the grandiosity, I think our guy is so convinced he's smarter than us that he'd take the bait."

"Worked with BTK," Darger said.

Bohanon came striding out of the office looking pleased.

"Betty says to email whatever we've got, and she'll make sure it's on every outlet in the state tonight, come hell or high water."

"That's great," Darger said. "I can forward it right now."

While Darger sent off the press release, Loshak hobbled over to the window that looked out on the parking lot. He nudged the blinds aside and frowned.

"Damn. It's getting dark already," he said, stepping back from the window. "I was hoping we'd be able to get out to see the scenes in person after the meeting, but I guess that'll have to wait until tomorrow."

Bohanon clicked his tongue.

"I hate to be the bearer of bad news, but I don't think you'll be walking the scenes in person tomorrow or any time in the near future."

"Why's that?"

Bohanon pointed at the brace on Loshak's knee.

"I think you're underestimating just how rugged the country is out there. It's hard to tell in the photos, but there are rocks and cliffs and mud. I mean, far be it from me to tell you your own business, but I'd think twice about going out there with a knee in that condition, personally."

Head bent, Loshak scowled down at his knee.

"Well, shit."

Darger had been listening in while she sent the email to the National Forest Office of Communication.

"So while I'm out hiking in the bush tomorrow, you can start sifting through all the juicy tips that pile up tonight," she said.

Loshak pressed his lips into a hard line and grunted.

"Oh goody. Desk duty."

He looked so sulky Darger had to hold back a laugh.

"Don't be such a grump."

"Easy for you to say."

It was true. Darger hated not being able to go out in the field. Besides, working a tip line detail was always a slog.

"I promise to call you from each scene, and we can video chat the whole thing," Darger said.

"Oh, there's no cell reception where we're headed," Bohanon said, looking amused. "You're lucky if you can get radio transmission in some parts. But I'll have a sat phone with me, so we can at least check in intermittently."

"See?" Darger said, patting Loshak's shoulder. "It'll be like you're on the scene yourself."

"I'm sure."

CHAPTER 11

When the task force meeting broke up, Bohanon offered to take Darger and Loshak to the best local restaurant and pub, The Prospector. They readily agreed and even managed to entice Chief Rhodes to tag along.

The bar looked like an older building, with wood siding painted barn red and a moose skull hanging over the front door. They followed Bohanon up a flight of wooden steps and through the entrance. The interior was dim, lit mostly with the ambient light coming from the neon beer and liquor signs decorating the windows. Three pool tables lined the back wall.

Loshak scooped up his menu and pulled a pair of reading glasses from his pocket.

"Nice specs, Grandpa," Darger said. "First the cane, and now this. You're turning into an old man before my very eyes."

"Don't be ageist, Darger. It makes you seem unsophisticated."

Darger snorted.

She and Rhodes opted for the fish and chips while Bohanon chose the fried shrimp basket. Loshak was the last to order, hemming and hawing a bit before settling on the halibut hoagie.

They ate then, and the food lived up to the hype. Loshak made a mess of his hoagie, but he sang its praises from first bite to last.

Darger had just taken her last bite of fish when Rhodes pointed at one of the TVs mounted over the bar.

"Hey look, it's our press release."

Everyone turned to look at the screen.

"Tonight, authorities are asking for your help to catch the brutal killer known as the Tongass Butcher. In conjunction with the FBI, local law enforcement has released a criminal profile in the hopes of generating new leads in the case," the female news anchor said.

What followed was a succinct summary of some of the more easily digestible details from the profile.

"Well, I think you got their attention," Bohanon said, gesturing at how almost everyone in the place had stopped what they were doing to stare at the TV.

There was a decent crowd in The Prospector that night, with every stool at the bar occupied and only a few tables open. Darger supposed there were probably only a few places to choose from in a town of this size.

Loshak rubbed his palms together and smiled.

"Oh yeah. The tips will be flooding in tonight. That's always how it goes. A big rush right at the beginning and whenever another news segment airs. We should have plenty of juicy nugs to sift through in the morning."

Darger sipped at her cream ale and noticed two men at the bar staring at their table. When they noticed Darger looking, they quickly turned away. She wouldn't have thought anything of it except that a few minutes later, she spotted a different cluster of people eyeballing their group. This time, they pretended to be focused on the TV mounted on the far wall, but every few seconds, they snuck a surreptitious glance.

Darger was starting to get the impression that word had gotten around about who they were. She thought on it for a few seconds and then considered that word maybe didn't even need to get around. In a town this small, strangers probably stuck out like a sore thumb.

That got Darger thinking about what that might mean in terms of their investigation. Would people be wary of them as outsiders? Reticent to talk? Or would they be curious and eager to help? She assumed it would be the latter, but sometimes isolated communities like this were protective of their own, resentful of outside influence, and hesitant to spill the dirty little secrets of their town.

Darger took another drink and glanced at their two local companions from the corner of her eye. So far they'd seemed helpful, open, and honest. More welcoming than plenty of jurisdictions they'd visited in the past. That was something. But ultimately, it didn't matter all that much whether they were friend or foe. Because Darger would find the killer, with or without them.

CHAPTER 12

They had just finished their food and put in an order for
another round of beers when the front door opened. Cyrus
Haywood and Donnie Struthers, their interview subjects from
earlier, entered the bar. Donnie sidled up to their table,
grinning.

"Well hello there again, Agents. You know, I was just
thinking about what we talked about earlier. Or should I say,
what we *didn't* talk about earlier, if you know what I mean."

He waggled his eyebrows.

"Donnie, you dumb son of a bitch. Were you raised in a
barn?" Haywood said, hooking his hand around Donnie's
elbow. "You don't just barge into someone's private fuckin'
conversation like that. You could be interrupting something
sensitive."

"Oh, it's fine," Loshak said, eyes glittering. "In fact, you
fellas should pull up a chair! Join us."

It took Darger a moment to realize that Loshak had just
used the term 'fellas,' a word she'd never heard him utter
before. She studied him for a moment, took in the rosy cheeks
and glassy eyes. Ah yes, the painkillers. Coupled with even the
tiny amount of booze, he was probably feeling more than a bit
tipsy.

Not needing any more of an invitation, Donnie set about
nudging the nearest table closer.

"I'll go get us some beers," Haywood grumbled and headed
for the bar.

When Donnie had seated himself, Loshak fixed him with a

mischievous look.

"Donnie, my man, let me ask you something. Have you ever heard of the Mothman?"

Donnie was almost aghast.

"Have I heard of the Mothman? Have I, Donnie James Struthers, heard of the Mothman?" He slammed his hand on the table. "Mister, I'm from Pittsburgh, where they filmed the movie about it. I was probably fifteen then, and me and my friends used to go watch them shoot. My friend, Greg Kaminski? Well, his older brother, Benji, got to be an extra. You know the scene where Richard Gere and that other guy are walking around Mellon Square?"

"Of course," Loshak said, and Darger knew he had to be lying. It was an interview tactic they used often. Play along on the minutiae to keep them talking.

"There's like three seconds where you can see Benji Kaminski walking behind them. Whole side of his face is right there over Gere's shoulder. Anyway, I've probably watched that movie two hundred times. So yeah, I think I've heard of the Mothman."

There was a pause then, and Donnie seemed to get an idea. His eyes went comically wide, and he leaned in the same way he had at the Driftwood Inn.

"Are you saying that this here is the work of the Mothman?" he whispered.

Haywood had returned with two bottles. He set one down in front of Donnie before taking a swig from his own.

"Here we go again," he said.

Donnie carried on, unperturbed.

"See, I always thought of the Mothman as belonging to that particular slice of Appalachia. Being that the Sasquatch legends are more common here in the Northwest and Canada, I naturally assumed that's what we were dealing with, but now you got me thinking." He shivered dramatically. "Woo! I just got the chills! Look at them goose pimples on my arm."

He stuck out his forearm and pushed up the sleeve of his flannel shirt. Then he shook his head.

"I'm just not sure this is a climate tolerable to a Mothman. It's too wet, I think. Our winged man? He's not equipped to live in a temperate rainforest."

Loshak nodded as if taking all of this very seriously.

Donnie capped his thought.

"I mean no disrespect, but if I'm being completely honest, I think you're better off focusing on the Sasquatch exclusively."

The waitress returned with their second round then.

"Did I hear you say something about Sasquatch?" she asked.

Donnie scowled.

"Show a little class, Trixie. You can't just barge into people's conversations like that. I mean, not to be rude, but we're having a sensitive discussion here."

"Well, just so you know, there aren't Sasquatches on P.O.W.," Trixie said.

Donnie smirked and winked at Loshak.

"Of course there isn't," Donnie said.

"This is Kushtaka territory."

"What the hell is a Kushtaka?"

"Shapeshifters in the Tlingit legends," Trixie explained. "Kushtaka means Land-Otter Man. My grandmother used to tell me and my sister stories about the Kushtaka to scare us into behaving. If we were being really wild, she did this three-note whistle. Low, high, low. Claimed it was the way the Kushtaka communicated with one another, and that she was going to call them to her and have them take us away. That always got us acting right, real quick."

Donnie crossed his arms over his chest and scoffed.

"So what, he's some kind of half-man, half-otter? Don't sound scary to me. Sounds kinda… cute."

"You say that now, but just wait until the next time you're out there at the lumber camp. I know how you singlejacks work. Out there in the woods by yourself. No one else in sight. Maybe within shouting distance of another jack, if you're lucky. That's when the Kushtaka finds you. See, they like to prey on people lost or wounded in the woods. Sometimes they even imitate the sounds of a crying baby or the screams of a woman to lure victims into isolated locations. Either way, once a Kushtaka has you, there's almost no hope for escape. They either turn you into another Kushtaka, doomed to wander the woods for eternity, or they rip your body into pieces. Sound familiar?"

Donnie licked his lips, suddenly looking a bit more uncertain.

Trixie put one hand on her hip.

"Anyway, people tend to confuse the Kushtaka with the Salish Sasquatch." She shook her head. "Two very different beasts. Sasquatch aren't violent, for one. Not unless they feel threatened."

Donnie opened his mouth to reply but was interrupted by the sudden scraping of a bar stool. One of the men at the bar had scooted closer to their table.

"I hate to be a Nosy Nelly, but I couldn't help but overhear your conversation. And I just wanted to say if you really want to know what's going on out in those woods, you should look into the Norse legend of the berserker."

He was an older man with a shaggy white beard and caterpillars for eyebrows.

Loshak, looking delighted to have someone else joining the

conversation, waved the man closer.

"Go ahead. Enlighten us."

"Well, 'berserker' translates literally to 'bear shirt.' So some of the stories say they were human warriors who wore bearskins as armor. But other stories say they weren't fully men at all, but half-man, half-bear. It was said that the berserkers were immune to edged weapons and fire, and that only clubs and other blunt instruments could be used against them."

Donnie scratched his jaw.

"A werebear. Now *that's* interesting."

The old man nodded solemnly.

"I heard them bodies were all tore up. Now, that don't sound human to me. But leavin' 'em out like they were, that ain't exactly bear behavior, neither. So... maybe it's both."

"There are quite a few Native American stories about bear people," Bohanon said. "Most of the tribes wouldn't hunt bears, either. They called them 'Uncle' or 'Grandfather,' and they were revered as healers and protectors. It was forbidden to kill one and was usually said to bring bad luck on the tribe if you did."

Darger sighed and drank her beer as the men continued debating what supernatural beast was responsible for the murders here on the island. If she'd hoped to get anything useful out of the locals tonight, all the *X-Files*-type talk had clearly derailed it.

She turned to Chief Rhodes, who'd been noticeably quiet for the last several minutes.

"What do you think about all of this?"

"Me? Oh, I'm not one for tall tales, really. I know why people cling to those kinds of stories, though. It's easier to believe some kind of monster did this than a regular old human being."

Darger nodded.

"That's a wise assessment."

Rhodes smiled sheepishly and tried to cover it by taking a drink. When she set her glass down, she seemed to steel herself for something.

"Can I just say, I found your presentation today really enlightening? The things you're able to glean just from looking at a crime scene is like something out of Sherlock Holmes."

"Well, I'm not sure we're all that impressive, but I'm glad you got something out of it."

There was a faint *pitter-patter* sound as Rhodes drummed her fingers against the table.

"Does the FBI have any sort of... classes on that?"

"Sure. The National Academy is a training program specifically for state and local law enforcement. There are a few classes in the program that focus on profiling and crime scene analysis," Darger said.

"The National Academy," Rhodes repeated. "I'm gonna write that down."

Watching the chief tap out a note to herself on her phone, Darger got an idea.

"Officer Bohanon is taking me up to look at some of the scenes in the morning. Would you like to come along?"

Rhodes blinked and rose taller in her seat.

"Absolutely. I mean, if I won't be in your way, that is."

"Not at all."

An elbow thudded on the table, and Haywood's face appeared over the policewoman's shoulder.

"You're going up to the camp?"

Darger bobbed her head once.

"Tomorrow morning."

"Would it be alright if I tag along?" he asked. "I left some of my gear up there. Figured we'd only be out of camp for a day or two. But at this rate, who knows when we'll be cleared to start work again."

"I don't have a problem with that. It could be useful to have an eyewitness on hand, actually. You could walk us through what you saw."

The conversation about bear people and wereotters seemed to have petered out, and now Donnie was staring at Haywood.

"I can't believe you're volunteering to go back up there, Cy," he said, his voice coming out in a hiss. "After everything that's been said here tonight?"

Haywood's jaw hardened.

"I told you. I ain't scared of your campfire ghost stories."

"Fine, but… you know there's *something* out there." Folding his arms over his chest, Donnie shook his head. "I don't like it. I don't think you should be going up to that camp, Cy."

"What are you? My mother?"

Donnie sniffed, a wounded expression on his face.

"Well excuse me for caring."

"He won't be alone," Darger said, feeling as though she were arguing with a child about whether there was a monster under the bed. "Me, Officer Bohanon, and Chief Rhodes. We'll all be there. And we'll be armed."

Donnie only shook his head again, unconvinced. Then he sat up straight.

"Hang on. I've got something in the car."

He darted off. Wove through the crowd and rushed out of the building.

About a minute passed. Just as Darger had forgotten about him, the door opened and Donnie came bounding across the bar. He jerked to a stop in front of Haywood.

"I got something for you, Cy."

He held out his fist and unclenched his fingers to reveal a miniature bottle, only slightly larger than Darger's thumbnail. He held it out, gesturing that Haywood should open his palm.

Haywood did so, and then squinted down at the small object Donnie placed there.

"What the hell is it?"

"It's a spell jar. One of my exes made it. She was into witchcraft and all that. White magic only, of course. The good kind." Donnie's eyes sparkled. "She made it specifically for good luck, and it's never let me down. She put all the lucky stuff in there. Special herbs like cinnamon and nutmeg. Some clover. A little chip of tiger eye. It's even got a drop of urine in it."

Haywood recoiled.

"Oh Jesus Christ," he said, tossing the bottle back at Donnie.

It bounced off the younger man's chest, and he spent the next few seconds struggling to pin the minute vial against his person. When he finally regained his hold on it, he clutched it protectively.

"Careful, Cy! This is irreplaceable."

Haywood dusted his hands off wordlessly, his top lip still curled in disgust.

"I want you to take it with you," Donnie said, holding the bottle out again.

Haywood's hands went up into a defensive position.

"Fuck no. I don't want your girlfriend's tiny piss bottle."

"It's not— It's like a microscopic amount of pee, Cy. It's not like she hosed the thing down. And anyway, it's good luck, I'm telling you."

"Fuck off," Haywood said, his tone unyielding.

"Cy, please. It would mean a lot to me to know you were

protected when you're up there."

"I'll take it," Darger said.

She didn't believe in this kind of thing, not even a little, but she had a feeling Donnie wasn't going to let this go until someone agreed to take it, and she wanted to finish her drink and get going.

Donnie made to hand it over, then held back.

"To be clear, this is a loan. I'm expecting you to return this."

"Of course," Darger said.

"I mean it." His face went even more serious. "You have to promise I'll get this back."

Darger nodded.

"I promise." When that didn't reassure him, she added, "Cross my heart and hope to die."

He sighed, as if those were the very words he'd been waiting to hear, and deposited the bottle into Darger's hand.

She tucked it in her pants pocket and turned back to her drink.

CHAPTER 13

It was a little past nine when Bohanon dropped them back at the Driftwood Lodge, promising to return in the morning. A fog had settled over the water, and the moon was a blurry orb behind the haze. Darger paused there in the parking lot, watching the mist shift and billow like wisps of gray silk.

It was beautiful. And eerie. And also unbelievably quiet. When the rumble of Bohanon's SUV had faded into the distance, there was only the faint whisper of the wind rustling through the trees and the hushed lapping of water against the shore.

The humid island air congealed into something frigid at night. Icy fingers prodded at every inch of Darger's exposed skin, spurring her to seek shelter after only a few seconds.

She jogged to catch up to Loshak, who was almost to the front door of the lodge. As Loshak's hand made contact with the door handle, some kind of bird called out, maybe an owl, and it sounded almost like laughter. A chill bristled over Darger's scalp.

"It wasn't very nice of you to mess with that kid about all the creature lore," she said as they crossed the lobby, heading for their rooms.

Loshak turned to her, eyes glittering.

"Who said I was messing with him?"

Darger rolled her eyes, which elicited a chuckle from her partner.

"Don't you miss being younger and being scared of that stuff?" he asked. "When I was maybe eight, I saw this movie

77

called *Creature from Black Lake*. Scared the complete bejeesus out of me. I'm sure if I saw it now, I'd laugh my ass off, but back then, when I was a kid? I thought it was just about the freakiest thing I'd ever seen. Gave me nightmares for months."

They'd reached their rooms now, and Darger stopped just shy of her door.

"Donnie Struthers isn't eight, Loshak. He's gotta be in his thirties. Too old to believe in this stuff." She twirled the keyring around her finger. "You shouldn't encourage it."

"Ahh, what's the harm?" Loshak yawned. "Man, I'm bushed. And my knee is starting to kill me. Think I'll take a Vicodin and probably pass out."

Darger unlocked her door.

"Same. Minus the Vicodin." She opened the door halfway and stopped. "Isn't it against regs to take heavy medication while in the field?"

Loshak made a dismissive sound.

"Oh please. Like you haven't done the same." Loshak pushed into his room and then turned back to face her. "See you in the morn for some of that complimentary breakfast."

"Goodnight," Darger said and closed her door.

She'd intended to head straight for the shower, but she found herself standing in front of the window, transfixed by the view again. Down by the dock, a floodlight cast a weak glow into the mist.

Something moved on the water, causing ripples to radiate out in circles just a few yards out from the end of the dock. Darger couldn't help but think of Trixie's otter people. What had she called them? The Kushtaka.

Darger shivered and then snorted at her reaction. It was always easier to contemplate such things in earnest in the middle of the night. Something about being alone in the dark made even the most rational brain wonder, *what if?*

But tomorrow… tomorrow she'd see the scenes in broad daylight. And the stories of Sasquatch and man-bears and trickster otter-folk wouldn't even enter her mind.

The monster they were hunting was all too human.

CHAPTER 14

Bright and early the next morning, the Ford Bronco rumbled down the dirt logging road, tires juddering over a washboard of ruts in the muddy track. The rough ride shook the occupants of the SUV in their seats like Mexican jumping beans.

Darger sat in the backseat on the passenger side, glugging down her coffee. It had cooled from scalding to lukewarm along the ride, but it was still delicious. The best hotel coffee she'd ever come across.

To her left, Chief Rhodes perched in the middle of the backseat — a spot she'd been relegated to as the smallest of the travelers. She looked only mildly uncomfortable wedged between Darger and Cyrus Haywood, the lumberjack who had followed through on his promise to ride along.

Officer Bohanon drove the vehicle, and a supervisor from the Tongass Lumber Company, Dennis Wishnowsky, sat in the passenger seat — he'd likewise volunteered to help show them around the other crime scene, the logging camp near where Nicole Baird's body had been put on display. In his mid-fifties, Wishnowsky wore a fussy beard and small, wire-rimmed glasses that reminded Darger of Steve Jobs.

"I reckon we're about ten minutes out now." Bohanon glanced over at Haywood. "That sound right?"

The lumberjack nodded.

"Prolly less than that now."

Darger's heart beat a little faster. Almost there.

A case never felt fully concrete to her until she'd walked the scene. Saw it with her own eyes. Felt its atmosphere. Smelled its scent.

She perceived the experience as more or less downloading the setting and all of its details into her right brain, giving her imagination something tangible to work with as she lined the crimes up with the profile. Those granular details seemed to foster new intuitive leaps, set off chain reactions in her instinctual mind. She thought maybe she'd picked the habit up from Loshak, but she wasn't sure.

Bohanon slowed the SUV to a crawl, rolling gently down into a pothole roughly the size of Darger's Prius and then up the other side.

Thank God for four-wheel drive.

It wasn't the first time the road conditions had forced them to progress at a snail's pace, and yet, to Darger, the hour-long drive out into the wilderness had gone quickly. Maybe it was the caffeine.

She tipped the cup to her lips. Dumped cooling coffee through the little plastic nozzle and into her maw. Then she went back to looking out the window.

Pine walls encased the road. The trees formed shear vertical lines going straight up, many of them stretching a hundred feet into the air. Darger craned her neck to try to see the one narrow slice of sky visible from her vantage point, catching only a flutter of cloudy gray up there, a strobe-like flitting of light between the tops of the trees.

The vehicle scuttled up one last hill and rounded a corner that leaned them all to their left. Then it parked them in front of a row of three buildings.

She chugged the last of her coffee and climbed out of the Bronco with the others. Feet stepping down onto a hard-packed sandy driveway flecked with gravel.

Crisp air surrounded her the second she left the SUV. It

was the kind of cold that stung her cheeks on contact. Made her lips and nostrils tingle.

OK. I guess this really is Alaska.

The morning chill would die back quickly enough now that the sun was climbing, but the frigidity in the air felt like an important reminder of where she was, what she was doing. An icy slap in the face. Refreshing if unpleasant.

Darger turned her attention to the cabins. The two on either side were double-wide trailers similar to the ones she'd seen from the seaplane on the flight in, but the one in the center was a more traditional cabin, with a high peaked roof that jutted up into the break in the trees and caught more sunlight than anything else around — a spot of brightness among all of the shade.

The treated wood siding was an orangey-brown shade not so far from the hue of the sand on the road. A red metal roof gleamed above that, smooth interlocking panels angling up at a steep pitch. It reminded her of a miniature version of the Driftwood Inn, though she suspected this cabin was modular, and thus, portable.

And then Darger's eyes drifted past the handsome structure of the cabin. Snapped to something incongruent in the distance.

She could see another break in the trees on a hill not so far off. A naked place where the logging had stripped one part of the land — a bald spot on the slope facing them. Stumps and broken branches and puddles of sawdust littered the ground, and the stark patch trailed out of sight over the hill. It looked very wrong with all of the untouched forest still hung up around it. An injured spot on the earth. Shaved and shamed.

They walked toward the center building, boots and shoes grinding into the gravel. Officer Bohanon led the way up a slight incline toward the front porch.

As they reached the door, Haywood stepped to the front of the pack. He tugged at a lanyard looped around his neck, slipped it over his head. Used a key dangling from it to unlock the door.

The singlejack pushed stringy hair out of his face, then waved them inside.

"Welcome to our humble abode," he said, walking deeper into the chamber.

Chief Rhodes filed in with Darger just behind her. Bohanon stepped to the side and waited to go last with both hands gesturing toward the doorway like some old-fashioned gentleman or maybe a bullfighter.

Darger's eyes took a second to adjust to the shade inside the building. Everything shadowed at first.

Then she saw the skeletal frames of the bunk beds take shape. The bunks took up most of the floor space in what was essentially one great room buoyed by thick round posts in a few places.

"Open floor plan, as you can see," Haywood said, sweeping his arms one after the other like a model on *The Price Is Right*.

A kitchen occupied the corner to the right. Commercial kitchen appliances huddled beyond an island, stainless steel hulks penned in on all sides by butcher block counters.

A small recreation area lay beyond the kitchen, where a ping-pong table squared off with a pinball machine, and a couple of couches sat before a flat-screen TV.

Haywood kept a brisk pace, leading them toward the rear of the building.

"And this is where the magic happens," he said, pointing a pair of finger guns at the bunk beds as they passed through them. "Yeah, sex is cool or whatever, but you ever get seven hours of uninterrupted sleep after a whole day sawing through old-growth timber? 'Cause that's the real magic."

Darger sniffed a little laugh.

"Just gimme one second," he said, jogging around one of the beds.

He opened a metal footlocker and pulled out a pair of heavy-duty safety earmuffs.

"You came all the way up here for your earmuffs?" Rhodes asked.

Haywood slipped the muffs around his neck.

"Hey, these aren't just any earmuffs, OK? These are top-of-the-line. Cost me a pretty penny."

They proceeded to a back door, where Haywood snapped a deadbolt out of the way. Nudged the thick oak door from their path.

And then they moved back outside, heading toward the crime scene.

"I hope it's OK that we're seeing the scenes out of order today, Agent Darger," Bohanon said. "See, the one crime scene back in Craig is technically the first, chronologically, but we've got what looks like a doozy of a storm blowing in later today. Flood warnings and everything. A road like this is almost sure to get washed out with weather like that, so I thought it'd be in our best interest to head out here to the two more remote crime scenes first thing. Check those off the itinerary before any inclement weather rolls in."

"It shouldn't be a problem at all," Darger said. "Besides, you know the lay of the land better than I do. I trust your judgment."

A mossy backyard squished underfoot like thick carpet, Darger's boots sinking into the plush green. A few smaller trees occupied the cleared land along the building, but the area still felt strangely barren compared to everything else around. Hollow. Naked.

They stepped through a tangle of weeds along the perimeter of the woods and crossed into the shade beneath the canopy of trees — that perpetual twilight that hovered just above the forest floor like a low-hanging fog. A bed of dead leaves and pine needles replaced the moss along the ground, not as squishy as the green carpet, but soft even so. And the earthy smell here held pungent tinges of mold or mildew, Darger thought. That made sense. This was a much wetter forest than what she'd grown up with in semiarid Colorado. All that humidity blew in off the sea and pelted the region with heavy rain.

The morning chill seemed to sharpen here underneath the trees, once more penetrating Darger's cheeks like icy needles, drawing her skin taut to the point of aching. Her breath congealed into twirling steam in the air before her lips and then vanished as quickly as it had formed.

Haywood trudged twenty or thirty paces into the thicket beyond the yard, ducked under a flap of yellow crime scene tape, and stopped. Angled his head down to the ground.

"He was right here. Well, part of him… Never did find the arms and legs, of course. Or the head."

He swallowed then, and something visible bobbed in his throat, made the sheet of skin ripple there.

The others closed on that cordoned-off piece of the forest. Bohanon held up the crime scene tape like the rope around a boxing ring, and Darger, Rhodes, and Wishnowsky crouched under the tented place.

All eyes turned toward the disturbed section of ground. Everyone going quiet as they looked.

The leaves had been swept back, and gouges raked lines

into the naked soil. A hole dotted the center of the turmoil, the punctured spot where the carved pole had jabbed into the ground.

The body was long gone, of course, but Darger could still see it, her mind transposing the grisly crime scene photo onto the reality before her.

An impaled torso jutting upright from the ground. That spike running through it like a skewer. Head gone. Arms and legs gone. Hacked off.

Ghastly.

She turned to look back the way they'd come. Squinting to pick out the cabin behind them through the plant life.

Even partially obscured by the foliage, it was only maybe one or two hundred yards from the back door. Ballsy to display it so close with something like three dozen men so nearby.

She tried to picture him out here in the dark hours just prior to dawn. Even with lumberjacks fanning out through the woods in a haphazard search party, he'd dismembered and displayed the body barely more than a stone's throw from the building. The feat seemed more striking as she stood here and looked at the logistics of the scene up close.

He knows his way around these woods, that's for sure. Comfortable even in the pitch black of night.

A faint chill tickled between Darger's shoulder blades and made her twitch. She glanced around to see if anyone had noticed, but all eyes were still trained on the ground.

They all stood there, looking. Thinking. Quiet.

Rhodes finally broke the spell, ducking under the police tape and striding deeper into the woods. She spoke over her shoulder as she disappeared between a couple of pine trees.

"The actual kill site was off this way."

CHAPTER 15

The group hiked another few hundred yards into the woods, following Rhodes's lead into the thicket. All those boot treads tromping waffle-like prints into the soft forest floor.

Darger fell in behind Bohanon toward the front of the pack with Haywood and Wishnowsky bringing up the rear. She looked back to make sure they were keeping up.

The singlejack seemed solid enough — his confidence plain in his body language — but the supervisor from the other camp looked a little listless and pale. Something queasy evident in the folds around his lips and eyes, reminding Darger of someone who'd eaten bad scallops.

Haywood caught her examining the two of them and gave a nod. Then he pointed two fingers at his eyes and pointed at Wishnowsky. Wound a finger next to his temple and shrugged.

So he was keeping an eye on Wishnowsky, too. Sensing the same weakness there that she did. Well, that was good at least.

The sun glowed brighter ahead — a gap forming in the canopy above, gray light streaming down in a visible shaft like a tractor beam. And then Darger's eyes traced lower, to the cause of the interruption.

An upturned behemoth of a Sitka spruce tree lay sprawled on the ground, the fat trunk several feet across. It'd fallen over, a mess of roots ripping out of the ground and leaving a crater in the dark soil. They veered left to go around it.

"That there is what you call a widow-maker," Haywood said. "Big ol' tree that comes down all at once. Could easily take out an entire campsite, you know? Flatten everything in the vicinity like a flapjack."

"Does that happen a lot?" Darger asked. "Trees just falling over, all by themselves?"

"Oh yeah. I mean, trees go down here all the time. Usually they're dead or dying, but you'll even see some healthy, living trees topple if the soil gets ate away by the rain. Erosion and excess moisture ain't a great combination far as a 15,000-pound tree's roots are concerned."

He shook his head and made a sucking sound with his teeth.

"Here," Rhodes said, somewhere up ahead.

Darger hustled that way. Found Rhodes and Bohanon standing in a small clearing. This time they stayed outside the small border formed by the yellow crime scene tape.

Another disturbed patch of ground spread outward from their feet. Pine needles scraped away in messy swoops, revealing haphazard patches of rich black soil.

Divots and gouges gashed lines in the loam like finger painting smears. Muddy spots formed puddles here and there where the black soil looked more brown. Clumped funny in a way that reminded Darger of kitty litter, like the dirt had been wet and went gummy as it dried.

Blood, she realized.

She slitted her eyes. Tried to imagine the scene.

The killer huddling here. Right here. The killing and dismemberment taking place in total darkness, under cover of night and trees. The blade's edge working in pitch blackness. Cutting. Slicing. The victim's feet and fingers scrabbling at the dirt and then going still.

That chill climbed up her spine again.

Haywood stalked off, his ankles beating through some shrubs as he strode away from the scene. Leafy explosions ringing out with every step.

The sound was enough to pull Darger back to the present. She blinked and looked at the others.

"Any insights?" Rhodes said, her eyes tracing up and down Darger's face.

The agent shrugged.

"I don't know. More than anything, the logistics are sort of shocking, right? He did this out here in the dark?"

Bohanon nodded.

"He lives out here," he said. "That's what I think. Who else could know the woods so well? Be so confident operating out here?"

Lives out here.

The idea triggered a burst of fresh ideas in Darger's head. A new puzzle piece that snapped together with the rest of her profile.

"Holy shit," she said. "He lives out here. He must."

Bohanon looped his thumbs into his belt before he went on.

"I know these woods about as well as anyone. Camped all up and down these hills. Have most of the maps memorized."

He shook his head gently before he went on. His eyes staring off into the middle distance.

"I would have told you that nobody knows the forests on this island like I do. No one. But this person, when it comes to experience and confidence out here... they're off the charts compared to me. It's not even close."

Wishnowsky whimpered a little and tried to cover it with a cough, perhaps as uncomfortable as Darger at the notion of someone's nature expertise outranking Bohanon's.

Her throat suddenly felt dry. She dug her water bottle out of her coat pocket and took a sip.

Rhodes squatted down and narrowed her eyes at the vacant

crime scene. She cleared her throat, but her voice still came out low and whispery when she spoke.

"He cut the corpse up right here. So where the hell are the body parts?" She jabbed a stick into the dirt. "I mean, why take them at all?"

And then they all held still, held quiet. Staring at the empty ground. Digesting Rhodes's question.

After a moment the silence was broken by Haywood. His voice was hard and came from somewhere behind them.

"Fucking. Huge."

Everyone turned that way to see him, some twenty or thirty yards off, pointing at the ground.

"Huge pile of bear scat here. And tracks headed off this way. Looks, uh… well, enormous."

Darger blinked. Not sure what to make of this development.

"Wait. You don't think…?" Rhodes said.

Haywood met her gaze and nodded. Made an affirmation noise deep in his throat.

Wishnowsky gasped, and Bohanon's eyebrows slowly climbed his forehead, reaching up for the brim of his campaign hat.

The quiet tension seemed to swell among them. A palpable discomfort growing taut until the air almost crackled with it. Nobody moved.

After a second, Darger understood what they meant.

CHAPTER 16

Haywood tracked the bear another few hundred yards into the woods, and the others followed. The trees tightened around them as they advanced, spruce and cedar boughs clustering together, the trail cinching so tight they had to move along in single file.

Darger walked behind Bohanon again, his broad shoulders seeming to plow a way forward for the both of them, parting the branches. She found herself oddly comforted to have him here. He knew these woods, possessed an impressive array of survival skills.

She could even imagine him living out here indefinitely, just like their killer must be. Hunting. Gathering. Building a permanent shelter of some kind. Starting fire with nothing more than two dry sticks and a shoelace or something.

Perhaps more important than all of these other characteristics, however, was the satellite phone tucked into a holster on Bohanon's hip. That was their lifeline out here where no cell phone tower could reach.

She should call Loshak soon, let him know about the theory that the killer was living in the woods. Her gut said he'd appreciate the thesis, probably agree with it. And it might give him something else to go on when he was digging through the tips.

"Well, lookie here," Haywood said.

The rumble of his voice shook Darger back to the present.

Haywood pointed at a depression in the soil, a place where the leaves and pine needles had been mashed flat, the dirt itself sunken in a few inches.

"A den. Sort of," Bohanon said. "The bears will sleep in these little half-dens during the warm months. They build something more elaborate, more permanent, come winter. A real shelter, usually in the ground or in a cave. Sometimes even in a tree. Takes 'em three-to-seven days to build a legit den, as a matter of fact."

"So is that the end of the trail?" Rhodes asked after taking a sip from her water bottle.

"Naw. Keeps on going this-a-way."

Haywood flicked his hand down a faintly visible game trail ahead.

Wishnowsky cleared his throat. He kept his eyes on the ground as he spoke.

"Is, uh… is there a reason we're, you know, tracking a bear?"

The others exchanged glances. Rhodes was the one who answered him.

"I think… Let's just say we suspect our bear may have tampered with the scene, in a sense. Just a quick look is all we want."

Wishnowsky didn't say anything to that. A fly buzzed around his head and he swatted it away.

Haywood led the way once more.

"What kind of information do these tracks tell you?" Darger asked.

Bohanon tilted his head to the side before he answered, a gesture that reminded Darger of a curious dog.

"I'd say we're looking at a male black bear. A big 'un. At least a 1,200-pounder. Maybe bigger."

"Damn."

"Black bears. Those are the scaredy cats, right?" Rhodes

asked.

Bohanon shrugged.

"Yes and no. Generally speaking, they are the smallest and least confrontational of the bears we have around here. That said, they are also the most likely to attack, in my experience."

"Jesus Christ," Wishnowsky hissed through his teeth.

"The least confrontational yet the most likely to attack? How does that work?" Darger asked.

"Of all the large game we have out here, the black bears are the least predictable. You just don't know what you're going to get. I'd say 90% of the time, they go sprinting off when they see a human. Just skittish that way. But sometimes they don't. There have been some very high-profile black bear attacks. Like I said, they are the toughest to figure. Grizzlies will let you know a lot quicker. They get really aggressive around their young and around food. But they rarely actually attack human beings.

"With black bears, there are variables to consider. First of all, this time of year is tough. In the run-up to winter and hibernation, some of the animals are starving, and that makes them desperate. There's also a thing called a predatory bear. Some black bears, males exclusively, learn to prey on humans. The belief is that it starts with campers not storing food properly. The bears learn to see the humans as a source of food, as weak, and they no longer fear them. That makes them far more likely to attack. With black bears in particular, a predatory bear attack is more common than a bear protecting cubs or food."

He tilted his head again before he went on.

"There was a couple in Canada who got attacked that way. A young male black bear grabbed the wife at the campsite and started dragging her away. The husband stabbed the bear repeatedly with a Swiss Army knife to no avail. See, he'd heard that you can just scare a black bear off, that they're scaredy cats like Claudia said, and he just wanted to hurt the animal enough to get him to go away. But this was a predatory bear. He saw the humans as prey, period, so he wasn't running. Later, the husband said if he'd known, he just would have cut the bear's throat. He'd had ample opportunity to do it, but it had never crossed his mind in the heat of the moment."

Everyone fell quiet for a beat. Their feet crunched over the bed of leaves, and the rest of the woods held silent in all directions around them.

"Did she make it?" Wishnowsky asked, his voice small. "The wife, I mean. Did she survive the attack?"

Bohanon thumped out a few more footsteps before he answered.

"The husband wrestled her away from the bear and got her onto a boat — a canoe, I think — to try to row to safety… but she bled out while they were on the water."

Haywood sighed, and then that expansive quiet seemed to swell around them again. The woods felt vast. Stark. Hollow.

But not empty.

Darger looked at the strange markings on the ground. Divots where giant bear feet had pressed into black soil. Toes visible in the soft earth. Claws poking dots in the dirt in front of them. The pads of the back feet much bigger than those of the front.

No. Not empty, these woods. They were not alone out here at all.

"So… we're just walking into the bear's home?" Wishnowsky asked.

Bohanon unhooked the can of bear spray from his belt and wiggled it in the air before him.

"I've used this stuff twice in my career. Sent bears sprinting away both times."

"It's like pepper spray?" Rhodes asked.

"Pretty much. Supposed to be stronger than what they pack in the stuff intended for humans."

Haywood turned around to ask a follow-up question.

"They come at you, those bears you sprayed?"

"Not exactly. They got close, but they weren't necessarily being aggressive. I think sometimes they're wandering around half asleep — just bumbling along. Like you can almost tell that they don't fully know or really grasp that you're there, even when you're yelling and whatnot. But when a thousand-pound bear keeps coming at you, you've got to turn 'em away, one way or another."

Even with the calmness in Bohanon's voice, Darger could feel a growing dread as they followed the tracks deeper into the woods. More depressed beds of pine needles marked the way — indented places, she assumed, where a bear or another large animal had slept.

They walked in silence for another stretch. She could feel her pulse battering away in the side of her neck.

"Aw, hell," Haywood said.

Darger turned her head that way but couldn't see him. Bohanon's shoulders were in the way, forming a human wall.

Then the big ranger stepped aside, and the way came clear.

Bohanon stood next to Haywood. Shoulder to shoulder. Both of their heads angled toward the ground in front of them.

A pungent scent filled Darger's nostrils as soon as Bohanon got out of her way — a musky, animal odor. Smelled like dog with a touch of extra funk to it.

She followed the gaze of the others.

And there it was.

The entrance to the bear den hung wide open. A gaping black hole under the base of an immense cedar tree. The tunnel trailed away into a rumpled spot that rose up from the ground next to a thick mess of roots. Lumpy. It looked like a cave mouth opening into a shallow grave.

And a human femur jutted out of the hole.

CHAPTER 17

Loshak yawned. He and Whipple had been going through tip line calls for several hours now, and he could tell his mind wasn't as sharp. He'd need a break soon.

Most of the calls had been crap so far, as expected. One woman called in certain that her stepdad was the Butcher — it even sounded reasonable enough at first, except that then she revealed that the suspect was a 76-year-old man. Several other tips mentioned suspects who lived thousands of miles away. And there were even a couple Donnie types calling in about Sasquatch sightings and the like, certain that large, mythical beasts were to blame for it all.

Yep. Loshak had to wade through a sea of trash in hopes of finding the one precious gemstone buried in the muck. If it was there, he'd find it.

He clicked the next call and hit "play," scanning the lines of text as he listened to the recorded message.

"The police need to speak to Jeremy Maddox." It was an older woman's voice, clipped and matter-of-fact. "He lives with his aunt at 14 Sunset Drive, and if there's anyone I know who could do the things they talked about on the news, it's Jeremy."

She hesitated. Her breath sounded like shaky wind blowing into the phone's microphone.

"I suppose I should just get this part out of the way right off the bat. Jeremy is my son. It brings me no joy to make this call, but I believe he could be the man you're looking for."

She took another breath before she went on.

Loshak pressed his headphone speakers tighter to his ears

like he might miss something important.

"The thing you have to understand about Jeremy is that he's always… had what I guess you'd call a fascination with dead things. He once brought home a raccoon he'd found dead on the side of the road and skinned it."

Loshak sat up straighter, suddenly feeling wide awake.

"Right there on our dining room table," the woman was saying. "You can imagine the scene it caused when I got home from work and found my grandmother's antique Hoosier cabinet splattered with blood.

"Then there were the fights at school. The shoplifting. The drugs."

She swallowed.

"When he was seventeen, he stalked a girl from school, and she ended up getting a restraining order against him. That was when he started to get bounced around to different psychiatrists, each with a new set of diagnoses. Seems like they had him down for every psychiatric disorder you can think of, at one point or another. After the bit of trouble with the girl, I thought it'd be best to send him away for a while, like maybe he could get a fresh start somewhere else.

"So he went to live with my sister. She's trying her best, but…"

She seemed poised to say something else but stopped. Sighed. When her voice came back, a tremor came with it.

"I'm… I'm not saying I think Jeremy did it. I just… well, I wouldn't be able to live with myself if I didn't say anything… in case he did do it."

There were three tones at the end of the recording, signifying that the caller had hung up. Loshak had taken notes while he listened, and now he glanced down at his pad.

A fascination with dead things.

A history of mutilating animals.

Fights at school.

Unstable home life.

Multiple diagnosed psychiatric disorders.

He was about to hit play again, to listen to the call a second time, when he noticed Whipple waving at him from across the table.

"You got something?"

"Not sure. Just felt like this one had something to it, maybe. More than the others, anyway."

"I think I have something, too, but you go first," Loshak said, wheeling his chair closer.

Whipple unplugged the cord from his headset and turned the volume up on his laptop before playing the call.

"Hello. My name is Maya Volk. I'm not sure if I'm supposed to give my name, but… I guess it's too late now."

The girl's voice fluttered as she spoke. Adrenaline. Rather than sounding on the verge of tears like the last caller, this one was either nervous or scared. Or both.

"I don't even know how to say this. It sounds so crazy when I try to say it out loud. But I had this feeling when I saw the news report about the… the murders. The one about the lumber cabin, in particular. I thought I was going to pass out."

Breath whistled in her nostrils.

"Because Walton Banks, he talks a lot about how all these different people like to pretend they own this island. The lumber companies and the tourism groups. But they were wrong, because this was *his* land, his birthright, and it had been stolen. And he said that one day they'd all get what was coming to them."

Silence hung on the line for a second. Then the woman's voice came back.

"One time, we were camping up on Klawock Lake, and we saw some people out on the water, fishing. Walton got really angry about it. Called them trespassers. He picked up his rifle and aimed it at them and pantomimed shooting them. I begged him to put the gun down, and when he finally did, he said if you find someone on your property, you have a right to do whatever it takes to stop them."

There was another long pause before she spoke again.

"That's… um… that's all. I apologize if I've wasted your time. Thank you."

The call ended, and Whipple swiveled to face Loshak.

"Now, I know we talked about the idea of someone having a vendetta against the lumber companies, and you didn't care for it. Said the crimes felt more personal."

"This particular vendetta sounds awfully personal," Loshak said, nodding.

"Also, if I'm not mistaken, Nicole Baird used to take people up to Klawock Lake sometimes for her survival classes. If this Banks fella frequented the area, he might have seen her up there at some point."

"OK. I'd say Walton Banks definitely makes the shortlist." Loshak scooted back to his computer. "Come listen to this one."

He played the message left by Jeremy Maddox's mother and watched Whipple's eyes go wide when she mentioned the part about skinning a raccoon on the dining room table.

"Do you know him? Jeremy Maddox?" Loshak asked.

"Doesn't sound familiar to me, no. But hot damn. Two suspects just like that."

Whipple closed his laptop and hopped to his feet.

"Who should we talk to first?"

"Well, we have Maddox's address. I say we start there."

CHAPTER 18

Rhodes snapped photos, squatting close to the den to get a good clear shot of the head of the femur. Darger crossed her arms and squeezed herself in something of a self-hug as she looked on that knobby ball where the bone ended.

"Jesus. I mean, how does this work?" Wishnowsky asked. "Should we, like, take the bones with us?"

"No," Rhodes said, not looking up.

Wishnowsky stammered a second, his face going a little red before he could get the words out.

"Those are the bodily remains of a logger. If it were one of my men... his wife... she'd, you know, want it. Or them. Or whatever."

"It's evidence," Rhodes said. "For now."

She took a couple more pictures and stood up, flicked through the photos on the viewfinder and seemed satisfied.

Bohanon put a hand on Wishnowsky's shoulder and patted a few times to try to calm him down.

"The task force already arranged for cadaver dogs to come in from Juneau, but they won't be out here for another day or two," he said. "So we'll take pictures of what we find, make sure not to disturb anything, and we'll head back and report it. For now, this remains an active crime scene. Later on, once the case is in the books, I'm sure the remains and any belongings will be turned over to the family. Does that make sense?"

Wishnowsky gave a single nod.

"Right. Of course."

After a second, he pushed up his glasses and went on.

"So is it wise to be, well, hanging around a bear den like this? Didn't we just learn that once a, uh, black bear thinks of a human as prey it becomes much more dangerous? Predatory and whatever. Sure as hell seems like this one would be by now."

Haywood scoffed.

"Buddy, believe me, if the bear was around here now, we'd know it."

"We won't dally long," Bohanon said, his hands sliding into that belt-at-the-hips cop stance again.

"But we should take a quick look around, right?" Darger said. She didn't want to voice her other thoughts just yet, so she didn't. "There could be more bones."

Rhodes made firm eye contact with Darger and nodded. Maybe she knew what the agent was thinking.

"A quick look couldn't hurt," Bohanon said.

He clapped Wishnowsky on the shoulder once more and joined the others as they fanned out to kick at the bushes.

Darger leaned down next to the gaping mouth of the bear den. Up close it seemed immense. Cavernous. Had to be big enough to fit a 1,200-pound black bear, she supposed. That pungent stench was stronger here. Like bad breath and rotting meat and some strong musk blending into one distinctly animal odor.

"Aw, Christ," Wishnowsky said, shuffling back. His voice cracked as he went on. "Don't go in there!"

"Just looking," Darger said, leaning in closer still.

She flipped on the flashlight on her phone and shined it into the black hole. Swept the beam over the interior of the den.

Tree roots and matted dirt walls stared back, dead leaves smushed into the earth all along the perimeter. She couldn't help but picture the bear taking a week to build this thing like

Bohanon had said, nose and paws shaping this cave like a sandcastle on the beach. This, of course, was where the creature would sleep the cold Alaska winter away. Hibernating for months.

"No bear," she said.

Wishnowsky sighed like someone had let the air out of him.

"Just dirt and roots and leaves," she continued. "No. Wait."

She brushed her light back to the elongated shape on the floor of the den, along the back wall. It looked like a stick. Spindly. But the bone shone gleaming white when the light touched it. White as a bleached tooth.

"Shit. Found another bone. A fibula or tibia, I think."

Then she saw the duller object just next to the bone. A dark lump. Thick. Maggots crawled over the exposed meat along one edge.

She gagged and pulled back from the den mouth. Pressed the back of her hand to her lips.

"And most of a foot. Flesh still on it."

Wishnowsky squeaked and shuffled back some more. His hands curled in front of his chest in a pose that reminded Darger of a Tyrannosaurus rex.

"Got something over here," Haywood called.

Darger jogged over to where he stood. Traced the line from his pointy figure to the stick of white down in the ferns.

Ellinger's arm, most of it stripped of flesh. Another cluster of maggots crawled over the few places that hadn't been eaten away.

Darger tore her eyes away from the grisly sight and glanced over at Bohanon.

"So… is it normal for a bear to drag a carcass back to its den?"

A furrow appeared between his brows.

"I've never heard of it. They'll drag a kill from open ground into some sort of cover. And sometimes they'll even bury a partially eaten kill under moss and leaves. But they usually keep their dens clean. They don't defecate, urinate, or eat inside it."

Wishnowsky scoffed.

"Well, obviously this one did."

Darger looked at Rhodes who gave her another firm nod.

"Not necessarily."

Wishnowsky licked his lips. Eyes darting back and forth.

"What do you mean, 'not necessarily'?"

"Maybe someone brought the body parts here," Rhodes said. "On purpose. To feed the bear."

CHAPTER 19

On the walk back to the cabin, Darger called Loshak on Bohanon's satellite phone. She felt a little like Zack Morris from *Saved By the Bell* pulling the telescoping antenna up and holding the chunky plastic brick to her ear, but once she filled Loshak in on their skeletal findings in and around the bear den, the conversation pulled her out of any sense of awkwardness.

"Sounds like quite a haul, evidence-wise," Loshak said. "And the bear angle is… bizarre. Can't say I've ever seen anything like that before."

Darger nodded along as he spoke.

"I know what you mean. When are the cadaver dogs going to be here?"

"It was supposed to be in a few days, but Whipple's going to call and see if we can't get them out here sooner than that. It may not do a whole lot for the investigation, but I think it would mean something to the families to find the rest of Alice Carr and Nicole Baird."

Darger ducked under a tangle of pine boughs as Loshak talked. She had slowed her pace on purpose, falling behind the others to get a little privacy on the call.

Now she scanned the trail ahead and didn't see them anymore. Her breath hitched.

She stopped. Her head swiveled. Gazed on only empty forest in all directions.

Had she lost them that quickly?

Would she be able to find her way back to the cabin on her own?

Her heart knocked in her chest. A thudding kick drum echoing under Loshak's words.

And she couldn't help but think of the 1,200-pound black bear with a growing taste for human flesh, perhaps somewhere behind her right now. Snuffling the air and knowing that fresh meat lurked nearby.

Wobbling branches drew her eyes at last. A whip-thin sapling still quivered from someone having passed by recently.

Darger hustled to catch up to the bobbing trees, and Wishnowsky's pudgy back appeared up ahead.

He turned sideways to sidle between two hemlocks. Disappeared into the shadowy cleft between the needles.

A faint sigh spilled out of Darger's lips as she pressed into those same boughs a few seconds later. Needles scratched at her cheeks and swished over her jacket.

She broke through to the other side, and the whole crew reappeared up ahead. Laying eyes on Bohanon's hulking figure in particular eased her worries — his knowledge of these woods would keep them safe. She could believe in that.

"I've got something else I wanted to run by you, actually," she said into the phone. "Officer Bohanon suggested that perhaps our unsub is living out here. Full time, I mean. Seeing these crime scenes up close, seeing what the perpetrator was able to pull off in total darkness… He'd have to know the land extremely well, be comfortable out here, day and night. And it'd fit the territorial angle of the profile. We're always more protective of home."

There was silence on the other line, and Darger thought she might have lost the signal.

"Loshak?"

"Sorry, I just started thinking about how we could use that. Figuring the crime scenes and dump sites, we might be able to triangulate a fairly tight search area. And there'd potentially be natural shelters we could check first. Did your hotel room have that brochure about all the caves on the island?"

"Yeah, I glanced at it last night," she said.

"Well, I'll get in touch with the folks at the Forest Service office, see if they have some ideas on likely spots where someone could hide out. And I'm thinking we should consider calling in a fugitive apprehension team with a K-9 unit. I mean, if he's living out there, it changes the game. Between the cadaver dogs and scent dogs, we might just be able to flush this guy out."

"Good idea," Darger said, looking out over the vast forest floor. "How are things going on your end? Get anything from the tip line?"

"A couple good leads, yeah. We're heading out to speak to a potential witness right now."

"That was fast."

"I figured it would be," Loshak said. "It's a small town."

"I'll let you get back to it, then." Darger skirted around a massive spruce. "And if I don't call at the next scene, I'll fill you in when we get back."

"Sounds good."

As Darger ended the call, she caught sight of the camp up ahead. A feeling of intense relief overcame her, and she suddenly understood just how tense she'd been since discovering the bear den.

She noticed a subtle relaxation in the body language of the two other LEOs as they approached Bohanon's vehicle as well. So she hadn't been the only one feeling uneasy.

She turned and looked back. The forest had a solemn eeriness to it. The vastness. The isolation.

And the bears weren't the only killers in these woods.

CHAPTER 20

On the way to speak with Jeremy Maddox, Loshak and Whipple stopped off at the pizza place in town and ordered two meatball subs to go. Whipple drove and ate with the experience of someone who was used to this particular brand of multitasking.

Maureen Hilyer, Maddox's aunt, lived in a log cabin-style house at the end of a dead-end street. A small vegetable garden occupied the south side of the yard, and there was a patch of fading fireweed out front. The spruce trees bordering the property cast long shadows over the gravel driveway.

Before they made it to the front steps, a woman was at the door. She was around forty, with long dark hair braided down her back and square frame glasses.

"Can I help you?" she asked, peering out from behind the door.

"I sure hope so," Whipple said. "I'm Bill Whipple, Craig chief of police. This is Agent Loshak from the FBI."

"What's this about?"

"Ms. Hilyer, do you have a nephew by the name of Jeremy Maddox?"

"Yes."

"And does he live here with you?"

"Yes."

"Is he here now?"

"He's at work."

"Where does Jeremy work?"

"At the cannery in town."

"OK." Whipple jotted this down. "Do you happen to remember his whereabouts on Friday?"

"He went to work, got back around 7:30, as always. We ate dinner. He went to his room and played video games. His normal routine." She crossed her arms. "What is this? What do you want with Jeremy?"

"Ms. Hilyer, we got a call from your sister. It seems she thinks there's a chance Jeremy might have something to do with the recent murders."

"Oh for Christ's sake." She threw her hands in the air and then turned back to the door. "Come on. You might as well come inside."

They entered a tidy kitchen area with a small breakfast bar and two stools. The back end of the house was an open living room with tall windows facing the stand of Sitka spruce trees at the back of the property. A woodstove huddled in the corner with a neat stack of firewood beside it.

Ms. Hilyer went around to the sink and began filling a tea kettle with water. She lit the stove and set the kettle over the flame.

"Look, my sister, she's not a bad person, but she doesn't really understand Jeremy," she said, moving back to the sink. "My sister is big on appearances. It's important that her family look 'normal' to everyone else. And Jeremy… well, he's just not. But that's not his fault. And it's certainly not a crime to be a little odd."

Ms. Hilyer pulled the top off a French press coffee pot and used a wooden spoon to scoop the grounds from the pot into a canister marked "COMPOST."

"It sounds like you have a lot of empathy for your nephew," Loshak said.

She gave a little shrug.

"I'm on the spectrum, so I know what it's like to feel like no matter what you do, you just don't fit in. And I know what it's like to live with someone who treats you like a freak." Her face tensed. "You know, my sister was so embarrassed of me when we were in school, she told everyone we weren't actually related. That I was adopted."

The water was boiling now and Ms. Hilyer shook her head. She scooped fresh grounds into the pot and poured the hot water over it. A cloud of steam billowed into the woman's face, fogging up her glasses.

"Anyway, my point is that Jeremy may be strange, but that doesn't make him dangerous." She set a timer and then took off her glasses to wipe them clean. "He's never been violent."

"What about the fights in school?" Loshak asked.

"That was self-defense. Jeremy got picked on a lot, on account of being different."

"And the stalking?"

"A misunderstanding," she said, selecting two mugs from one of the cabinets and setting them on the counter. "I know that sounds like I'm downplaying it, but I don't mean to. Jeremy does a lot of what they call 'magical thinking.' He noticed this girl at school and something inside told him he had to know her for some reason. That she was 'special,' somehow. So he'd follow her around school and keep notes on her. What she was wearing. What she ate for lunch. Who she talked to."

"Pardon my saying so, but that sounds like stalking to me," Whipple said.

Ms. Hilyer sighed and pressed down on the plunger of the French press.

"I know how it sounds. But he didn't have an endgame. Not the way most stalkers do. He didn't believe they'd end up in a

110

relationship. In fact, he specifically didn't want her to know him at all." She poured coffee into the cups and pushed one to Loshak and the other to Whipple. "There was no possessiveness. No romantic notions. No intent to do anything at all, other than keep his little notes. I'm not saying that makes it OK. But Jeremy sometimes needs help in scenarios like that to understand that what he's doing is wrong."

Loshak ran through bits and pieces from the profile, lining up the ones that fit Maddox. Fraught relationship with his mother. Stalking behavior. Trouble at school and with his peers. History of mental illness. Criminal record.

"Could we see Jeremy's room?" Loshak asked.

His aunt's mouth twitched.

"You have to promise not to touch anything. One of the ways I've built trust with Jeremy is giving him his own space. I don't go into his room without permission, and I never move his things around. I won't let you violate that."

"Not a problem," Loshak promised.

They took a narrow flight of stairs down to the basement. Half of the space was a utility area with a washing machine and dryer. Jeremy's "room" was cordoned off with a row of sheets stapled to the joists overhead.

Loshak held one of the sheets to one side so they could enter the space.

There was a twin bed shoved into one corner, sheets and blanket left unmade. A garment rack laden with hangers appeared to be mostly unused. The majority of Jeremy's clothes were strewn about haphazardly in piles along with other random detritus: notebooks, pens, books, and video game cases.

A small TV perched on a table at the end of the bed with an older model Xbox, the power cords and charging cables in a tangled mess.

The one point of neatness in the room was a bookshelf next to the bed. On top of the faux wood veneer was a careful arrangement of small animal skeletons.

Chief Whipple glanced from the odd collection and over to Loshak. He turned to Jeremy's aunt.

"These are… interesting."

"Look, Jeremy has a fascination with death, but he didn't kill any of those animals. He finds them already dead. In the woods, on his hikes. Roadkill on the side of the road. Sometimes my cat brings dead mice and ground squirrels around. Jeremy gives them funerals and buries them in the yard, waits a few months for nature to do its thing, and then he digs up the skeletons.

"I know that sounds like a macabre interest, but it's not hurting anyone. And he's surprisingly gentle about the whole thing. Look at how tiny some of those bones are, and not a single one broken."

She pointed at one of the skeletons.

"Besides, you name me one place in this town that doesn't have some kind of taxidermied head hung up on the wall. How is that any different?"

Whipple took one last look at the collection and turned to face the woman.

"You mentioned hiking. Jeremy spends a lot of time outdoors?"

The woman stood up straighter.

"He does now. His mother was content to let him rot away in front of the TV, but I've made it a point to encourage him to spend more time in nature. It seems such a waste to live somewhere like this and not take advantage of all it has to offer. We hike together sometimes, but he's also taken to exploring the island on his own. I think it's done wonders for his mental health."

"Does Jeremy own any firearms? Crossbow? Things of that nature?"

"Absolutely not. I dislike weapons."

Loshak tried to get a feeling from the room. A sense that this was the living space of a murderer. But a bedroom wasn't like a crime scene. Even if there were evidence of something more sinister somewhere here, he'd probably have to dig around to find it. And in this case, that would require a warrant. Warrants required probable cause, and right now, the only thing they knew for sure was that Jeremy Maddox was a strange young man.

What he needed was to talk to Jeremy in person. That would give him something, even if it was just an inkling that the kid could be their guy.

He gave Whipple an almost imperceptible nod, indicating that he was ready to go. They thanked Ms. Hilyer and headed back out the way they came.

On the walk to the car, Whipple was the one to break the silence, keeping his voice low like Hilyer might be listening in.

"We going to the cannery to talk to Jeremy?"

"That's right."

"Seems like a weird one. Still, the aunt sure doesn't think it's him."

Loshak nodded, but he didn't voice his next thought out loud.

The lady doth protest too much, methinks.

CHAPTER 21

The Bronco sliced its way down another dirt logging road into nowhere — a winding path that cut like a river between two steep slopes of trees. With everything set at dramatic angles, all the opposing textures of the foliage — supple green leaves, spiky pine needles, the withered husks of the growth already gone shriveled for the winter, and the puckered dry of the bark — gave it the feel of an oil painting.

The serpentine road also made Darger think about going on the log ride at Elitch Gardens as a kid, sliding around that snaking track of water before the big plunge at the end.

Her belly rumbled. Thankfully it wasn't too audible over the sound of the tires juddering over the rough road. She dug in her coat pockets hoping to find something — candy or a piece of gum, maybe a pack of those neon orange crackers Loshak sometimes brought on the plane. Pocket number one held a pair of nitrile gloves and some plastic zip tie FlexiCuffs. Pocket number two contained a BIC lighter.

Third pocket's the charm.

But when her hand rose out of that last pocket like a vending machine claw, she found only a balled-up tissue in its clutches.

She glanced around at the other faces in the car. Took them in one by one.

Bohanon's jaw was set. Brow scrunched like a predatory bird's. He kept a death grip on the steering wheel. Fighting with it every time a pothole or rutted spot tried to pull them off the road.

Haywood and Rhodes both wore blank expressions. Eyes flicking over the wilderness out their respective windows.

Wishnowsky seemed to have some color coming back to his cheeks, the ghostly paleness that had afflicted his face out near the bear den receding to its normal semi-rosy shade. That was good.

They were heading onto his turf now, and though the crimes committed near here were just as grisly as the more recent murder, from what Darger understood, they were less likely to happen upon anything too dramatic at this scene today. The techs and dogs had already crawled through the woods here and turned up very little.

Darger checked her pockets one more time. Fingers fishing into those fabric flaps. Digging around in the shadows.

Nothing edible.

And then the SUV pulled up hard. Brakes squeaking faintly. The vehicle stopped short with a jerk.

It made the agent lean forward. She ripped both hands out of her pockets to brace herself against the front seat.

The inertia let up all at once, Darger fell back into her seat, and the Bronco settled. Bohanon killed the engine.

The stillness seemed to jump up around them all. Pouncing. An almost violent motionlessness. Striking and strange after all that forward momentum.

Darger's head snapped around. Her eyes flicked everywhere. Looked for the camp. The bunkhouses. Any buildings or signs of civilization at all.

Nothing.

Just trees in all directions. Forest so thick it looked impenetrable. The road forming that lone strip of mud that cut through it all, trailing up a hill and rounding a bend away from them.

"Is this it?" she asked.

Bohanon tucked the keys under the visor as he answered her.

"Not quite. Road is washed out."

Wishnowsky chimed in then, his voice sounding surprisingly confident in Darger's ears. He really did seem to have bobbed back to normality after his minor panic session in the woods.

"This stretch of road is a recurring problem for us," he said. "Washes out just about any time we get a substantial amount of rain. It's not a big deal, though. We'll have to hoof it over the rough patch, but there's a cart we can take the last two or three miles up the hill. We use it to schlep the workers up the slope every fall when the road gets nasty like this."

Looking out the window again, Darger could see matted grass with bald sandy patches out the passenger side — the makeshift parking lot used during the wet season.

Everyone climbed out, and Darger watched Haywood toe up to the wounded section of the road. After a second, he shook his head.

She moved that way and stood alongside him, gazing down into the breach.

A gouged place in the sand gaped back at her, about eight feet across, alternately jagged and muddy. A few craggy rocks just bigger than bowling balls peeked up from the slitted place where the dirt had been washed away almost completely, a craggy canyon where the road should be. From there, the divot continued into the foliage, a delta mouth of sorts spilling into a cluster of ferns.

Haywood sucked his teeth before he spoke.

"Damn. We get our share of bad roads back at our camp, but nothing quite like this. How deep do you think the worst of it is? Five feet? Six?"

"Gotta be at least six," Rhodes said, now standing beside them as well.

"Can't you just picture some hot dog racing through here, not seeing the gorge until it was too late?" Haywood said, laughing a little as he spoke.

Darger imagined the front end of the Bronco tipping into the ravine. One fender plunging into those rocks and wedging there. She shuddered. They'd need a crane to get it out.

"Over here," Bohanon said.

The officer stood off to the opposite side of the track with Wishnowsky just behind him.

"It's wet as a creek bed in the low spot, so we've got some flagstone here to walk across," Wishnowsky said. "We used to lay down boards, but they washed away a few times. So far the stone has stayed put, though the silt covers it over every couple months."

Bohanon went first, walking across the footpath awkwardly like he was walking on a balance beam. When he reached the other side, he turned and looked back.

The others followed then. Haywood hopped across the stones like he was a kid crossing a river.

They hiked up the hillside, the muddy road going dry and sandy again underfoot, the sloppy mush sound of their footsteps turning back into a gritty crunch.

The land pitched upward into a steeper angle. Darger could feel her calves and thighs go harder and harder with each step, muscles flexing and taut.

Just around a bend in the road, they found a small carport tucked back in the trees. What looked like an oversized golf cart sat underneath the angled awning.

"Here we go," Wishnowsky said.

He jogged over and jumped into the passenger seat, then waved the others over. Smiling now.

They piled in after him. Darger found it mildly amusing that Bohanon had been more or less conscripted to drive again, with everyone else falling into the same seating arrangement just like school kids with assigned desks.

The dashboard looked more like a computer than anything. A big touch screen jutted from the center of it.

Bohanon punched a circular button next to the steering wheel, and the vehicle whirred to life with more of a humming sound than the rumble of an engine.

"Sounds exactly like firing up the Dell desktop my parents had in the 90s," Haywood said, grinning.

Wishnowsky pushed his glasses up onto the bridge of his nose before he responded.

"It's electric. Crazy to think that in just a few years, ICE vehicles will be obsolete. Every car and truck will sound more or less like a computer."

"ICE vehicles?" Rhodes said.

Wishnowsky gave a faint smile.

"Internal combustion. Gas engines. They'll all be EVs sooner than later. California already passed a law about it. 2035 is the cutoff, I think? Shoulda bought some Tesla stock after all, eh?"

Bohanon muscled the steering wheel, and they veered out from under the carport, juddered over a rough patch, and then they were on the sandy road and the ride smoothed out.

The little cart whirred, a fluttery sound. It reminded Darger of the noise of the flying cars from *The Jetsons*, perhaps crossed with the churn of an electric can opener she'd once heard as a kid.

"Not too bad," Bohanon said, tapping the steering wheel

like a dog's head. "Rides a little smoother than my old Bronco, I'd say."

A series of switchbacks took them up the biggest hill they'd encountered so far. The electric cart managed the hairpin turns well enough, and it did seem that Bohanon wasn't fighting as much with the steering wheel here.

After a few miles zigging and zagging up the hill, the camp appeared before them, seeming to rise from the flatland atop the slope.

It was set up similar to the previous camp — several trailers and a prefabricated cabin — but the buildings here were clearly newer. Neither the red metal roof nor the stained wood siding of the cabin had been worn by the elements, and even the lines of the trailers seemed somehow more modern. An array of solar panels sat at one side of the cleared lot, a tripod angling them all toward the sun.

"Oh, damn," Haywood said. "Y'all's place is nice. I heard you had solar up here. Must be sweet to not have to run generators all the time."

Wishnowsky nodded once, and Darger thought she could see a little pink dusting his cheekbones.

"The solar panels were my doing. They cover all the energy requirements for the cabins and the cart. They're on a timer, so they angle directly at the sun at all times."

"Nice," Haywood said. "Real nice."

He clapped Wishnowsky on the shoulder, and now Darger was certain the camp's supervisor was blushing.

"Well, it's certainly a boon to have access to amenities that don't require a constant supply of fossil fuels."

"I can fuckin' imagine," Haywood said. "Last fall, we had a timber transport truck get stuck in the mud. Blocked all the traffic to camp for days, including our resupply truck. We had to ration our fuel for necessities only, and that meant shutting off the hot water. It was a rough three days, and not just because cold showers suck butt. Some of the guys just quit showering altogether. You ever share a bunkhouse with a dozen unwashed lumberjacks?"

He let out a low whistle.

"Stinky doesn't even begin to cover it. Whole place smelled like Swiss cheese and ass."

One more switchback shifted the camp out of view for a second. Planted a wall of lodgepole pines in their way. And then they wheeled around the final corner and parked out front, the cabin towering over them.

Wishnowsky practically leaped out of the cart, and the others followed. He speed-walked a few steps toward the main cabin, and then he turned back.

"Now, before we head out," the supervisor said. "Who wants lunch?"

Bohanon stopped shy of the doorway and spoke up.

"Actually, I'm going to swap out some memory cards in the trail cams we've got out here real quick. It'll only take me ten minutes or so, and it'd save me another trip out this way."

"We can all go together, after we eat," Wishnowsky said. "I'm sure no one minds."

Bohanon glanced up at the sky.

"With the weather coming in this afternoon, I'd rather we not linger up here any longer than we have to." He waved his hand, as if to shoo Wishnowsky into the cabin. "You folks go ahead and eat. I'll wolf down whatever's left when I get back."

CHAPTER 22

On the drive back to town, Chief Whipple drummed his fingers against the steering wheel.

"What'd you make of all those skeletons in his room?" he asked. "That gave me the goddamn willies."

Loshak balanced his cane between his knees and cocked his head to one side.

"I dated a girl in college whose favorite hobby was taking hikes into the woods to look for animal bones. She was a biology major, though, so it didn't seem so strange. It's like the aunt said, we accept a fascination with bones and death in certain contexts. Science. Taxidermy."

"I guess so," Whipple said, sounding unconvinced. "Still seems awfully creepy to be sleeping in a room with that stuff."

They zoomed past the station, heading for the westernmost point of the island where the cannery was located.

Whipple made a right turn, and they rumbled down a rutted dirt driveway and parked. Loshak had gotten whiffs of the cannery before now, but the smell here on the premises was ten times stronger. Pungent and fishy.

There were seagulls everywhere, swooping through the air and waddling over the ground, each one hoping to scoop up some free grub.

Whipple led the way over to an industrial-looking building made of corrugated steel. He tugged open the door, and they entered.

If Loshak thought the smell was bad outside, it was overwhelming inside the cannery. The odor of dead fish in the air felt thick enough to suffocate. He breathed through his mouth and tried to focus on not gagging.

He followed Whipple down the assembly line, past a big metal chute dumping fish onto a stainless steel table. Loshak watched the first worker on the line slit open the belly of each fish before passing it on. The next guy thrust fish two at a time into a machine that automatically took the heads off.

There were several dozen people working, and most wore waterproof overalls and rubber boots. The workers nearest the "cutting" area were also decked out in yellow rain slickers, which were smeared with blood. Everyone wore thick gloves.

One part of the floor was covered in foamy pink guts. He and Whipple gave this area a wide berth. Finally, they located the foreman. He wore the same rubber boots and overalls as the other workers, but he sported a thinner pair of gloves and clutched a clipboard.

He was a stout man with a graying beard and wild eyebrows. Loshak couldn't help thinking that he looked like a stereotypical sea captain. He imagined the man standing in front of the wheel of a ship, a pipe clutched in his gritted teeth.

When he spotted the two men approaching, his caterpillar eyebrows gave a little jump.

"Chief Whipple, what can I do for you today?"

He had to shout over the noise coming from the various fans and machinery.

"Hey, Mac. Can we step outside for a moment? We have a few questions for you."

Mac held up a finger and tapped the nearest worker on the shoulder.

"I need you to take over the count for a minute or two," he hollered, handing over the clipboard.

Then the three of them headed for the door with the

foreman's rubber boots squeaking and squelching the whole way.

Loshak could still hear the rumbling of the machinery outside, but it was duller now. And despite the stench he'd noticed from the parking lot only a few minutes ago, after being inside, the air here now seemed the crispest and freshest he'd ever inhaled.

"John Mackenzie, this is Agent Loshak. He's with the FBI."

"No shit? And what's the FBI want with Knutson's Cannery?" His voice was raspy, but the tone was friendly enough.

"Does Jeremy Maddox work here?"

"As a matter of fact, he does," he said, pulling off his gloves. "But I'm guessing you already know that."

"And he's here today?"

"Actually, no." Mac scratched his beard. "He was supposed to be, but he called off Friday and took the next few days off. He tends to take his sick days all in a row like that."

Loshak and Whipple exchanged a look, which caught Mac's eye.

"This doesn't have anything to do with them people butchered out there in the Tongass, does it?"

"We can't really talk about it," Whipple said. "But if it were, what do you think about the idea of Jeremy doing something like that?"

Mac's mouth moved as he seemed to literally chew the question.

"Well, I don't like to talk out of school, mind you. But if I had to pick anyone I've worked with… shit, make that anyone I've ever met, it might just be Jeremy."

"Can you elaborate on that?"

"Guy's just kinda off, you know? I mean, he's never been

violent or anything like that. I should make that clear from the get-go. I wouldn't even say I don't like him. He keeps his head down and does his work. Never had a problem in that regard. But it's like when you try to talk to the guy…" He swiped his hand back and forth over his face. "There's nothing behind the eyes. Just blank."

He cupped his chin in his hand and continued.

"One time we had a rat in the cannery. Don't know where the hell it came from, but all a sudden it was scampering right down the line. It was mass chaos inside. Half the people were trying to catch it. The other half were runnin' from it like it had the plague. Anyway, it gets chased down the line, heading straight for Jeremy's post, and in one lightning flash movement— BAM!" Mac pantomimed a stabbing motion. "He speared the thing right through the middle with his boning knife. The thing was still moving, its little legs squirming. And Jeremy just holds it up in front of his face, looking at it with this absolutely dead-eyed expression. Like there's not a shred of emotion."

Mac crossed his arms over his chest.

"Now, I don't have any problem killing vermin. It's a part of the job, really. We can't have that kind of contamination. But this was just… brutal. So cold. Gave me the damn creeps."

Loshak listened as the man spoke, thinking they were getting a picture of a different Jeremy from the one his aunt had described.

"Any idea where he goes on his days off?" Whipple asked. "If he's not at home, I mean."

"I haven't the foggiest."

Loshak figured it was a long shot, but he asked anyway.

"Does Jeremy have any friends in there who might know?"

Mac shook his head.

"Nah. Like I said, Jeremy keeps his head down. He comes to work, and that's it. Never been one to socialize with the others, not even a little."

Whipple nodded.

"Would you happen to have a phone number for Jeremy?"

"Sure. Though technically it's his aunt's number—"

"Jeremy doesn't have his own phone?"

"Nope. He don't usually have much to say, but one thing he'll talk about at length is how the government is tracking the lot of us through our phones." Mac rolled his eyes. "Says anyone with a cell phone is a sheep."

"Well, I know you're busy, so we'll get out of your hair," the chief said. "Call us if you hear from him or see him, will you?"

"You can count on it," Mac said and headed back inside.

Back in the car, Whipple turned to Loshak.

"Lying about his whereabouts. Refusing to own a cell phone." The chief raised his eyebrows. "The plot thickens."

"It certainly does," Loshak agreed. "And I'm more than a bit curious to know what Jeremy does on these impromptu days off, and why he's been lying to his aunt about it. We should plan on heading back to her house around 7 so we can be there when Jeremy gets home."

Whipple tapped the steering wheel with his fingertips a few times.

"And until then?"

"We still have another potential witness to talk to." Loshak checked his notes. "Maya Volk."

"I'll give her a call," Whipple said, pulling out his phone. "See if she's free for a little chat."

CHAPTER 23

Bohanon clunks over the deck on heavy feet. Boot treads pounding the planks. Boards groaning a little as they flex beneath his bulk.

He can already picture the trail cams he seeks, their tripods hooked around tree trunks, their memory cards waiting to be swapped out. He wonders if they've snagged any footage of the killer prowling these woods, though he's careful not to get his hopes up — it's a long shot. In truth, he's in no particular hurry to get to the cams.

He lifts his head to look out over the land. Slopes full of trees tilting up toward the heavens, gray sky shearing off the tops of the hills like an uneven flattop.

The dirt drive slits an open place in the wall of forest. A vacancy that bends out of view as it stretches back down the hill. Like empty space on a painter's canvas, a void that creates compelling contrast with all the solid objects around it.

And some faint twinge of excitement flutters like moth wings in his chest as he moves for the woods.

He wonders why it never gets old. Being in nature. The thrill of walking among the trees, the searing bright concentration it seems to wire into his head, the renewal of his attention span, of his mood — none of these feelings fade. Ever.

His boots grind into the sparse gravel now. Carry him to one of the game trails off to the east side of the cabin.

He elbows through some vines. Strides into the hollow forest beneath the canopy, where that carpet of brown needles and dead leaves squishes under every step.

The effect, that magical spell nature seems to cast over him, seems greatly intensified when he walks these woods alone as he does now. With others around, it's there but muted. Its alchemy blunted in some way.

The truth is, it feels good to be away from them all. Not just the other law enforcement officers and lumber workers back in the mess hall of the cabin, but away from humanity in general.

Alone. In motion.

Nothing feels better than to walk alone. It's something he's felt since he was small, something that makes him feel kind of guilty.

Should a person want to be apart from everyone? Is it wrong to only find joy on these trails that snake through the vast wilderness?

The stand of cedars ahead catches the corner of his eye. It surprises him a little. Already here. Even ten feet out, he can't see the camera, but he knows it's there, tucked back near the trunk of one of the trees.

He stalks close to the prickly things. Grips a spruce sapling for balance. Jams the other mitt into the needles and roots around until he finds the angular object he seeks.

The flexible tripod wraps around the trunk of the tree like spider limbs clenched tight. It takes him a moment to unhook each of the legs, and then he plucks the camera from the boughs.

He powers the device up. Flicks a finger across the screen to scan through the thumbnails. He's not going to take the time to review it all now, but a quick look couldn't hurt.

His heart beats a little faster as his eyes flit over the screen, but it's the same static image over and over for the most part. That frame of pine needles forms a border around each shot. A few have birds perched in the branches, some near and some far. No silhouette of a man or anything of the like.

The usual. He sighs.

He ejects the memory card from the side of the device. Tucks the tiny disk into his breast pocket. Plugs in a new one.

Then he leans over to reattach the camera to the tree. Putting it back is somehow always faster than removing it.

He plods on toward the next camera. Veers hard to his left, heading more north than east now.

The going gets a bit rougher. Pocked land. Pitted and choppy and strewn with deadfall. He's off the path for now, but he'll hit the next game trail soon enough.

Once again his fingers find their way into his breast pocket. They wriggle past the plastic baggie holding the memory card to find what's tucked beneath it.

The pack of Juicy Fruit comes out just long enough to slide a piece out, and then it disappears back into its hole.

He unwraps the slice. Folds it into his mouth. Balls up the foil wrapper and rolls it around between his fingers and thumb, squishing it into something tighter and tighter.

This is his vice, he realizes. Sugary gum. He solely partakes in it in secret like a junkie.

Juicy Fruit. Bubble Yum. Shredded pouches of Big League Chew. Even those six-foot rolls of Bubble Tape. He loves it all.

As bad habits go, it's nothing compared to smoking or drinking or even gambling, but he has had three root canals so far, so it's not without its consequences.

His eyes sharpen. Focus. Find the faint ribbon of the game trail, that mahogany strip that creases the rug of the forest floor with a bare band of dirt.

He steps onto the trail. Picks up speed. Almost done.

He'll be back with the others in less than five or seven minutes, and he'll feel better the rest of the day for having had these few minutes in the woods to himself. Almost like his version of meditation or yoga or something.

He blows a bubble. Pops it with his lips. Lets the thin flap of gum rest on his tongue for a few seconds before he starts chewing again.

Then he ducks under a couple of low-hanging branches that reach out over the trail like outstretched arms. Feels the mottled bark skim across his back.

Just as he gets upright something crunches behind him.

A dry twig snapping. The percussive pop loud in the quiet. Sounds like a breaking bone.

His shoulders jerk up in a wince. An involuntary shrug that freezes at the top.

He stops. Listens. Feels that flap of gum gone motionless on the side of his tongue.

He realizes that the birds, too, have gone quiet. Nervous. Waiting.

He turns around. Feels a shaky breath drawn into his chest.

His eyes crawl over every inch of forest that he can see. Slowly scanning from left to right.

Green and brown leaves wag a little as a breeze kicks through. Dark tree trunks jutting up everywhere.

Nothing else there. Not that he can see.

But he's not alone. He can feel it.

His hand reaches down. Fingers brushing the top of the can of bear spray.

The quiet intensifies. Sharpens to a spiky point. Needle pricks that creep over his skin.

Another breath comes rolling in. Swells his ribcage. Vents through his nostrils.

He blinks. Sets his jaw. Squishes that wad of gum tight between his molars and holds it there.

And something lurches in the distance.

He cranes his neck. Fastens his eyes to the dark blur ahead and above.

A squirrel leaps from one tree to another. Snaps a dead branch as it jumps, another of those dusty pops ringing out over the emptiness like a small-caliber gunshot.

The critter flips its tail around once it lands. Cracks the bushy fur thing like a whip a few times, to the right and then to the left. Then the creature skitters down the trunk and disappears.

Bohanon shakes his head. Releases his hold on the bear spray. Turns and continues to the next cam.

The next breath that heaves in feels loose, relaxed, and those needle pokes on his skin feel more bubbly than biting now. Almost pleasant.

The trail slopes downward at a slight angle, and he can see the birch tree with the camera nestled around its trunk just ahead. Nearly done.

He steps down onto the lowest point of the trail. Feels just the slightest tug at the crook of his shin, the lightest touch like a fern frond or creeper brushing there.

Something cracks to his left. Louder than the dry twig. Thicker.

He has just enough time to turn his head that way.

And then something bites his ankle. Cinches around it. Pulls so taut it feels like it might rip his foot off.

He looks down. Barely has time to register the brown coil trussed around his pant leg.

Rope.

The cord yanks. Whiplashes him off his feet. Rips him off the ground.

A snare.

130

A trap.

Everything flips upside down. That rope jerks him by the ankle. Keeps pulling. Lifting him up and up.

His eyes swivel everywhere. Trained down at the blur of the forest floor as it zooms away from him.

Both his arms dangle between his head and the leaf-strewn ground. Limp limbs somehow over his head and beneath him all at once. Confusing.

He feels the blood rush to his temples, prickle along his scalp.

Feels the rope strangling his ankle. Impossible strength in the cord's grip.

Feels his stomach press toward his lungs, toward his neck. Somehow heavy in this upside-down state.

The rope reaches the end of its run. Bounces him hard once.

Then it sinks him back toward the ground gradually.

He dangles there. Rotates to the side. Spinning as the cord twirls.

Trapped.

Something flutters then. A yellow blotch drifting toward the ground.

The pack of gum. Spilling from his pocket. Falling away from him.

He reaches for it. Fingers grasping far too late. Clutching at emptiness.

And then he hears the crunch of heavy footsteps rushing toward him.

CHAPTER 24

Five plates sat on the table. Forks and knives splaying at odd angles. Semicircular smears of sauce and salad dressing looking like finger paint on the white ceramic. Darger couldn't help but notice that only Officer Bohanon's remained untouched entirely.

"Where the hell do you think Bohanon is?" Rhodes said, as though reading the agent's thoughts.

Darger shrugged. She'd been wondering the same thing for a while now, but she hadn't wanted to say anything about it — like maybe bringing it up out loud would jinx it.

"He said it'd be ten minutes or so."

She checked the time on her phone.

"But it's been at least twenty now. Probably more like thirty."

Haywood paced back and forth near the front of the cabin. Peeked out the windows on each side of the door every few seconds. His tension seemed to spread through the room, slowly infecting the other three who still sat awkwardly at the table.

"Easy to miscalculate time out here. I'm sure he'll be along any minute," Wishnowsky said. "In the meantime, I can get this place cleaned up."

The supervisor stood then and started gathering the dishes. After a second, Darger joined in and then Rhodes. They packaged Bohanon's uneaten portion in a disposable storage container to bring along and then loaded the dishwasher.

Haywood kept up his patrol at the windows, seemingly

oblivious to all they did. Something almost rodent-like twitched in his body language. The nervousness plain.

Darger could understand it. There was something about Bohanon that made her feel safe out here. A strength, a sureness — his absence felt surprisingly visceral, like cool air touching an open scrape.

Wishnowsky squirted in a load of liquid dish detergent that looked like strange aqua-tinged cream. Then he closed the stainless steel door and tapped a button along the top of it.

The machine beeped once and gurgled to life. A deep humming accompanied the sloshing sounds like a vent fan in a bathroom.

The camp supervisor turned their way. Noticed Haywood at the window.

"Any sign of him?"

Without looking away, Haywood shook his head.

Wishnowsky leaned over to clean the lenses of his glasses with the hem of his shirt. Slid them back on. Glanced up.

"Well, I might as well lock up here. We can wait for him outside. Like I said, I'm sure he'll be along any minute now."

Haywood grunted something, though Darger couldn't tell if there were any words involved. The lumberjack pushed through the doorway, and then his footsteps thudded down the steps.

The others followed after a beat, filing through the cabin door one by one and spilling down the stairs into the driveway. The day seemed brighter after spending time indoors — that gray sky veering closer to white, or so it seemed to Darger.

They milled around in the lot for a few minutes, before Haywood let out an impatient breath.

"This ain't right. He shoulda been back by now."

Rhodes pulled her phone out. Started swiping through her

contact list with flicks of her index finger.

"Hang on. I can call him real quick…"

She jabbed the screen with her thumb. Then she blinked hard, eyes going wide as she realized her mistake.

"Oh. Right."

Her cheeks bloomed to a pink the shade of salmon as she slid the phone back into her pocket.

"Yeah, no service out here," Wishnowsky muttered.

Haywood stalked closer to the tree line and cupped a hand around his mouth. He yelled through the half-horn of fingers there, his voice catapulting out into the woods.

"Bohanon!"

They all waited. Listened. Eyes flitting along the border between the dirt driveway and the forest.

No response.

The lumberjack yelled again. Louder this time. His voice breaking up at the end.

"So… what do we do if Bohanon doesn't come back?" Rhodes said, keeping her voice low.

"He'll show up any second now," Wishnowsky said. "Probably just a bad judge of how long it'd take to check his cameras. Men have a terrible sense of time, or so my wife is always telling me."

"Sure. Yeah. Hopefully." Rhodes worried at her bottom lip with her teeth. "But let's just say he doesn't. What would we do?"

Haywood shuffled along the perimeter of the woods. Leaned his head back like a wolf and yelled again.

Again everyone looked that way as though Bohanon would come bounding out of the woods when called like someone's pet German shepherd. The foliage held still.

"We'll go look for him, I guess," Darger said. "And if that

doesn't pan out… we'll call back into town and get more people out here to search."

"Shit," Wishnowsky said, the word hissing out between clenched teeth.

Darger and Rhodes both looked at him, speaking in unison. "What?"

"I just realized that Officer Bohanon is the one with the satellite phone. If he doesn't come back…"

The supervisor's eyes met Darger's then flicked over to Rhodes. None of them spoke, but the gravity of the situation started sinking in. Bohanon going missing, even for a few minutes, was scary enough. The idea of being cut off from contact altogether…

Haywood passed by them. Crossed in front of the cabin again heading the other way. Disappeared behind the building.

Darger had just enough time to wonder what he was doing before Wishnowsky interrupted again.

"The CB in the Bronco would have to be pretty heavy-duty as far as its range, no? The Forest Service guys are always way out in the middle of the wilderness. A handheld radio like the one Chief Rhodes has will only reach a mile or two, but I'd figure a VHF radio built into a vehicle would probably have a range of at least twenty-five miles. That should get us in touch with someone. I'd hope. If we don't happen upon Bohanon before long, we could try to call for help with that."

His face brightened considerably as he spoke, and Darger felt a little something loosen in her own neck and shoulders. She almost immediately felt guilty over the sense of mild relief with Bohanon still out there, that whipped dog feeling she sometimes got when she binged on junk food.

"Uh, guys. Got a problem over here," Haywood called from a distance.

Darger bolted like a startled deer. Rushed over to see what the singlejack had found, the others following close behind.

She rounded the corner and Haywood came into view. Standing. Staring at nothing, his head fixed toward the stark gravel lot.

Darger's legs jolted to a stop beneath her. Right away she knew something was missing, something important, but it took her a second to realize what.

The vacant parking lot shifted from benign to somehow wrong, somehow threatening as she stared at it.

Rhodes drew up alongside her and gasped, obviously seeing it, too. Wishnowsky brought curled fingers to his lips.

They all gaped at the empty space. Frozen. Unblinking.

Haywood was the first to say it out loud.

"The cart is gone."

CHAPTER 25

Paralysis gripped Darger's chest for the span of several heartbeats. Held her breath and stilled her voice.

How?

Why?

The confusion spiraled in her head. Somehow growing. Rippling outward.

She blinked then and remembered to breathe, to focus on the inhale and then the exhale. In at the diaphragm, out at the nostrils. She let her breath bring her back to the present this way. Blinked a few times and looked at the driveway and the cabin and the shocked faces of the others nearby.

"Would Officer Bohanon have ridden down to his Bronco?" she said, her voice sounding calmer than she felt. "Maybe he left something in the vehicle. Or wanted to take the memory cards from the camera down to keep them secure."

Hearing these words out loud, Darger found she didn't like them. These were plausible enough motives for Bohanon to take the cart, but they didn't feel right. At all. A sour taste crept into her throat.

Still, she kept talking, somehow unable to stop the stream of language pouring from her lips.

"The ride down and back might be — what? — twenty minutes or so. Maybe a little more."

She looked down the hill as she spoke. Eyes tracing along that spot where the road veered out of sight like the cart might appear there any second.

It didn't.

Haywood clicked his tongue against the roof of his mouth.

"Ranger— er, I mean Officer Bohanon seems, to me, like the kind of dude who'd say something to us before he ran off like that. I only met him recently, but that's what I think."

Wishnowsky cleared his throat. He sounded surprisingly confident when he spoke.

"Look, this time of year, the sun sets early, and darkness will fall in the woods long before that. I'd estimate we've got two hours. Maybe less. I say we hike down the hill. If Officer Bohanon is down there, great. If we meet him along the way, great. If not, well… he has the satellite phone to call for help, and we can call it in on the radio in the Bronco. We can find out if they've heard from him. Get some help looking for him if need be. He left the car keys under the visor, so even if we have to drive back down a bit to get in range for the radio—"

Rhodes scoffed.

"He goes missing for ten minutes, and we're just going to leave him here?"

Wishnowsky put his hands on his hips. Something fierce flashed behind the lenses of his glasses.

"I didn't say that. First of all, we don't even know if he *is* missing. But we do know it's going to storm tonight, and we don't want to be out here when it does. You saw that washed-out spot in the road down there. Well, this flood warning tonight could rip up ten more patches of road just like that and pen us in here. Maybe for days. No one wants that, do they?"

Nervous glances passed among them all, but no one said anything. Wishnowsky went on.

"We have plenty of time before the rain hits, but I don't fancy the notion of trying to hike down the twists and turns of this hill in the dark. I figure on foot it's about a forty-minute trek back to the Bronco, give or take. If we head down now, we can be at the vehicle with plenty of daylight to burn and decide how to proceed from there."

The more Darger thought about it, the more logical it seemed. Then another thought occurred to her.

"OK. Wait. If Bohanon didn't take the cart down the hill, who did?"

Rhodes's eyes blinked faster. Wishnowsky gulped. Haywood's mouth hung open a couple of seconds before he spoke.

"I mean…" the lumberjack said, trailing off. "Do we really think that's possible?"

The question hung in the air. Of course it was possible that the Butcher was out here with them, right now. But no one seemed to want to say that out loud.

Wishnowsky grunted, apparently getting a second wind of confidence.

"It's not about what's possible, but what's *likely*. And it's obvious to me that for one reason or another, Officer Bohanon took the cart and was waylaid somewhere along the way. Perhaps the battery died. It happens. That's why I think we should hike down and see. We cover all our bases that way, and nobody has to panic. The sooner we pick a path forward, the sooner we get through this."

Everyone held still again. Exchanging glances without speaking.

Rhodes nodded first, the tiniest flick of her chin. The gesture seemed to grow stronger the second time she bobbed her head.

Then Haywood shrugged and nodded as well. Darger couldn't tell if she could see a smirk or a half-smile on his lips.

All eyes fell on the agent then, and silent reverence stretched out over the woods. Haywood's eyes went a little

139

wider, something curious in them.

Darger took another breath. Deep inhale. Long, slow exhale.

Then she nodded as well.

Wishnowsky seized upon the consensus, perhaps sensing its fragility. He started walking down the dirt track, waved a hand over his shoulder to beckon the others.

"Let's get a move on."

Darger fell in behind him, walking alongside Rhodes with Haywood bringing up the rear. Their footsteps pattered at the muddy road, slapping and squishing like the sound of a dog eating spaghetti.

She stared at the tree line in the distance even as the earth tilted downward beneath her. Her eyes traced back and forth along that threshold where the pointed pine tops sheared off into the gray sky.

That zigzagging dirt road led them down the slope, and the forest suddenly felt much colder.

CHAPTER 26

The sun crept toward the horizon, and the shade thickened around them as they moved down the hill. Darger figured they were about halfway to the Bronco, though it was hard to be certain, and she found the dimming light ominous.

Shadows pooled everywhere beneath the trees on both sides of them. Dark gauze strung between prickly pine boughs. Gloom puddling beneath deciduous behemoths.

According to Wishnowsky, they still had about an hour and a half until dusk fully hit, and another half hour or forty minutes after that until the sun was down completely. Aside from this update about the daylight left, no one had spoken since they started down the track.

Their feet pounded at the dirt. Stabbed at the patches of dry sand. Scuffed against flecks of gravel. Sank a little wherever the moisture still gripped the dips in the grade.

Taken together, the footsteps made a strange beat. Some rhythmic gallop of scrapes and slaps and thuds. Hypnotizing.

The hike and the clapping throb of their footfalls seemed to have a lulling effect over time. Tugged Darger's mind away from the here and now and set it out into the stillness.

She found that icy feeling of fear had receded, that all of this had begun to feel more and more routine. Normal. Just a walk in the woods.

The crisp fall smell strengthened in her nostrils. The sharp scent of the pine needles. The earthy tone of the trees.

Untouched nature always smelled so clean to her. Bright and pure. It refreshed her in some way. Focused her. Helped her drop the white noise of daily life until that static buzz of society was gone entirely and her head was finally clear.

But, positive as it was in so many ways, that clarity brought along its own set of quirks. Somehow it always made her think of TV commercials from when she was a kid, some guy standing in the hills of Ireland, taking a pocket knife to a bar of Irish Spring soap. Funny how that worked. Corporations had invaded every cell of her brain until even standing in miles of pristine wilderness made her think of products to buy and their associated marketing campaigns.

Images planted deep in her synapses. Stored dreams of hand soap wired into her being, ready to fire off at the slightest touch.

As cynical as the notion made her feel on one level, the absurdity also brought a small smile to her lips. The ridiculous image flared in her head again — the aerial shot swooping over the lush green hills of Ireland, the close-up of the stupid knife slicing through the block of soap, shaving it like butter. Ludicrous.

The sudden giddy feeling made her think of the look on Loshak's face as he talked about the Mothman. The excited glee of a kid etched into his grin. That strange hush coming over his voice like someone might be listening in.

But then she thought of Bohanon again. Remembered how just a couple of hours ago he'd led the way through much of the first scene, his broad shoulders blazing a trail through the woods not so far from here. His bulky presence and wilderness expertise making her feel safe.

She hoped he was alright, that there was some normal explanation for his absence. It still seemed the most likely outcome to the part of her brain that calculated such things.

But she couldn't quite believe it.

And what did that really mean for the rest of them? Were they in danger now? Being watched?

Even after all she'd experienced in her career, it felt somehow childish to ask herself those questions. Melodramatic. Absurd.

But she knew it wasn't. She knew it better than anyone.

They weren't alone out here.

She stared into those dark spots in the woods again. Eyes trying to penetrate the pitted places between the trees, unable to see anything there but the shapeless void, a wall of black holes surrounding them.

She wondered which one he was hiding in.

CHAPTER 27

The soles of Darger's boots skidded down a vertical slab of sand along one of the hairpin turns. Her arms splayed out to her sides for balance, and she broke into a couple of steps of a running stumble before she caught herself.

Then she stopped a second. Bent slightly at the waist. Eyes fastened on the roughness of the road. Happy to have the ground feel solid underfoot once more. For just a second, as she was falling, she'd felt like a plane about to take off, those outstretched arms just needing to catch the wind to lift her.

"You alright?" Haywood said, coming up behind her.

Her heart still beat rapidly from the stumble.

"Yeah," she said. "Just lost my footing, I guess."

The dirt leveled out some again, falling back to a more gentle downward tilt, and they kept moving, but Haywood's question somehow seemed to have shaken them out of their stretch of silence. Rhodes was the next to speak.

"Weird as today has been, I've gotta say, it's really beautiful out here. I mean, I've lived on the island a while now, and I've driven by the forest countless times, but I guess I've always been something of an indoor person. Air conditioner blasting. Screen in my face. I need to get out here more. Go hiking or camping. Or both. Enjoy all this while it's still here."

Haywood chuckled. Flashed a big smile gone faintly yellow before he responded.

"Yeah. Well, you could maybe wait until y'all have got this, you know, psycho killer in custody, at least. That's my professional opinion, anyhow."

Rhodes's expression flashed back to worry.

"Oh yeah. Yeah, I'll, uh, wait a bit. Kind of cold and rainy of late, anyway. Maybe next year or something."

Haywood spat on the ground.

"Sorry, I don't mean to make light of it or nothing. I just… Hell, I work out here, day in and day out. I love these woods with all my heart. But it's weird being out here right now. Like there's static in the air, a charge that follows you around."

He shook his head before he went on.

"Usually it's so peaceful, so quiet. Tranquil and shit. Right now you can feel the danger, you know? Lurking and looming. Just waiting to get you alone."

They fell quiet again for a few steps. Darger thought about Bohanon as she supposed they all were now.

He'd been alone, and now he was gone.

"Shit. Sorry," Haywood said. His head hung down between his shoulders, bobbing a little with each stop. "I didn't mean to go all dark like that."

Wishnowsky interrupted, that assertive tone spilling out of him again.

"We're ten minutes out, I think. For better or worse, we'll know more soon. I'm still holding out hope that Officer Bohanon will be down here at the Bronco. Until we know otherwise, I think that's the best mindset to try to hold onto."

Another few paces crunched past without talk.

"Either of you two ever go camping out here?" Darger asked, trying to redirect the conversation to what Rhodes had brought up in the first place.

Haywood snapped his Zippo open. Lit a hand-rolled cigarette before he answered.

"Oh yeah. There are a buncha good spots near the water. Some cliffs and interesting rock formations there to explore.

And if you like a deeper woods experience — the whole mountain man type of deal — I think the opposite side of the island is really nice. Shielded better from the wind, you know? Kind of, uh, what's the word? Placid."

Wishnowsky walked backward for a few paces to face the others while he chimed in.

"I love camping, but not if you're talking about getting eaten alive by mosquitoes in a flappy tent. Sleeping on the cold ground and whatnot. I do it the modern way. I've got an RV. Go to one of the campgrounds and hook up the sewer and power. Best of both worlds that way. You've still got the trails for hiking and ponds for fishing right there, but you sleep on a soft bed. Maybe watch a ball game in the evening. It's a delight."

Rhodes smiled.

"So, basically, you go glamping?"

Haywood snickered, a pulse of hisses squishing through his teeth like a cat laughing in a cartoon.

Darger's eyes stayed trained on the distance as the others spoke. She watched a curve in the dirt track ahead, the trees seeming to slide out of the way like curtains to reveal the next slab of road.

"Glamping?" Wishnowsky said.

Rhodes nodded once.

"Combine glamorous and camping, and that's what you get."

"Oh… I mean, I don't know if I'd say that."

"What you do ain't exactly rugged outdoorsman-type stuff, though, is it?" Haywood said. "Air conditioning? Watching TV? I mean, it's a *little* glampy, no?"

Darger squinted, no longer listening to the chatter. She'd spotted something.

A dark shape slowly formed in that growing gap between the trees ahead. Something large sprawled on the ground, lying right in the middle of the road. Center stage.

She swallowed hard. Felt a lump bob up and down in her throat. Eyes still fixed on that dark object ahead.

Then she drew her weapon and bolted for it.

CHAPTER 28

Darger zipped down the road at a full sprint. Boots stabbing the sand with scraping sounds like the point of a shovel striking the earth over and over.

Her eyes flitted over that form in the road ahead. Swiveled over contours and lines she couldn't quite make sense of yet.

She had to know. Had to see. Had no choice.

Dimly aware of the others behind her. Their confusion.

Wishnowsky's voice sounded behind her, already seeming distant, seeming small.

"What the hell?"

Everyone fell quiet after that. The glamping conversation killed off in a single stroke.

The silence between them felt huge. Felt wrong. A shuddering, awful hollow that hung between Darger and the rest.

Probably all gaping at her back, she thought. Confused.

Didn't have time to explain.

She wondered if any of them had seen it yet, that lump in the road. Probably not. She would know when they did, surely.

She lifted her free hand as she ran. Smeared the back of it over her forehead, finding a thin film of sweat there already.

She looked down at her slicked hand. Blinked. Shifted her gaze to stare ahead again.

She couldn't focus on the shape. Couldn't see it right. Couldn't process it.

Maybe it was shock. Maybe it was the distance or the choppiness of her gait. She didn't know.

She squinted hard at the form in the road. Still couldn't see it right.

Soon it wouldn't matter. Soon she would be there.

She would know.

She kept running. Kept pressing forward toward her destination, for better or worse.

Gasps spilled from the others behind her. One wheeze setting off the others in a chain reaction. Horror torn from their throats. Awe expressed through a series of sucking sounds.

Wishnowsky's voice came out in a raspy falsetto. Wavery. "Oh, Jesus Christ!"

And the object in the road came clear all at once. Darger could see it now. Confirming what she'd known all along.

Goosebumps rippled over her flesh. Drew her skin taut from head to toe. She gripped her weapon with both hands now.

It was a body.

Officer Bohanon's body lay face up on the road with his feet pointed toward them. The taupe Forest Service uniform stark against the darker mud of the logging track.

Darger's vantage point kept his top half obscured for now. Left her only a view of his legs. Unmoving.

She sprinted up to him. Heart thudding. Everything moving in slow motion, swimmy along the edges of her vision.

A strange feeling fluttered and heaved and lurched in her head, sloshing like waves in a choppy sea. Panic.

She forced deep breaths to fight it. Ribcage shaking. Lips and nostrils wrenching in great lungfuls of humid air. Tumbling them in her chest and letting them go.

Her mind whirred through possibilities. Tried not to think the worst. Tried again to offer a palatable explanation for all of this. Anything.

He could have tripped and fell.

Could have fainted.

Could have had a heart attack or a stroke.

She swallowed hard. Spittle sucking into her dry throat.

But where's the cart?

It doesn't make sense without the cart.

And then she was on him. Gliding by his feet. Kneeling by his shoulder.

She was on autopilot now. Assessing the damage.

Instinct drew one hand from her weapon. Reached for his neck to check for a pulse. Fingers stretching for that column of flesh beyond his collar.

But her hand recoiled before it got there. Jerking back like she'd touched a hot pan on the stove.

She blinked. Gaped. Tried to make sense of what she was seeing.

The neck was just there. No more than a foot from her flailing arm.

But there was no head attached to it.

CHAPTER 29

Shock vibrated through Darger. Numbed her limbs. Choked off her breath. Emptied her mind of all but that primal revulsion.

No head.

Instinct made her shrink away from the gory display of the cleaved neck. Crab-walked her back a couple of feet, the heels of her hands squishing into the soft dirt of the road — the Glock, too, scraping through the mud.

No head.

She blinked, and more words finally came to her. Some understanding dawning.

Headless.

Killed.

Butchered.

Just like the others.

She fought the inertia gripping her chest. Hitched her throat. Took a deep breath again. Her training reminding her to do that, to try to stave off the shock the best she could.

The words came again.

Headless.

Killed.

In broad daylight.

He's out here.

Right now.

And he's close.

She whipped her head to the right and left. Tried to stare into the murk between the trees. Saw nothing there but the shadows.

Instead the dark places gazed right back into her.

And suddenly she felt exposed. Vulnerable. Naked in the open.

She scuttled off the dirt track like a beetle. Tucked herself into the edge of the woods. Brambles picking at her pistoning arms and legs as she crawled into the thicket.

Then she stood to face the others. Held up a hand. Eyes swiveling everywhere, shifting from face to face.

They'd stopped. Stood and watched this whole time.

But now they started in motion again. Haywood picking up into a jog.

She wanted to tell them to stay back. Wanted to warn them off the road, out of the open.

But the words wouldn't come. The noise in her head too loud.

All she could do was breathe and hold up her hand like a crossing guard. Wild eyes swiveling in her face like marbles. Shaking her head. Trying to tell them, *No. Stop. Stay back.*

Haywood raced up next to her. Head angled down toward the body. His eyes going wide when he saw it.

"Aw, Christ."

He heaved once like he was going to vomit right there. Then he pulled himself together. Shook his head. Said it again, voice cracking this time.

"Aw, Christ."

Rhodes and Wishnowsky approached, not quite jogging. Both veering away from the body but then turning and looking from a few feet away. One of them whimpered a little, but Darger couldn't tell which.

"We need to get out of here," Darger said, her voice cutting through the panic and surprising her, coming out loud and sharp.

The others just stared at her. Shocked and confused and trying to catch up.

Haywood got it first. Eyebrows lifting as he did.

He scooted off the dirt track. Stepped into the foliage beside her.

"He might still be out here," he said to the others, his lips all wet.

With a flick of the wrist, he beckoned the other two. They followed the motion and got off the road, maybe out of habit more than thought. The gesture somehow cutting through the confusion.

Darger balled her hands into fists and took a deep breath. Forced her thoughts to slow down.

"The Bronco," Darger said. "We need to get to the Bronco."

She turned toward where the SUV must be, somewhere down the winding road ahead. Stared like maybe she could see through the wall of trees and spot the vehicle.

"We'll stay just off the road. Hidden in the trees," she spoke just above a whisper now. "And we'll make our way back to the SUV."

She looked from face to face. Felt her pulse twitching in her eyelids.

Blank faces stared back at her. Baffled. Dazed. Listless.

"You with me?"

After a second, the heads nodded one by one.

"Let's go," she said.

She took one step forward.

And then the crossbow bolt thudded and twanged into the tree trunk just next to her.

CHAPTER 30

Darger ran into the dark of the forest.

Ran away from the direction of the crossbow bolt.

Ran away from where the Bronco was parked.

The woods opened up before her. A hilly landscape with dark tree trunks jutting everywhere.

Moss and dead leaves flecked with sparse growth down low. That canopy of leaves, some alive and some dead, strung up like Chinese lanterns on the spindly branches above.

Motes burst inside her head as she ran. Flashes like tiny fireworks playing over her field of vision.

Haywood ran along her right side, arms pumping to form a throb of fists out of the corner of Darger's eye.

Rhodes loped off to the left and a little behind her. Something uneven hitched in her gait, the right leg seeming to have a longer stride than the left, but she was keeping up alright so far.

Darger swiveled her head. Cranked her torso to look behind her. Eyes scanning everywhere, scanning everywhere.

She couldn't find Wishnowsky.

Instantly she pictured him lying facedown in the scrub, two blunt quarrels blooming out of his back. Trying to crawl through the foliage. Blood pulsing out around the shafts of the arrows buried in his flesh.

She turned back in time to dodge around a spruce bough. Shoulder brushing against its needles.

She kept going. Ignored the current surging in her head, panicked whispers speaking in fast motion, telling her to turn back, to find the bespectacled man somewhere behind them. Maybe hurt. Maybe already dead.

Blood pulsed in her ears, beat in her temples. Clunked in her head like a speed metal drumbeat.
She looked back again.

Wishnowsky appeared in the distance. Wheeling around a cluster of saplings.

Thank God.

Darger closed her eyes for a second. Felt the sense of gratitude seep into her brain.

But it was just a glimmer of warmth fighting through the icy adrenaline snaking through her system. Momentary. There and then gone again.

Bright light shined down through a broken spot in the rooftop of leaves overhead. A shaft glowing through the opening where another widow-maker had fallen.

Darger veered away from the light. Feared the exposure. Moved off to the left.

She led them up another slope. A knoll steep enough to make her feet slip some beneath her, though she kept upright.

She felt a faint jolt of relief as they rushed down the opposite side, her stomach lifting from the downward motion, like flying down a hill on a roller coaster. The slope put earth between them and their stalker — if he was even giving chase.

They ran and ran and ran.

A fire slowly built in Darger's chest. Lungs feeling wet and scorched at the same time.

But she pushed herself. Kept going. Kept checking to make sure the others were keeping up.

They tromped through the woods for what felt like a long time. Weaving through trees. Kicking through scrub.

When she couldn't take it anymore, Darger found the

biggest tree she could and ducked behind it. Slid her back down the trunk until she was sitting there.

The others joined her one by one. Haywood finding his own tree. Wishnowsky and Rhodes sharing a fat red cedar about a man and a half wide.

They all sucked wind. Chests quaking. Heads bobbing. Blotchy faces with mouths opened wide like trout.

Darger's insides felt gooey. Burning and heavy with wet.

As soon as she could stand it, she held her breath and listened. Trained her ears beyond the sound of the others drawing ragged breaths.

At first, she heard nothing, really. The whisper of the wind in the leaves. The periodic groaning of the trees shifting.

She glanced at the others. Saw their fish faces mottled with flushed spots. Each of them still struggling to breathe.

Next she stared into the woods. Tried to make any kind of sense of where they were now — in relation to the Bronco or in relation to the cabin — but she found only indecipherable plant life staring back in all directions. No landmarks. No sense at all. Just that choking crush of trees and hills that stretched on and on without meaning.

Could they be lost so quickly? With it growing darker by the second?

She licked her lips. Reminded herself that the others had collectively spent quite a bit of time in these woods. Surely they wouldn't be so quick to get turned around.

A patter joined the other sounds, the normal sounds. Something new. A rhythmic tapping that stood out from the rest.

She sharpened her ears again. Focused on it.

Footsteps?

She didn't think so.

Too many taps. Too fast. Too light.

A drop dabbed at her shoulder. Another at her knee.

She held out her hand. Cupped palm facing the heavens. Felt the cold wetness rap at her fingertips two times in rapid succession.

It was starting to rain.

CHAPTER 31

On the drive up to Klawock, where Maya Volk worked as a hairstylist, it began to rain. Just a light sprinkle, not even enough to warrant more than a periodic swipe of the windshield wipers. Still, Loshak couldn't help but think of Darger's group tramping about in the woods. He hoped they were staying dry.

Whipple parked his vehicle outside the salon. Tiny flecks of water peppered Loshak's forehead, cheeks, and neck as they crossed the parking lot.

A bell jangled over the door as they entered. It was a small place, with two chairs facing a mirrored wall and glass shelves of products stretching to the ceiling.

A young woman with curly red hair was in the middle of blow-drying an older woman's hair.

"I'm just finishing up Mrs. Burns, and then we can talk," she said, raising her voice over the sound of the hairdryer.

Whipple stepped closer to one of the shelves, scanning the various gels and conditioners and mousses. He plucked a small amber bottle into his hand and squinted at the label.

"Multi-peptide hair serum," he read aloud.

He carefully replaced the bottle on the shelf and turned to Loshak.

"See, now… I never understood why ladies seem to need a specific bottle of goop for every body part. My wife, she's got a serum for her eyes. A different one for her lips. The other day, she comes home with one for her fingernails. I thought she was pulling my leg!" He shook his head. "Don't even get me started on the hand cream and foot cream. I mean, it's gotta all be the same stuff, right?"

Loshak ran his fingers through his hair.

"I'm the wrong person to ask. I use one of those all-in-one bottles of shampoo and body wash."

"Exactly! I mean, soap is soap and lotion is lotion, right?" Whipple narrowed his eyes at the rows of products. "I think the whole beauty industry is a big con."

The conversation ended abruptly when the whirring of the hairdryer suddenly cut out. Maya removed the protective smock from her client's neck and escorted her over to the cash register.

"Oh, can I get another bottle of the leave-in conditioner?" the woman asked. "I'm almost out."

Whipple raised his eyebrows at Loshak as if to say, *See what I mean?*

Maya escorted the client to the door, locking up behind her and turning the "OPEN" sign to "CLOSED." She paused in front of a pair of windows facing the street for a moment before spinning back around.

"OK," she said. "I'm ready… I think. I'm kind of nervous."

"No reason to be nervous. We're just going to ask you a few questions."

"Right." She picked at her cuticles and forced a smile. "It's just that I don't know what I can tell you, really. I mean, other than what I already said on the phone."

A row of three chairs formed a makeshift waiting area near the door. Loshak angled them so that they would be facing one another and gestured that she should sit.

"Why don't you start with how you met Walton Banks."

Maya took a deep breath, her shoulders shaking slightly.

"Well, I moved here with my mom the summer before

159

tenth grade. I've never been the outgoing type, and I didn't know a soul here on the island, so I spent the first half of that summer by myself. Most days I'd go down to the water and watch the boats or look for rocks. That was how I met Walton. I was skipping stones on the beach, and he came over and said hello."

She stared down at her hands as she spoke, periodically glancing over at the windows.

"By the time school started, we were officially dating, but I'd only met one of Walton's friends. Taylor Higgins. It was only once I was in class for a few weeks that I realized Taylor was his *only* friend. The other kids at school didn't like Walton much, because well... he was kind of a bully. And it wasn't just the other kids. He'd backtalk the teachers, too. He even made our English teacher cry once. But no matter what kind of trouble he stirred up, his family somehow always got things smoothed over."

Loshak began checking off various details from the profile in his mind. *Lacking social skills. Trouble at school.* So far so good.

"People avoided Walton, which meant they avoided me in turn. And any time I did manage to start making a friend, Walton would scare them off. I didn't realize it at the time, but now I think he did it on purpose. Kept me isolated from other people. He wanted to be the only one who had any sway over me. He was the same way with Taylor."

"What was Walton's home life like?" Loshak asked.

"Good... or so I thought. They owned so much land on the island, Walton was always talking about it. One of his grandfathers had all this acreage going back to some mining operation from the 30s or 40s. Old money, or what passes for it in Alaska. But they weren't as rich as I thought... or as happy."

She shrugged. "Things changed during Walton's senior year. His parents started having problems, and Walton's acting out at school went from bad to worse. He started picking fights. I think he got suspended at least three times in the first semester alone. And then he attacked Mr. Childs, a math teacher. Broke his nose. There was talk of expulsion, but as usual, his dad got him out of it."

This was the first hint at Walton being overtly violent in his past, and Loshak was eager for more details.

"What exactly happened with the teacher?"

"Mr. Childs tried to confiscate Walton's iPhone. I didn't see this, mind you, but I heard the story enough times. Walton lurched at him. Pulled the teacher's shirt up over his head, kind of like a hockey fight, and then he kind of got him bent forward and punched him. Broke his nose. Poor guy bled a big red stain through his white dress shirt."

Loshak jotted this down in his notes and gestured that Maya should go on.

"Right around this time, his dad sold all the family property and bought a house in Hawaii. A beachfront mansion. Walton was their youngest, and once he graduated, his parents decided they were going to leave Alaska for greener pastures."

Her eyes stared into the middle distance as she remembered.

"Walton was furious. Ranted about it nonstop. The way he saw it, his parents had pissed away his inheritance. Sold it off so they could live in paradise. Left him high and dry."

Loshak checked another mental box. *Hostile feelings toward his parents.*

"Once Walton felt like something was his, that was it. No one else was allowed to touch it. He confronted his dad one night and ended up going after him with a hammer. That was

161

the last straw. I think his dad finally saw that Walton was completely out of control, that the family always covering for him had taught him all the wrong lessons.

"He gave Walton a choice: join the military or face the assault with a deadly weapon charge. Walton chose the Army. He left the day after graduation."

She shook her head.

"Pathetic as it seems looking back, I was a mess when he left. I wrote to him and emailed him hundreds of times, but he never wrote back. I still had a year of school to get through, and I felt completely alone. But I did eventually manage to make a few friends, without Walton there to push people away. I graduated and went to cosmetology school and came back here to open my own business. I moved on from Walton Banks.

"Or so I thought."

CHAPTER 32

Maya blinked, and her eyes refocused, flitting from Loshak to Whipple.

"I'm sorry. I didn't mean to vomit out our entire history like that."

Loshak gave her a warm smile.

"No need to apologize. The details are helpful." Loshak let his eyes fall to his notepad. "So Walton left for the Army… How long was it before you saw him again?"

Her face tightened.

"Almost ten years. One day last year, I was shopping at the Town Square Market, and there he was. I was caught so off guard, I just stopped and stared. And he smiled and said, 'Hey, Maya. What's up?' Like no time had passed at all.

"I thought he'd apologize for ghosting me, but Walton's never been the type to apologize." She sniffed a little. "But he did seem different. Older. More mature. At least, that's what I thought at first.

"The only time the mask slipped was when he was drinking. Because he was still mean. Meaner, even."

Maya tugged at the sleeves of her sweater, pulled them down so only the tips of her fingers were visible.

"Anyway, he asked me out to dinner, and I said no. I didn't know why at first. But he wore me down over time. Kept talking about how he had no one left in the world who cared about him. His family has pretty much cut him off, financially and communication-wise."

"Because of the hammer incident?" Loshak asked.

She frowned.

"I'm sure that was part of it, but I got the impression that there was a more recent falling out. Walton never said what it was, and even if he had, I'm sure he would have only told his side of the story. He has a way of painting every conflict as if he's an innocent victim.

"Still, I felt sorry for him. So I agreed to let him take me out. Just as friends. I should have known better than to say that to him. He always did take any sort of boundary like that as a challenge."

The sound of a car rumbling past drew Maya's gaze to the window again.

"So he pushed me, an inch at a time. Wore me down, like I said. First it was a hug. Then a kiss. And then…"

She trailed off there. Let the implication hang.

Loshak sensed an internal struggle in Maya. It was something he'd seen before with people who were in abusive relationships. They had the common sense to know that the best thing would be to leave, but they felt powerless to do so.

"And so eventually you two ended up back together?" Loshak asked gently.

Maya's shoulders slumped.

"Yeah."

"Are you still seeing him now?"

"No. Not after what happened at the lake."

"That's when you went camping, and he pointed a gun at someone?"

Maya nodded.

"Yeah. There's that wilderness retreat up there, on the far side of the lake, where they rent out kayaks and stuff. That particular piece of land is one of the ones his parents used to own, so Walton had been grumbling about it the whole time.

At night, we could see their fire from across the lake, and he'd go stand by the water and just stare at it with this hateful look on his face."

"What happened when he pulled the gun? Was there some kind of altercation?"

"No. That was what was so strange about it. I heard a sound and glanced over and there he was, standing with a rifle in his hands, aimed at two people in kayaks out on the water. I didn't even know he'd brought a gun. I asked him what the hell he was doing, and he said he was about to teach some cocksucking tourists a lesson. Then he jerked the gun and made noises with his mouth like he was shooting."

Loshak would guess the two people in the kayaks had no idea a gun had been trained on them, which was an eerie thought. And it lined up with their theory that the killer was stalking his victims. Sneaking up on them and taking them by surprise.

"The people in the kayak paddled out of sight, and Walton finally put the gun down. Then he said that in the movies, when someone kills someone, they show them have all these feelings about it. Remorse and guilt and whatever. But he said that was all Hollywood bullshit. That he'd killed in Afghanistan, and he didn't feel anything."

This anecdote filled Loshak with a strange mixture of giddiness and unease. Giddiness that Banks was sounding more and more like a suitable suspect and unease at the sheer callousness in his words.

"The whole time, he had this look in his eyes," Maya was saying. "Something electric. It reminded me of the look a cat gets when it's about to pounce.

"That was it for me. *My* final straw. Even if it came years later than it should have."

"You ended things between you?" Loshak asked.

"Yes. But not right away. We were supposed to stay up in the woods for a few more days, and I didn't feel safe breaking things off when it was just the two of us alone. So I pretended I felt sick and made Walton pack up and take me home. When we got back, I sent him a text the next day. Told him it was over. Usually I think that's a cop-out, breaking up by text. But I didn't trust him not to do something crazy."

Another vehicle trundled down the road beyond the windows. Maya stopped talking to watch it roll by.

"Maya?"

"Sorry." She shook herself. "Talking about this makes me jumpy. Every time a car goes by, I can't help but imagine that it's him."

"You said you were worried he'd do something crazy. Did he?"

She chewed her lip and nodded.

"He showed up at my house, banging on the door, demanding an explanation. I threatened to call the police, and he left. The next day, he showed up at my work and started cussing me out in front of a client. That time I really did call the cops, but by the time Chief Rhodes got here, Walton was gone.

"I thought he took the hint, but then maybe two weeks later, I noticed him behind me on the road when I was driving home from work. I should have known he wouldn't give up so easily. Once he decides something belongs to him, he never lets it go. So instead of going home, I called my best friend and drove over to her house. When I got there, her boyfriend was out in the front yard with a shotgun. Walton took one look at Roger and kept driving. That was the last time I saw him."

"And when was this?"

"A few months back. The end of July, I guess."

"Does he have any other weapons that you know of?" Whipple asked. "Besides the rifle he had up at the lake?"

"I'm not sure, but I'd guess so. He's always been big into bow hunting. He used to say that was the true sign of a master woodsman. Not using a gun, you know?"

Whipple nodded.

"Do you know where Walton is living now?"

"He was crashing at Taylor's after he got evicted."

Loshak glanced up from his notepad.

"The same Taylor from high school?"

She nodded.

"I guess they've been together more or less this whole time. Taylor joined the Army a few months after Walton. And then they came back here together."

"OK, so where does Taylor live?"

"Well, that's the other thing. Taylor was living back home, with his mom. But then I guess she caught them stealing from her, Taylor and Walton, and she kicked the both of them out."

Loshak started thinking about the timeline. An eviction, a break-up, and then another eviction. Precipitating stressors.

"Any idea where they might have gone after that?"

"There's this old abandoned house we used to hang out in when we were kids. It was on one of the pieces of land the Bankses owned before, or so Walton said. Word around town is that the two of them have been camping out up there."

"And where is this?"

"It's off the logging road that runs up near Crab Creek."

Whipple bobbed his head and locked eyes with Loshak.

"I know the place. We used to call it the Miner's Cottage."

"Well…" Loshak said, checking his phone. "We still have time before Jeremy Maddox would get back to his aunt's house. Let's go take a look."

CHAPTER 33

Darger pressed her shoulder blades tightly to the rough bark of
the tree at her back. She tried to stay out of the drizzle the best
she could, the branches overhead shielding her at least
somewhat.

Dusk had bloomed around them quickly, its murk
spreading through the air like squid ink. The encroaching night
purpled everything little by little. Made the fractured shards of
the horizon they could see between the branches more and
more indistinct. Walls of darkness closing around them like a
fist.

The wind had picked up even faster than the nightfall.
Frigid gales gusting off and on like deep breaths, making
Darger's lips and cheeks feel chapped. It beat the branches
around in pulses, shook the leaves and made them hiss and
scrape and spit.

The heavier rains would come along with the bitter cold
front — a potentially deadly combination.

They couldn't stay here. Not in the cold and the wet. Darger
knew that, but she couldn't make herself move, couldn't make
herself speak.

Instead she tried to listen over the wind and patter of the
rain. Ears sharp. Breath shallow. Focused on any unnatural
sound in the distance. The crack of a branch. The beat of
footsteps. Anything.

Her eyes flitted over the forest around her as she listened.
Watched wagging branches, flapping leaves, swaying pine
boughs. She searched the empty spaces for his silhouette,

standing or squatting, running or still, the dark shape of the one coming after them, the one who'd killed Bohanon and taken his head.

But she saw only the woods. Heard only the wind and rain. Nothing.

She wondered how long they'd been sitting here, huddling in silence. Cowering. Twenty minutes? Thirty? Probably less than it seemed. Maybe as few as ten.

Wishnowsky cleared his throat. Broke the silence for the first time since they'd settled under the trees to hide, his voice coming out in a husky whisper.

"The temperature will drop quickly as soon as the sun is all the way down," he said, fiddling with his glasses. "Low is going to be under forty tonight. That's more than cold enough for hypothermia to be a real risk, especially if we're all soaking wet. A couple campers got caught out in a storm like this a few years ago. Froze to death before they could find shelter even though it was only about 35 degrees out. The wet is no joke."

Darger could already feel the chill in the air, that icy wind swirling around her ankles, swiping at her neck.

"Christ," Rhodes said. "My clothes are already almost soaked through from just sitting here."

They held silent for a beat.

"So what do we do?" Haywood said.

Darger took a deep breath, felt her chest shudder at the apex. Then she let the air seep out slowly.

If he was coming, he'd be on us by now.

We have to move, before the cold gets worse.

When she spoke, her voice came out dry and small.

"Well, we have two choices, right? We either go for Bohanon's vehicle, or we go back to the cabin."

Haywood sucked his teeth.

"I hate to be a Debbie Downer, but it seems to me that he was waiting for us to go for the Bronco when we got ambushed. So I don't particularly love the idea of heading *toward* the psycho."

Darger swallowed, and her voice came out stronger this time.

"I don't really want to head toward him, either, but the Bronco has the radio, right? The sooner we can call for backup, the better."

Rhodes nodded once.

"Makes sense to me."

Haywood took a big breath. Shoulders rising and falling.

"Yeah. Yeah, I guess you're right."

All heads turned toward Wishnowsky, who had fallen quiet for some time. His lips fell open a fraction of a second before words came out, the pregnant pause making Darger uncomfortable.

"There might be a radio at the cabin," he said.

"Might be?" Haywood asked.

"There are boxes of old equipment in one of the storage closets. We have a stash of emergency provisions, just in case something happens and a crew were to get stranded out here for a while. MREs, first aid, and so on. The last time we did inventory, I remember seeing a heavy-duty radio setup packed away in there. One of those old-school base stations."

They all fell quiet again, processing this information.

As much as Darger liked the idea of getting to the vehicle and getting the fuck out of here, the notion of a warm building held its own appeal. And if they could call for help from there…

Haywood turned his head and looked out into the trees before them.

"The cabin would be closer. We basically ran straight toward it when we fled the road."

Rhodes hugged herself and nodded.

"Then my vote is for the cabin."

Darger started to stand. The chief interrupted her.

"Wait."

Rhodes leaned forward and pulled a small revolver from an ankle holster.

"My backup weapon. Either of you know how to shoot?"

Both men nodded, but Wishnowsky spoke first.

"I do."

"Take this then. Just in case."

Rhodes handed the gun over, and the camp supervisor blinked at the silvery object in his hands. Then he stood and tucked the weapon in his belt.

Darger swiveled her head to take in the darkening woods around her once more. Tried to get her bearings about which way the cabin was from here.

Haywood stood and lifted his arm. Pivoted it like the hand of a clock before himself, pointing off at a diagonal to the left.

"Cabin's that-a-way."

CHAPTER 34

The Miner's Cottage looked like a soggy thing in the half-light of dusk. Peeling paint formed fissures all over the facade, the flaked spots in the enamel exposing gray splotches beneath.

The wood had gone spongy around the window sills, swollen and bulbous. It reminded Loshak of something growing on the seafloor.

The agent walked up the wet sidewalk leading to the front door. Cane punching into the pale concrete. Rain spitting down.

On the drive up, Loshak had spotted only one other house on the road, miles back. Not a bad spot for a hideout, even if the place looked in poor repair.

Whipple strode alongside the agent. Got his flashlight out as they mounted the steps and crossed a rotting porch.

A big piece of weather-stained plywood covered the window on the front door. There was something deeply uninviting about the image, as though the building had been nailed shut for years.

Whipple glanced at Loshak, who gave a quick nod. The chief rapped on the door with his free hand.

"This is Chief Whipple with Craig PD. This is private property, and anyone inside is guilty of trespassing."

It wasn't a bluff. Whipple had tracked down the current owner of the property, who had not only been dismayed to hear rumors of squatters, but also gave Whipple permission to search the place.

"Come out now, and we'll let you go with a warning."

They waited, listening for any sound at all. A response. A whisper. Even the scrape of footsteps on floorboards. Loshak squinted as if that might allow him to hear better.

After another few seconds of silence, Whipple knocked again.

"Final warning. We're coming in."

His hand moved to the doorknob, gave it a twist. Unlocked.

They hesitated a second at the threshold. Gazed at the open door. Then they stepped into the darkness inside.

The search began. Whipple's flashlight sweeping everywhere.

It took Loshak's eyes a second to adjust to the gloom inside, even with Whipple's light whipping around.

The ruins of a living room slowly populated his field of vision, trash everywhere. A shag carpet the color of rust peered up from the bare patches of floor, stained and frayed in the few places Loshak could see clearly. A couch slouched against the back wall, so beat up that it sat crooked like a broken-down car abandoned in a junkyard.

Silver and yellow cans coated the floor just beyond the door's reach. Made little pinging and crinkling noises as they waded through them.

A sour beer stench pervaded the place, intermingled with the standard mold reek of a long-abandoned house. Loshak cupped a hand over his mouth, grossed out at the notion of all the various spores he must be breathing in.

They kicked around the living room like that for a couple of minutes. Cataloging decay more than any kind of evidence.

"Don't see much of interest here," Whipple said. "Wanna check out the rest of the place?"

"Not really," Loshak said. "But I will."

He hobbled toward one of the doorways leading out of the

living room. Peered through the open rectangle there.

A big hole in the roof cratered the ceiling of a back bedroom. Blackness radiated from a bulging spot of plaster above, the popcorn ceiling gone mushy and dark. The taint reached down the walls all the way to the floor, like Loshak could see the corruption spreading into this place. Thankfully the room lay empty entirely. No reason to go in.

The next bedroom looked pristine by comparison, though the carpet had been ripped out. Ugly subflooring gazed up from underfoot.

A bare mattress lay up against what looked to be the driest of the walls. Loshak limped over toward the bit of bedding. Navigated through a bunch of empty Doritos and Funyuns bags and shredded magazines of both pornographic and *Soldier of Fortune*-type content.

Only one piece of decor showed on any of the walls: a dartboard with a photo attached to it. Riddled with holes.

Loshak stepped closer and found it was a family photo, one of those professional shots taken in a studio. Father, mother, daughter, and son. He recognized the boy in the photo as a young Walton Banks.

Still harboring a grudge against his family, it seemed.

Orange cylinders among the debris caught his eye — a bunch of empty prescription pill bottles. He slowly bent down, felt the pressure well up in his knee as he got low. Then he started gathering up the pill bottles. Tilted them toward the lone window, reading the labels in the fading daylight.

The name on all the labels was Walton Banks. No surprise there.

He recognized a few of the medication names. Lexapro, a mood stabilizer. Ambien, a sleeping pill. He looked up the two drugs he didn't recognize.

Aripiprazole, an antipsychotic.

Lisdexamfetamine, a stimulant used to treat ADHD.

The Lexapro and aripiprazole were clear indications of mental illness, which fit the profile.

Loshak jabbed the cane into the floor and pushed himself up. His knee ached as it unfolded, but it felt better as soon as his leg was straight, some kind of pressure draining from it rapidly.

He shuffled out of the room. Checked the kitchen briefly. More trash cluttered the floor and counters — food wrappers, empty plastic shopping bags, more beer cans. The fridge lay empty save for a single squeeze bottle of French's mustard, which also looked empty. He opened a few cabinet doors to find them bare as well.

One more bedroom. Loshak took a single step in and heard a loud crunch under his foot. Peered down at the black specks all over the wood floor here.

Whipple swung the flashlight down. Let the spotlight reveal the details.

Centipedes. Hundreds of them.

Curled up crunchy things that must have hatched in one of the walls and come spilling out. They were dead now, in any case.

"Aw, no way," Whipple said, backpedaling. "No way. I'm not walking in… in… that."

"Just shine the light in," Loshak said. "I'll take a look."

A sun-bleached Chicago Bears blanket had been nailed to the lone window here in lieu of a more traditional curtain. It made this the darkest room so far. Something about it struck Loshak as noteworthy. It felt off to him.

Why cover this window?

Whipple toed up to the threshold. Speared his light along

the floor.

The beam swept over wooden planks. Then it glinted on a blue throw rug. A busted-up dresser with all the drawers pulled out sat atop it.

Empty. You could see that from across the room.

The light kept crawling forward. Brushed over piles of dirty clothes crowding one corner.

Then it shifted along the wall. A big trunk sat in the opposite corner. A glossy black thing that looked antique.

Loshak crunched across the room. Centipede corpses popping under his feet and cane. He threw open the chest.

More clothes lay there. A few t-shirts, a pair of jeans, some socks that looked worn but not yet holey. The laundry smelled surprisingly clean, some detergent scent trapped here in the chest.

Loshak got low again and ran his hands along the bottom of the trunk. Searched for any unnatural lump or hardness.

Nothing.

He stood. Held still for a few seconds. Thinking.

"Nothing, huh?" Whipple said. "No surprise, I guess. Hell, we gave it a shot."

He swung the light out of the room. Started looking around in the kitchen again.

Loshak stood in the darkened bedroom. Something wasn't right.

He hobbled over to that broken dresser, the one sitting on top of the throw rug.

The only rug in the house. And it's pinned under a dresser in a room that looks mostly unused.

Why?

Loshak slid the dresser aside, a surprisingly easy task with drawers ripped out of the thing. Light and skeletal.

The rug scooted along with the broken bit of furniture, bunching a little at one point. Slowly revealing whatever lay beneath.

With the dresser out of the way, Loshak stared down at the shadowy floor. He couldn't tell what he was seeing.

"Can I get some light back here?"

The footsteps thumped over the linoleum. Coming closer.

The light plunged into the room once more. A glowing shaft lancing into the planks at Loshak's feet.

Dark lines cut a rectangle of seams into the floor where the rug had been. Something knobby above them, like a lumpy snake.

A trapdoor.

Chained and padlocked.

CHAPTER 35

They hiked up the slope, Haywood out in front now. The singlejack's body swayed a little with each mounting step. Each leg kicked to find footing in a loose zigzag, shoulders shimmying, the steep incline rocking his gait back and forth.

Rhodes and Wishnowsky slalomed along behind him just the same, and Darger brought up the rear. Watching all of them in the dying light.

The rain picked up as they walked. Fat droplets drumming at the leaves above them. Pelting them with watery explosions.

The ground squished under Darger's feet, that already soft layer of needles and moss and leaf mold now going soggy. Soon it'd be slick mush, a layer of watery oatmeal slipping and sliding beneath them. Somehow it made her think of the wood chips at the bottom of a hamster's cage — maybe because, for the moment, they were trapped here. Penned in by miles and miles of forest, all the trees sticking up like the bars of a cell.

No one spoke now. Everyone jumpy. Nervous. Quiet.

The land leveled out some, and they trudged on. Boot treads smacking and slurping against the ground like wet lips.

Angry wind kicked up and whipped rain into their faces. Flung droplets hard enough to sting. The gale worse now that the ground was flat.

Rhodes pulled the collar of her jacket up over her nose and cinched it shut there. Tried to stave off the rain that way. Eyes squinted to slits above the rim of polyester and cotton.

Haywood had his hood up, but it already looked sodden, draping funny around the dome of his skull. Darger doubted it was much help.

Her own jacket had claimed it was "water-resistant," but she could already feel the dampness seeping through. Apparently water-*resistant* wasn't the same as water*proof.*

The last pops of color had been sucked out of the world around them. No more green in the leaves. No more red visible in Wishnowsky's coat. Everything withered to grayscale. Shadows swelling to engulf all.

Another gust sprayed Darger in the eyes. Cold rain. Made her stop a second to blink and flush the wetness away.

She clenched her teeth.

Just need to get to the cabin, to the radio.

Even if it takes time for help to get up here, we'll be safe inside. And dry.

She lifted her shoulders again. Took a deep breath. Hustled to catch up with the others. Feet skidding in the hamster mush.

The land tilted upward again, that hill once again testing them.

Darger found the going slipperier than it had been just seconds before. The layer of soil beneath the mulch going as soft as creamy peanut butter.

She slipped. Hard. Jabbed a palm into the ground to catch herself. Hand cold and wet. But she stayed up. Kept going.

Wishnowsky lost his footing a second later. Shoes careening out from under him. Arms waving uselessly in the air at his sides like flapping sparrow wings.

He hovered there for a second. Flailing. Falling but not yet fallen.

And then gravity ripped him down.

He landed flat on his ass. Butt cheeks clapping at the mud. His spine compressing into a slouch on impact, something ragdoll and wrong about it.

He skidded a few feet down the slope. Then he sat still. Shoulders curled toward his knees. Chest heaving in a couple of breaths.

His yell came out between clenched teeth. Both hands slapping at the slop he was sitting in.

"Goddamn it!"

Haywood looped a hand under one of the fallen man's arms, and Rhodes grabbed the opposite wrist. They hauled him up like that. Water dripping down from his backside.

"Let's keep going," the lumberjack said, his tone soothing.

Wishnowsky smeared the wet from his glasses with the hem of his shirt. He shook his head.

"Christ. I could wring myself out like a dishrag."

They pressed on. Climbed the gloopy hill without speech. The wind and rain making enough noise for any of them.

And the last of the light fled the sky all at once. The gray hue above dimming to inky tones over the course of just a few seconds, like a movie fading to black at the end.

No moon. No stars.

They walked into the dark.

CHAPTER 36

Loshak stared down at the chain fastening the trapdoor shut. It ran through three clasps, forming a triangle of fat links. Reminded him of something from a horror movie.

"Chain looks pretty heavy-duty, considering where we are," he said. "The lock, not so much."

The padlock seemed thin next to the thick chain. Cheap and weak.

Whipple walked across the room at a clipped pace. Footsteps heavy on the wood.

"So what do you think?" the officer said as he drew up next to Loshak. "Root cellar or something?"

"I don't know. Old house like this? It could be anything. Root cellar. Crawlspace. Full basement."

Whipple ran the flashlight beam along those dark seams at the edges of the panel set in the floor.

Loshak watched the glow crawl over the planks. Then he gazed at the flashlight wiggling in Whipple's hand — a Maglite about the size of a baguette, except heavy.

"Let me see your light," the agent said, careful to keep his voice neutral.

Whipple's eyes swiveled up from the floor. Locked on Loshak's.

"What… what for?"

Loshak held out a hand.

"Just give it."

Whipple hesitated. Stared at the open hand and then at Loshak's eyes again.

Loshak drummed his fingers against his palm. Impatient. Saying *gimme* without saying it.

The glow shifted over the wall as Whipple relented and snugged the tube into Loshak's palm. The Maglite's metal frame felt warm from the cop's fingers.

Loshak knelt quickly. Felt cords in his bad knee shift.

He twisted the little padlock into place. Then he hammered down on it with the end of the Maglite. It thunked, loud in the small space, but it didn't break.

"Hey, whoa," Whipple said. "Should we... I mean, aren't we..."

Loshak glared up at him. Held quiet.

"I mean. I guess the owner did give us permission to search the place," Whipple said. "And, uh, probable cause. And whatnot."

Loshak banged the lock again. This time the hooked shank ripped free of the body. The top edge of the steel had busted and delaminated.

"Huh," Loshak said, pulling the lock free and looking at Whipple. "Found it this way."

Whipple nodded. Spoke almost under his breath.

"Yeah. Yeah, that's it. We found it this way."

Loshak snaked the chain through the trio of hasps and set it aside. Then he took a breath.

"Wanna help with this part? Don't want my knee to buckle on me."

Whipple shuffled over to the other side of the trapdoor, which suddenly seemed much bigger now that they were about to lift it.

"One. Two. Three."

They heaved opened the trapdoor, the hinges squawking like a pair of gulls. The heavy plank of wood leaned up against the wall.

And then the stink hit them square in the nostrils. It reeked, even from the top of the stairs. An earthy smell mixed with rot.

"Aw, Jesus," Whipple said, cupping both hands over his nose. "What the hell?"

Loshak couldn't help but laugh.

"Dead rats, probably."

"Christ. How many?"

"Who knows? I watched a viral video where someone put a python in a hole in some drywall, and within a minute fourteen rats had piled out of the hole into a waiting bucket. To get away from the predator, you know? That was fourteen at once. Who's to say how many might have been in this place over the years. Living. Breeding. Dying."

"Sick."

Loshak pushed the Maglite's beam down the wooden steps. Damp cement was visible at the bottom. Glossy in the glow of the flashlight.

"Looks like a full basement," he said. "Shall we have a look, then?"

Whipple stared at him with wide eyes, hands still clasped over his nose and mouth.

"You finking out on me, Whipple?"

Whipple blinked.

"I mean... there's probably nothing down there, right? Except for hundreds of dead rodents, allegedly."

"Uh-huh. I'll just take a quick look then," Loshak said.

He started down the stairs before Whipple could protest or waffle about it. Cane tapping alongside.

The smell grew worse with each step down — the stench of decay overtaking the mold, overtaking the mildew. The odor triggered memories. Old cases coming back to Loshak in a montage flurry. Peeling up floorboards. Finding human remains in the muck of the crawlspace.

God, I hope it's just rats this time.

When he hit the bottom, his feet scuffed on the wet concrete. The light swept around, kept swaying back and forth like he couldn't keep it still. An out-of-control fire hose spewing illumination.

Most of the floor looked clear. Empty. Relatively clean, at least in terms of clutter, which seemed at odds with the smell. The cinder block walls etched a perfect grid around him.

He took a few paces into the vast chamber. Finally relented and brought the collar of his shirt up over the bridge of his nose.

A small bulk lay in the center of the floor ahead. It took Loshak a second to figure out what he was looking at.

"I think I found the source of the smell," he said over his shoulder. "Got a dead raccoon down here."

It was the ringed tail that gave it away. Otherwise the thing was so desiccated it looked partially melted, a puddle of fur with some lumps in it where the bones must be.

Cobwebs festooned all the corners toward the back of the room. Thick tufts strung there like gauze.

Milk crates huddled on the floor. Full of water-warped paperbacks and old VHS copies of blockbusters like *Back to the Future* and *Star Wars*. A few dated board games mixed in. Cultural artifacts from the 70s and 80s, which was likely the last time this place had been legitimately occupied.

He limped across the concrete expanse. Weaved around the support posts. Headed into the darkness at the back of the single room down here.

He heard flies buzzing as he neared the back wall, a little surprised that any were still alive this late in the year.

Probably feasting on the rodent and raccoon cadavers.
Old Cottage Buffet.

He moved toward the insectile sound. Toward the last shadowy section of floor.

Soon he saw the flies circling, circling. Black specks flitting in the air.

He aimed the light lower. A clump there behind all the milk crates, snugged up against the wall.

The buzzing had led him straight to...

The dead body lay belly down on the concrete slab. The head was turned almost backward atop the neck.

Loshak jumped back.

Dropped the flashlight. Its glow cut out when it hit the ground.

Darkness.

CHAPTER 37

Loshak stared into the blackness. Moaned a little. Scuffed his feet over the bare cement. Flies buzzing everywhere, buzzing everywhere.

Alone.

In the dark.

With a corpse.

He squatted. Felt that aching cord in his knee pull taut again like a drawstring.

He patted his hands over the cement. Fingertips brushing at the cool smoothness.

He imagined accidentally touching the corpse. A cold, fleshy thing, rotting like soft cheese down here in the basement for weeks. Maybe months. He moaned again.

The edge of his palm butted into the hard tube of the Maglite. His fingers scrabbled over the thing like spider legs. Gripped. Lifted.

He jabbed the button. Twice. Three times.

Nothing.

Broke the bulb.

Fuck.

Then it hit him.

He jammed his fingers into the inside pocket of his coat. Found the angular plastic of his phone case there. Pulled the thing out and flipped on the light, the beam swinging upward like a cutlass as he got upright again.

He wobbled against the cane. Then steadied himself. Held still a second.

It made him realize how heavily he was breathing. How hard his heart was pumping.

He pointed the beam at the body. Slid the circle of light upward from the booted feet. Over the blue jeans, up the trunk.

And then the glow touched that slashed neck again. He held the beam steady on that backward head. Took in the details.

Jaw hanging wide. Eyes rolled up in the sockets so only the whites showed through the drooping lids. Flesh going purple around the eyes and mouth.

The black specks of the flies careened in and out of the shaft of light. Funneling out of the wounds, spiraling in the air a while, and then returning to the feast.

Loshak took a breath. Smelled the stench of putrefaction, stronger now than ever.

He swept the light back down again. Brought it to rest on the blue jeans — the backward head somehow more disturbing as he focused on the backs of the legs.

He found the bulge in the back pocket of the jeans. The corpse's wallet.

Loshak leaned on the cane. Tottered forward a few paces. Managed to get the wallet free without trouble. Flipped the leather flap open.

The smiling face on the photo ID was only vaguely identifiable as the body in front of him. But the name told him exactly what he expected.

The dead man was Taylor Higgins.

CHAPTER 38

Rhodes clicked on her flashlight. Lifted it into that standard cop pose, hand raised beside her head. Pointed it before them.

The beam swept over a slice of forest indistinguishable from any other. Fluid trickling everywhere.

Tree trunks glistened. Leaves bobbed where the rain pattered at them. The muck underfoot seemed to be congealing into something like soup. Beef barley from the look of it.

No sign of the cabin. No sign of the road.

The officer clicked the light off, and the walls of black re-formed around them. Afraid to leave it on, probably. If the Butcher was anywhere nearby, the shaft of light would be like a beacon, making their position on the hill visible from a great distance.

Darger's eyes readjusted to the darkness, and the gray sky above slowly regained definition. The clouds seemed to hold a small glow themselves — that glimmer of light the only thing saving them from impenetrable darkness every time the flashlight clicked off.

"We're still good," Haywood whispered somewhere in the gloom. "It's not much farther."

Darger shivered. The wet had gotten to all of her now. Soaked every stitch of clothing. Glugged around in her boots with each step.

And the cold had settled quickly. That wind blowing in frigidity along with the rain. She remembered what Wishnowsky had said — that it'd be under forty degrees tonight, that hypothermia would be a risk if they stayed wet for too long.

Her faith that they would find the cabin was slowly diminishing. Seeping away along with her body heat.

Uneasiness rose to replace her confidence, seemed worse whenever that flashlight flicked on and showed them that they were still in the middle of nowhere. Vast forest stretching out on all sides of them.

What if we're lost?

She didn't let herself entertain the hypothetical question for long. Better to keep going.

The foliage gripped at the ankles of her pants now. Brambles and thin vines like strands of licorice grabbing for her, ropy tendrils trying to hold on like insect limbs.

The undergrowth thickened. Forced her to pick her feet up higher.

It took a second for the meaning of this to sink in.

The thickest undergrowth they'd encountered had been in the areas where the canopy let in the most light. The places where big trees had fallen down. Natural clearings. And the edges of the forest.

She snapped her head around. Squinted like it might help her see into the nothingness.

The best she could make out were some trees to her left and right, faintly darker columns reaching up among the blackness like veins of coal in the wall of a mine.

"Here," Haywood said.

Darger could vaguely make out his arm waving in the dark, somehow recognizing the motion though the details remained indistinct.

"Let's get some light," the lumberjack said. "Just for a second."

Once again Rhodes clicked on her Maglite. Lifted the dark

tube up like her arm might be about to throw a dart or a football.

The beam pushed over the ground, slicing through ferns and some kind of creeping vine. She brought it higher. The glow lanced through the edge of the thicket, the oval of light stretching over gravel and mud laid bare just beyond the woods.

A clearing.

The road.

"The cabin should be off to our left," Haywood said.

Rhodes swung the light that way. There.

The building glistened. Metal roof glossy with moisture. More water beading on the darkened windows.

Wishnowsky hissed then.

"Turn the light off!"

The light juddered as Rhodes flinched. After a fraction of a second the glow cut out.

"What is it?" Haywood asked, his voice going whispery to match Wishnowsky's.

Everything held quiet for a second.

Darger's chest felt tight and hollow. She blinked a few times to try to help her eyes adjust faster to the dark again, though she doubted that it actually worked.

Wishnowsky finally spoke.

"Just… I thought I saw something. I'm… I'm sure I did."

"What was it?" Haywood said.

But the question hung unanswered between them. Tense. Uncomfortable. Like a song ending on a sour note.

Again when the talk fell away the patter of the rain rose up to fill the quiet.

Darger spoke next.

"Let's just wait here a moment. Wait and watch. We're

close now. Better safe than sorry."

She squatted down and felt the others do the same alongside her.

And she trained her vision on the black clearing just beyond the woods. Watched as it slowly, slowly came back into view as her eyes adjusted.

First lines formed in the void. Thin strands like spiderwebs somehow stark against the rest of the black.

Then those lines fleshed out into contours. Apart from a couple of tree trunks and the vague box of the cabin itself, they remained mostly meaningless shapes for now, but the new shadows added body, added bulk to the darker bits, like charcoal shading providing dimension to a drawing.

Details populated the world next. Textures and outlines sharpening to help Darger see the door at the front of the cabin. The windows cut into the walls. The raised ribs separating the panels on the roof.

She let her eyes drift over the middle distance, the empty space separating the woods from the steps leading up to the cabin. Taking it all in as new specifics revealed themselves. Various fronds and leaves jutted up from the ground. Rises and dips visible in the grade of the driveway.

Then she saw it.

Her breath caught in her throat. Eyes going wide.

She blinked hard once.

There was someone there.

A silhouette huddled low in the dark. Ducked into one of the dips in the wide parking area just in front of the building.

She batted the person next to her on the shoulder, not even sure who it was.

She tried to point in the dark. Hoped they could see her.

But then she looked again at the person squatting in the

distance.

Squinted.

Really looked.

And it wasn't a person.

Just a scraggly bush or something. She could see the stalklike bottom of the thing after all, thin as a stick. The bulbous bushy part set on top of it.

"What?" Haywood whispered.

"Nothing. I thought I saw someone, but… it's just a plant, I think."

She thought about it as the words came out. Had there been a plant right in the middle of the parking area like that? She thought not.

"The… thing jutting up in the middle of the driveway?" Wishnowsky whispered.

"Yeah."

"Whatever it is, I can promise you it isn't there normally." They fell quiet for a few seconds.

"Should I shine my light on it?" Rhodes said.

Darger and Wishnowsky answered in unison.

"No."

While at the same time Haywood said: "Yes."

Someone sighed. Frustrated. Maybe Rhodes.

Darger tried to peer through the murk. Tried to see the faces of the others there in the shadows. Found only the vaguest humanoid shapes in the dark instead.

She spoke up at last.

"We're about to cross a big open space. We'll be more vulnerable than ever. I say no lights from here on."

"Agreed," Wishnowsky said.

"I mean, when you put it that way… Hell, that's fine by me," Haywood said.

"OK," Rhodes said after a second.

There was a little slithering sound then. Probably Rhodes putting her Maglite away, Darger thought. The agent went on.

"So I say we creep up on the building slowly. Quietly. Stay along the edge of the woods until we're even with the porch and then make a break for it. We can check out the… thing… in the driveway along the way, but we won't get too close."

"Sounds like a plan to me," Haywood said. "You guys on board?"

Rhodes answered right away.

"Yep."

They waited for the camp's supervisor to respond.

"Wishnowsky?" Darger said.

"Yeah. Yeah, I'm in."

Darger sucked in a deep breath. Held it a second at the apex. Then she let it out slowly.

"OK," she said, getting to her feet. "Let's go."

CHAPTER 39

Loshak climbed the steps slowly. Moved toward the open rectangle above, a portal leading him out of the basement.

And he felt that mix of feelings he often felt on this job. Shock and revulsion at having found a corpse. A renewed resolve to see it through. And satisfaction, too — a sense of clear progress in their case.

He'd identified the killer. He had no doubt of it now. Walton Banks.

Whipple was smiling when Loshak reached the top of the steps, but his smile faded immediately when he saw the look on Loshak's face.

"What is it?"

Loshak handed him the dead Maglite.

"I'm afraid I busted your flashlight."

Whipple shrugged, looking confused.

"Well that's no big deal. I've got a spare."

"Also there's a dead body."

"A what? Where?" Whipple's head whipped back to face the open trapdoor. "Down there?"

Loshak nodded.

"Holy shit."

Loshak started walking back through the house, Whipple practically dancing alongside as he tried to keep up.

"So wait. What does that mean?"

Loshak shrugged.

"Well, the ID on the body says Taylor Higgins, and the other person who was supposed to be living here — Walton

Banks — is nowhere to be found. I'd say that makes him our number one suspect."

A pained expression flashed across Whipple's face. "Did he... is the body... like the others?"

"Not quite, but his head is cut almost clean off."

Whipple went quiet at that. Stared at the floor as he walked.

"Did you know him?" Loshak asked.

Whipple blinked, but he only seemed to half break out of his daze.

"Taylor? Only vaguely. But his mother... well, everyone knows Shirley. Jesus. I'm going to have to tell her."

Loshak led the way across the porch and down the front steps. As soon as they were out from under the shelter of the overhang, they started jogging through the drizzle.

"We'll have to wait for the M.E. to weigh in on a time of death," Loshak said. "But given the state of the body, I suspect this happened before all the other murders."

"So this was a... catalyst, of sorts?"

Loshak nodded. He climbed into the passenger seat before he went on.

"It seems the most likely explanation to me. Killing his only friend... I mean, it just makes sense for that to come first. Everything after has been a desperate act. A final flailing of a man who's come completely unhinged."

"Final."

Whipple wasn't asking a question.

"It fits the profile. This kind of crime almost always involves emotional triggers. He gets evicted. His girl dumps him. Maybe that triggers him to snap when he gets into an argument with his friend. And that murder only triggers him further still, to the crimes that have come after. And if he moved out into the woods — well, he certainly had a reason to go into hiding once he'd killed Taylor, even if nobody found the body until now."

Whipple let out a breath, shaking his head.

"Anyway, you wanna do the honors and call it in?" Loshak asked.

"Oh," Whipple looked startled. "Right. It'll probably take at least a few hours to get a team of techs out here, so yeah. Better call it in sooner than later."

Whipple gripped the CB mic. Pressed the button. Started relaying the info.

That left Loshak to the privacy of his own thoughts.

The good news is that we know who our killer is now.

He stared out the window at the darkening sky.

The bad news is that Banks is still out there, and he has nothing left to lose.

CHAPTER 40

Darger led the pack now for the first time that she could remember. They slinked out of the woods, one by one. Proceeded from there in single file.

She kept them to the deepest shadows, stayed just along the perimeter of the forest. The open space felt vast around her. Unnerving. But at least with that wall of woods standing tall to her right side, she felt like she had somewhere to run and hide if it came to that.

They crept along like that. Slow. Careful. Soundless.

Every fifteen or twenty feet, Darger would duck down and listen, and the others would follow suit behind her. Everyone falling into a frog squat and holding still.

She stopped again. Let her ears focus.

The rain fell heavier now. Big drops that patted at the damp ground and thumped at her shoulders. The wetness plastered a swatch of hair to her forehead that she kept flicking out of her eyes.

The rhythmic tapping of the precipitation seemed a gift and a curse to Darger. All the extra sound provided a certain amount of cover, shrouded whatever faint clicks and thuds they made in a blanket of white noise. But it also made it harder to hear their foe, should he be nearby.

Through the years, she had found that in these heightened moments of tension, she trusted her senses above all else. She didn't think. Didn't have time to. She acted in accordance with what she saw, heard, felt, smelled. Immediate reactions. To have one of those crucial senses diminished now made her uneasy.

Her eyes scanned the area around her in slow motion, moving from right to left to track from the edge of the woods all the way to the building. The scene remained unchanged. Immobile save for the wind-whipped branches and the places where she could see the rain falling through pinprick shafts of moonlight streaming down through the clouds.

She heard nothing. Nothing but the rain.

She lifted herself and slogged on. Boots squishing cool wetness between her toes with each step. The soggy fabric of her pants and shirt slithering against her body.

She shuffled another twenty feet closer to the building. Then she ducked down again. Only a hundred or so feet to go, then they'd cut hard to the left to cover the final distance to the porch in a sprint.

A stiff breeze kicked up as she moved. Flung rain into her face like flecks of cold spittle. The wind was still there, but the rough stuff from the first wave of the storm front had smoothed out into something calmer, something softer.

She snuck a peek at that strange object in the driveway, but even up close, she couldn't make it out. The tilt of the light and shadow somehow seemed to swallow it from this angle, absorbing it into the black background beyond it. She wouldn't even know it was there had she not already seen it.

She glanced back. Counted the heads behind her. They were all there, though she couldn't quite tell who was who.

Then she picked up again. Lurked another fifteen feet forward.

They were close now. Treading on the muddy driveway instead of the grass and weeds along the side of the woods. The ground squelched with each step. Darger could feel the hard rocks in the slop, jagged stone edges pressing into her boot treads like teeth.

She could feel the ground sloping down underfoot as well. Another dip in the land carrying her lower and lower.

This time, when she stopped and listened, she found that the soundscape had changed.

Water gushed from the downspouts on the cabin, sounding frothy as it jetted out of the metal tubes, and the rain plinked and sizzled where it struck the puddles at the bottom. The roof itself pinged when pelted with drops, little high-pitched metallic sounds.

Her heart punched faster in her chest. It felt good to be this close, close enough to hear the building there. But the new noise further clogged her ears, further stripped away her defenses.

She took a breath. Felt her chest inflate, ribcage shuddering, and then the wind flowed out of her lips, out of her nostrils.

OK.

OK.

This is it.

She looked back at the others again. Lifted a fist into the air with her arm locking into a 90-degree angle at her side, realizing she was half-mimicking Rhodes's flashlight pose.

She looked for any movement among the three of them, maybe some nodding or some other kind of acknowledgment that they saw her hand motion. She could make out the shape of the three heads there but little else, everything melting into blackness beneath that.

If I can't see them, can they see my gesture? Probably not.
Shit.

She looked around again. Let her gaze dance across the full field of her vision.

Branches still wagged in the woods. All those arms waving

at them endlessly. Leaves flipping and twisting in the breeze. Mashing together when the big gales blew in. Dead stuff flitting down at a steady clip like falling snow.

The building itself looked dead. Empty. No lights there. No motion discernible.

That should be a good thing, she knew, but she found it somehow ominous nevertheless. That rectangular threshold of the door tantalizing and terrifying all at once.

She kept turning. Scanning.

The object in the driveway took shape again. Coming clear finally.

Darger choked in a breath. Throat scraping like a pulled drawer. Unable to hold the sound in.

Her eyes stayed locked on that *thing* in the middle distance.

The stick-like bottom jutted out of the muddy driveway, dead center in the dirt track. And the bulbous object bulged atop the spiky piece of wood.

Darger could see the hair running across the rounded dome now, just like the hair she could see on the heads behind her.

The others turned. Saw what she saw.

Horror pulsed through the lot of them. Gasping. Gaping. Snorting.

Everyone knew what it meant. Everyone saw what protruded there from the road.

Officer Bohanon's head mounted on a wooden stake.

CHAPTER 41

Darger's shoulders jerked. The wave of shock rolled through her, a tremor that wouldn't let up. It sent a chill over her rain-slicked skin, a cold touch that somehow transmitted a range of feelings through her flesh.

Awe.

Disgust.

Terror.

She brought a shaking hand to her side. Slid her gun out of her holster. Heard the tiniest hiss of Rhodes doing the same behind her.

She swallowed hard. The gulp loud even against the patter of the rain, the sizzle of the puddles.

She tried to stop her chin and neck and arms from shivering. Willed the muscles to stop twitching. Couldn't.

Breath jetted through the gapped place between her teeth. Air thick and cold and damp on her lips.

A swamp smell thickened on the wind. Like the rain was leeching something out of the ground now. Releasing it into the atmosphere to waft around.

Her eyes snapped back to the building. Zeroing in on the oblong rectangle of the door there, just visible in the shadows.

So close.

No more than a twenty-yard dash.

Mere seconds.

She swallowed again. A painful lump yo-yoing in her neck. The walls of her throat somehow dry despite the ever-increasing deluge of rain.

Sopping on the outside. Dry on the inside. Of course.

She changed her clasp on the gun. Felt her wet palm suction itself to the grip like a tongue.

Then she blinked and refocused on the cabin, on the door. Her nerves swelled again. Bile climbing her esophagus. It all felt wrong.

He could be waiting here.

A trap.

But what choice do we have?

She took a deep breath again. Or tried to. Her chest convulsed, inhibited the effort some. Ribcage squeezing out the breath before she wanted it to.

Breathing didn't seem to help. Not this time. But she forced herself up finally.

Her legs tottered beneath her. Felt more like something outside of her than her own limbs just now. Weird sticks of meat and bone propping her up, barely keeping her balance.

The plan had been to rush to the building. Sprint for the door. Duck inside. A way to get out of the open quickly.

But she didn't like the plan anymore. Didn't think she could run right now even if she wanted to.

"We'll take it slow," she whispered, her throat sticky with dryness.

Talking felt weird. Felt wrong. But if he was still here, the sound wouldn't matter now, she thought.

She braved that first step forward. Felt the little fountains of water flex between her toes again. Colder now.

She lifted the gun before her. Kept her arm taut to try to minimize the shaking.

He was either lying in wait just ahead or he wasn't. There'd be a confrontation here and now or there wouldn't. All the hiding probably hadn't mattered.

He was fucking with them. Enjoying himself. He wasn't going to come straight at them, at least not for now. Where was the game in that?

She took another step. Boot sinking several inches into the muck. Arms and legs still quivering like plucked harp strings.

She heard the sloppy patter of footfalls behind her. Smacking and sucking. The others following. Good.

The next few steps came faster. Wobblier. Delivering her to the beaten path that sloped up to the steps.

She realized that she could feel Bohanon's head behind her. Perpetually aware of its presence like a mild electric current jolted from his skull to her back. A prickly sensation. Orienting her to it always.

She slid around in the loose muck with each step now. No rocks to hold the earth still here.

Her boot lifted. Reached out. Landed at an angle on the point of the first riser.

She gripped the handrail with her free hand. Pulled herself up onto the steps. Almost astounded to feel the solid plank of wood beneath her again. Something miraculous in the firm, flat plane supporting her weight.

Then she looked up. Peered over the deck ahead. Let her eyes lock on the door some handful of paces before her.

Fresh adrenaline flooded her brain. Coursed through her system. Chilled her hands to something icier still.

Nausea roiled in her gut as she crossed those few boards standing between her and the threshold. Bubbling in her middle.

Then the others appeared alongside her. Fanning out. Approaching the door walking four wide.

Wishnowsky pushed a key into the deadbolt. Cranked it to the right. A metallic click sounded as the bolt retracted.

Then the camp supervisor twisted the knob, and the door swung into the cabin.

Everyone held still for a moment. Breathing. Watching the dark rectangle before them, the shade inside the structure too thick to see anything through.

Darger's heart hammered in her chest. A fluttery feeling lurched and whipped in her stomach. Blood pounded in her ears.

She stepped into the darkness.

CHAPTER 42

Darger edged one foot in front of the other. Short strides. Careful.

She pressed deeper into the murk of the logging cabin like that. Slow and steady. Eyes wide. Staring hard into nothing.

Her gun pointed the way forward, though she couldn't see it. She swept the Glock all the way to her right. Then swiveled it slowly to the left from there, panned it all the way across the room.

She could just make out the shapes of a few of the windows in the distance. Fingers of light shining through the gaps in the curtains. Enough illumination to give her a vague sense of things more than letting her actually see them.

The quiet inside the building bloomed around her. Strengthened with each step she took. The constant patter of the rain growing fainter through the open door behind her. Tinnier and insubstantial.

She could hear her breath. Little shudders spasming in and out. Shallow yet somehow loud here in the stillness. Right on top of her.

She stopped. Waited. Listened. Cold feelings crawling over her. Icy electrical current touching every tiny follicle on her arms and legs and neck.

Her eyes slowly adjusted to the gloom. The kitchen island formed hard edges to her right. Skeletal bits of the bunk beds congealed into solidity across the room.

Nothing moved in the shadows before her. Nothing that she could see, anyway.

"Entryway is clear," she said, keeping her voice low. "I'll cover you."

Footsteps jostled behind her. Wet shoes skidding onto the glossy veneer of the wood planks inside. Thumping and squeaking.

Darger turned back in time to see a meaty arm extend over the wall a few feet away. Wishnowsky, she knew. She could hear his soggy hand swishing over the drywall.

His fingers found the bank of light switches. Flipped all six of them in two strokes.

After a second, the LED bulbs flickered and came on overhead. Lit the vast interior of the cabin, instantly making it feel bigger.

Bright light speared Darger's pupils. Ice picks. She brought the heels of her hands to her slitted eyelids. Pressed them there. The butt of the Glock jamming into her brow as she did.

"Christ."

Footsteps thundered into the space now. Emboldened by the light.

Darger forced her hands down. Watched the motions through rapid-fire blinks.

Rhodes and Wishnowsky stormed for the storage area beyond the kitchen. Something aggressive in their body language, even if their rain-soaked clothes made them both look like wet rats.

Rhodes kicked open the door. Jutted her gun into the opening.

Wishnowsky swept his arm in beside her. Hit the lights. The little snub-nosed gun dangling at the end of his arm.

Then they both disappeared into the glowing doorway. Footsteps almost hitting some galloping rhythm as they beat into the floor.

"Clear!" Rhodes yelled two seconds later.

And then Darger was moving. Crossing the plank floor. Shuffling through the maze of bunk beds.

She held her breath every time she jutted her Glock around a corner among the bunks. Felt her heart leap in her chest.

Nothing there.

Haywood whipped a few hanging blankets out of the way, and then the both of them got down and checked under the beds, Darger jabbing her gun into the dark places along the floor.

Again, clear.

That left one room to check — the bathroom.

Darger and Rhodes moved for the final doorway. Rhodes again kicking it out of the way, this time flipping on the lights herself. Harsh fluorescence flickered to fill this space, an unpleasant tremor visible in the glow.

Darger shuffled into the room, Rhodes just behind her. Their footsteps echoing funny off all the smooth surfaces, slurring applause accompanying their every move.

The shower room to the left was easy. A big open space with a few dividers to cut it into loose stalls. Tiny mosaic tiles covered the floor and walls. Pale blue squares surrounded by white grout. Looked like something in a dorm.

Clear.

They moved past the shower doorway. Pressed into the main bathroom.

A handful of sinks jutted out of the wall to the right. White bowls with chrome faucets and handles protruding from them. Silvery mirrors hung up above.

The urinals looked like porcelain medicine cabinets set low on the opposite wall. Urinal cakes like pink hockey pucks in each of their maws. Smelled like disinfectant mixed with lavender and bubble gum.

The stalls were last. Two of them leading into the back corner of the room.

Darger got low. Saw nothing along the floor under the stall doors. No shoes. No signs of moisture as though someone had walked in here with wet feet.

She glanced at Rhodes. Gave a nod.

The officer took a breath. Chest protruding and then deflating.

They moved for the pair of pale green stalls. Slowly. Quietly.

Darger's heart thudded harder than before, that crooked fist knocking in her chest like it was trying to beat a hole through her ribs.

She kicked open the first stall door. The plank bashed into the empty space. Ricocheted off the wall and came rebounding back.

The crack of the impact shivered in the air. Echoed off the tiles. Loud.

Nothing there.

They waited a few beats. Let the silence resettle over the space.

Darger felt sick from the adrenaline. Nausea rumbling through all of her torso, somehow spreading up through her neck into her head. Even her face somehow felt nauseous. Cheeks and mouth aching with it, bitter with it.

Rhodes took charge on the second door. Booted the slab. Flapped it out of the way.

Both of them thrust their guns into the narrow seafoam doorway. Shoulders squishing together so they could both fit.

The empty throne of the toilet gaped back at them, mouth open wide as though surprised or embarrassed.

Clear.
Darger allowed herself to breathe.

CHAPTER 43

Bunny-suited crime scene techs swarmed the abandoned house, fluttering like moths. The bulk of the CSIs disappeared into the open mouth of the trapdoor, pounded down the wooden stairs into the basement where the corpse lay — belly down and face up.

It was dark now. Raining steadily. Loshak and Whipple lingered at one side of the kitchen, gazing out the window from time to time at a sky gone black. The water tapped on the roof and dribbled down from the ceiling of the ruined bedroom.

Camera flashes split the darkness above the trapdoor every few seconds. Rapid-fire flares of brightness that drew Loshak's gaze.

The agent watched through the open doorway, feeling oddly removed from the strobing rectangle, the hole cut into the floor that led down into the dark. He could still remember how it felt down there, the damp concrete scuffing under his feet, the rot smell swelling to unbearable as he crossed the space. But now he was two doorways away, like the thresholds themselves somehow kept him safe.

A gas generator whirred to life outside. Engine throbbing out a throaty drone. A pair of techs bustled inside, orange extension cords snaking behind them. They dragged in half a dozen portable halogen work lights that slowly but surely beat back the gloom throughout the house as each one was plugged in and switched on.

The last light and its accompanying orange cable slithered down into the trapdoor itself, to replace the battery-powered lights the techs had originally carried in. Loshak edged over to the hole into the basement. Watched the dark swirling around the steps give way to gray.

Let there be light.

The illumination, on the whole, didn't do the house a lot of favors. Every flaw gleamed in the harsh light, glistened like a brown tooth. The rotten drywall in the leaky bedroom looked otherworldly, almost apocalyptic — black and textured like some cross between burnt skin and papier-mâché.

"Christ, it's going to be a long night," one of the techs in the living room said, voice a little muffled by his gear. "All of this garbage to sift through."

Loshak took that as his cue. He wandered over to a lonely corner in the bedroom where the trapdoor lay. Fished his pill bottle out of his pocket and popped one. Washed it down with a lukewarm slug from his water bottle.

The bitter taste bloomed on his tongue. Almost pleasant now. Part of the ritual that ultimately killed the pain.

He looked down at the plastic bottle in his hand. Licked his lips.

Take two. They're small.

He spilled another pill into his palm. Cupped it into his mouth. Rinsed it over the gorge with more lukewarm Aquafina.

Then he checked his phone. He'd been texting with one of Whipple's guys back at the station. Requested all the files they could find on Walton Banks. Criminal. Military. Even school records, if they could dig them up. Anything and everything.

Nothing yet. Of course, this late at night, he wasn't surprised at the delay. Being optimistic for once, perhaps due to the drug-induced endorphins flooding his system, he hoped everything would be available in digital format. Didn't want to end up digging through folder after folder of pages this time.

But given the locale, he knew the most likely outcome was a little of both.

Flicking around on his phone, he suddenly remembered Darger. He'd called and left a voicemail about their discovery at the abandoned house, but she hadn't gotten back to him yet. Probably worn out from all the hiking. He imagined her getting back to the Driftwood Inn and sacking out immediately.

He fired off a quick text:

Early night for you?

He stared at the screen for a few seconds. Expecting a snarky reply along the lines of *some* people having the luxury of sitting on their keisters all day.

Whipple pushed his head into the bedroom doorway then. Eyes stretched wide, something between shock and a smile in them.

"Jesus. Been looking all over for you. You gotta come see this," he said, and then he darted away again.

Loshak shoved his phone back into his pocket and hobbled in pursuit, nearly colliding with a tech as he rounded a corner. The woman's vinyl suit crinkled as she dodged out of his way.

"Excuse me," Loshak said. "Sorry."

Up ahead, Whipple burst through the screen door. Thudded down the steps and took a hard left toward the back of the house.

Outside? They found something in the yard?

Loshak stepped through the doorway. Jabbed his cane into the forgiving wood of the porch.

The generator blared out here. An endless grind hurling from the machine's innards. Louder by an order of magnitude as soon as he stepped beyond the shelter of the house.

He hustled after Whipple as best he could. Rain pelting the vinyl flap drawn up over his head.

A tripod shined six square bulbs onto the techs huddled in the backyard. Angled the brightness down at them so it cut out a triangular wedge of the darkness like a slice of pizza.

One of the CSIs stabbed a shovel into the dirt. It clanged on something metal.

"Got it," he said.

Loshak picked up speed as the group bent down and brushed the few inches of topsoil away.

Something buried in the backyard.

"Come on," Whipple said, waving a hand to the agent. "They found some disturbed land out here, and…"

Whipple's words cut out. His head angled toward the ground.

Loshak got up to the hole just as they cleared the last of the dirt away. He gazed down into the shallow hole.

It was a metal box about the size of a coffin.

CHAPTER 44

Darger stared at the empty bathroom stall as the door swung back into place, the metal of the latch clattering as it did.

The echoes faded. The room fell still again.

Darger blinked. Unmoving. Still gazing at that blank seafoam green plank.

She breathed. Deep. Smelled the urinal cake sharpness as it pervaded her nostrils and sucked up into her sinus cavity. Felt pins and needles prick to life in her hands and feet and spread down the length of the limbs, throbbing as they climbed the cylinders of meat and lanced into the trunk of her body.

Disconnected words rang in her head. Trying to knit themselves together and penetrate the shock settling over her.

Empty.

Vacant.

He's not here.

The whole building is clear.

We're safe.

For now.

Her mind flashed to the dark silhouette outside — Bohanon's head mounted in the yard. Stick jabbed into the sheared-off neck. Rain plastering the hair flat to the head.

Rhodes reached out and put a hand on Darger's arm, and the agent rocked back a step. Overwhelmed by the touch, by the space around her, by the shuffling echoes fluttering in this room.

"You OK?" Rhodes said.

Darger blinked again. Finally tore her eyes away from the

stall door and looked into the other woman's face, gaze flicking over her chin and nose and cheekbones, constant motion, too stimulated to maintain eye contact.

"Yeah. I just... I think it's all catching up with me now. The reality of it all."

Rhodes pulled the wet hat off her head. Shook it toward the floor and flung droplets that way.

"I know what you mean. All that buildup for an empty building… somehow makes me uneasy, even if it's what we wanted."

The ess sounds of Rhodes's words peeled off the walls. Hissing echoes. Cutting.

"Right. Exactly."

They stood another couple seconds, Darger's chest heaving though she wasn't winded. Rhodes keeping a side-eye on her.

"You ready to head out?" the chief said.

They moved for the door. Rhodes pulled it open, waved a hand, and then Darger passed back into the main room. It felt like being funneled through a chute, sound and space opening up around her once more.

"All clear?" Haywood asked from across the room.

He stood amid the bunks, his eyebrows lifted high, creasing his forehead into a pile of wrinkles.

Darger nodded once.

Right away the tension fled the lumberjack's body. Forehead smoothing. Shoulders sagging. Relief palpable.

Wishnowsky cleared his throat behind her. She turned to find him standing in the doorway to the store-room.

"I think you should all see this."

Rows of floor-to-ceiling shelves held boxes and boxes of provisions a camp like this would need to operate so far from civilization. Cleaning supplies and laundry detergent. Paper towels and toilet paper. Batteries in various sizes. Cans of corn, green beans, and tomato sauce. Bulk bags of flour and sugar. Costco-sized boxes of Frosted Flakes, Raisin Bran, and Quaker Instant Oatmeal. Tetra Paks of shelf-stable milk. Massive jugs of cooking oil. Various sized pots and pans and baking trays.

"Over here," Wishnowsky said, leading them to the back of the room.

An open cardboard box lay on the floor. The side read, "EMERGENCY 2 WAY RADIO" in permanent marker.

On top of a nearby filing cabinet was a metal console, about the size of a lunch box. Black and chrome with a variety of knobs and switches on the front, and a handheld microphone attached via a black spiral cable.

A thick black cord ran from the back of the radio to an outlet on the wall.

Wishnowsky flicked a metal switch on the radio.

Up. Down.

On. Off.

Nothing happened. No lights. Nothing.

"Could it be the outlet?" Darger asked, taking a step closer.

"No. I think… I took off the back cover, and I can see that several of the tubes are missing."

"And you don't have any spares?"

He shook his head.

"The emergency kit was put together by my predecessor, and I just assumed it would be functional. But the truth is, we've never needed to use it. When the worksite is active, we have regular walkies for communicating within the camp, and then there are always two designated safety officers with satellite phones for emergencies." He swallowed. "I'm sorry."

Darger ground her molars.

We should have gone for the Bronco when we had the chance

216

and gotten the fuck out of these woods.

She opened her mouth to speak but stopped herself when she saw the look on Wishnowsky's face. He looked on the brink of tears.

"This is… I mean… I can't apologize enough."

Darger inhaled through her nose. Let it out.

"It's OK. We're safe, and we're dry." She stared down at her sodden clothes. "Or we will be here in a bit."

Relief washed over Wishnowsky's face. He nodded to himself, seeming to regain his composure.

"Alright, so… we don't have any way to reach out for help at the moment, but someone's bound to figure out that we're missing, right? And soon," Wishnowsky said. "It's getting late. When all of us don't get home here in a bit… I mean, someone will notice and put two and two together."

They exchanged glances.

"Shoot. No one's waiting on my ass," Haywood said. "Obviously."

"My husband is out of town on business all week," Rhodes said. "He's at some IT conference in Chicago."

Darger closed her eyes.

"My partner may or may not notice if I don't check in," Darger said. "He's… well, he's recovering from knee surgery, and, uh, heavily medicated, especially at night. So it's just as likely that he'll pass out before he can think anything of it."

All eyes shifted to Wishnowsky. Darger's eyes flicked down to his left hand and found a golden band cinched around his ring finger.

"I'm recently separated, so…" the big supervisor said, looking down at the floor.

His eyes flicked back up.

"What about Officer Bohanon? Was he—"

Rhodes cut him off.

"Not married."

Everyone went still. Glassy-eyed.

The silence screamed in the office around them. Buzzed in the fluorescent tubes overhead.

When Wishnowsky spoke again, his voice came out tiny and tight. Almost high-pitched.

"So no one will even know we're gone."

CHAPTER 45

The techs chiseled dirt out from around the top of the metal box. Working the perimeter with shovels and fingers alike.

Rain rattled against the lid. Little pings that sounded hollow.

With most of the dirt cleared away, Loshak could see now that the thing was an earthy green. Riveted and vintage. Possibly an old military relic of some kind, though he had never seen a container quite like it before.

Finally, one of the CSIs looped his fingers into the gap. Pulled.

The lid sprang up. Dirt bursting along the edges in a powdery explosion.

Everyone leaned forward, craned their necks, Loshak included.

A tangle of automatic weapons filled the box lengthwise. Loshak recognized a couple of AR-15s and saw at least one AK-47 beneath that. It looked like there were more as the box trailed away into the shadows.

"A whole arsenal," Whipple said.

"No surprise," Loshak said. "This kind of guy… he likes stockpiling. Hoarding, at least when it comes to things he associates with strength, with survival. Probably has similar caches out in the woods. Ready and waiting."

The cameras started flashing again. Photos snapped from every angle. A tech with a video camera got down on hands and knees to film the weapons up close, mud imprinting the white of the bunny suit.

Finally, they started hauling out the guns. Bagging and tagging.

"We've got something else down here," one of the techs near the hole said. "Looks like, uh, personal effects, I guess you could say."

A few shirts and pairs of jeans lay along the bottom of the box.

"What do you think?" Whipple said, looking at Loshak.

"I think we're looking at Taylor Higgins's clothes."

They both held silent for a second. Loshak pictured the corpse in the basement again, head just about twisted off like a screw-top bottle cap.

"Now, why the hell would he leave the body in the basement and bury the clothes?"

Loshak shrugged.

"Empathy works in strange ways for a person like this. We tend to think someone with sociopathic traits lacks empathy entirely, but I think it's better said that they have a warped version of it. Stunted so badly that it's hard to conceive. They can muster a cartoonish version of someone else's interior world. A crayon drawing. Borderline nonsensical.

"Maybe, to Banks, something about his friend's clothes, the material possessions left behind, felt more real than the dead body, than the actual loss of life. They made him feel whatever muted version of guilt or grief that he's capable of, so he buried them here, where he thought no one would see. Under guns. Under dirt."

CHAPTER 46

Fresh dread coursed through Darger's gut. Weighed her belly down and clenched there like a fist.

No one knows where we are.

And no one will be able to do anything in time.

She pictured Loshak at the small desk in his room, cane at his side, poring over paperwork, scrawling notes in the margins. Probably totally unaware of the clock. Then tipping his head back and dumping an orange pill bottle into his mouth. Crunching up a mouthful of Vicodin like Smarties.

Even if her partner sussed out the scenario and called in the cavalry, it was unlikely they'd be able to do much of anything in this storm. Not until morning. And if the roads ended up washed out, then what?

She balled and unballed her fists. Tried to force feeling back into her palms and fingers.

Her fingernails pierced the thick flesh near the heels of her hands, and the pain brought her back to the moment. Sharp. Real.

She realized that she was shivering again, shoulders and jaw shimmying, even in the relative warmth of the building. Her wet clothes clung to her like soggy clods of seaweed.

Her eyelids fluttered, and then she looked at the room around them.

Shelter. They had that, at least. Warmth, too.

She turned her head. Looked over Wishnowsky's shoulder at the doorway leading out onto the main floor of the cabin.

Beds. Food. Dry clothes. Electricity, even.

Yes.

She would take a hot shower. Get warmed back up. She shivered a little harder at the thought, but the hope still lifted her spirits.

By tomorrow morning, someone would become aware of their absence, even if the rescue efforts were on the prolonged side from there.

Then her eyes swiveled to the dark window before her. A pane of glass cut into the wall, dappled with droplets of rain.

The blackness beyond the glazing held him somewhere out there, enfolded him in its gloom. Maybe near. Maybe far.

A prickling sensation rolled over her palms. Stole back the sensation from her fingers. Crawled up her arms and wormed into her core.

Hours and hours of night still lay between them and dawn.

He was out there. Angry. Driven. Toying with them.

Knowing that, knowing what he'd already done, how could they rest? Eat? Shower?

And she realized that she felt exposed under the glow of the lights, in the window. Vulnerable. Utterly visible while all outside held dark, concealed.

She jerked instinctively away from the glass pane, suddenly afraid.

Is he out there now?

Is he watching?

And Darger's skin went colder still. Frigid. Numb from the neck down. Like her head was just floating there in empty space, totally untethered from the rest of her.

Haywood noticed her reaction, seemed poised to ask what was wrong.

And then his eyes went to the window, and he lurched into motion. Stuck his face right up to the glass. Both hands resting on the sash, then lifting to cup around his brow and cut the glare.

He stared out for a few seconds and then jerked into action again. Head doing a half swivel. Then he shuffled off to the left of the window. Grabbed a steel filing cabinet there about four feet tall. Hugged his arms around the sides and slid it over in front of the glass.

His head twisted again to take in the rest of the room. His shoulders squared on a second filing cabinet in the opposite corner, a two-drawer model about a third shorter than the first. He stacked it on top of the other, blotting out the window almost entirely.

The words arrived in Darger's head a beat later than perhaps they should have.

He's barricading the room.

By the time she thought it, Haywood had moved back into the main space. Striding past them with urgency.

The others stood still. Dumbfounded. Staring at that gaping doorway between them and the rest of the cabin.

Within seconds, they heard the sound of heavy furniture scraping over the wood planks.

Darger looked at Rhodes. At Wishnowsky. And then they went out to help.

CHAPTER 47

Darger wandered toward the bunk beds on bare feet, tightening the towel wound around her head as she walked. A baggy t-shirt draped down from her shoulders, some 3XL thing that fit her like a tent, hanging almost to her knees — she'd found it in one of the footlockers now barricading the windows. When she'd first pulled it on, the dry fabric had been shocking against her skin. Warm and soft and not even faintly damp.

"You're up," she said to Haywood, who nodded and hustled off toward the showers.

Then she sat on one of the bottom bunks, the mattress and supports squawking at her touch. The thin padding cupped her like a hammock. Comfortable in its own way, but she doubted she'd be able to sleep much.

She closed her eyes for a second. Heard her pulse squish in her ears, that accelerated beat conveying how she really felt.

She tried to will herself to relax. The building was secure. There were four of them, and they had three guns. She needed to calm down. Rest. Be ready for whatever tomorrow brought.

Her body still radiated heat from the shower. Warmth stinging in her hands and coiling outward from her core.

Even having vanquished the chill, she'd taken extra time drying. Toweling every inch to try to compensate for the soggy feeling that had slowly seeped into her skin over the past few hours.

Her fingertips were still shriveled and pale, vaguely opalescent — white raisins stuck to her hands — and she found her skin still felt strange, somehow waterlogged and soft. She balled her hands into fists, felt that oddly velvety skin pull taut like it might snap.

She opened her eyes. Saw the bulbs burning above. Then let her vision drift lower to scan the room.

First, she looked over the fortified points of entry. Furniture snugged against every window and door. Some of the small blockades were braced with heavier objects. Other makeshift ramparts had been roped together or lashed with bungee cords — Haywood's work.

When she was satisfied with what she saw there, she took a breath and checked out what the others were doing.

Rhodes leaned over and toweled her hair on one of the other bunks.

Wishnowsky stood in the kitchen area, filling a glass at the sink. He brought his hand to his mouth and then took a big swallow of water. Probably sore from the hike and popping a Tylenol.

The shower sizzled in the distance, the high-pitched sound of the spray just audible over the drone of the vent in the bathroom. Glancing that way, Darger could vaguely discern wisps of steam coiling in the doorway and dissipating.

Then she realized she could hear Haywood singing — crooning some Tom Jones song, softly at first. He got louder and louder as he went, really getting into it.

Rhodes busted up laughing as the lumberjack hit a ludicrous level of intensity, and the giggling quickly spread to Darger and Wishnowsky. Infectious.

Finally, the agent focused on her immediate surroundings. The thin mattress. The scratchy green blanket spread over it.

Her wet clothes hung off the top bunk, dark garments draped over the rail there, looking elongated. She'd put her jacket near one of the electric heaters built into the wall, hoping that might actually get it dry by morning, though she wasn't overly optimistic about it.

She plucked the towel from atop her head. Let her damp hair swoop down into her face, dark strands like squid tentacles swinging into her field of vision. She looped the towel over the rail above, let it hang alongside her clothes.

Then she laid back on the bed. Stared up at the ribbed pieces of metal running across the mattress above her.

Her sore limbs and back took great pleasure in sprawling out. Somehow aching and blissful at the same time. No more strain of holding up her weight, of trudging around in the muck.

Still, her heart beat too fast for sleep to seem feasible. Electricity burned bright behind her eyes, even if exhaustion spun gritty sand in them.

She pulled the top sheet up over her mouth. Let the cool of it seep into her lips.

The linens and laundry all smelled incredible. Some lavender detergent scent she typically would think nothing of suddenly made precious against that soggy swamp smell she'd endured the last few hours. Clean and dry.

She closed her eyes again. Let herself listen to the sounds of the space. Empty and quiet apart from the muted sounds the others made.

Rain drummed on the metal roof. Steady tapping that was external, not part of the quiet inside the space.

Her mind still whirred. Flitted from topic to topic.

Thinking about how sore the hike had made her caused her to vow to get in better shape. Something like this shouldn't have kicked her ass so thoroughly, some touch of softness having crept in of late. She couldn't let it take hold.

The image of Bohanon came next — his broad shoulders

blazing that trail out in the woods. Showing them the way. Leading them as he had led so many over the years.

She wondered what Loshak was doing now, whether or not his leads had gotten him anywhere, and whether or not he'd found a decent slice of banana bread along the way.

She imagined Owen, 4,000-some miles away and probably passed out in front of the TV with the cat asleep on his chest.

The shower's hiss cut out. Haywood and Wishnowsky traded places, the lumberjack still humming "It's Not Unusual" as he walked out among the bunks, though much more softly than the wailing he'd done in the shower.

Darger kept her eyes closed and drifted into some state in between waking and sleep. Some of the urgency receded in her thoughts, and before long the voices in her head lay still. Quiet.

Some part of her still tracked the noises of the others.

The squawk of Rhodes's mattress as she climbed into bed.

Haywood fussing with his blanket before he finally lay still.

Wishnowsky's shower cutting out and the slap of his bare feet against the glossy planks of the floor.

The sharp click when he turned out the lights before climbing into bed himself.

The room fell fully quiet then, and the stillness swelled in the cavernous area. Walls expanding. Ceiling opening. Like the night sky yawned above them — clear and still, unlike the clouds and rain filling the heavens outside.

Darger's eyes opened. Stared at the blackness hung up above, thickened by all the objects they'd piled in front of the windows.

She lifted her head. Scanned the dark expanse between her and the front door.

Nothing.

She let her head plop back to the pillow. Waited.

The breath of the others evened out. Turned peaceful.

The rain still patted at the roof. Pinging sounds somewhere up above in the murk.

She blinked and breathed.

It occurred to Darger how much space they'd given each other, leaving at least one empty bunk between them.

Maybe that was human nature. To give each other elbow room. To leave each other be.

She picked up her head again. Scanned. Looked for movement in any of the windows — what little of them she could make out. Let her vision sweep over the black nothing in all directions.

The shadows seemed endless.

CHAPTER 48

Loshak drifted in and out, sleep and the pain meds swelling warmth into his cheeks. Holding him under.

He woke to find himself in the chair in his motel room, soft light spilling from the lamp on the opposite side of the bed. An open folder full of papers sprawled on his lap — the rap sheet, military history, and other miscellaneous papers relating to Walton Banks.

Bits of the files came back to him now. It'd been dry reading. Banks had suffered his share of minor infractions — assault, drunk and disorderly — and more than a few reprimands for brushes with authority in his military time. All of it paled compared to what he was up to now.

Loshak blinked and looked around the room, eyes catching on the alarm clock next to the bed. He blinked again as he processed the information.

It was late. After 3 A.M.

He checked his phone. Darger had never responded.

Guess she really did call it an early night.

He scratched at the stubble shrouding his jaw. He should probably check—

He stood then, and his knee twinged. Bad.

The pain blinded him for just a second. Then it flared steadily, bolts of it shooting from the joint up into the meat of his thigh.

He leaned over to grab the orange bottle on the nightstand. Shook a couple of Vicodin into his palm and knocked them back with the help of his bottle of water.

He took a few breaths and waited for the pain to recede, his consciousness seeming to exist only in that throbbing connective tissue in his knee for this moment.

His heart knocked. The alarm clock's red digits rolled over from 3:11 to 3:12. And then the drugs hit. The sharpness of the hurt pulled back into a dull ache quickly. Some chemical bliss swirled anew in his head, though it failed to beat back the exhaustion.

His chest and shoulders loosened up. Allowed some deep breaths to enter and exit.

Thank Christ.

He stripped and got into bed. Clicked out the light. Felt a thin sheen of sweat on his forehead and the back of his neck from when the pain had hit. Damn.

Right away he drifted toward sleep. Slipping deeper and deeper.

What had he been thinking about before all of this?

Darger. Right.

Well, whatever Darger might have found, they'd figure it all out tomorrow morning.

For now? Sleep.

CHAPTER 49

Darger woke to feet shuffling over the floor, thudding underscored by faint chirps and screeches from the bending floorboards. Part of her mind realized that the sound of the rain had died out before the other sounds fully registered.

She jerked her head up. Breath hitching. Eyes opening wide.

Bright light assailed her pupils. Smeared her vision. Bulbs overheard burning white orbs.

Then she saw him.

Haywood digging through one of the footlockers they'd pushed against the front door. Pulling out a thermal undershirt and holding it up to gauge the size.

Darger lay back. Felt the cool of the pillow against the back of her neck.

Some twinge of embarrassment coursed through her, though she didn't know if it was a reaction to her moment of panic or the notion that Haywood had gotten up before her, that she'd slept right through it.

He's a singlejack. He probably gets up before daylight every day.

A soft thump drew her eyes to the bathroom door where Rhodes appeared. She was fully dressed, and even though Darger knew it was impossible, it looked like she'd put on makeup.

Darger gritted her teeth.

Sheesh. Haywood and Rhodes both got up before me.

A voice spoke up from the kitchen. Wishnowsky.

"Usually I'd offer to make breakfast, but I'm afraid I don't have much of an appetite after what we've seen."

Oh God. I'm the last one up?

For some reason, the thought made Darger squirm with vulnerability.

"Me neither," Rhodes said.

"Still, we should all eat something," Wishnowsky went on, holding up two blue boxes with white lettering on them. "So what'll it be? I've got Strawberry or Blueberry."

Darger squinted. Realized what the boxes in Wishnowsky's hands were: Pop-Tarts.

"Let's see what we got," Haywood said, holding up two hands.

The supervisor tossed one of the boxes to Haywood underhand, who caught it cleanly and then looked down at it and scowled.

"No frosting? Is this a joke?"

He glanced up through stringy hair, chin tucked, that sneer still fixed on his mouth and wrinkling his nose. He threw the box back.

Disturbed by your lack of frosting, Darger thought, almost laughing.

Wishnowsky sighed. Turned and rifled through one of the cabinets. He found another box toward the back and threw that one to the lumberjack.

"Frosted Cherry," Wishnowsky said. "That good enough?"

The lumberjack's face lit up. He looked like an excited kid as he tore open the foil sleeve and started wolfing one of the rectangular pastries down. From across the room, the frosting looked almost neon pink. Broken crumbs tumbled from the corners of Haywood's mouth.

Rhodes scoffed.

"You're not even going to toast it first?"

Haywood shook his head, smiling as he chewed, pale pastry chunks bobbing around in his mouth.

"Better this way."

Rhodes scoffed again.

"I'll have mine toasted, thanks. Strawberry, I guess."

Wishnowsky nodded. Then he looked at Darger.

"What kind you want?"

Darger rubbed her eyes before she answered.

"I mean… the frosted kind."

Haywood stopped eating long enough to do a fist pump.

"Yes! See? Agent Darger gets it."

"Toasted?" Wishnowsky asked.

"Yes, please," Darger said. "Sorry, Haywood, but not toasting a Pop-Tart is insane. It's just… insane."

Haywood chuckled and took another big bite.

Darger kicked her legs out from under the blankets. Felt the cool floor against the soles of her feet.

She checked her pants, which hung to her left. Fingers squeezing up and down the seams on both legs. Dry. Good.

She stood and slid them on, leaving the oversized t-shirt on for now.

Then she padded over toward the kitchen where the scent of toasting Pop-Tarts swelled. It smelled more like flour than anything to Darger, but there was something nostalgic about it. Even better than that was the scent emanating from the coffee pot.

Wishnowsky was already eating his first pastry. Chewing the edges off his Pop-Tart with little munching motions like a chipmunk, then finally biting the center.

The toaster clunked. Four Pop-Tarts jumped up, heads poking out of the caged slots.

"Breakfast is served," Wishnowsky said, sweeping a hand

toward the toaster and the plates sitting on the counter before the appliance.

Darger plucked two of the pastries from the toaster. Felt the ribbed imprints on the back of the dry things as she put them on one of the plates. Then she poured herself a coffee and added two tiny cups of shelf-stable creamer.

She sat at the same table where they'd eaten lunch the day before. Soon enough the others joined her, everyone falling into the same positions again as though the seating had been assigned.

They ate in silence. The Pop-Tarts seemed sweeter than Darger remembered. Made her mouth feel arid and sticky.

She found her eyes continually drifting to the spot where Bohanon's plate had sat. Empty now like a socket where a tooth had been.

When Wishnowsky finished his breakfast, he leaned back, took one big breath, and broke the silence.

"So I've given it some thought, and I think we should hike down to Bo— to the Bronco. Rain did some damage to the roads last night, no doubt, but it'll be exponentially worse after another full day of rain, should we wait around. The SUV is a 4-wheel drive. We might be able to get out if we go now. If not, we should be able to call for help on the radio, right?"

Wishnowsky let his gaze fall from face to face as he went on.

"If we stay off the trail, slow and steady, it'll probably take us an hour, hour and a half to get down to the vehicle."

Rhodes shook her head.

"In a search and rescue scenario, the recommendation is to stay where you are."

"Yeah, that's if you're lost in the woods, and there's no loony with a crossbow huntin' your ass down," Haywood said.

Rhodes spread her hands wide.

"Look, we've got shelter here. Food. Electricity. At some point this morning, someone will notice that we're missing. There'd be some communication between the other members of the task force, and once they realize that both Agent Darger and myself are absent… I mean, they'll have to figure it out at that point."

Darger knew it was true, but part of her couldn't help but wonder if Loshak would be too busy lusting after banana bread to notice she was gone. She *had* promised to call Owen today, but she hadn't said when, and it wasn't exactly out of the norm for her to be so busy with a case that she'd forget.

"I hear what you're saying," Haywood said, opening another sleeve of Pop-Tarts. "But I'm with my man here. The longer we're stuck here, the more rain that falls. The more rain that falls, the higher the chances that they can't get us out for days even if they want to. I mean, hell, if it floods like they say, the road will be impassable. I've been up here when the road is out. It's a mess. Can take days to repair. We'd have a better chance getting out with canoes. There's a reason this is the tail end of the logging season."

Wishnowsky chimed in again.

"Besides, even if they organized a search party right this second, they don't know exactly where we are. Not even accounting for the time it takes to drive up here, they might kill an hour or three searching all the wrong places. And all the while, the road conditions continue to deteriorate."

Haywood scratched the back of his neck.

"And to be honest, I kinda feel like a sitting duck here. Don't like it."

They all fell quiet after that. Silent except for Haywood chomping on raw Pop-Tart.

"Well... it's a 2-1 vote at the moment," Rhodes said, looking at Darger. "What do you think?"

Darger looked around the space again. Saw the makeshift barricades piled up in front of the doors and windows. She felt safe here, for the moment, but she didn't want to stay another night in the woods if they could help it.

Before she could speak, Wishnowsky cleared his throat.

"OK, I didn't want to have to bring this up but... I have epilepsy. It's well-controlled... *if* I take my medication. But missing a single dose puts me at great risk of having a seizure."

Haywood let out a breath.

"Shit, man."

"Why didn't you tell us about this before?" Rhodes asked.

Wishnowsky shifted in his seat, not making eye contact.

"It's not something I like to talk about."

"Why? It's nothing to be embarrassed about."

His eyes snapped up, something fierce in them now.

"You think so? The first seizure I ever had, I was in college. One second I was in the middle of a Sociology lecture, and then the next thing I knew, I was on the floor with the TA and a bunch of my classmates standing around. As I struggled to figure out what was going on, I realized I'd wet myself. I was 21 years old. Fished out and pissed my pants in front of my entire class. So I don't know. Guess I don't always volunteer that kind of thing when I first meet people."

Rhodes winced.

"Sorry. I didn't mean to... I'm sorry."

Haywood scratched at his beard.

"So this might be a dickish thing to ask but... don't you keep an emergency dose of your medication on you?"

"Of course," Wishnowsky said. "But I took it last night."

Darger suddenly flashed on Wishnowsky standing at the

sink, washing something down with water. She'd assumed it was aspirin or Tylenol at the time.

"We have to get to the Bronco then," Darger said, her gaze moving around the table. "It's the only way."

CHAPTER 50

A heavy cabinet and one of the bunk beds slid over the wood floor, one and then the other scraping over the planks just far enough to be out of the way. Haywood and Wishnowsky squatted into the pieces of furniture, looked like they were pushing a car.

When they were done, they stepped back, and everyone stood facing the threshold laid bare.

The heavy wooden slab of the door stood naked before them. Oak with a dark veneer.

Discomfort roiled in Darger's gut at the thought of that single sheet of wood being the only thing between them and the Butcher's crossbow.

All three of the guns were drawn. Darger's Glock. Rhodes's Beretta. Wishnowsky's borrowed snub-nose.

After a moment of hesitation, Wishnowsky stepped forward. Flicked the deadbolt. Clutched the knob. Twisted and stepped back.

The door swung aside, and the doorway gaped. A rectangle cut out of the wall.

Gray light filtered through the opening. The sky cloudy but bright compared to the shadowed interior of the cabin.

Everything held still for a second. Soundless and fixed.

And then Haywood shuffled up to the open door. The others stepped forward to peer out, shoulder to shoulder.

An expanse of driveway lay before them. Gravel embedded in exposed dirt. All of it looking dark from the residual moisture.

Beyond the lot, a few feet of overgrown grass sprawled, and then finally that wall of forest rose from the earth. Tree trunks jutting toward the heavens. Branches crisscrossing. Leaves enmeshed.

Darger's eyes flicked around. Snapped back to the middle distance.

And there it was.

Bohanon's head facing them. Ghastly. Skin bleached grub white by the rain.

Eyes open but no intelligence in them. Pupils looking in slightly different directions.

Flesh sagged around the orbs. Pulled down by the wet to expose too much of the whites. Droopy like hound dog skin.

The carved pike holding the severed head in place looked the shade of a toothpick. Whittled to smooth perfection. An impossibly skinny stick jammed up into the ragged throat.

Darger ripped her gaze away and swallowed. Eyelids fluttering. Head tilting down toward the stony dirt of the drive, to the few wooden steps between her and the ground.

She didn't like even looking at the open land there. Dreaded all the more crossing it to get under the cover of the woods.

Her skin felt tight. Drawn taut over her flesh.

Her eyes flitted between the trees. Looked for him there. Wondered if he was watching them now. Lying in wait. Ready to spring a trap.

Even in broad daylight, shadows pitted the places between the trunks. Held much of the woods beyond her eyesight. Kept it dark and secret.

They all stared out. Unmoving. Unspeaking. Surveying the ominous landscape. No one daring to break the silence.

Tension wavered in the air between them and that threshold of the doorway. A barrier. A portal. They could all feel it, Darger knew.

They'd drawn straws to determine who'd go first, and Haywood had come up short. But suddenly that felt wrong to Darger. She had a gun, after all. The only thing Haywood had was a can of bear spray they'd found in the supply closet.

"I think I should go first," Darger said.

Haywood shook his head.

"No. I drew the short straw. Fair is fair."

"But you're the only one without a gun."

"Yeah, so the three of you can cover me."

He cranked his head back, and his eyes searched all of their faces. Waited like that for a few breaths. When no one spoke, he turned back to look out over the land.

"OK, just… move quickly. When you hit the tree line, find cover. We'll be right behind you," Darger said. She turned to the other two. "As soon as he's into the woods, that's our cue. Out the door and down the stairs."

Haywood took a few deep breaths. Checked himself from head to toe. Patted at his jacket pockets where foil Pop-Tart wrappers crinkled. He squeezed the garbage bag tucked under his right arm like a clutch — it held a set of dry clothes he'd dug out of one of the footlockers.

Finally he stepped through the glowing doorway. His silhouette darkening the frame for just a moment, casting a shadow that leaped over all of them like a spider.

His feet thudded over the deck. Thumped down the steps. Footsteps going crispy as he moved onto the gravel.

He started across the sea of stones and sand. His back to them. Head angled toward the dirt.

He looked wrong out in the open. Exposed. Light assailing him from every angle. Igniting the yellow part of his jacket so it almost looked neon. Laying him bare.

Darger swallowed. Felt something tremor in her neck. Itched under her chin with the fingernails of her free hand.

She let her gaze drift past the shrinking figure. Eyes crawling over the grassland to that shadowy wall beyond.

She scanned the edge of the woods. Looked for any threat there. Any sign of movement in the shade.

Nothing.

No one.

Haywood picked up speed now. Bounded over the last of the driveway and stepped into the ankle-high grass. His arms pumped at his sides. Stride bobbing him up and down.

He pushed through the grass. Hit the wall of the woods. Kicked through the weeds there and strode beneath the canopy, the shadows swallowing him, sucking some of the yellow hue out of his jacket right away.

The lumberjack stopped there just a couple of feet into the thicket. His upper body swelled — a big breath going in. Tension melting from his shoulders as he let the wind go.

Then he turned. Locked eyes with her in the doorway. Smiled. Gave a little wave that somehow read as cocky.

Wishnowsky spoke then, keeping his voice low.

"OK. Well… are we ready?"

Darger checked her coat. Found the water bottle nestled in her inside pocket. The alternating silver and gold foil wrappers of the Pop-Tarts and protein bars Wishnowsky had foisted on her in another.

Rhodes finished her check first.

"All good."

Darger spoke just after her.

"I'm set."

Wishnowsky licked his lips. Looked like a nervous labradoodle wearing glasses.

He had a small bag with extra waters in it, the handle looped around the crook of his elbow. Every move he made with it was somehow awkward, constantly shifting the angle of his arm.

"OK," he said, getting the thing under control. "Let's go."

Darger bit her bottom lip. She didn't wait around for him to finally make a move.

She stepped forward into the light.

CHAPTER 51

Darger glided down the wooden steps. Felt every minute degree of give in the boards beneath her feet.

She stepped away from the building. Moved out of its shadow. Her breath going still a moment as she strode into the direct light.

Into the open.

Into the void.

She turned for just a second when the door clicked shut behind her. Saw Rhodes on the stairs, Wishnowsky fumbling to lock the door.

She kept moving forward. Let her focus drift ahead to the gloomy barrier of the woods where Haywood huddled in the bushes.

The forest didn't seem to be getting closer fast enough. The gap between her and cover staying too wide. A sensation that reminded her of wading through a pool, her momentum locked into slow motion no matter how hard she churned her legs.

She looked at the ground. Watched the mud slide by. Mushy sand gritting beneath the treads of her boots. She saw Haywood's footprints there now, which somehow made her feel better.

No other footprints around. That's good, right?

Finally, she stepped off the gravel-flecked sand. Grass reached up around her ankles for the next few paces.

She took a big breath as she crossed into the woods. The shade blotted out much of the daylight all at once, shrouding her.

Haywood clapped her on the shoulder. Then they both turned and watched the others cross the foliage barrier.

Rhodes high-stepped through the growth, and then Wishnowsky stumbled through a few paces behind her. His face already looked pink, breathing a little heavy, just under a minute into the journey.

All four of them held still for a couple of seconds just inside the walls of the forest, looking at each other with blank faces, as though considering whether or not they were really going to do this.

"Everybody ready?" Haywood said.

The heads bobbed one by one, and the lumberjack struck out before them, looking back and smiling over his shoulder as he did. Trying to reassure them, Darger thought, somehow thankful for the effort even if it wasn't working.

Wishnowsky spoke up as the others lurched into motion.

"If we keep the road just off our right shoulders, it'll take us straight down to the Bronco. It'll be slower going than taking the road directly, of course. I'd guess maybe ninety minutes? Hopefully less."

And so the hike began. The ground gently sloped beneath their feet, the earth sliding down toward that jagged ravine where the Bronco was parked. The soil and its coating of mulch remained soggy from last night's rain. Spongy in many places.

The trail winnowed as they proceeded. Darger took up the spot just behind Haywood in their single-file formation, with Rhodes just behind her and Wishnowsky bringing up the rear, still huffing.

They plunged down the hill that way, weaving around trees and shrubs, walking in those barren places where the leaves above had choked out all undergrowth. Darger felt the treads of her boots dig in when the grade grew steep, somehow finding purchase in the slushy ground cover.

They stayed quiet. Kept their movements more careful than usual. Avoided the crunch and snap of speed, though Darger wasn't sure it was much of a help. Better than crashing through in a dead sprint, she supposed.

She thought about the profile again. About all they'd learned about the Butcher.

He must be a master tracker, a master hunter. Very comfortable in this environment. Very patient.

If he was near, he'd hear them. She held no illusions about that.

Even so, Haywood's confident body language kept her spirits up a little. Upright posture. Bounce in his step. She realized that he'd slid right into Bohanon's role, a leader both literally and emotionally, something that took some courage considering what had happened to the big ranger.

The slope sheared off all at once. An almost vertical drop opening up before them.

They toed up to the steep spot and stood side by side, looking around.

"Yikes," Wishnowsky said, staring down at the chasm between his feet.

"Do we try to slip 'n slide down this thing?" Rhodes asked. "I mean, I'm only half kidding."

"Uh, no thanks," Darger said.

"It's what? Twenty, thirty feet?" Haywood shook his head. "Too much risk of a snapped ankle. Then we'd really be fucked."

Everyone fell quiet again. Wishnowsky pointed out a beaten spot off to their left.

"There's a game trail here that seems to lead down. It'll take us farther from the road than I'd intended, but that's OK." He pulled a compass from his pocket. Checked it and seemed satisfied.

Haywood nodded and led the way down the new trail.

They edged along the drop-off. Fell into the worn spot where the animals had gashed a line in the soil.

They started their descent. The land tilting and tilting beyond what seemed possible.

Darger's footsteps went choppy. Arms and legs flailing to help her keep her balance.

Again, she felt her boots dig into the slop, punching through the soft stuff to grip at the solid ground, the treads sliding a little with each step but somehow finding traction and keeping her upright. Still, each step felt precarious, gravity threatening to rip her balance away at any second and tumble her into the abyss. She moved with great care.

A touch of heat made its way to Darger's cheeks as the exertion seemed to build. The shade kept the sun off them, at least. That permanent dusk under the canopy was good for one thing, in any case.

The path slowly veered around something of a gentle switchback and then another. Guided them down the steepest of the mess.

Then the decline went straight down on them again, like the ground dropped out from beneath them all at once. Everyone jogging now involuntarily. Skidding. Bouncing. Splaying their arms like wings.

And then they were bunched up at the bottom. Clustered together like bowling pins. Shoulders lightly knocking together.

It was over. Back to the gentle slope of earlier. Just like that.

Darger's head went light. Scalp prickling hard.

Looking around, she could see she wasn't alone in the feeling. All of them went a little giddy all at once. Rhodes smiling. Wishnowsky chuckling through that red face. Haywood hissing a strange laugh between his teeth.

Darger screwed the cap off her water bottle. Tipped her head back. Felt the cool liquid traverse her mouth and spill down her throat. Crisp. She wanted to drink more, wanted to feel the cool cascading into her, but she made herself wait, made herself save it.

Wishnowsky consulted the compass then and stuck his arm out.

"If we continue on this way, we should hit the road again in no time."

Haywood pressed on, wading through a narrow trench of muck at the bottom of the drop-off, and then the grade returned to something manageable going forward. Darger stepped in behind him, and the others followed as before.

Wet smooching sounds accompanied their footsteps for the next stretch. The mud was thicker down here, loose pudding beneath their feet. Darger supposed that made sense — the runoff would've gushed down the steep slope and pooled at the bottom, creating a miniature swamp in the process.

They marched through the slime. Kicked through thicker undergrowth for a while. Lush fern fronds waving endlessly around their ankles.

That flash of jubilation that had bloomed around them briefly slowly drained. The quiet brought solemnity back over them. The gravity of what they were doing here settling in again with each step.

The swamp receded in time, and the grade started angling downward again. Slouching once more toward the Bronco, somewhere below.

Darger peered up through a break in the canopy. Saw the gray skies roiling above, a mass of clouds scudding by, looking darker on the edges. She wondered how long until the rain would begin again. Hoped they were long out of here by then.

A chill crawled up her back like a claw.

Then she gazed at the woods around them. Dead leaves still clung to most of the branches. Shades of green and brown flecked with the darker threads of the boughs. All of the strands wove together. Glutted the space. Blotted out even the vaguest glimmer of the horizon.

Walls of plant life penned her in on all sides. Unfamiliar. Unknowable. She hated how she couldn't see very far, how the stalks and stems and thick tree trunks choked out her view all the way around, how the boughs all seemed to lean over their path, limbs reaching for them.

And that icy claw scraped up her spine again in slow motion. Colder than before.

She checked the time. It had already been almost an hour and a half since they'd left the cabin. She swallowed before she spoke.

"How much longer, do you think? Seems like we'd be close now."

The group exchanged glances, all eyes eventually settling on Wishnowsky.

He was cleaning his glasses with the hem of his shirt again, and when he looked up and realized everyone was staring at him, he jumped a little. Slid the glasses back on and checked the compass.

"Um... Wait here a sec," he said.

He tromped off to the right and disappeared into the shady thicket.

The rustling brush grew quieter as he moved away. Soon they couldn't hear his steps.

Darger sipped her water. Relishing the cool feeling on her

tongue, in her throat. Again, she screwed the cap on the bottle before she wanted to. Forced herself to conserve.

They all gaped into the narrow gap in the trees where the supervisor had gone. Silent. Motionless.

Darger felt the adrenaline seep into her bloodstream. Hackles rising. Eyes burning bright.

Then something popped in the distance. A single sharp sound ringing out over the soft forest din.

Darger checked on Rhodes and Haywood out of the corner of her eye. Saw that both of them were frozen, staring, upright, and rigid like spooked deer.

She waited.

Listened.

The crack of sticks and crunch of leaves faded back in. Moving toward them.

The branches started shaking in that parted place in the distance. And then Wishnowsky appeared in the middle of the foliage.

His face looked ashen as he drew closer. That pink complexion drained to gray. Skin slick with sweat.

He blinked hard before he spoke. Wrinkles surrounding both eyes and then vanishing.

"The road. It's not… uh… not there."

They all held quiet for a beat. And then Darger's voice squeezed out of her.

"What?"

Wishnowsky's head angled down toward the ground as he responded. He pulled the compass out of his inside pocket again and cupped it in his palm in front of himself.

"I can't find the road. It should be just off to our right. I'm not… I don't…"

Haywood interrupted.

"We're lost."

CHAPTER 52

Loshak woke. Blinked. Stared up at a tongue-and-groove wood ceiling that was entirely foreign. An alien texture rendered in half-light. Incongruous.

He sat up. Swiveled his head.

Light filtered in around the edges of the curtains — a rectangular glow that somehow caught his mind up.

Oh. Right. I'm in Alaska.

Yep.

He'd been having a weird dream. Trying to text Jan but his fingers kept typing the wrong letters. Churning out gibberish that he'd backspace over again and again. Seemed like he was taking forever just to say hi.

The clock on the dresser said it was almost 10 A.M. He'd slept later than he intended, but between the time change, the jet lag, and the pain meds, it made sense.

He plucked his phone from the bedside table. Checked it. Still no word from Darger.

Well, well, well. It appeared he wasn't the only one sleeping in today.

He took a breath. Stretched his arms. Heard something pop in his shoulders and upper back. Then he leaned back again.

There was still plenty of time before today's meeting, in any case. No need to rush.

He'd take a quick shower and go wake Darger up. Maybe even run into town and grab some donuts first. A wake-up call always went better if you arrived bearing gifts that were high in both sugar and saturated fat. The perfect combination.

He swung his legs off the bed, his knee twinging again when his left foot hit down on the carpet. Damn it.

He popped a couple of Vicodin and hit the shower.

CHAPTER 53

Rhodes spoke through clenched teeth. Bit off her words at the end. Her eyes bored into Wishnowsky's, looked demonic.

"The track has to be there. A road can't just disappear."

"Give me the compass," Haywood said.

Wishnowsky just stared at the compass in his hand. Face pale. Top lip twitching. He watched the needle like it might suddenly lurch in some new direction.

"We probably just veered off course a bit after coming down into that ravine," Darger said.

Haywood held out his hand toward the supervisor and flapped his fingers.

"Wishnowsky. Give it."

Still the man didn't look up from the round object in his mitt. Eyes still fixed on the needle. Eyebrows scrunching and unscrunching in cartoonish scrutiny.

His lips parted as though to speak but only breath came out. Nothing more.

Haywood snatched the compass out of Wishnowsky's hand. Held it out before himself. Lip curling in either a snarl or a smirk as he looked at the thing and then glared at Wishnowsky.

"This way," the lumberjack said, pointing his arm off at a diagonal.

He started walking without missing a beat. His pace accelerating. Something aggressive in his gait.

"How do you know?" Rhodes said, falling in behind him.

Haywood grunted and kept walking down the hill. Didn't answer.

Darger held back. Waited and watched Wishnowsky stare at his empty hand where the compass had been.

"Wishnowsky," she said just above a whisper.

He started. Gazed at her without recognition in his eyes.

"Let's go," she said, tilting her head toward the others.

His head snapped toward Rhodes. Then he grumbled something unintelligible and fell in, hustled to catch up.

Darger took up the rear this time. Felt better being able to keep an eye on Wishnowsky.

They walked for what felt like a long time. A tense silence rang out among them now, punctuated by the crunch of their footsteps falling in and out of time with each other.

Darger could feel her jaw clench in rapid pulses. Jaw muscles flexing. Molars squeezing together.

She kept straining to see the horizon before them. Eyes once more trying to look through the wall of trees. Trying to see any glimmer of light beyond them.

The opening where the road lay.

A flash of white from the Bronco's enamel.

Anything.

She realized that her upper back was slowly knotting up. The stress manifesting in those muscles. Constricting them. She rolled her neck from shoulder to shoulder, heard strange crackling up and down the bone like gristle popping.

Something about the feeling made her think of Bohanon's head mounted in the lot again. Neck sheared off in a ragged line. Flesh of the face gone the gray-white of a dead fish.

She shuddered.

It was still out there even now. That head on a skewer. Watching over the cabin. Those eyes looking in slightly different directions. Too much of the whites exposed.

The grim image pulled her away from the immediacy of the

woods. Sent her thoughts back to the night before. Walking along in the rain, in the dark. Wet and cold and miserable. Only able to make out the barest outlines of the things around her, the wet angles that shone in the dim light.

The trauma of it all seemed to prickle to life inside of her again. As if the misery had left some kind of mark, a kind of echo of itself. Fragmented movies ready to play over and over again in her head.

He left the head there because he wants us scared. He's playing with us. Taunting us.

Voices pulled her back into the moment. Haywood's raspy voice. Something frantic in it.

Frantic excited? Or frantic panicked?

"Here! It's here!"

They must have finally found the road.

Darger jogged to catch up. Realized she had fallen behind a bit as her thoughts wandered. Felt another pang of that strange guilt she'd felt in the morning when it occurred to her that she'd slept through everyone else waking.

The red of Wishnowsky's jacket caught her eye through the foliage. Just a glimmer poking out of the brown and green. Enough to steer her the right way, though.

The others stood with their backs to her. Stopped there. Facing the break in the trees in a loose semicircle.

Nobody moving.

Nobody talking.

When she reached them, she saw what they saw.

The slightly orange shade of the road sprawled there at their feet, that slit of sand that slashed a line into the woods. The open ground looked strange after so much time enclosed by the trees. Somehow inviting.

But it was what lay on the roadway itself that everyone was

staring at.

The SUV sat funny on the dirt. Uneven. The front end tilted slightly to the left like a listing ship.

Darger's eyes sought an explanation. Found it when they swept low.

All four tires slashed and flat.

Then the rest of the scene came clear.

Hood hanging partway open like the vehicle was mouth breathing.

Ripped-out wires dangling from the open space where the battery should have been, that spot now an empty socket between the radiator and the engine block.

He'd trashed the Bronco.

CHAPTER 54

The clerk leaned over the glass case. Pointed to another group of donuts bunched there, cordoned off from the others by plastic dividers.

"These here are the apple cider donuts. Real popular. Made with the real deal. Cider from a mill right here in Alaska. Fresh, you know, squeezed or whatever."

Loshak licked his lips. Stuck his face right up to the glass. Eyes dancing over the plump confections.

We only put truly precious things behind glass. Like jewelry, priceless artifacts, and fresh donuts.

"Damn. This is a tough choice."

The clerk chuckled a little.

"Hey, take your time, bud. I ain't exactly got anywhere better to be. They pay me by the hour, ya know?"

Loshak shifted to the left and caught his reflection in the glass. Smiling. Eyes all wide and perhaps slightly crazy-looking.

He was high. He could feel the drugs spiraling in his skull, throbbing in his hands and face, numbing the tip of his nose.

Knowing this somehow didn't help him speed up the decision.

He scanned the fried circles of dough again. Pudgy-looking things. Frosted in various shades. Glazed and glossy. As golden and perfect as flesh straight out of a tanning bed.

"Let me get a... uh... strawberry cheesecake. Two strawberry cheesecakes. Wait. Make those birthday cake instead. No. Wait."

The clerk wheezed out a laugh again. Spit hissing between

his teeth.

"Sorry. Guess I kind of want to try 'em all."

As Loshak continued the internal donut debate, it occurred to him that he was glad no one besides the clerk was here to witness this. Especially Darger. She'd give him one of those judgy looks again.

Bet she won't be so disapproving when I show up at her door with fresh donuts.

Yeah.

That would show her.

CHAPTER 55

Darger broke away from the others. Stepped into the light of the open. The sky strangely vast above her now without the meshwork of leaves and branches above.

She crossed the road. Boots treading over the barren sand, aggression bouncing in her gait.

She walked up to the SUV and ripped the driver's side door open. Leaned into the gap.

Her eyes took a fraction of a second to make sense of what she was seeing inside. Blinking. Focusing.

The radio had been ripped out of the console. Another mess of wires visible in the hollow recess where the thing had been.

Of course.

She checked under the visor.

No keys.

Of fucking course.

Not that they'd do any good with the state the rest of the vehicle was in. But it still somehow added to the injury that they were gone.

She slammed the door. Heard the crack of metal on metal echo out into the woods, the sound swooshing outward, reverberating, somehow reminding her of a boomerang. She regretted the volume of it for a second.

But then a fresh wave of anger surged inside her like a black tide and washed the regret away. Hot, clean rage that made her jaw clench so tightly that her teeth quivered against the insides of her cheeks.

She stormed back to the edge of the woods. Drew up on the rest of the crew.

The others still stood in the same spot. Listless. Faces grim.

She stayed in the road. Not wanting to lower herself into cowering among the trees and weeds again.

Better to die on your feet than live on your knees.

Her hands crept to her hips and fastened themselves there, seemingly of their own accord. She tried to fight back against the fire inside, at least enough to sound civil when she spoke. But the words came out bitter anyway.

"So... now what?"

She looked from face to face. Knowing that she was glaring. Practically challenging them, whether she meant to or not.

Wishnowsky stared at the ground again, the most lethargic-looking of the group. Nevertheless, he was the first to speak.

"We should go back."

Haywood's head snapped upright on his neck. He got out his angry retort before Darger could.

"Back?"

Wishnowsky's eyes swiveled over the ground. Two blank marbles in his head.

"Back to the cabin. Barricaded inside, with weapons. We'll be safe there."

"Jesus fucking Christ," Haywood said. "It was your idea to leave in the first place!"

Darger bit her tongue. Forced herself to breathe.

"Look, I don't want to get stuck out here for days if the weather turns again. Especially not with my condition," Wishnowsky said. "But what choice do we have? Hiking down to the main road would take something like eight hours. And that's if we stayed on the road."

Haywood turned away, the frustration clear in his body

language.

"There's food and water at the camp. Enough to last us however long we need it to," Wishnowsky said. "And there's not really any other option, is there?"

They all held quiet for a beat. A few bugs chirped somewhere in the distance. And the wind sucked along between the trees.

Rhodes spoke up for the first time in a while.

"I don't know. We could try to find that little cart. Maybe figure out a way to bridge that washed-out spot in the road. And—"

"Ride out of here at 12 miles per hour," Darger said, regretting the tone as soon as the words were out.

The officer's shoulders sagged.

"I don't know. Maybe he's right. Maybe going back is the only choice."

Haywood started off down the road. Practically stomping. Arms pumping at his sides.

"Where the hell is he going?" Wishnowsky asked.

Darger shook her head, eyes tracking the lumberjack's progress. The memory of Bohanon going off by himself and not coming back occurred to her, and fresh discomfort wriggled in her gut.

"We can't let him run off on his own. Come on."

She led the chase after Haywood, the other two spilling out of the woods onto the road behind her. They ran up on him.

"Haywood," Darger said.

He spun back all at once. Face red.

"What?"

Darger dug a foil sleeve of Pop-Tarts out of her pocket. Held them out.

"Here. Maybe eating something will help."

A grimace still wrinkled Haywood's top lip. He eyed the shiny rectangle in Darger's hand, fury still plain in his gaze, in his body language.

"Are these the fuckin' cherry?"

Darger nodded.

He hesitated another second, but then he took them from her. Tore open the crinkly sleeve.

His expression changed, softened, as soon as the bright pink frosting shifted into the open. The sunlight caught on the red sugar sprinkled over the icing, made it twinkle like glitter. Haywood relented, let his scowl fade, and crammed both pastries into his maw just about as fast as he could, chewing in big circular motions with crumbs all stuck to his lips.

People talk a lot of shit about junk food, Darger thought. *But it kinda solves most of life's problems.*

"Maybe we should all have something to eat before we schlep ourselves back up the hill," Rhodes said, unsheathing a pair of Pop-Tarts of her own.

Wishnowsky sucked down a Nutri-Grain bar. Blueberry goo visible at both ends of the mushy-looking log.

Darger peeled open a protein bar. Ripped off a bite of the dense thing by jerking her head back like a vulture tearing meat and sinew away from a carcass.

She chewed the mealy thing, felt its toughness slowly give between her teeth. It tasted like some kind of compressed cardboard composite, but it did seem to take the gnawing dread in her gut down a notch.

They ate like that in relative quiet for a few minutes. Wrappers crinkled. The wind hissed and whispered and rattled through the dry leaves.

A menagerie of sweet smells wafted in Darger's direction now and then. The candy smell of Haywood's frosting as he

262

tore into another sleeve. The unidentifiable perfume note accompanying Wishnowsky's Nutri-Grain bar. An almost syrupy scent coming from the brown sugar and cinnamon Pop-Tart that Rhodes ate.

Darger gazed down the dirt road as she chawed on another leathery piece of protein bar. Looked over at the Bronco sitting at an angle there, tires all smushed flat along the bottom.

Just seeing the white vehicle made her grit her teeth. That black tide lurching against the sides of her skull again.

Our way out seems so close. So close. Right there.

But it's not a way out.

It's nothing.

Beyond the SUV, the rough breach in the dirt track showed jagged and wrong even from a distance. Washed out much worse than it had been yesterday, new gouges and grooves bored into the sand.

She turned to look the other way. Scanned the dirt road trailing off toward civilization, eyes spearing the empty space cut out of the woods.

A washboard of ruts assailed the road top, some of the dips still holding muddy water, but she couldn't see any severe damage, at least not from here. If it wasn't too bad yet, help would make it to them before the second wave of the storm hit. She hoped.

The protein bar hovered before her lips again, the automatic action of eating feeling entirely involuntary for the moment. Not quite able to break her out of her daze.

That cardboard taste coated her tongue again. Jaw working hard to break it down.

Eyes still staring off into the distance. Examining the road for damage. Licking along the curve where the woods swallowed the dirt track up once more.

Rhodes gasped.

A sharp sucking sound that made Darger jump. Blink. She almost choked on a wad of protein.

All heads turned toward the officer.

The chief's eyes shifted skyward. Some kind of awe plain in the expression.

When she spoke, it came out quiet, slightly raspy.

"Look."

A black line twirled upward from the tree line in the distance, a thin ribbon rising into the air, snaking from side to side as it did.

It took a second for the image's meaning to register in Darger's mind. Eyes soaking it in blankly before her brain could process it.

Smoke.

CHAPTER 56

Loshak balanced the flat box of donuts on top of the coffee carrier. Lifted his free hand to knock on the door to Darger's room. Gave it three good raps, something vaguely jaunty in the rhythm.

He took a step back. Made sure to keep the box of sweets between him and the door like a lion tamer holding out a chair. Even if he were rudely waking her, she couldn't be mad at him, not with the donuts there. No way.

The door held still. A blank piece of wood painted a gray-blue.

No answer.

Hmm...

He swiveled his head around as though she might be walking up behind him, but the hallway was empty.

He turned back to the door. Hesitated there. Couldn't decide if he should knock again or...

He pulled out his phone. Thumbed her number. Pinned the phone to his ear with his shoulder, almost tipping the coffees over in the process but balancing things at the last second, clamping the boxes between both hands like someone catching a Frisbee.

The phone gurgled in his ear. Quickly went to voicemail.

No answer again.

OK, there were plenty of explanations for that. Her battery was dead. She turned her ringer off while she slept. But there was something about the whole situation he didn't like. It wasn't like Darger to be incommunicado for this long, especially not when she probably had juicy details to relay from her field trip up to the crime scenes.

He scrolled through his phone, found Officer Bohanon's number, and dialed.

One ring and then straight to voicemail.

Oh, shit.

CHAPTER 57

Darger slipped in the mud. Boots not quite able to keep a firm grip in the slop anymore. Unearthing black chunks of soil and leaving behind divots every time the treads failed to hold on.

They climbed the opposite slope from the cabin now. Weaving through the woods on land not quite as steep as the hill they'd just climbed down.

The growth here, however, seemed thicker. Vines coiled over everything. Thick green ropes choking trees and ferns. Spongy-looking moss creeping up the tree trunks and carpeting the ground.

The land flattened out for a stretch, and they stopped for a quick water break.

Darger's eyes scanned the heavens again as she drank. Looking for that undulating black tendril of smoke.

She couldn't find it. They were too close now, and the trees blocked her view. That sweaty, clammy feeling of being lost smeared itself against her again for just a second.

But Haywood had noted the direction on his compass, she reminded herself. He knew the way. She trusted that.

"So... are we sure this isn't a trap of some kind?" Wishnowsky said between water glugs.

Haywood shook his head.

"Smoke looks like it's not far from one of the hiking trails that winds around Klawock Lake." He spit on the ground. "There are a few spots off the trail that are real popular for camping. It's a rugged hike and an even more rugged spot to camp. No cell service or amenities, but... some people like it that way."

Rhodes nodded.

"There are cabins over at the wilderness retreat. For campers, you know? Well, one of my nephews, who is heavily into outdoorsy stuff, mentioned that he was going camping for Labor Day weekend last year. I asked if he was renting one of the cabins, and he looked at me like I'd killed a kitten. Said he only does 'rustic camping.' No cabins. No electricity. No nothing."

Wishnowsky still looked doubtful, eyebrows all crushed together.

"I've run into some campers who strayed off the protected land, wandered into our logging area," Haywood said, smiling a little. "Real tough-guy types, you know? Almost something competitive about them, like they were pretending they were on *Survivor* or some shit. Cargo pants. Buffs on their heads. Big *Crocodile Dundee* knives holstered in leather sheathes at their sides like they might need to harpoon a walrus or something out here. Kind of hilarious in a way."

Wishnowsky tilted his head. Finally spoke, his voice small and steady.

"Well I think it's a trap."

He looked around at all of them. Nervous and sweaty. Reminded Darger of someone in a horror movie, which she supposed they basically were.

Wishnowsky licked his lips and went on.

"He cut off our way out, and now he's funneling us toward that smoke so he can pick us off. Sure as you're alive."

Everyone looked away from him then.

Rhodes angled her head down to the ground.

Haywood shifted his weight from foot to foot. Looked uncomfortable.

When no one said anything, Wishnowsky elaborated.

"We know he has ranged weapons. He could be waiting somewhere up high. Drawing us into a clearing to take us out."

Haywood spat on the ground again before he spoke up.

"Dude already had us cornered in a cabin if he wanted us. Could have gotten us as we walked out the funnel of the front door, right? Why go to such elaborate lengths when he already had us pinned down?"

Wishnowsky huffed, eyes swiveling in his head again, looking at everything and nothing. He didn't respond.

"We'll keep going, but we'll take it slow," Darger said. "Quiet. We still have three guns to his one, at most. He'd be stupid to come at us in broad daylight, considering that."

"Yep," Haywood said.

Rhodes nodded.

Wishnowsky grumbled. Then he nodded as well.

They started up the slope again. Walked in silence for a long time. Slow and steady.

Darger found herself more tuned in to the present now. Focused solely on the here and now. Watching the shifting tree branches ahead, listening to the sounds of the woods sprawling out around her.

Her mind stayed blank. No more stray thoughts. No more abstractions. Only the concrete forest details were real now.

The woods thrummed with life. Singing birds. Flitting boughs. Buzzing flies.

She watched Haywood rise and fall before her. Walking over something.

She climbed up onto the big log a beat after him, crossed it like a small bridge, then stepped down on the other side and kept going.

The smell of smoke hit then. The clean woody scent of a

campfire. Not the polluted stink of smoke in the city, that acrid stench of melting plastic or factory chemicals. This was wood and wood alone.

They were close.

Her senses sharpened further still. Pointed her head in the direction her instincts told her the smoke was coming from.

Haywood must have sensed it as well, as he also turned that way. Adjusted their course a hair to the left.

Light shined through the leaves there, a lacework of gray and green. But Darger couldn't see the camp yet. No signs of people or of the fire itself.

They pressed onward. Slowed their pace even more. Slicing through foliage without sound.

Darger drew her weapon. Saw Rhodes do the same out of the corner of her eye. Knew Wishnowsky would be doing the same, though she didn't turn her head far enough to confirm it.

She kept all of her attention tuned to that narrow gap in the boughs in front of them. Leaves wagging there gently in the breeze.

Something moved.

A flash of blue between the tree limbs that made Darger's heart leap.

It shifted again. Someone's shirt coming clear through the foliage.

Darger stared.

A blue t-shirt sharpened into focus first. Then she could see a gray hoodie laid over it.

But then the clothes darted back. Slid out of view.

Silence.

Nothing.

Darger felt her sweaty palm squirm against the grip of her Glock.

They stepped forward in slow motion. Silent things drifting toward the parted place among the trees.

Then the fire caught Darger's eyes. Thrashing orange flicking up from the ground. Her next step revealed the logs and a few sticks forming into something of a cone at the fire's base. Another pace showed that it was surrounded by a circle of rocks.

It was a campfire. Small. Normal.

The vinyl tent took shape beyond it. Pale green polyester with gray accents along the zipper and seams. It flapped gently in the breeze, made a sound like a flag pulling taut.

Darger felt herself breathe. Realized that she hadn't for a second there.

She poked out her foot. Took another step forward. And that was when she heard the voice up ahead.

Small. Almost squeaky.

"Grampa, can we have pancakes?"

CHAPTER 58

"No fun to be stranded out here without supplies. I know all about that first hand, believe me."

The old man smiled at Darger over the campfire. He smoothed a hand over the top of his shaved head where a hint of sweat seemed to have beaded, probably due to the proximity of the flames. He went on.

"Well, I'm glad you stumbled upon us. I'm Shepard. Joe Shepard. This is my wife Marilyn. And these two little rascals are Sadie and Kira. My granddaughters. I'm teaching 'em everything I know about the great outdoors. Ain't that right, girls?"

One of the girls nodded while the other stared off into space. Dark hair. Heart-shaped faces. They looked enough alike that Darger thought they might be twins, but she couldn't be sure.

Marilyn was tall and had one of those bony faces so packed with angles that it seemed like she might have been a model in her younger years. Sharp nose. Spiky chin. Bladed cheekbones. A cardigan the shade of a plum slung over her scrawny frame. Cat-eye glasses set over brown eyes, something gentle and intelligent in them.

Shepard, like his wife, looked to be in his late 60s or 70s. His pale blue eyes seemed to glow out from the sunbaked skin of his face and scalp, a deep tan coating all of him like a lacquered piece of antique furniture. The hound dog sag in his cheeks was juxtaposed with a chiseled jaw speckled with stubble.

An army green t-shirt swaddled the old man's barrel chest, and the cargo pants below came replete with the leather-sheathed Rambo knife just as Haywood had predicted. Darger almost chuckled and pointed when she saw it, but she reined herself in.

Shepard's eyes flicked down toward the fire. He leaned toward the cast iron pan hovering over the orange coals.

Clear egg snot slowly congealed into white rubber around the yellow orbs of the yolks. The old man sprinkled salt and pepper over the food and shook the pan gently.

"You want to have breakfast with us before we head out? The Jeep is maybe a mile hike from here, but we've got plenty of food if any of you are hungry. Eggs. Bacon. There was talk of pancakes, but we should probably hit it sooner than later. Get you folks back to civilization."

One of the girls huffed at that, but Shepard locked eyes with her, and her gaze fell to the ground.

Darger exchanged glances with Haywood and Wishnowsky. Rhodes leaned in close and muttered just loud enough for Darger to hear.

"I don't think they're grasping the gravity of the situation."

Darger nodded. Spoke up.

"How long have you been out here? In the woods, I mean."

Shepard started dishing up the food as he spoke. Sliding the fried eggs onto plates where buttered toast already sat. Grabbing a couple of bacon strips from another plate where they were wrapped in greasy paper towels.

"Coming up on two weeks. First we set up over closer to the coast. Stayed there maybe a week. Did some whale watching. Then we packed up and drove inland to Klawock Lake. Spent a few nights at a spot a couple miles east of here, closer to the lake. But we were a little too low elevation-wise. The rain flooded our camp, so we had no choice but to pack everything up and move to higher ground. Drove into the hills and hiked up here just before nightfall last night. Lucky we found such a nice spot given the time crunch we were in."

He spread his hand over the small clearing they'd camped in. Flat and grassy. It was a nice enough location, with views of some of the taller slopes not so far off, but Darger couldn't appreciate it much just now.

She swallowed. Studied the man's face, like the lines etched there might convey the information she sought.

"Have you been checking the news at all?"

Marilyn chimed in before Shepard could answer.

"Joe has a rule when we go on our trips, whether it's Alaska or Hawaii. No phones. No radio. No news. Just the peace of the land."

Darger nodded.

"So you're not from around here?"

Shepard smiled like the notion was ridiculous.

"Here? Lord no. We're from Ohio."

He doesn't know. Doesn't know about the storm. Doesn't know about the killer.

She chewed her bottom lip. Watched the kids sop up runny egg yolk with their toast. Didn't want to spook them.

"Mr. Shepard, could I talk to you for a second?" She jabbed a thumb toward the thicket to her left. "Alone."

CHAPTER 59

Shepard's face went pale even before Darger was finished speaking. He took a couple of ragged breaths.

"My God, I had no idea."

He said it as much to himself as to her, so Darger didn't say anything.

"We've been out here this whole time, not knowing…" His eyes whipped back over to his wife and granddaughters. "My girls."

And then he was moving, striding across the campsite with purpose. He rushed toward the tent and disappeared inside for a second, pulling himself in backward so he looked like a turtle retreating into its shell.

He emerged a second later with two backpacks and started shoving bits and pieces into them. Plucking socks and a t-shirt from a makeshift laundry line. Grabbing some of the cooking items from near the fire and wrapping them in towels, both cloth and paper, before he shoved them into one of the bags.

"Alright, girls. We're packing it in," he said. "Let's go. Right now."

Haywood and Marilyn joined in right away. Pulling sleeping bags out through the zippered mouth of the tent and then rolling them up.

"Wait. Are we really not going to have pancakes?" one of the girls said. "I thought you were teasing me."

Shepard's lips scrunched into a hard line, all pressed together. His voice came out in a growl, the struggle for restraint plain in it.

275

"Not now, Sadie."

Somehow the delivery of the three benign words conveyed intense anger. Dark feelings that rippled through everyone in the camp.

Everyone fell quiet and focused on getting the camp packed up.

Darger folded up the two camp chairs and leaned them against a tree. Beneath one, she found a pair of small, pink Converse All Stars. Her eyes went to the girls, noticed that one was barefoot. She plucked up the shoes and carried them over.

"Here. I think these are yours."

"Oh," the kid said, her voice sounding shy. "Thanks."

"You need help getting them on?"

The girl shook her head.

While the kid wrestled the shoes on, Darger glugged down the last of her water. Let her vision stretch out over the hills in the distance, focus panning over all of those trees poking up from the slopes. Spiky pine tops. Skeletal husks that had lost their leaves.

He's out there now. Somewhere.

The tent deflated as Shepard removed the poles. Exhaled as it did, the sound and motion drawing Darger's attention back to the campsite.

The old man gathered up the flattened piece of vinyl and went to work rolling it up and snugging it into a drawstring bag. Handed it to Marilyn, who shoved it down inside her pack.

Rhodes stepped forward, hand wriggling in her coat pocket. She dug out a sleeve of Pop-Tarts and handed them over to Sadie.

"They're not exactly pancakes, but... Share with your sister."

Both those heart-shaped faces lit up. Smiling. Eyes dancing.

For more than a few seconds they just stared at the silver foil clutched in the small hands. Seemingly too excited to even open it.

Shepard pulled the straps of his pack onto his shoulders. He stomped over to the fire. Dumped a five-gallon bucket of water on the coals.

The fire hissed and steamed and struggled through its death throes. Then it held still. Snuffed out for good.

"Jeep is maybe a mile back this way," Shepard said, pointing his arm off into the woods. "If we hustle, we can be there in fifteen, twenty minutes. Go on and get the rest of your things around, girls. If you leave anything out here, we're not coming back for it."

"Wait. No frosting?" Sadie said, looking down at the bare pastry of the Pop-Tart in her hands. Little holes on the top of the flesh-toned thing revealed the strawberry goo inside. Made Darger think of Bohanon's stumped neck.

"Aw, hell. Here," Haywood said, offering up a new foil sleeve. "These here are the good ones. Frosted. Cherry, I believe."

The silvery rectangle hovered in the space between them, glimmered where the sunlight caught it.

Shepard leaned down to spread the soggy ashes of the campfire with a stick.

A whooshing sound buzzed toward them. Fluttering and humming.

Something thwacked a tree trunk nearby. Split and thunked into the wood. The small hole seeming to appear in the tree all at once, just about the trajectory of where Shepard's head had been a second before.

The gunshot cracked and thumped in the distance behind them a heartbeat later, the noise trailing the bullet. The air disturbance sizzling around the other sounds like a sparkler. Echoing funny over the hills.

Three words rang in Darger's head.

Sniper rifle.

Close.

CHAPTER 60

The rifle fired somewhere off in the hills again. Cracked and sizzled and thumped.

And then the panic took hold.

The whole group stampeded like frightened cats. Fled into the woods in varying directions.

Darger found herself running blindly. Tree branches whipping into her face.

Something involuntary pistoning her legs. Propelling her into the forest.

No thoughts in her head.

Just fear. Frenzy. Hysteria.

She craned her neck. Looked back for just a second.

Saw the others bursting outward from the campsite like motes of shrapnel thrown in all directions.

And then they disappeared into the foliage. Gone from her sight all at once.

The campsite held still. Vacant.

And that heightened the terror again. Thrust a word into her head at last.

Alone.

She turned back to the maze of vegetation before her. Redirected her trajectory to dodge a tight cluster of saplings.

Arms and legs swinging, loose, floppy, as she rushed back down the slope. Glock floundering along with her gait. She didn't even remember pulling from its holster.

Gravity ripped her downward over the steep stuff. Head leaning out in front of her feet. Faster, faster.

Ragged breath heaved into her open mouth. Rushed over her bottom teeth.

She plunged down another drop-off. Feet barely touching the ground. Toes skimming over the muddy slash in the mulch.

Pine boughs reached out. Tried to hug her to their trunks. All of the green enfolding her. Swallowing her.

She caught herself again as the slope leveled out a touch. Gravity relenting some. The treads of her boots digging in.

One second of relief shuddered through her. Rapturous. The notion that she'd put this hill between herself and the rifle occurring to her. Soothing her. Then ripping its comfort away just as quickly.

The sounds of the rifle played in her head again. She focused on that fraction of a second between the crack of the bullet's sound wave and the thump of the rifle itself. Not long enough.

He was close. Maybe a few hundred yards.

Too close.

He could be over the lip of the hill already. Hurtling downward.

Closing on me.

She glanced back. Saw the faded green boundary hung up there like a curtain. Dense leafage.

At least that should conceal her. For now.

She pushed herself harder. Spilled down the hill. Thrashed her arms through the thicket, batting away branches and leaves and stalks and stems.

She lost her footing as soon as she burst through the edge of the woods. Tipping forward over the land gone suddenly flat again.

Weightless.

She hit down. Hands and arms folding up under her. Teeth

clacking together hard.

She skidded on her belly onto the dirt logging road. Chest and elbows juddering over the sand. One cheek brushing over the road top.

The world went shaky and strange. Mud filling half her field of vision. The rest of it sideways. Bouncing. Nonsensical.

But then she was pushing herself up. Hands and knees scrabbling. Running into that crooked world. Watching it straighten as she got her feet under her.

She wiped a wad of mud out of her eye. Cranked her head around again. Looked behind her. Left. Then right.

No one.

Nothing.

Alone.

She tried to gaze up the slope. Saw only that wall of woods in the foreground. Blocking her view.

She got the faintest sense of the shade between the trees. Empty places filled only with dark.

Wherever the others were, she couldn't see any of them.

Alone.

CHAPTER 61

Wishnowsky runs out in front. Haywood trails a few steps behind him, one of the little girls hoisted into the lumberjack's arms.

The supervisor leads them away from the campsite. Takes a circuitous path through the foliage. Weaving down the hill on a diagonal.

Cabin.

Shelter.

At first that's all he can think. Those two words pulsing in his head in screaming whispers. Pounding like hammer blows over and over. A mantra gone violent.

Cabin.

Shelter.

Cabin.

Shelter.

It goes on like that a while before it registers that he's running that way. Leading them back toward the cabin. The thought arriving late, suddenly, revelatory, and almost baffling to him in some way. Like a long-held mystery that's finally been explained, the meaning laid bare at last.

Going to the cabin.

Well... that makes sense, doesn't it?

Wishnowsky's feet skid out from under him then. A muddy gash in the forest floor loosening the grip of his shoes.

His steps go choppy. Arms splayed at his sides. Balance thrown to one side and then the other.

But he stays upright. Tromps through a gauntlet of quaking

aspens, swims his arms through the tightly packed trees, all those straight trunks jutting up from the ground, his jog building back into a run as he slaloms through.

When he's back in the clear, he brings a hand to his face. Smears the heel over the sweat beading on his forehead. Finds the meaty part of his mitt shockingly cold to the touch.

He looks back again. Half expects Haywood and the girl to be gone, but they're still there. Still there.

Wishnowsky eyes the girl a second longer. Can't remember her name, either of their names. She's young and stick thin. Maybe ten. Maybe younger than that.

And he can't block himself from wondering:

Will she slow us down? Get us killed?

He moans a little at the notion. Wishes he hadn't thought those words. Wishes even harder that the panicked part of him didn't believe that she would do both of those things. That she *would* slow them down. That she *would* get them killed. And sooner than later.

He banks around another patch of mud. Takes a wide turn. Hurdles some deadfall.

Fatigue catches up with Wishnowsky all at once. His breath wheezing. Temples throbbing. Throat dry and painful. Lungs turned to two wet bags in his chest.

He stops. Leans up against a tree. Lets his head sink lower and lower until he's bent at the waist.

He breathes.

Wind rasping into his neck.

Somehow painful. Useless. Like his body can't absorb the oxygen anyway. Like maybe he'll never catch his breath again.

Faint black splotches strobe in the corner of his left eye, flickering along with his pulse.

Haywood and the girl squat down nearby, mostly concealed

behind a shrub dotted with white flowers that look like cups. The lumberjack is heaving, too, though not as bad as Wishnowsky.

The girl looks like she might burst into tears. Eyes squinted and blinking rapidly. Lips turned down.

Wishnowsky clenches his jaw.

Perfect. Go on and bawl and pitch a goddamn fit and get us crossbowed and dissected like frogs already. No need to do all this running if we're only gonna get it in the end.

Haywood coos to the girl, his voice very low. Even just a few feet away, Wishnowsky can only hear bits and pieces.

"You're gonna be alright now, darlin'. We'll get you back to your family before you know it, Kira. Me and Wishnowsky here, we'll make sure of it. Ain't that right, Wishnowsky?"

Both heads whip around to face the supervisor, Haywood lifting his eyebrows.

Wishnowsky feels his eyes swiveling around, looking everywhere but right at the girl. He finally pumps his head once in a nod.

"We're headed for the cabin?"

The supervisor nods again.

"I figured so. See, I figure the Butch— er, our guy — will want to cut off the vehicle first. Shepard's Jeep. Seems to be the pattern for him so far, anyway. I reckon we can get a good head start before he moves on from that. Hopefully."

Wishnowsky finds himself breathing easier as the lumberjack speaks.

Thank Christ I'm not out here alone.

He guzzles some water from his bottle. Then he finds himself speaking.

"You think the others will head for the cabin, too?"

Haywood tilts his head to the side. Looks out into the

woods as he answers.

"Some, yes. Probably. I think the vehicle will be awfully enticing, but it doesn't feel right to me, I guess."

Wishnowsky knows what he means, though neither of them dare speak it in front of the girl.

Feels like a trap.

A trap that your grandma and grandpa may well be falling into right now.

Something in Haywood's body language tightens. His neck elongates like a spooked bird's. Then his head goes rigid.

Wishnowsky lifts his own head. Pushes his glasses up higher on his nose.

Listens.

The quiet is alive around them. An open, airy thing. Tinkling leaves. Whispering wind.

In this moment, Wishnowsky can hear the space of it, the vastness of it, the open places between the trees stretching out for miles. The yawning nothingness that sprawls upward from the land and reaches out into the heavens.

He shudders thinking about it. All of that space.

But there's nothing else there. No footsteps. No voices. Nothing. Just the woods.

"We should move," Haywood says, getting to his feet. "You ready to go, baby doll?"

Kira sighs. Then she, too, picks herself up. Dusts herself off. Her expression still looks forlorn, but the tears no longer look imminent.

They walk on. Now the lumberjack holds the girl's hand instead of carrying her.

At the bottom of a hill, the decline gives way to an expanse of flat land. When the light starts to grow around them, Wishnowsky suspects he knows where they are. Finally.

The last of the trees come and go, and the road lies open at their feet. They stop at the threshold. All of their heads rotating to take everything in.

The open space looks vast. The woods on the opposite side somehow appearing far away like a distant shore. The sight makes Wishnowsky's stomach wad itself up like a meat rag and crawl up toward his throat.

Haywood takes the first step into the breach. Drags the girl along about a half a pace behind him.

Wishnowsky follows. Stomach clenching tighter still. Nerves coursing lightness into his thighs. Making him feel somehow breezy atop his legs.

Their shoes scuff ever so faintly at the dirt. Gritty sounds that sound loud in the sprawling quiet around them. The tiny crunch and echo right on top of them.

They pass into the woods on the other side, cross the tree line and step into the shady undergrowth, and Wishnowsky feels better after that. Gut unclenching to let him breathe freely again, the air somehow sweet passing over his lips.

Relief floods into him. That lighter-than-air feeling only swelling. It feels for all the world like he's hovering up the slope toward the cabin. A mote of light floating, floating.

He mops at his brow again. Sleeve swiping the forehead this time.

He knows it's still a long hike to the cabin from here — a couple of miles or so, most of it just about straight uphill — but they should have a good lead on the Butcher by now. If he'd gone for the Jeep, he'd be miles off in the opposite direction.

They walk in silence for some time. Wishnowsky can see that dirt track just beyond the edge of the thicket, the light of the open once more shining bright just beyond the tree line.

They duck and weave through thicker growth here. Turn

sideways to squeeze between saplings and brambles. Wishnowsky gets out in front again, helping to bend branches out of the way for the lumberjack and the girl.

"Dang. You know what this reminds me of?" Haywood says, keeping his voice very low.

Wishnowsky squats to walk under a bough, waits for Haywood to go on, to answer his own rhetorical question by telling them what this reminds him of.

But he doesn't.

No further words come.

He never finishes his thought.

Instead there's just the faintest thump and whoosh. A sound like a plucked string somewhere in the distance.

Wishnowsky turns. Gapes.

The crossbow bolt blooms from Haywood's left eye all at once.

Just there.

A blunt shaft protruding from his face. Green fletching jutting from the end of the bolt like feathers. The aluminum nock glittering in the light trickling through the trees.

The lumberjack's lips twitch a couple times, like the rest of that sentence is still trying to get out by way of instinct.

And then he topples forward. A floppy thing. Arms and legs already limp.

He collapses into a clump of ferns. Totally motionless.

CHAPTER 62

Darger walked down the dirt road. Moved away from the cabin in a brisk march. Her gut told her the Butcher would gravitate toward the building, figuring that once he'd flushed them out of the brush like rabbits, they would scurry for shelter.

Such is the nature of prey, and no one would know that better than a predator.

The treads of her boots ground at the sand. Made powdery noises that were stark against the hush of the woods. Sharp and grainy.

Her head snapped around. Looked for any sign of movement. Any sign of anything.

The woods held still like an animal playing dead. Remained impenetrable to her eyes. Shadowy. Unknowable.

She found her gait slowing involuntarily. That prospect of being out here alone looming large once again. God, what if she didn't find any of the others? Would she end up out here all night by herself?

She swallowed. The juicy sound loud and sort of pathetic in her ears.

She made a fist with her free hand. Clenched the gun tighter with the other.

Fresh fear welled in her now. Vulnerability. The sound of her footsteps suddenly seeming to expose her position, the open air around her offering no cover, laying her bare.

She obeyed the whims of the instinct, even if her rational mind didn't believe that the Butcher was close. She veered off the road and ducked into the woods again. Parting the foliage with her hands and stepping through like it was a curtain.

The shade under the trees enveloped her. Veiled her once more in gauzy half-light.

She'd tromped just a few paces under the canopy when she heard the splintery explosion of a stick cracking.

Close.

She got low. Shrouded up to her shoulders in shrubbery.

She adjusted her fingers on the Glock. Palm greasy. Slithering against the grip.

And she waited. Listened to the forest breathing. The gentle moan and grumble of bending branches in the wind.

Instinct told her to run. To flee. Her limbs twitched with it, ached with it.

But the stillness told her to wait. To be more patient now than ever. And she listened to the calm voice inside instead of the fear.

When it felt right, she moved toward the sound. Staying low and quiet. Eyes scanning everything.

Shallow breaths. Soundless in her mouth, in her throat.

Creeping.

Every rustle of the leaves sounded huge now. Each gust of wind plumping fresh goosebumps on her skin.

She kept moving. Squat walking through floppy leaves. Slow.

A faint whimpering sound caught her ear. High-pitched and muffled.

She froze.

Waited.

Motion blurred just a few feet before her. Something low to the ground darting between two trees.

She swung the gun that way. Let her finger slide off of the trigger guard and squeeze. Wrist flexing. Hand clenching.

Then she jerked her hand. Stopped herself just in time. Tipped the muzzle of the gun toward the ground.

One of the little girls — Sadie — stepped out into the open.

CHAPTER 63

Chief Rhodes sprints through the forest. Blind panic pushing her forward into the branches. Prickly pine needles brushing at her cheeks, at her shoulders. Tendrils and vines rapping at every inch of her.

She follows the back of the person in front of her. Lets the dark cardigan there blaze a trail, slender shoulders knifing through all the plant life, finding gaps, running to daylight.

Rhodes gives chase without thought. Pumps her arms. Pistons her legs.

Only panic pulses in her brain. The animal instinct to flee, to run, to get away. Nothing more.

Then she blinks. Her scattered mind realizing all at once that it's Shepard's wife, Marilyn, cutting through the forest before her.

Not Darger.

Not Haywood.

Not even Wishnowsky.

She's following an old woman whom she just met.

Rotating her head around now, she sees none of the others. Just the still of the woods, shades of brown and green, the world choked with trees and brush in all directions.

Christ. At least she's not alone.

They weave through pines. Leap over the small logs crisscrossing the landscape. Sticking to a single file.

They keep up on the ridge. Avoiding gravity's pull, which Rhodes can feel just to her left, trying to tug her down the hill, slide her to where the grade sharply gives way. It'd be so much easier to sprint down the slope, let herself get swept up in the momentum.

And then what?

Run for the cabin?

Some instinct forbids it out of hand. Doesn't like the prospect of going back, cowering, hiding. To pretend as though the wooden structure might keep them safe.

Eventually, he would go for the cabin. Only a matter of time.

For the first time, that surging tide of panic pulls back a touch. Allows Rhodes to consider more than the notion of escaping, fleeing blindly into the woods.

It occurs to her, at last, to wonder where they are going.

She cuts around a fallen fir and gropes after their destination. Finds darkness in her mind where that information could or should be, like a missing chunk in the middle of a jigsaw puzzle that leaves the image indecipherable.

Where the hell are we going?

She immediately rephrases the question to herself, tightens the focus of the query.

Where would Marilyn go?

Her mind tumbles what little she knows of the woman. Replays snippets of the scene around the campfire. A montage of images, sounds, smells.

Shepard's smiling face. Ice blue eyes inlaid like jewels within the sunbaked skin of his face.

Marilyn's angular visage likewise smiling at his side. Something refined about the woman's long, bony face. Kind eyes. Burning bright with intelligence. Sensitive and aware.

The smell of smoke comes next. The clean wood smoke of a proper campfire.

Then the cast iron pan with eggs congealing inside. Clear goo going opaque before her eyes.

The blistery feel of the heat radiating outward from the glowing coals. Hot on her cheeks. Slowly seeping into the fabric of her clothes.

The little girls talking about pancakes and Pop-Tarts. Vacillating between disappointment and excitement so rapidly the way kids do.

They were going to hike out of there, she remembers. Just about to take off. Breaking down the tent. Rolling up sleeping bags. Packing things up.

And then it hits her.

The Jeep.

Marilyn is running for the Jeep.

Her mind stirs over these new pieces. Snaps them together little by little. Lets them build up into something bigger.

A vehicle. A way out.

We're not just running away. We're getting away.

The fresh hope flushes heat into her face. Makes her pick her feet up higher. Push off from the soft mulch underfoot harder.

Marilyn presses through one more barrier — a cluster of sumac trees — and then she spills into the open, into the light.

Rhodes races. Shoves through the stick-like trunks of the small trees. Steps into the clearing.

The dirt lot cuts a small brown patch out of the forest, and another logging road runs off it in a coiling strand like a muddy river.

The Jeep is there. Parked at an angle. Bright yellow enamel with a black hardtop roof, matte against the glossy paint.

Rhodes half expects to see the vehicle in the same shape as the Bronco. Tires slashes. Hood ajar. But it looks fine.

Oh thank God.

They dart toward the vehicle. Boots squelching across the

lot. The rain has turned it into a miniature swamp. Rhodes feels her right foot sink up to the ankle but barely notices.

Marilyn jumps into the driver's seat, Rhodes into the passenger side. The older woman pulls a set of keys from her pocket and fumbles with them for a moment, trying to find the right one.

She inserts the key. Hand shaking. Fires up the engine.

Rhodes could almost weep at that sound. The sound of salvation.

Marilyn puts the Jeep in gear. They lurch forward a few yards and then stop.

Rhodes doesn't understand what's happening until she hears the thrum of the Jeep's engine grow louder, higher in pitch.

She glances at the side mirror and sees mud spitting out from the rear tire.

Marilyn switches to reverse. Guns it again. The Jeep moves a few inches backward. Halts again. Brown sludge geysering out from the front wheels now.

Marilyn puts in it drive and cranks the wheel. Desperate now. But Rhodes already knows it's no use.

They're stuck.

CHAPTER 64

The Butcher strides up on the dead body. Feels that tingle along his scalp of the adrenaline peaking.

The hillbilly-lookin' corpse lies in the weeds. Most of him covered over in fern fronds.

He edges right up on it. Gives it a little kick in the shoulder.

No response.

Of course.

He eyes the woods around him one last time. But the others cleared out right away. Ran for it.

It's all quiet now.

He puts the toe of his boot under the stiff's shoulder. Rolls it over onto its back.

The body flops into its new position in an uneven lope. Going up slow and coming down fast. Something limp in the motion. Dead weight.

His eyes crawl over the fallen thing. Focus on the shaft protruding from the orb of the eye socket.

He sucks his teeth.

Ho-lee shit.

Look at the way the goddamn bolt comes straight out of his eye. It's a thing of beauty.

Some dizziness of freedom assails him as he gazes upon the corpse. A floating kind of euphoria in his head and hands. Bliss.

He adjusts his grip on the crossbow, turns it sideways so it's parallel to his body. Then he squats to get a closer look.

The tip of the bolt runs about four inches deep into the

dude's head. Juts out in a stiff, uncompromising way. Not like some Hollywood special effect. This is real life. Gruesome and incredible. An unforgettable image.

Crazy.

He shakes his head and just stares at the sight. Eyes tracing that point of threshold where the wood enters the skin.

He looks down at the crossbow in his fingers and shakes his head again.

The rifle strapped over his shoulder is a tool — a neat piece of equipment that does its job well. Useful. Efficient.

But the crossbow?

It's something else altogether.

What it does is art. To him, it is art. Striking and strange. Primal. More than just a tool doing a job. Using it is an act of expression.

Inflicting.

Projecting.

He leans forward then. Reaches out a hand in slow motion like the body might lurch up like a largemouth bass and bite him.

He fingers the place where the bolt enters the eye socket. Prods along the soft edges.

Then he grips the shaft just beyond the fletching. Yanks on it. Hears just the slightest sucking sound from inside the skull.

Could use the bolt if he can get it back.

But the son of a bitch is stuck in there pretty good. Probably ain't coming out.

Part of him knows this. Knew all along that the bolt wouldn't budge. With animals you're better off pushing the bolt through.

Can't exactly push the thing through the back of his skull, though, can I?

So what am I doing?
Do I just want to play with it?
Marvel at my handiwork?
Get up close and personal?
Lay my hands on it?

He tries one more time. Jostles the arrow back and forth like it might rip loose.

And his hand slips. The force whips him straight back.

He overcorrects. Tries to get his balance back. Tips forward. Almost lands facedown right on top of the dead body.

But at the last second, he reaches out to catch himself. Flattens his palm against the corpse's wound. Feels it squish beneath his hand. Lukewarm and juicy.

Then he recoils. Shuffles back. Holds up a hand that looks like it's been dipped in ketchup.

Dude.

Gross.

He feels his top lip pucker. Teeth exposed.

Christ. Who knows where this dirtbag has been?

Then he chuckles to himself. Finds his own response absurd.

He's cut up bodies. Skewered them on spikes. Toted the wounded bits all around these woods to feed the bears.

And now he's grossed out by a little blood on the heel of his hand?

But he wears gloves when he works, doesn't he? Mostly keeps the wetworks off his skin.

And this one here? A dirtbag, like he said. One of those scummy timber workers. Drinking and whoring in all his free time. Probably has any number of sexually transmitted diseases, some of that nasty shit wriggling in that red slop on his hand even now.

He stands. Holds the soiled hand out in front of himself as he tromps back into the woods. Watches a red rivulet weep down over his wrist.

He can wash up in the stream.

CHAPTER 65

Wishnowsky bolts into the woods. Mind on fire. So full of fear he can't really think straight.

He bobs and weaves through the forest thoughtlessly. Gets white-hot flashes of that image in his head — Haywood with the crossbow bolt jutting out of his face, lips twitching, before finally bellyflopping into the scrub.

Gore.

Death.

He knows the moment will loop in his head for the rest of his life, however much longer that might be.

Something crunches behind him.

He whirls around. Just about throws the little snub-nosed gun as he flings it up in front of himself.

A light shape darts there. Small.

It's the girl. Kira.

The white noise in his head had stripped her from his mind. Reduced all of reality to a panicked throb in his skull.

But she's there. Right behind him. Keeping up.

It's ludicrous in a way. Snaps him back to himself some.

And part of him wants to giggle. To cackle. To gibber like a chimp flinging poo at the glass walls at the zoo.

Jesus.

Maybe I was wrong about her.

He keeps an eye on her as he hustles on. Observes her skills out here. Impressed despite his earlier misgivings.

He's faster than her. He's pretty sure of that.

But she's slippery. Nimble. Quick to sidle through tight

299

passages in the foliage. Agile around all the turns and switchbacks.

Light on her feet. Loping like a gazelle.

He's clumsy by comparison. An oaf fumbling through the narrow places. Losing his footing. Getting whipped in the face by all types of forestry.

What he accomplishes with brute force, blunt will, she does with care and skill. Craft. Grace.

Yeah. I was wrong.

And selfish.

Jesus. Shit.

Poor kid.

I have to make sure she gets out of this OK.

He runs for the daylight. The gaps between the trees.

He doesn't know, anymore, if they should try for the cabin. It feels like a target.

He pictures those familiar walls closing around him. A wooden shell surrounding both of them.

That tempting shelter. Somewhere off behind them.

But no. No.

He imagines himself and the girl there, barricading the place, this tiny gun the only means of protecting them. The image brings him no comfort.

Just run for as long as you can. Stay one step ahead. Live in the now.

The rest will happen later, can be worried about later, for better or worse.

The gravity of this idea weighs on him. Heavy on his shoulders, in his gut.

Whatever happens from here on — to me and to the girl — I have to live with it. I have to find a way to deal with it.

Our fates are bound now. Intertwined in a way that can

never be undone.

If I survive, today will be with me until the end.

They sprint another few hundred yards into the indecipherable woods. Trees and scrub blur past. Still endless. Still meaningless.

The fatigue catches up with him all at once. Clogs his throat and lungs with what feels like coarse grit sandpaper.

He lets his run slow. Kind of falling forward in a stagger until he finally stops.

Then he leans over. Hands on his knees. Sucking wind into a burning chest. Face all flushed and clammy with sweat.

He closes his eyes. Forces deep inhales.

It feels like his breath can't catch up. Lungs all wet and heavy. Aching inside.

Runnels of sweat drain down from his brow and drizzle off the tip of his nose. The salt of it there at the corners of his mouth.

He squats down fully. Lets the foliage swallow him up.

Tries to find faith that his breathing will slow in time, that this pain in his throat and heat in his face will recede. Some panicked whisper inside telling him that it won't.

He closes his eyes again. Clears his head.

And his breathing does even out a little. Steadying.

Four more big breaths.

Then he opens his eyes. Starts to look around. To listen.

He turns around and around. Lets his gaze flicker over the woods.

Nothing looks familiar.

Just miles and miles and miles of the same landscape repeated.

He sees the killer in every dark shape. Tree stumps. Deadfall. It all looks like the shape of a man for a second and then morphs into some bit of foliage.

He looks at the girl. Feels his gut weigh down with leaden responsibility. How is he supposed to take care of a kid? He can barely take care of himself out here. And if he ends up having a seizure…

His lips tremble. He almost wants to cry. Wants to scream. Wants to lie down in the ferns, crawl into the shadows and wait for death.

They're lost. He knows that now.

Maybe he could get them back to the cabin. Back to the road. Given enough time.

But it's just as likely that he couldn't.

Shit.

All I can do is try.

Try to do right.

It's all any of us can do in this life, in this world.

He stands. Stretches.

And he starts forward. Walking now instead of running, though he wants to keep a brisk pace.

He tries to think. To strategize.

Rain is coming. Soon. And darkness will fall soon after.

Where can we go?

The land slopes down underfoot, and he looks off to the horizon. Sees the mountains jutting up toward those dark clouds in the distance.

And he thinks he has an idea. Something worth trying. Something even he could find his way to, no matter what.

He feels something prodding at his hand. Looks down to see Kira lace her fingers into his.

They walk on holding hands.

CHAPTER 66

The police convoy scuttled up the first incline, one car after another bobbing up and over the dip in the dirt track, then disappearing behind the hill. A single-file line of cars, SUVs, and trucks, almost all emblazoned with the logos of various law enforcement factions.

Agent Loshak watched the crawling procession from the backseat of Whipple's Expedition. A full load of occupants alongside him, all waiting for their turn to mount the rise and shoot down the other side. It almost felt like waiting as the chain clicked up the first hill of a roller coaster, Loshak thought. That slow, peaceful build somehow more suspenseful than almost anything he could remember. Strangely unnerving.

He slurped at a coffee gone lukewarm. It tasted like shit, but the caffeine would still work, and he needed something to fight back the drowsy spell the pills had given him. Purely a physical thing, he thought. His eyelids had gone a little heavy, though his mind was still sharp.

The Expedition crested the hill. Seemed to slide in the mud a bit as it coasted down the slope on the other side.

The logging road wove a circuitous path through the hills. For now they rode along a ridge, a steep drop off to their right showing them a vast expanse of treetops, neatly tufted things from this angle that reminded Loshak of heads of broccoli.

They speared into the guts of the forest. Making better time, so far, than anyone had thought. It appeared that this section of road had held up to the first wave of the storm.

As soon as Loshak committed this observation internally,

the convoy came to an abrupt stop. Brake lights flared all the way down the line, that red glow clicking on one by one from one end of the snake to the other.

"Well… shit," Whipple said from behind the wheel. He muttered something into the radio. Seemed to be conversing, though Loshak couldn't make out what was being said from his spot way in the back.

After a bit of back and forth on the CB, Whipple turned to face those riding in back.

"Sounds like we've hit our first problem area, I guess you could call it."

Loshak couldn't help but picture love handles highlighted in graphic red on some ab-blasting infomercial. *Problem areas.*

"They think they've got it handled, though. Guess we'll see here in a minute."

Loshak watched out the window. Toward the front of the line some officers bustled out of their vehicles. Pulled long boards out of the back of a truck there.

They toted the planks up to a muddy gash in the road and laid them down. Loshak could only actually make out part of the activity farther up the road, but it was enough to suss out what they were doing.

One of the men stood and waved the cavalcade forward.

The first set of brake lights gave out, the red glow shearing off all at once. The truck crept forward. Slowly. Carefully.

It seemed to work.

The rest of the line got moving again. Inched forward little by little.

When the Expedition made its way to the point of the *problem area*, Loshak watched intently as the vehicle lined itself up with the boards set out in the mud. The ride felt different for the next thirty or forty feet. Tires gliding over flat wood that squelched in the gooey roadway.

Then they moved back onto the dirt track and kept moving. All the short-term excitement used up just like that.

Huh. Not so bad.

Loshak leaned back in his seat. Tipped his head back and dumped the rest of the tepid coffee down his gullet.

CHAPTER 67

Shepard hides in a bush. Squatted down in the innards of the thing. Leaves flapping in his face. A few sticks jabbing into his belly, clawing at his clothes.

But the old man doesn't move. Doesn't breathe.

He watches the Butcher stalk past. The big murderer surprisingly light on his feet. Nearly soundless as he glides through the brush.

The Butcher's chest heaves slightly with each breath. Oversized ribcage expanding, bulging into something of a barrel chest. Then he exhales and his torso thins back to something V-shaped and lithe.

The killer has some bulk to him. Meaty substance. But he remains visibly lean despite that. Every detail tapered and toned. Skin drawn taut over riveted musculature. Face all hard angles.

When his lungs ache beyond what he can tolerate, Shepard dares a breath. In and out through his lips. Quiet.

The Butcher swings his head around. Stares right at the bush where the old man is hunkered.

But he glances away just as quickly. That head swiveling another second before he looks back the way he's going.

He can sense me. But he can't see me.

The killer's broad shoulders turn sideways. Knifing through a cluster of saplings.

He's a soundless thing, like a ship's prow cutting through still water.

A moment later, he passes out of Shepard's view.

Disappears into a gap in some pines. A few shivering branches are the only sign that he was ever there at all.

The old man lets himself breathe freely. Chest shuddering.

He thinks of the girls then and swallows. He hopes Marilyn has taken them straight to the Jeep. Gotten the hell out of here.

It had all happened so fast… some primal panic overtaking all of them. Pushing them apart.

When everyone else ran away, Shepard ran toward the shooter. Every instinct in his body told him it was best to do the unexpected. Go straight at him.

He took a flanking angle, stayed low moving through the brush. Hooking at this motherfucker like a bowling ball barreling at the headpin.

The good news is that he'd tracked him here. Kept eyes on him this whole time. Even watched him fire the crossbow bolt, close enough to hear the soft thunk of the thing, even if he couldn't see what or who he was firing at.

Not until later, anyway.

The bad news is that all he has for a weapon is a survival knife. Not much good against a muscle-bound maniac with a crossbow in his hands and a rifle strapped over his shoulder. But if he knows where the Butcher is, he's safe. Might be able to help keep others safe, too, if he is clever enough.

But the girls…

Nothing he can do about it now. Better to focus on the variables he can control.

He waits several seconds after the killer has disappeared from his vision. Notes how calm his heartbeat is, how normal his breathing is. Good. Needs to keep them that way.

Finally he pulls back from the bush that has concealed him. Shuffles after the killer.

He winds through the pines where the Butcher vanished.

Shrouded in prickly boughs for a second. Comes out the other side. Finds the forest empty.

Where did the son of a bitch go?

He creeps forward. Keeps low.

After another twenty yards, he hears the trickle of the stream. Thinks he knows what's happening.

This might be your chance. Your only chance.

He follows the decline in the grade underfoot. Feels the land tilting to where the stream must lay before he can actually see the water.

A veil of trees slides out of his way as he presses forward.

And he's there. The Butcher is there. Trodding on the muddy banks of the stream. Feet smacking a little against the muck.

He's going to wash off the blood.

Shepard jogs close. Then he gets right down on his belly to conceal himself among the ferns, the foliage thicker near the water.

The old man watches through the gaps in the gently swaying fronds. All those little pinnules flicking in and out of the way like so many green fingers.

The Butcher ducks down into a crouch. Dips his hands into the water.

Shepard leaves his cover. Draws his knife. And creeps closer.

CHAPTER 68

Kira squeezes Wish's hand tighter. Feels the warmth of his fingers against hers.

His name is something different than that. Something longer. But he said she could call him Wish instead, and so she does.

They've been walking for so long now. It's hard to imagine these woods could ever end.

But then she thinks about the ocean at the island's edge, how eventually the trees cut off and the water stretches out to the horizon, reaches all the way out to lap up on beaches in China or Russia or Mongolia or something. Maybe all of them, in a way.

Wish lets her hand go, ducks under a gnarly birch branch, and Kira follows his lead. Feels leaves tousle her hair.

She picks herself back up on the other side. And look what's beyond the tree limb.

More woods.

Her hand feels empty and cold now. She finds his fingers again and clenches them.

Better. But not that much.

She wants to go home, but she knows she can't.

They walk on for what feels like forever. Endless plants clutching at their ankles.

After so much quiet, Kira hears the soft babble of a stream in the distance. A flowing sound that seems to change subtly with every second, never quite the same.

Wish stops dead next to her. Stands bolt upright for a split second.

Then he ducks down. Glasses sliding down toward the tip of his nose as he jerks himself lower. Lips pulled down in a grimace that exposes mostly his bottom teeth.

She squats next to him. Then follows his gaze. Sees the dark man at the stream.

The Butcher. That's what Wish called him.

The big angular body leans over the top of the creek. And he swishes his hands around in the water. Holds the fingers up and examines them.

Then he cups water and dumps it over his wrists. One and then the other. Slowly washing away blood that creeps halfway up his forearms.

Little musical sounds accompany every slosh and trickle of the water. Tinkling like wet wind chimes.

The man's hand goes cold in Kira's. Somehow she knows this is how frightened he is, palms and fingers going icy due to fear.

Wish shuffles back. Staying low. Yanks her along with him. Jostles her shoulder around in its socket.

Then he's lifting her. Clutching her to his chest and carrying her a ways. Setting her down just next to a thick oak tree.

He looks at her for a second. Licks his lips. Eyes scanning back and forth over her face. Like he's trying to measure her in some way.

He leans forward then. Whispers in her ear.

"You have to listen and do exactly what I say." He takes a breath. Licks his lips again. "You're going to climb that tree. Climb at least fifteen feet up. Hug yourself against the trunk and don't make a sound. I'll come back if… when I can."

Panic clenches in her belly. A wild clawing feeling.

He's going to leave me.

But then he's hoisting her up. Hands under her arms. Pushing her up over his head.

She folds her waist over a thick branch. Bark rough against her belly.

She wobbles. Balances. Gets a grip. Moves into a seated position.

She looks down at him. Wants to ask why.

But his eyes look big. Scared. He mouths, "Climb."

And so she does.

Puts one hand above the other. Grips branches. Pushes off with her feet. Zooms up the tree with relative ease.

He's ditching me.

Abandoning me.

Probably thinks I'll slow him down. Get us both killed.

And the water fills her eyes. Throat goes tight. Choking back the tears. Not letting them out. Never letting them spill.

She won't. No matter what.

Still, snot weeps down from her nostrils. She smears it away and keeps climbing.

Once she's a good twenty feet up, she hugs the trunk. Looks down just in time to watch Wish run off.

She feels empty, like letting a balloon go. Watching it float away, soar up until it's just a tiny red dot in the sky.

At first, Wish stays quiet. Doing a kind of funny jog. Making very little sound.

She sees him take off his jacket and hang it up in the branches way off to her left.

Then he darts out of view at last, and her stomach sinks further. She feels her bottom lip trembling, and she bites it. Won't let herself cry. Not now. Not ever.

Branches snap and pop and echo everywhere.

Wish. Loud. Crashing through leaves like he's windmilling his arms as he runs.

She realizes he's drawing the bad guy away. Trying to… what?

The dark man stands along the water. Snaps his head around. His eyes go straight to the jacket.

And then he's up. Barreling that way. A grin twitching on his lips.

He, too, disappears into the weeds beyond the jacket. Gone.

And Kira hugs the tree tighter. Closes her eyes.

And waits.

CHAPTER 69

Loshak stood at the edge of another washed-out spot in the road. Gazed into the trough of mud before him that must have once been a passable stretch.

The quagmire stretched a good thirty feet beyond his position. Hardly recognizable that it'd ever been a legit dirt road. Looked more like something scantily clad people should wrestle in.

Some parts looked scooped out, cupped and wet like a giant ice cream dipper had gone to work here. Reminded Loshak of a bunch of open mouths, pointed toward the sky and half full of water.

They were a few miles beyond the first lumber camp. Having found no sign of their people or Bohanon's Bronco there, he and Whipple had parted ways with the search teams at that point and continued up the road as planned. And now they were stopped. Again.

He leaned over and used his cane to poke at the muddy furrow. The tip sunk straight into the mud, as if the stuff were quicksand, and Loshak tipped forward. Wobbled.

At the last second, his cane struck solid ground somewhere beneath the glop, and he caught himself.

Jesus. Do not fall into the death pit.

A series of beeps sounded somewhere behind the agent. Ripped his attention away from the muck.

He turned to see the bulldozer backing off the trailer. Slowly churning its way down the ramp and swiveling once it reached the flat ground.

The people along the mud pit all stepped back, Loshak included. And the big piece of equipment rumbled through the gap where they'd just stood.

The blade lowered itself to the slime and went to work. Plowing forward. The muck swept up into the concave blade, looked like melted chocolate ice cream.

The bulldozer shoved a big sloppy wad of mud up into the edge of the woods. Then it spun and did the same thing back the other way.

The progress was slow and steady. The stench of swamp in the air now that the muck was being flung about.

Still, Loshak found the process fascinating. Like watching some arcane process detailed on the Discovery Channel. A bunch of Marshmallow Peeps pressed out of a machine and shuttled down an assembly line or something. Except dirty and smelly and gross instead of puffy and sugary.

The knee-deep mud was reduced to ankle-deep mud.

The bulldozer kept working. Back and forth and back and forth.

"Looks like they're just about done," Whipple said, slapping Loshak on the shoulder. "We should head back to the Expedition so we're ready to roll."

Loshak nodded, and they tromped back to the vehicle.

A few moments later, the procession was moving again. Loshak stared down at the mud as they traversed the section of road that had only minutes before been more akin to a bog. He found himself clenching his cane as though nervous that it'd get stuck in the muck. He didn't release his grip until they were well past the trouble spot.

They trundled on at what felt like a snail's pace. Around every bend, Loshak prayed they'd catch sight of the Bronco. That he'd see Darger and the rest waving. But there was no sign of them.

Another few miles down the road, along a ridge with a sheer drop on the right side, Whipple brought the Expedition to a screeching halt.

"Oof," he said, staring out through the windshield. "I don't think a bulldozer or some boards are going to cut it this time."

They got out for a closer look.

"Looks like Paul Bunyan came along and took a big ol' bite out of it," Whipple said.

A sedan-sized section of the road was simply gone, washed away into the ravine. What remained of the road was a narrow path just wide enough to walk across but certainly not enough to drive across. And Whipple was right. The concave shape of the void did remind Loshak of a bite taken out of a cookie or a piece of bread.

He gazed beyond the cavity, straining his eyes to see what lay in the road ahead. But it was empty. No Bronco. No Darger.

"I know you really wanted to try to make it up to the second camp, but we have to turn back. Don't see as we have much of a choice."

Loshak massaged his forehead, nodding.

"It's fine. We'll just launch the missing persons search from the lower camp, like we talked about. It might take a little longer, but we'll find them."

He took one last look at the road before turning back to the Expedition.

"One way or another, we'll find them."

CHAPTER 70

Shepard glides forward. Ducks low so that the ferns brush at his arms, at his chest.

His feet flex. Walking heel to toe. Every step careful. Placed among the plants with precision, with skill. Slow-motion progress.

And the Butcher's broad back is just there along the stream still. Maybe twenty feet before him. Maybe less.

Drifting closer. Closer.

His forearm ripples. Fist gritting around the hilt of the knife.

This is it.

Right here and right now.

He needs only to drag this sliver of metal over the Butcher's throat. One clean stroke of his blade to slit the soft flesh there. Make a cleft that cannot be repaired.

And the killer's life will come spilling out all at once. Gouts of thick red gushing into his fingers. Drizzling into the stream.

It's here. Right here. Ready to happen now.

Shepard can feel it. The energy of it tingling in his hand, in his arm. The knife an electric thing ready to jump, to go ripping.

He stalks on. Maybe ten feet between them now.

The stream babbles louder here just near the banks. Covers any little sounds he might be making.

He splays his arm out to his side. Ready to launch himself. Draw the blade over that thick neck wide open before him.

Something crashes in the forest ahead.

Shepard freezes.

Sticks explode somewhere across the stream. A flurry of loud cracks echoing over the land. Violent against the stark quiet that has hung over these woods for so long.

The Butcher's spine stiffens. Lifts him up taller.

And Shepard flops to his belly again as soon as the killer moves. Involuntary. Instinct triggering some reflex.

Facedown. Submerged in fronds. Partially tucked behind a log.

He holds his breath. Ribcage stiff against the soft earth here near the water.

The Butcher takes off. Bolts into the woods.

What the fuck?

CHAPTER 71

The Butcher bounds across the creek. Hurdles the waterway and plants his foot in the muddy bank on the opposite side. Boot sucking as he pries it free.

He scurries up the sloped land there. Feet skidding in the muck. Eyes locked on that pop of color in the distance. Hurtling himself through the foliage toward it.

The forest knits itself tighter around him. Clogs the way with a twining green mess. Makes it harder to see.

But he parts the layers. Races forward. Levers his way through the congestion.

And the way ahead comes clear at last.

His eyes go wide when he sees it better. That smile playing at his lips dies all at once.

It's just a coat. Empty fabric. Draped over a pine bough. Flapping gently like a flag.

Shit.

He doesn't slow. Presses onward. Adjusts his trajectory on the fly. Wheeling off to the left to give chase to whoever is crashing through the brush.

He builds speed. The crossbow pumping along with his arm, hovering there before him, a coiled black thing like a snake about to strike.

The crashing sounds grow louder. Closer.

The beat of footsteps crushing at the forest floor. The pop of broken twigs as someone runs through them.

And his eyes scan everything. Flitting everywhere. Looking for movement or color or both.

One part of his mind stays wary. Tries to sense if this could be a trap of some kind.

But he doubts it very much. Doesn't feel right. Not based on what he's seen from them so far.

The ranger and the lumberjack are dead. That leaves two lady cops, an elderly couple, a fifty-something man with doughy dad energy, and two little girls.

All of them scared shitless. Untrained. Soft.

Running for their lives.

Fish in a barrel, more or less.

There's no way any of them have the balls to come at him. Not now, anyway. They might find courage later, but he still has the edge for the moment. Shock and awe.

Better to press that advantage, then. Run straight at them and leap right for the goddamn jugular.

Attack.

Attack.

Attack.

No mercy. Not a chance.

Fortune favors the aggressor.

He steps through a curtain of pine boughs. Pushes into the deeper shade. Eyes taking a second to adjust to the fresh darkness.

And there he is.

A portly man weaves through trees in the distance. Chest heaving. Stumpy legs churning.

Ah, yes. The fleshy one. Panicking. Making all kinds of noise. Hilarious.

CHAPTER 72

Heavy footsteps trail Wishnowsky into the thicket. Boots stomping, trampling, encroaching.

This is it.

He whirls. Lifts the little snub-nosed gun. Points it into the woods. Muzzle poking toward the gap in the pines where the Butcher will soon appear.

Or so he hopes.

He exhales. Ruddy cheeks quivering as he lets the air go. Something scraping in his throat. A sound like a cat coughing up a hairball.

Jesus.

Oh, Jesus.

This is it.

The gun trembles at the end of his outstretched arm. The silvery nickel plating of the weapon gleaming in a shaft of light filtering through the canopy above.

Electricity prickles over his scalp. Tiny pinpricks tingling over the backs of his arms and legs.

This is the feeling he gets before a seizure sometimes.

He forces himself to ignore the tingling sensation in his limbs. Refocuses his attention on his surroundings.

His eyes try to drill through the foliage. Crawling over the branches. Licking along the edges of the shadows.

Nothing.

He backpedals a couple of paces. Head swiveling atop his neck. Cranking hard to the left and then the right.

What if he flanks me?

Circles around behind me?

His shoulders hunch up toward his neck. An involuntary gesture. Someone pulling the puppet strings taut. Tightening the muscles in his back.

No. No.

Stick with the plan.

He'll come the way I thought he would. Run right through that gap in the pines.

And I'll blast him.

Chilly air swirls around his sweaty figure. Plasters his shirt to his back. Glues a strand of hair to his forehead.

He realizes that he feels naked without his coat. Exposed. Not so much a missing armor feeling as a lack of his security blanket. Pathetic as the notion seems just now.

And still the gun jitters like a moth. A hovering thing in front of him.

He gapes into the woods. Breath wheezing in and out. Pulse battering his neck.

Something stirs the boughs before him at long last. Needles convulsing. Then the branches themselves wagging, arcs growing bigger and bigger as the footsteps punch closer.

Wishnowsky's throat scrapes again. Clamps shut this time like a fleshy valve at the back of his mouth.

He straightens his arm, which somehow makes the tremor worse. Feels the strength in his wrist. Feels his hand flex.

The Butcher bursts through the greenery. Broad shoulders wedged just a second between the pine boughs, and then the trees seem to eject him and thrust him forward into the open.

Wishnowsky squeezes the trigger.

The gun jerks in his hand. Pops and barks. Snorts a little flicker of flame.

He steadies his arm. Squeezes it again. Feels the power

pulse through the weapon. Thrashing in his hand.

The figure doesn't slow. Plows right at Wishnowsky. Even the crack of gunfire doesn't seem to faze him.

Jesus.

Wishnowsky backpedals another couple of paces.

Aims.

Squeezes again.

The gun leaps. Still clutched in his fingers. Lifts his arm like it's shaking his hand.

The Butcher chews up the ground between them. Thundering ahead with his head down. He lifts the crossbow before him.

Wishnowsky lines the weapon up with center mass the best he can. Fires his fourth round. Two to go.

Another step back.

Another step back.

The Butcher's hands caress the crossbow. He lines up his shot.

The weeds grip Wishnowsky's ankle. Coil around and tug.

He almost squeezes the trigger. Stops himself to save the round.

Falling.

He hears the crossbow *shunk* as it's fired.

Hears the whoosh of the bolt going right over his head.

He crashes down on his ass. Flops onto his back. Squirming. A box turtle stuck upside down.

He gets the gun up again.

And then the killer is on him. Weight crashing onto his thorax. Flattening him to the dirt. Pinning him down.

He squeezes the trigger.

But the killer shoves Wishnowsky's arm up just as he shoots. The shot goes high. Flits off into the trees.

One bullet left.

And then hard fingers are scrabbling at his. Impossible strength overtaking his hand. Pointing the gun off into the brush.

They struggle for the weapon. The killer rakes it loose and then Wishnowsky's flailing hand slaps the weapon, volleyball spikes it down to the ground.

It skitters somewhere off to their left. Glitters in the light for just a second. Disappears into the weeds.

It's gone.

The gun is gone.

Wishnowsky blinks. Stares into the spot where the brush swallowed the weapon. Out of sight. Out of reach.

He knows now that he's dead.

His eyes stream over the Butcher's torso. No blood. No wound. Unmarked.

He missed. Five times he missed.

And then the killer has a crossbow bolt in his fist. Lifts it over his head and brings it ripping down.

Jams it straight into Wishnowsky's throat. Punches it through the skin.

Cold metal spears his neck. He chokes. Gags. Feels the shaft twist against the soft flesh as it's pulled out.

The blood is hot on his skin. Searing.

The Butcher stabs again and again.

A thrashing ball of muscle atop him. Plunging a cylinder of wood into his throat.

Something wild in the violence. Something out of control.

Ripping.

Piercing.

Mad with it.

Wishnowsky brings a hand up under the Butcher's chin.

Palm cupping the angular bone. Fingers curling up onto the stubble.

He tries to push the face away. Lifts his head and shoulders in the effort. Arches the back of his attacker. Slows the wild jabbing at his throat.

But it's too late. He knows it's too late.

And then cold creeps over all of him at once. An icy touch sweeping over his skin, coiling outward from that ragged hole in his neck, spreading like frosting over a cake.

And the dark comes closer. Gets bigger. Opens its arms to take him away from here.

Wishnowsky blinks again. Eyelids fluttering.

The woods become a green and brown smear around him. Blurry.

He lets his head flop back to the dirt. Neck limp. Face going slack like the rest of him.

And he looks out at nothing. Eyes pointed at the canopy above but not really seeing it.

Blood gushes from his neck. Spiraling out of the gaping hole there like water out of a bathtub faucet. Glugging over his chest in pulses.

His mind blocks the pain, though. Leaves him hollow. Somehow. Someway.

Numbness creeps over him. That icy nothingness taking him under little by little.

Submerging.

Becoming.

Death welling in his physical form. Claiming the cells of his body one by one.

The cold is clean.

The emptiness is tranquil. Serene.

He drifts into it. Flowing back from whence he came.

When Darkness Falls

His eyes swivel one last time. He looks into the light streaming through those branches up above. The glowing bars shining through the shivering lacework of leaves.

And he's not scared anymore.

CHAPTER 73

Loshak sat on a bench in the back of the truck. Another paper cup of coffee had attached itself to his right hand and periodically swooped toward his mouth to dump more caffeine into his maw. They had an urn brewing in the corner of the tactical truck, a big stainless steel thing that reminded Loshak of being at a potluck in the 1980s. Still, the brew tasted cleaner than the muck he'd brought with him from the station.

He took another drink now. Felt the heat zip down along his esophagus.

He sat alone in the truck. Wanting to give his knee a break while everyone else scurried around, getting ready for the search.

The radio babbled and popped at a low volume near the front of the truck. Snatches of talk and static. Not saying much.

The fingers of Loshak's free hand tapped at the rounded top of his cane. Fingertips drumming out a complicated rhythm.

He checked his watch. They should be taking off soon.

Release the hounds.

Loshak had gotten a look at the pack on his way to the truck — a bunch of smiling German shepherds with their tongues lolling out, clearly eager to go bounding into the woods to track their quarry.

This group was part of the fugitive apprehension team. The dogs would be given the scent from a bag of dirty clothes they'd brought from the abandoned house, and with any luck, they'd be able to track Banks down by way of smell.

Shortly after the dogs went out, a swarm of heavily armed

law enforcement would follow. Organized. A grid search. Thrashing through the foliage. Blood up.

A second, smaller group mostly made up of volunteers from the Alaska Search and Rescue Association would focus on the search for Darger and the rest. They'd be armed with bottles of water, first aid kits, and space blankets.

Lastly, there were the cadaver dogs, brought in to hopefully allow them to locate the last of the missing remains.

Yep. It was all about to go down. With any luck, they'd have their people back and the Butcher in cuffs before nightfall.

And Loshak would just sit here all the while. Knee dully throbbing. Thumbs-a-twiddling.

Hurry up and wait. I guess I know that game well enough by now.

He eyed the big buffet urn in the corner. A glowing orange button gleamed like a jewel just above the black nozzle.

At least the coffee is decent.

The back doors of the truck hung open enough that Loshak could see some of the officers outside. He scooted to the edge of the bench to get a better look, knee flaring up for just a second.

The horde of police was geared up as though for battle. Postures upright and stiff. Chests thrust out. Arms splayed.

The helmets and vests added bulk to each and every frame. Assault rifles cupped in their arms before them.

He could see the adrenaline in their eyes somehow. Something fierce there. Pointed. A shine.

A silhouette rushed toward the doors, and Loshak scooted back as though embarrassed to be snooping, though there was no reason to be.

Chief Whipple peeled the doors apart and stuck his head inside. A little smile curling just the corners of his lips, something mischievous in the grin, Loshak thought.

"There you are." The officer jerked a thumb over his shoulder. "I'm thinking about heading back to town. Kinda figure I ain't much use here on the front lines, but... Well, there's a pair of choppers coming in from Ketchikan. If we go now, we can get back in time to catch a ride in the helicopter, help try to spot something from the sky. What do you say?"

Loshak looked down at his cane. Thought about it for all of one-tenth of a second.

Well, well, well... Maybe I can still be useful after all.

He stabbed his cane straight down into the floor and stood. "Hell yeah. Let's go."

CHAPTER 74

Frustration grows. Blooms. A steady heat in the cheeks. A pulse of the muscles in the jaw, squeezing the molars tight.

The Butcher kicks through the brush. Looks for the silvery glint of the gun there.

Nothing.

He can picture the weapon. A snub-nosed pistol. Nickel-plated. Black grip.

He's pretty sure it would only have one round left after what just happened, but… Why leave it to chance, right?

It'd poke a clean hole in someone's guts just the same. Tattered meat. Perforation.

Better to find it. Better to take it.

Especially after how close that was.

The doughy man had laid in wait for him. Taken an open shot. Five open shots, in fact. He'd missed all of them somehow, but he shouldn't have.

Luck.

Stupid bullshit luck.

Fair enough. It happens.

But not to him, not out here. He shouldn't need it. Didn't want it.

Better to earn every inch of this land. Prove his dominance over and over. Reign supreme over the lesser beings.

Luck is for losers. Weaklings.

He breathes. Sucks wind through his nostrils. Feels it inflate his chest. Tries to hold onto the stillness of it.

And he watches the body out of the corner of his eye as he

holds his breath.

Flat on his back. Throat open wide. Blood stain making a bib shape on his chest. Glasses crooked. Legs splayed just a little.

Despite the evidence of violence, there's something peaceful in the man's expression. Features placid like a religious painting.

Then he returns to kicking at the weeds.

It should be there, the gun. Tucked somewhere in the green folds of the undergrowth. Probably buried in the straw-colored blades of grass at the very bottom, the dying stuff shorn low like hair buzzed off by clippers.

But it's not there. Just plants and dirt. Nothing of use.

Anger flares in him. A single flame rising in his head. A tear-drop-shaped thing, spouting like the fire from a lighter cranked all the way up.

Goddamn it.

A stick snaps in the distance, and goosebumps ripple over his skin right away.

He holds still. Listens. Stares hard into empty space. Replays the tiny pop in his memory.

A faint sound but unnatural. He knows the difference. Always knows the difference.

His body knows. All of his follicles flicked on, pricked up, by the unusual noise.

Forget the piece of shit gun.

He runs toward the sound.

CHAPTER 75

Rhodes picks her way through the roughage. Leads Marilyn into the thick of it.

It had taken some talking, but she'd finally convinced the woman that they had to abandon the Jeep. They'd taken turns standing in the muck, pushing the vehicle from the front and the back while the other person gunned it, but the tires had only dug in deeper.

Even after that, Marilyn still wanted to wait at the Jeep, certain that Shepard and the others would come. That perhaps with more muscle power, they could find a way to get the vehicle unstuck.

But as the minutes ticked by, it became clear that no one was coming.

So they trudge toward the road on foot. Or Rhodes thinks they do. Hopes so.

The road will help her reorient herself. Give them the option of faster travel should they want it. They could jog a ways on the open track and duck back under cover when they got tired.

And when — not if — the cavalry comes, we can flag them down.

Rhodes pictures it in a montage. The images vivid in her mind.

The convoy of police vehicles — cruisers and trucks alike — streaming down the track. A single-file line as far as the eye could see, a snake of cars and trucks stretching around a bend in the distance.

And then the two of them stepping through the curtain at the edge of the woods. Striding out into the open. Crunching onto the gravel. Arms flapping over their heads.

One of the vehicles veering to the side of the road. Stopping and picking them up.

Big smiles.

Slaps on the back.

Everyone happy.

All of this over.

A sound interrupts her mind movie. Startles her enough that her shoulders shimmy.

She clasps for her gun. Body trembling like a struck chime.

The sound comes again.

A sob and a gasp.

High-pitched. Breathy.

Rhodes turns. Sees the tears streaking the other woman's face.

Marilyn whimpers again. A choking sound venting from somewhere deep in her throat.

"We have to go back," the old woman says, grabbing the officer's arm. "Have to find them."

Rhodes blinks. Frazzled mind taking a second to catch up.

The girls. Of course.

"They're with Shepard," she hears herself say. "You know they are."

Hopefully they are. Who fucking knows?

Marilyn shakes her head. Eyes wide and wet.

"We have to go look for them."

Rhodes glances back the way they'd come, though she doesn't know why. The woods veil everything.

All the forest details look identical in all directions. Trees. Leaves. Plants. Chewed-up mulch on the ground — some of it bare, some of it covered over with growth.

Still, she thinks about it. Going back. Would that make any sense?

Maybe.

It's going to rain, and it's going to be cold.

We could make for the cabin. Seek shelter there.

But she feels sick when she thinks about it for more than a second. Much prefers the idea of keeping close to the road, waiting for help to come.

If it ever does.

"Let's try to find the road," she says, holding eye contact with Marilyn. "We'll get our bearings, and we can figure out what to do from there."

There. That'll buy me some time, at least.

Marilyn stares at the ground. Wide eyes blinking behind the lenses of her glasses.

A gunshot rings out somewhere in the near distance, and both women jump.

Marilyn grabs at Rhodes again, snatching at both of her arms in a way that reminds Rhodes of a baby monkey clinging to its mother at the zoo.

Another gunshot cracks like a snapped femur.

And then three more.

And suddenly Rhodes is surprised to find herself belly down on the ground, half shrouded in foliage. No memory of diving, though she knows she must have.

Marilyn squats next to her.

"Oh God," the old woman gasps. "Oh my God."

They fall quiet then. Staying low. Listening. Some kind of creeper coats this swath of the ground like green shag carpet, and a bed of wild blackberries clogs up the earth just to their left, prickers crisscrossing in thick tangles.

Rhodes can't hear anything now. Only her pulse pounding in her ears, in the hollow of her skull.

Marilyn adjusts her position. Rocks back off the balls of her feet. Snaps a stick with a descending heel.

The crack rings over the emptiness like another gunshot. Impossibly loud. Percussive. Echoing funny.

They freeze again. Not breathing. Not even daring to look at each other.

Rhodes blinks and listens.

Blinks and listens.

The silence holds at first. Seems like it might vanquish the loud sounds. The shots. The stick. Cover them over like a blanket of dirt.

When Rhodes hears the heavy footfalls coming, she crawls into the berries. Worms forward on her belly into the thickest of the brambles.

And Marilyn follows.

CHAPTER 76

Darger and Sadie kept to the side of the logging track, trudging through the woods with the dirt road just off their left shoulders. The sun poked through wispy spots in the clouds now and again, the light around them swelling and dimming at the whims of the ever-shifting heavens.

Darger didn't know where they were going. Had no destination in mind.

The cabin seemed like too obvious a target. Bohanon's head left in front of the entrance like a warning.

She'd briefly considered the Bronco. Even if it wasn't functional, it would at least provide shelter from the weather, but it'd be little to no help if the Butcher came upon them.

That left Shepard's Jeep, which Darger wasn't confident she could find, if it was even still there. She hoped instead that some of the others had made it to the vehicle and fled.

Still, it seemed important to keep going, keep moving, so she lumbered on. Picked her feet up out of the roughage. Placed them down into the mess of green with diligence, trying to stay quiet.

Part of her mind watched the flitting light where the woods broke up. Tried to see the road there.

Help had to be on the way. By now, the rest of the task force would have figured out their group had never returned. That none of them had made it back to town.

They could be close. Just around the next bend, even.

She stared at the place where the dirt track vanished in the distance, willing a vehicle to appear there. Loshak would be tucked in the backseat, waiting with a hot thermos of coffee and donuts.

Several seconds passed. The road remained empty.

Mixed emotions billowed in Darger's chest. She tried to push the negativity away, to hold onto the hope that it was only a matter of time before someone came for them.

If the roads are even passable at this point.

She looked down at the girl. Saw the peaceful expression on the small face, some kind of sanity present there, reason somehow shining through her innocent features. The child's demeanor calmed Darger some. Snapped her back to herself.

On they walked. Marching through teeming vegetation. Vines as thick as rope carpeted the ground, groping after every ankle they could. The clustered tendrils reminded Darger of a spider plant she'd had in her first apartment. Green hands with so many fingers.

The walk stretched on and on, like the woods themselves. Feet pounding at the plants. Progress a thing only vaguely sensed with the scenery never really changing.

Peeking through the foliage, Darger could see washed-out spots in the dirt road now. Nothing impassible so far, but there were clear wounds where the water had left gashes in the surface and worn away the edges of the track. Miniature Grand Canyons etched into the dirt.

Shifting darkness drew her gaze back to the sky. Roiling gloom.

Dark clouds scudded in from the horizon. Black cotton candy slowly filling the sky. The next wave of the storm closing on them little by little.

Well, that's nice and foreboding.

A distant gunshot shattered the silence. A spiky sound. Metallic and small, at least from this far away.

Darger's legs stopped dead underneath her. Froze her mid-stride.

Sadie hugged around the agent's waist. Bony arms encircling just over the hip bones.

Darger held her breath. Listened.

The birds had all gone quiet, she realized. Disturbed by the violent noise. Hushed by it.

For just a second, she thought she heard a scream. A fleeting thing, more sensed, felt, than truly audible.

Four more shots echoed through the trees. Her mind tuned into the details of it this time.

It wasn't the rifle. She was pretty sure of that. Sounded tinnier. Like a handgun.

Rhodes?

Wishnowsky?

She wondered if Shepard was armed, apart from the *Crocodile Dundee* knife attached to his belt.

Darger looked around. Eyes flicking to the black clouds rolling in, to the sound of gunfire somewhere back the way they'd come.

They needed shelter. From the wet. From the psycho.

But what were their options, really?

She gazed at the mountains in the distance. Trees jutted from much of the rugged land, though some bare rock faces were visible, the stony crags taking over more and more the higher up she looked. A dusting of snow even lined the crevices near the pinnacle of each peak.

Her eyes traced up and down the hills. Then she looked back at the section of woods where the cabin would lay, up a hill back behind them.

She took a deep breath and let it out slowly.

One way or the other.

She made her choice and strode on.

CHAPTER 77

Kira adjusts her arms on the birch trunk. Gritty bark texture pressing into the meat of her biceps. Not rough and pitted like normal bark but coarse in its own way. Grainy.

The gunshots still play in her head. Echoing thunderclaps with metallic clicks at the center of each.

Wish.

She knows, somehow, that he isn't coming back.

That he is dead.

And now she is alone. Stuck up here like the time the neighbor's Great Dane treed Peanut, their cat. Defenseless.

Her eyes creep over the ground below. Take in the details.

Tufts of green sprouting from the carpet of dead leaves.

The stream trickling along for no good reason.

That empty jacket draped over a pine bough. Motionless.

The woods lie vacant now. Hollow and still.

She hugs the tree tighter. Squeezes her eyes closed. Shivers against the living column of wood.

And now she is cold all over, just the way Mr. Wish's hand was cold when she was holding it. Seems like forever ago now.

She holds still. Listens to nothing screaming in all directions.

Tries to stay calm. To keep herself from shuddering.

Something rustles below. Raspy footfalls in the brush.

And she pinches her eyes tighter.

Is he coming back?

She pictures the bad man as she last saw him. Leaning over the babbling stream. Dipping his hands into the wetness.

Flinging cups of water over a bloody wrist.

The footsteps crunch closer. Closer.

Stop just underneath the tree.

And then the quiet comes alive again. A thrashing emptiness. The big nothing sucking, sucking.

The void.

Like a drain at the center of the universe that swallows all of us eventually. Pulls us through the grate and flushes us from this plane of existence into the nowhere.

A voice whispers below.

"Kira."

Her heart beats harder now. A galloping ball of meat in her chest.

She opens her eyes slowly. Blinks a few times. Looks down.

Her grandpa's tan face stares back up at her. Pale blue eyes gleaming within the folds of his eyelids.

The faintest smile curls his lips, but his eyes look grave.

When he speaks again, his whisper lets up some, lets a trace of the real timbre of his voice through.

"Come on down, little lady. We've gotta move."

CHAPTER 78

The helmet on Loshak's head looked like half a candy shell, its surface glassy and black. He already dreaded strapping on the harness-style seatbelt in the chopper. It'd fit funny with the Kevlar vest already bulking up his torso.

He shuffled over the concrete floor. Glanced at his reflection in the chrome trim around one of the hangar doors. Saw the faintly warped version of himself there in the glossy metal, mirrored aviators snugged on the bridge of his nose.

The sunglasses reminded him of Spinks. They'd been together when Loshak bought the shades — had consulted some college kids in an airport shop, rapidly coming to a consensus on the aviators. They made him look like General MacArthur, one of the kids had said. He smiled a little at the memory.

Whipple's voice shook him out of the nostalgia spell. Brought him back to the moment.

"You ready, Agent Loshak?"

Loshak gave a nod and a thumbs up. Felt his jaw flex once. Whipple nodded back.

The chief stepped closer. Fiddled with the vest strapped to Loshak's chest. Then he pounded him on the shoulder.

"Looks good. Sorry about the helmet. New regulation. Funny that we can take civilians up helmet-free, but any law enforcement officer boarding a helicopter in an official capacity has to pop on a hardtop. Them's the rules."

Loshak shrugged.

"I don't mind."

Whipple started for the door and waved an arm over his shoulder.

"Let's roll."

They passed through the hangar door and rushed out onto the tarmac. The sound of the chopper was immediately massive in the air around them as they stepped into the gray daylight.

Loshak kept his head down. Hobbled over the concrete with his cane working, his gait choppy due to his knee. He felt his feet clopping on the cement, though he couldn't hear them against the whir of the rotors.

He let his eyes drift up to the piece of machinery at last. A black thing, something insectile in the way the slender tail boom fit onto the bulkier cabin.

The wind whipped off the blur where the rotors must be. So much air, so much force, slamming straight down into the ground. Its pulse felt in every step Loshak took.

He ducked his head low as he neared the helicopter. Ran for the open cabin door. Vaulted himself up, Whipple grabbing his hand and pulling him inside the chopper.

Then he snugged himself down into his seat and laid his cane across his lap. Took a breath. Started strapping himself in, adjusting the harness to fit over his shoulders.

The chuffing of the propeller vibrated through Loshak's seat. Felt like the machine's rapid heartbeat shuddering through him.

When the last man boarded, the door slammed shut. A series of nods and thumbs-ups was exchanged between the pilot and the others on board.

The helicopter lurched up from the ground and rushed for the forest.

CHAPTER 79

Rhodes crawls deeper into the brambles. Feels thorns spearing her skin. Little spikes hooking and tearing. Reaching right through her shirt to scratch up the smooth sheet of flesh coating her back.

She wriggles. Belly hugging the ground. Knees and hands clawing at the soil. Torso squirming gently back and forth. Trying her best to stay quiet.

She can hear Marilyn behind her doing the same. Body scuffing over the dirt. Plants clinging and shaking. Breath sharp coming out of the old woman's mouth. Hissing with the pain.

The smell of the dirt swells as she crawls. Pungent. Earthy. Wet soil and green plants. Reminds her of pushing a cart through the garden department at Home Depot, all those white plastic bags of potting soil bulging at the seams.

When Rhodes has writhed to what she gauges to be about the center of the brier patch, she holds still. Breathes.

The air feels thicker under that crisscrossing carpet of green. Heavier and damp against her cheeks. Cool.

She turns her head. Peers through the gaps between the leaves and stalks and shoots. The little wedges of light flit along with the breeze. Open and close like so many chawing mouths.

She can't see much. A sliver of the sky. Scraps of the plants beyond the berries. None of the openings will hold still long enough for her to make sense of the objects beyond the berry patch.

She listens to those pounding feet nearby. Somewhat muffled by the foliage now. Dulled. They might be getting closer, but she's not certain. Hard to judge from this spot facedown under the thick bed of brambles.

Is it him?

It must be.

The others would be quiet. Hiding. Afraid. Like her.

He runs with abandon. Like he owns these woods.

Maybe he does.

The steps come clearer. Definitely getting closer now. Darting right for them.

He slows down as he gets nearby. Footfalls crunching differently. Stepping with some care now.

Like he senses us.

Rhodes holds her breath. Tries to stare out through the tiny gaps in the plants above again. That crisscrossing meshwork of plant and leaf, dappled with spots of light and patches of shadow.

The footsteps stop. The thump and crunch cutting out just shy of the blackberries, or so it seems.

Rhodes tenses. The hair pricks up on the nape of her neck.

She can feel her body wanting to shudder. An electric prickle spreading over all of her.

She shoves the feeling down. Squelches it with a flash of white-hot anger.

Feels droplets of sweat plumping on her top lip.

The briers shift, and she can see something out there.

Something dark and thick. Hovering right on top of them.

Shadowy. Colorless and indistinct.

Probably a tree trunk, but she's not certain.

She dares to move her hand down to her side. Lets it drift to her hip. Draws her weapon.

Part of her dreams that he will come into view. That she will be able to shoot him somehow, aiming through this mess of plants in her face. Which seems impossible. A magic bullet.

Marilyn gasps somewhere behind her. Starts thrashing against the brambles.

Would she have seen him?

Rhodes doubts it.

Probably claustrophobic. Stinging from the thorns.

Panicking.

Panicking at the worst possible moment. Goddamn it.

Rhodes tries to kick her. Give her a nudge to knock some sense into her. Snap her out of it.

She swings her leg. Misses.

Marilyn stops moving anyway. Holds still again.

But it's too late.

He has to know they're here. Has to.

The tree trunk hovering over them moves.

CHAPTER 80

Darger and Sadie hiked through the brush, slowly gaining altitude. The land shifted around them, morphed like time-lapse footage of a rotting peach. The soil grew stonier underfoot, chalky and gray compared to the rich black earth they'd encountered earlier. The lush green of the lowlands likewise gave way to khaki shades as the plants went scraggy fibrous higher up. All the plants became coarse like wicker. Woody. Veined. Elongated.

"How much longer?"

Sadie's voice startled Darger from her thoughts. It was the first thing she'd uttered in some time.

"Uh… I'm not sure. Are you tired? You need a break?"

"No. But I'm kinda hungry."

Darger wiped sweat from her top lip. She couldn't be sure — was operating totally on gut instinct, in fact — but she didn't think the Butcher was anywhere near them.

They were the lucky ones, she suspected, having veered away from trouble. If the gunshots had told her anything, it was that someone else hadn't been so fortunate.

"We'll stop soon and eat something, OK?"

Sadie nodded, her face surprisingly placid given what they'd been through.

Darger was impressed by the girl's nerve. It would have been understandable for her to shed some tears. To express fear or anxiety. But so far she'd marched on like a brave little soldier.

Darger retrained her vision on the rocky part of the

mountain in the distance, kept her shoulders squared on it. The trees in the foreground covered the peak over once in a while, especially the patches where the leaves were still intact and the canopy blocked out most everything.

But the mountain always reappeared before her. A hulking thing in the distance. The biggest mountain — that was their destination.

Just keep aiming yourself for the big mountain, redirecting as necessary.

And keep going.

Can't get lost. Can't go wrong.

So long as you can see it, you can get there.

A strange divot in the hill wound them around a twisted oak tree. It looked unhealthy. Stretched out. Mostly leafless. Bony and crooked like something in a Tim Burton movie.

When they stepped into the clear, her eyes crawled over the peak again. It was still a couple of miles off, she thought, though it was hard to judge distances out here.

She let her vision scan the craggy rock surface of the thing. It took her a moment to find the spot again. A dark cleft on the face of the mountain marking the breach there.

She scanned her eyes left, spotted another one.

Caves.

Her mind went to the pamphlet in her hotel room, the one advertising the range of tourist activities on the island.

"Prince of Wales Island features thousands of natural caves and caverns…"

The main focus of the brochure had been the guided tours available for El Capitan Cave, but what Darger was recalling now was a picture of the sheer rock face of one of the mountains and what looked like shadowy windows cut into the hard surface.

Part of her recoiled at the idea of going into a cave. Pressing into the dark stone walls.

But they wouldn't need to go in far. They just needed to be sheltered from the rain, when it came, and sheltered from the maniac running through the woods if and when he came. A cave in the cliffside seemed a good hiding spot, and it'd be an easy spot to defend, in theory.

After a flat stretch, the land sloped upward sharply again. Darger felt her feet dig into the mulchy ground.

She wondered if anyone else would have the same thought that she did — to get to the caves. Wait for the search and rescue team to come looking.

She could see Haywood considering the notion. He'd maintained a level of common sense about all of this.

And she didn't know much about Shepard, but he knew the land, seemed like a survivor. Maybe he would think of it, too.

Maybe they'd even run into someone on the way.

A sliver of the sun peeked out through the clouds now, that glowing orb already past its apex, ready to begin the downhill portion of its descent. It'd tuck itself behind the very mountains they were headed for sooner than later, bed down there for the night.

But for now it felt warm on her cheeks, on the backs of her arms. A gleaming brightness to cut through all the shadows. Reassuring.

The clouds mutated. The wispy stuff solidifying until it blocked out the sun once more.

Darger looked up at the black clouds rolling in. Thought about how soaked she'd been the night before.

She shivered at the memory.

CHAPTER 81

Shepard grabs Wish's jacket. Plucks it off the pine bough like it's a coat rack.

He runs his hands over the plush thing. Synthetic canvas housing some kind of soft stuffing.

Altogether it strikes him as high-quality. Made to weather the elements.

He hands the coat to Kira.

"Put that on. It'll keep you warm."

The girl slides her arms into the jacket. It fits her like a tarp, hangs down to just shy of her knees.

Then she rifles through the pockets. Pulls out another foil sleeve of Pop-Tarts and smiles.

Shepard leads the way on. Staying low and quiet. Progressing in fits and starts.

He jogs to where they can duck behind a cluster of deadfall. Gets belly down behind the mess of fallen trees. Waits there for what feels like a long time.

Breathing and listening. Patient. Heartbeat not even accelerated.

The woods keep still, keep calm. The leaves crinkle. The birds sing. But the noise stays level. Undisturbed.

Next they dart for a few leafy bushes. Shepard wades all the way into the shrubs. Squats there for a time.

Then he zips on. Sliding sideways into the center of a copse of pines. Takes Kira's hand as he slowly advances through a minuscule gap in the boughs, totally submerged in shadow and prickly needles.

When he reaches the edge of the branches, he sees what he knew he would. Stops and gawks for just a second as the image registers.

Wishnowsky's legs protrude from a patch of ferns. The plants swallow up his upper body so only those two limbs are visible. Blue jeans and sneakers jutting out of the fronds, feet set wide in a stance that might be reminiscent of a superhero in other circumstances.

So still. Eerie. Makes Shepard shudder.

His voice comes out husky. Sounds heavy in his ears.

"Wait right here, baby. I need to go take a look."

He swallows hard. Then steps forward.

A strange numbness overcomes him as he progresses toward the body. Feels like he's floating.

When he gets close, his eyes dance over the ragged wound laying the neck open wide in flaps of red. The two lenses of the glasses trapping the sightless eyes under glass. The expression on the corpse's face seems to him incongruously serene, staring up at the sky.

He kneels next to the corpse. Surprised to find himself getting choked up.

Working with care, he removes the glasses. Closes the eyes. Puts the wire-rimmed things into one of the empty hands.

Then he stands. Turns away. Moves on.

All we can ever do is move on.

He kicks through the brush next to the body. Somehow not surprised when he sees the pistol glinting there in the weeds.

He grabs it. Checks the cylinder.

Only one bullet left.

But it's better than nothing.

CHAPTER 82

Marilyn holds still. Eyes swiveling over the dirt, over the matted green of the briers above.

The brown berry canes weave over each other in dense patterns. All the leaves protrude from the stalks, ribbed with white veins. Red and purple dots strewn among the earthen tones.

She'd panicked. Lost control of herself. Thrashed against the brambles.

And the prickers had lanced her shoulders, her forearms, her scalp. Leaving marks everywhere they touched, gouging red grooves into her flesh.

Some of the little green spears remain stuck in her even now. Hooked ends curved into her arms. Caught.

Now she trembles. Belly pressed flat to the dirt. Open wounds aching where the air touches them.

Cheeks gone hot. The pink of them faintly visible at the bottom of her field of vision.

Embarrassed.

Embarrassed that she lost control. Embarrassed that she freaked out in front of Chief Rhodes.

Even here. Scared for her life. Facedown in the sand. A blanket of brambles draped over her. Embarrassed.

It makes no sense, but it doesn't have to. Nothing ever has to.

Something crunches outside the brier patch. Not the crack of a splintering stick this time. The crushing of something softer, probably something green.

But it's a footstep nevertheless. This is what Marilyn believes.

He's there. Right there.

And he knows we're here.

He has to.

Doesn't he?

She tries to see anything at all through the thorny mess above. Eyes trying to penetrate the tiny gaps in the thicket. Finding only the faded glow of the overcast light there. No other details that she can make out.

Nothing moves for a long time.

All quiet. All still.

She takes shallow breaths. Soundless. Smells the dirt in her nostrils. Tastes it on her tongue, faintly bitter.

Sweat seeps from her hairline and shoulders. Adheres her shirt to her back. Makes her feel soggy all over. The juice stinging where it touches her cuts.

Still she hugs flat to the ground. Doesn't squirm. Doesn't even dare a full breath.

She waits and listens. Waits and listens.

She tries to remember the sound she'd heard. That soft crunch she'd thought must be a footstep.

Could it have been something else?

If he were out there, if he knew they were hiding in the brambles, he would have done something by now.

She turns her head. Tries to look out through the mesh of briers one more time. Still can't see a damn thing.

She pushes up onto her elbows. Sticks her face right up to the berry canes. Peers out through the narrow hole there like she's looking through a periscope.

Her eyes snap to the bigger objects first.

Tree trunks jutting up from the earth. Branches extending

from each of the big bodies like outstretched arms.

Leaves wag in the breeze. Shadows shifting as the branches shake, light and dark lurching and dancing over everything in a kaleidoscopic way.

Nothing there. No one.

Just the woods. The same vast nothingness stretching out as far as she can see.

She lowers herself to the dirt once more. Muscles unclenching in her neck, in her back. Breath coming easier at last, rolling in and out of her like waves.

She lays her forehead right down on the cool ground.

Something lurches behind her. Clutches for her. Grabs her by the ankle and yanks. Hard.

The world slides beneath her.

Gliding on her belly.

Weightless. Powerless. Out of control. Skidding.

Her fingers curve. Scrabble. Claw at the dirt. Useless.

He rips her out of the brambles and into the light.

CHAPTER 83

Loshak's stomach did a little flopdoodle as the helicopter banked hard to the right. Beside him, Whipple jabbed a finger at the window.

"We're coming up on the Valhalla camp."

Half a minute later, Loshak spotted the clearcut area in the forest, and beyond that, the cluster of cabins.

Loshak adjusted the sunglasses over his eyes and stared down at the people bustling about among the vehicles parked there. Most of the search teams would be in the woods by now, but a small contingent would remain at the base camp they'd established. Overseeing each element of this operation.

A burst of chatter on his headset drew his attention away from the activity on the ground.

"We'll follow the logging road from base camp up to the Tongass Lumber work site," Whipple was saying. "With any luck, we'll spot the Bronco, and then we'll have an updated last known location for the missing persons search. Mackey, you take Sky Team Two closer to the lake to assist with the manhunt."

"Roger that," came another voice over the comm channel.

They veered away from the base camp. Down below, Loshak could just make out the faint line of the logging road between the breaks in the trees. A wet brown snake slithering to and fro through the forest.

His eyes zigged and zagged, hoping to catch a flash of white that would be the Ford Bronco, but the only thing he could see was a vast, unending sea of green.

Trying to find Darger out here was like trying to find a needle in a few hundred square miles of haystack.

But no. He knew that was silly. They would be found.

He just had to stay patient.

CHAPTER 84

The woman feels frail to the touch. Bony ankle. Birdlike frame gliding over the dirt.

Delicate.

He tears her free of the brambles. Flips her over onto her back with little more than a flick of his wrist.

Then he leans over her. Bent at the waist. Weapon poised in his hands. Ready to inflict damage.

She squirms. Scrabbles her arms and legs like a beetle stuck on its back. Bucks her hips as though to scoot away like that.

The Butcher brings the butt of the rifle down on the bridge of the old woman's nose.

The first strike splits her glasses. Dims the light in her eyes, even if they're still open.

The second bash splinters her nasal bone. Shatters it with a sound like peeling apart a cracked egg.

Blood weeps out from the point of impact. Jets from her nostrils. Sluices into the nasolabial folds like cracks in the sidewalk. Drizzles onto the plants below in an uneven patter.

He keeps pounding. Smashes the glasses to bits. Shatters the lenses and bends the frame. Embeds bits of glass into the pulp of her face.

She's gone fast. Out. Plucked from this plane.

Released from her service here.

Damned and delivered.

But he keeps going. Eyes wide. Blood up. Adrenaline pounding through every cell.

Some kind of hate gibbers in his skull. Eggs him on.

Aggression given voice there. A distorted scream that hands down commands. Wordless orders he somehow understands.

Maim.

Kill.

Destroy.

She's not moving now. Not blinking. No twitch of breath hitching in and out of her lungs. Nothing.

He stands a little more upright. His own chest heaving. Brimming with life.

Her eyes stare out at nothing. Gaze blank and vaguely skyward. The white orbs look wrong set in the bloody mess of her face.

Something flutters in the distance. A tiny churning sound that makes his breath cut off all at once. Makes him hold still and listen.

For a second, he thinks it's in his head. The blood churning in a thudding pulse inside, almost clicking along in his skull, in his ears.

But then the sound gets bigger, comes clearer.

CHUFF-CHUFF-CHUFF-CHUFF

A helicopter. Rotors chopping at the air louder and louder. Coming right this way.

Oh shit.

A grin splits his face.

This is it.

CHAPTER 85

Darger sat on a fallen birch tree, the girl straddling the pale trunk just next to her. Something about the positioning made it look like Sadie was sitting on one of those coin-op horsey rides outside of a supermarket somewhere, Darger thought, some wave of childhood memories occurring to her. Did those even exist anymore?

They'd finally stopped for a lunch break, or something close enough to that. The girl unwrapped another Pop-Tart, foil crinkling, and brought the uncooked pastry to her face, gummy red innards gleaming where her bite mark marred the rectangle.

Darger likewise peeled the wrapping away from her meal, if she were feeling generous enough to call it that. Her teeth sank into the dense protein bar, tore away another cardboard-tasting chunk. Chewed and chewed. The mealy thing disintegrating in her maw little by little.

Still, it felt good to sit. The ache in her legs and lower back almost pleasant after so long on her feet. A lightness coming over her, both body and mind.

And the woods seemed different, too. Disarmed somehow. No longer quite so ominous. Quiet and almost peaceful instead.

"Are you taking me to my Gramma and Grampa?" Sadie asked.

The question caught Darger off-guard at first. But of course that's how a kid's brain would work. She'd assume that, as the adult in the situation, Darger would have some simple, logical, concrete goal in mind. Find her grandparents.

"Um, yeah. Eventually," Darger said. "But it's supposed to rain later, and right now I think we should find somewhere that will keep us dry."

"Like a cabin?"

Darger popped the last bit of her protein bar into her mouth.

"Not exactly."

It wasn't really an answer, but Darger wasn't sure how the girl might react to the idea of sheltering in a cave.

"Do you think Kira is with Gramma and Grampa?" the girl asked.

Her face had gone suddenly grave, the little pink mouth pressed into a line.

This was the first time the girl had expressed any anxiety out loud, and it took a moment for Darger to recover from the sudden shift.

"Yeah," Darger said, having no idea whether it was a lie. "I'm sure she is."

"Good. Because she's too little to be out here by herself."

Darger realized she'd been a bit naive until now. Just because the girl wasn't trembling and tearful, that didn't mean she wasn't worried. Kids were capable of hiding their emotions just like adults were.

She wadded up the empty protein bar wrapper into a ball and shoved it into her pocket, fingers brushing against something in the folds of her pants. Something hard. Vaguely the size and shape of a bullet. Darger had no idea what it even was until she pulled it out.

It was the tiny "good luck" bottle Donnie Struthers had insisted she bring with them. Darger's first thought was that the charm hadn't brought her any luck at all. But that wasn't exactly true. Whoever had been on the receiving end of the gunshots she'd heard, for example, was having decidedly worse luck than she was.

And that gave her an idea.

She held the object out to Sadie, the glass glittering in the sunlight.

"Here."

Sadie grasped the chain and held the vial up to her face, her eyes going slightly crossed.

"What is it?"

"It's a good luck charm," Darger said, then lowered her voice to a whisper. "Made by a fairy."

Sadie scoffed.

"Fairies aren't real."

Darger brought a hand to her chest and pretended to look scandalized.

"Geez, don't let the fairies hear you say that."

When Sadie had finished off her Pop-Tarts, Darger took the empty wrappers and stuffed them in her pocket along with the rest of her trash. Funny how even in a life-and-death scenario, it seemed wrong to litter.

She glanced up at the sky then and was alarmed to see how dark it had gotten. They'd only been stopped here for a few minutes, but the black clouds on the horizon were noticeably thicker. The encroaching gloom of the storm.

Time to get moving.

Darger picked herself up. Her legs protested, muscles whinging and clenching in sharp bursts, but she ignored the pain.

She had no choice.

They had to find shelter before the rain hit.

CHAPTER 86

Rhodes creeps toward the edge of the brambles. Working her knees and elbows to wriggle over the land on her belly. Gun in her hand.

A tunnel of green and shadow lies before her — the cave mouth into the brambles glowing bright at the end. But she can see nothing in that half-circle of light just along the ground. Just more dirt and crushed leaves. Part of a tree in the distance.

Another slice of the woods just like all the rest.

She swallows. Presses toward the light. Feels her pulse quaking in the side of her neck.

He must not know I'm here.

Would have flushed me out by now.

If I'm quiet enough, careful enough, I can get the jump on him.

Maybe.

She hears the slap and thud of violence. Some kind of beating being administered, sounds close, though she can't see anything yet.

Needs to keep moving. Crawling.

The shaft of crisscrossing berry canes glides by overhead. Intertwining brown stalks like wires skimming in a slow-motion drift. Somehow makes it seem like the plants are moving instead of her.

The beating stops all at once. The silence swelling. She hesitates a second.

Listens.

Nothing.

She slinks forward. Her vision sweeping over the last of the gloom, closing in on the line in the sand where the daylight gleams bright.

And more of the world beyond the brambles slides into view, little by little.

She sees the textured blue of denim sticking up from the green. Marilyn's denim-clad legs lying over the ground. Not moving.

Rhodes resists the paralysis that creeps over her. A chill spreading over her skin that wants to stop her limbs, wants to hold her still.

She pushes herself. Knee forward. Elbow forward. Torso slithering over the sand, swaying gently back and forth.

His boots come into view. Combat boots reaching up over his ankles, laced as tight as footballs.

Holy shit.

She swings the gun before her. Arm shaking. Panic wobbling inside her skull, sloshing and leaping.

The sound of the chopper hits then. Rotors slicing, whomping, pulsing.

And he's gone. Bolts like a spooked rabbit. Darting off into the woods.

Rhodes blinks. Stares into the empty space where he'd been some five or six feet beyond the brambles. Maybe not point-blank range but close enough.

She listens to his footsteps rush off. Those crunching thuds fading. Fading. Gone.

Then she lets her head sink back to the dirt. Breathing dust. Empty.

The woods hold still beyond the brier patch. Hollow now that his presence is gone.

Rhodes stays facedown. Feels sensation slowly creep back

into her limbs, then her core. Realizes there's a thorn stuck in the flesh on the back of her neck. The tip of it seeming to flex into her skin like a single cat claw every time she takes a breath.

She turns her head to the side. Cheek pressed into the gray sand.

The violence is over.

The footsteps are gone.

Still, she waits a long time.

Not moving.

Not thinking.

Just breathing.

Feeling alive. Somewhat lucky to be so.

And yet terrified, too.

Finally she reaches up and removes that spiky bit of green from her neck. Feels relief with the thing out, though the wound stings as the air gets at it. Her fingers come away smeared with blood.

She crawls toward the edge of the brambles again, though part of her mind begs her not to.

Just stay here.

Stay hidden.

Keep your face tucked down in the berries until the rescue team comes.

If it ever does.

She stops again. That sobering thought clanging around in her head for a second before she can get herself to crawl forward once more.

No, they'll come. They have to.

Don't they?

The helicopter, she reminds herself. The chuff of the rotors replays in her head.

You heard the helicopter overhead. They're here now.

Looking for you.

She worms through the briers. More spikes scratching her, opening her skin.

Finally she crawls out. Moves into the light. Busts through a last line of brambles as she stands, one thorny cane sticking to her chest like Velcro, ripping out of the ground along with her upward motion. She pulls it free and tosses it aside.

She stretches her arms toward the sky. Feels the open air touching her wounds. Sharp.

She swallows then. Knows this next bit will be the hard part.

It takes a second to make her foot step forward. Her mind having to force the movement, somehow. Concentrating for a full two seconds to get it done.

She only has to walk a few paces to find what she's looking for. Those jeans laid out in the weeds. The bloody mess atop them only confirming what she already knew.

Marilyn is gone.

CHAPTER 87

Shepard and Kira wade into the thick woods. Tangles of vines and thorny bits everywhere, gripping and ripping at them with greater and greater frequency.

The mountains jut up from the land off in front of them. Stony peaks rising out of the dirt.

Shepard eyes the rocky bluffs every time they peek out from between the trees. Scans them for details.

Little dots of darkness pock the rugged peaks. Cliffs. Caves.

That's the only way Shepard can see for staying hidden and out of the wet tonight, trying to keep warm to what degree they can.

They'd headed for the Jeep first. Found it hopelessly stuck in the mud. So much for a quick escape. Still, they could have sheltered there and would have, had it not been so close to where he'd last seen the Butcher.

And so he leads them toward the highlands, toward the cliffs. Feels confident enough that they can get there before dark.

But he's taking a slight detour first.

He tears his eyes away from the horizon. Starts paying attention to the shrubbery around them. Finds some familiarity there in the growth — more a feeling, an instinct, than an absolute certainty of recall, but he knows.

They're close now.

He stalks through some thick ivy. Waxy leaves squeaking faintly under the treads of his boots.

There.

A rumple of rough material protrudes from the bed of dark leaves. This is the object he has sought.

He kneels next to the backpack. Rips something from it. Drinks from the metal canteen. Hands it over to Kira.

He'd dropped his pack here while tracking the Butcher. Feels a deep satisfaction at having found his way back to it, though he knows the feeling will be fleeting.

There's much left to do. Many dangers left to face.

He stands and hoists the pack onto his shoulders. Feels the weight settle over the muscles in his back. He walks on, carrying the bulk.

If he were going with the original plan, he wouldn't do that. He'd travel as light as possible, track the psycho and try to take him down.

Now that Kira is with him, though, the goal has changed. He has to keep her safe, and that means finding shelter sooner than later.

Unfortunately, the tent was packed in Marilyn's bag, and he doesn't like the idea of going back toward the campsite. The Butcher would expect that, he thinks. Would expect them to return for supplies or in hopes of regrouping. It'd be the perfect spot for an ambush.

That thought worms uncomfortably in his belly, and he silently prays that Marilyn will also put two and two together and avoid returning to camp as well. Hopes Sadie is with her.

Just hunker down somewhere and stay hidden, babe. Wait until help comes.

He sends this thought out into the ether, as though he might be able to beam it into his wife's mind.

He walks on. Staring off at the mountains again.

The caves. That's the plan for now. But it could change. It is important to stay malleable out here. Nimble. Ready for anything.

Shepard consults his compass. Veers to the north to avoid the sloppy swamplands. They'll take a gently curving route to the cliff face, stay out of the bogs.

They hike for what feels like a long time. Bashing their way through the undergrowth. Shepard consulting the compass now and again, changing trajectories as needed.

He had done some climbing here years ago, before his own children were born, let alone his grandchildren. Had bivouacked in one of the caves — more like a small, shallow chamber than a tunnel — and found it cozy enough.

Picturing it in his memory helps him reaffirm the plan. He knows firsthand there are caverns — at least a dozen of them honeycombing the rock up there — and figures it the only dry place to bed down for the night, should it come to that. Which it probably will.

Kira tugs on his backpack. Two quick pulls akin to a tap on the shoulder.

He wheels and looks at her. Mind already racing. Ready to leap into alarm mode. Expecting that she's seen something, heard something.

Instead, he's met with a placid expression on her face.

"I'm hungry."

She says it matter-of-factly. Something flat and entitled in the tone that he finds surprising and sort of hilarious.

"Heh. Uh, sure, kitten. Let me see what I've got."

He pulls off his pack and digs around in the front pocket. Hands over a little plastic baggie full of gorp.

The girl doesn't hesitate. She digs out a handful and starts chowing down. Jaw working in a circular motion. Crunching loudly.

Shepard figures he better have some himself. Keep his

blood sugar from crashing.

He dips his fingers into the bag. Snatches up some of the trail mix.

He doesn't realize how hungry he is until the salt of the peanuts hits his palate. The flavor of the raisins comes next, their bright and sweet interplaying with the saltiness.

He grabs another handful, bigger this time, and they both stand a moment and eat. Staring out at nothing. Surrounded by a tranquil forest.

But then Shepard hears something. Something unnatural breaking up the serenity.

He goes silent. Shushes the girl.

Her crunching cuts out. They both listen.

The churning grows louder. Closer.

He knows the sound.

It's a helicopter. Probably a rescue team out looking for those other folks.

It's heading their way.

His heart starts pounding. He drops the pack into a mess of creeper at his feet and rushes for daylight.

His legs motor beneath him. Chewing up ground. Slaloming through the trees with the girl just behind him. Their momentum slowing just a little as they take a slope.

He busts through the tree line. Hurtles out into a clearing on a hilltop.

The chopper is just there. Hovering perhaps thirty feet above the trees. Close enough that he can make out the shapes of the officers inside.

He waves his arms and jumps up and down. Yells though the chuff of the rotor swallows the sound almost entirely.

Kira copies him. Practically does jumping jacks next to him.

The helicopter hesitates a moment. Then it lurches their

way. Comes right overhead. Circles there. Now he can make out the details of the people on board. Someone wearing a pair of aviator sunglasses next to the pilot, smiling and waving out the window.

His skin goes cold all over. Pulls taut around him like a sheet of latex too small for his skeleton. Adrenaline rocketing through his system as though he'd just mainlined a syringe full of the stuff.

Jesus.

They actually see us.

It doesn't seem real. Spins a strange dizziness into his skull that reminds him of getting laughing gas at the dentist as a kid.

Still, he jumps up and down. Even with numb arms and legs, tingly and weightless all over, he jumps up and down. Doesn't know what else to do.

The giddiness seems to swell in his face. A smile there so strong that it makes his cheeks sting even through the numbness.

Joy renders itself physically. Floods the cells of his body. Fills him with lightness, with hope.

No. More than mere hope.

Faith.

Salvation.

The rifle crack comes from somewhere higher up on the next hill.

The windshield of the chopper cracks. Spiderwebs.

There's a bloody explosion on the glass. A dappling of red like a Jackson Pollock painting. And a strange void where the pilot's head used to be.

Shepard stops jumping. Feels a panting breath on his teeth, on his tongue. The whole world holding still for one second.

And then the helicopter veers off to the right. Tilting.

Falling away from him. Listing like a sinking ship.
It crashes into the next hill over.
And explodes into a fiery spray.

CHAPTER 88

Shepard rips Kira off the ground. Lifts her like a toddler, hugging her to his chest.

He lugs her out of the clearing at a dead sprint. Her gangly limbs flopping against him, bouncing along with his gait.

He only breathes when they're back under the cover of the woods. Shadows swallowing them, dimming the color of their clothes, of their faces.

His skin feels clammy. Panic slicking him with cold sweat.

He finds his pack where he dropped it. Sets Kira down and pulls the straps over his shoulders.

Then he sucks a few big breaths. Chest shaking. Jaw quivering.

"Will they be OK?" Kira says, her voice low. "The people in the helicopter. Will they be OK?"

Shepard doesn't say anything. Just looks at her. Mind blank for a second.

She stares back. Eyes wide. Expectant. He's the wise grandfather after all, supposed to know everything.

Part of him thinks he should tell her it'll be OK, that they'll all be OK.

But the reassuring lie won't form in his throat, won't rise to his lips.

Instead he grunts. A single syllable coming out, something choked and final in it.

She nods once and looks down at the lush forest floor. She seems to understand somehow.

His mind jumps around. Replaying the horror, the sound,

the fury. The heat of the explosion rolling off the fallen helicopter, the blistering whoosh swirling around him.

He takes Kira's hand, and they fall back into the woods. Veering further north.

He picks his way forward. Weaving through tightly knit forest. Stepping over the twisted undergrowth that pocks the ground with sprawling limbs and trunks here and there.

That shaken feeling won't quite leave him. A jittery throb that keeps washing through him.

Exploded.

Blown to bits.

Gone in an instant.

They jog down a steep incline, picking up speed for a moment. Then they start up the slope on the opposite side of the small valley, their progress slowing once more.

Thoughts pound in his skull. Pulsing there like a headache.

We'll still head for the mountains, for the caves. It's the only way.

Have to give the sniper's area a wide berth, though. Steer well clear.

He hears the rain before he sees it. Droplets plunking at the leaves above. Tapping. Thudding a little more heavily where they pelt the ground.

He hopes it's not what it sounds like. Hopes there's some other explanation. Anything.

But the hope fades when he feels a fat cold drop on the top of his shaved head. The water exploding on the rounded dome of his scalp.

CHAPTER 89

Loshak gaped out the window. Watched black smoke coil up from the ground, from the cluster of fiery trees there where the second helicopter had been only a minute before.

Shock prickled cold tendrils over his scalp. Wormed the icy strands down into his chest, into his belly.

If I had gotten on the other chopper...

The descent replayed in his mind. The helicopter whirling and tipping. Plummeting. Slamming into the earth.

It had looked like the thing disintegrated on impact. Instantly erased. Fire and smoke roiling where it had been.

Then the explosion had shuddered through the air. Sent a shiver through their chopper. The rumbling vibration felt through Loshak's seat.

Their own helicopter had veered back immediately. A sharp turn away from the crash site, away from its cause.

Chaos ensued inside the cabin. Loud and frenzied.

Raised voices tangling over each other. Some of the officers pointing into the trees. Talking about where the shots had come from.

Someone else frantically calling it in on the radio. Reading off coordinates from the navigation screen. Crackling static distorting the voices talking back to them.

They'd gone over a ridge. Put a slice of sloping land between themselves and wherever the shots had come from.

Still they could see the smoke spiraling up. Black tufts that looked wet. Almost oily. Winding their way toward the heavens.

Now the pilot reached up and flipped a switch overhead, a little red light flicking off as he did. He monkeyed with the controls. All those dials and knobs and switches on the console — it was all more or less meaningless to Loshak.

"OK, I need everyone to just settle down a minute," Whipple said over the snarl of voices on the headset. "It's not doing any good to have eight people talking at once."

When there was silence, he went on.

"Rossi, you called in the coordinates, yes?"

"Affirmative."

"Alright then. Fogelson, you relay those coordinates to the Fugitive Apprehension Team."

"Already done."

"Good. Have the paramedics at base camp on standby. From what I saw, I doubt there are any survivors, but you never know. Maybe we get lucky. As for us, we're going to continue on to our destination. We're still a few miles from the Tongass Lumber cabin. I'll radio in when we get there."

"Shouldn't we try to keep eyes on the hostile?" one of the other men asked.

Whipple sighed.

"Look, he already took one chopper down. It's obvious he's well-armed and well-camouflaged. Not like we could land this bird on top of a pine tree and get after him, ya know?"

They all fell quiet for a few seconds. Nervous glances flicking between them, the eye contact never quite holding.

The helicopter rotor pounded out that chuffing pulse. Thrummed its rhythm through the hull of the ship.

Whipple turned his gaze on the agent. Fixed a stare on him like he was trying to see through the aviators.

"What do you think, Agent Loshak?"

"I think you're right. Getting to the cabin should be our

priority. If we're lucky, we can have the rescue portion of this operation squared away and from there, put all our resources into the manhunt."

"Let's get it done," Whipple said, and the chopper gently corrected course.

Loshak stared down at the treetops, praying that Darger and the others would be holed up in the cabin. Safe.

CHAPTER 90

Rhodes searches Marilyn's body quickly. Chewing her bottom lip as she does.

Digging in the corpse's pockets feels almost like an out-of-body experience. Like it's someone else doing it. Like her mind has retracted from the awfulness, taken a good portion of her consciousness somewhere else.

A blank place. A nowhere place.

Knees down in the roughage. Fingers hooking into the hip pockets of the jeans, into the breast pocket of the shirt. Wriggling in the folds of fabric.

She doesn't look straight at what she's doing. Doesn't look at the body, at the blood. Lets her eyes gaze blankly into the ferns while her hands work. An unfocused stare.

The green blur just beyond the cadaver. Meaningless tangles.

Little breaths flutter in and out of her. The air whistling through.

The body has already gone cool to the touch. Some strange tepidness felt through her clothes. Flesh still pliable, awaiting the rigor to come. Reminds Rhodes of touching a freshly defrosted chicken breast, straight out of the microwave. Lukewarm meat.

How cold would Marilyn get lying here tonight? Out in the open?

Exposed to the rain. Exposed to the carrion birds and to the flies and maggots.

Rhodes cranes her neck. Looks up all of a sudden. Gazes

into the awning of leaves above that formed Marilyn's last view.

She leaves the travel wallet. Takes the small plastic package of Kleenex. Scoops a soft rectangle out of the breast pocket, and the smaller, harder cylinder next to it.

And then she's up. Stomping off into the woods. Running. Moving the opposite direction the Butcher had gone. Her haul still clutched in her hands before her.

When she's run some 200 yards or so, she turns back. Confirms that she can no longer see the body, can no longer see anything familiar.

She shoves the tissues into her hip pocket. Takes that soft rectangle and turns it in her hands. Reads the label.

A soft pack of Marlboro Light 100s. That tangy tobacco smell rolling out of the open top.

She plucks one of the long white tubes and perches it between her lips. Eyes crossing a little as she stares down at the thing so that for a second she sees two bleached cylinders protruding from her face. Double vision.

Then she cranks the lighter a few times. Swoops the flame close. Lights it.

Breathes smoke.

She hasn't smoked in over a year. Quit once she got word that her blood pressure wasn't the best.

But now?

Now she can't resist.

The smoke tastes funny. Not her brand. But the overall familiarity somehow makes the process feel urgent. Some part of her brain convinced that she can and will derive comfort from these tobacco sticks.

The nicotine rushes into her bloodstream. She feels it plainly after her third big puff, like a prickle in the blood vessels in her head.

The drug doesn't help. Makes her heart hammer in her chest. Makes her head go light and swimmy like that first cigarette behind the tennis courts when she was a high school kid.

She pictures Marilyn there in the woods. Face up. Arms wide. Waiting for the storm and wildlife to defile her body further.

She wonders if she should have covered her some. Laid boughs over her face, at least.

But no. It wouldn't mean anything. The rituals we use to try to shroud death, to diminish the blunt force of its savagery... none of them mean anything.

Marilyn got her face beat in for no reason. Nothing anybody did or said could soften that reality.

And it was never going to be OK.

Rhodes strides forward again. Picking through the foliage. Smoking and walking. Trying to think.

If she can find a clearing on higher ground, maybe she'll be able to spot the helicopter again. It had whirred out of range, no longer audible. But she could signal them somehow, she thinks. Build a fire, perhaps, though the thought makes her nervous. Whatever signal she sends to their rescuers she is also potentially sending to the Butcher himself.

Her throat feels a little raw now. And the cigarette tastes worse and worse with every hit. Some chemical note coming forward, getting stuck in her nose, on her tongue.

Still, she's glad to have the smokes. Glad for something to do with her hands. Glad to have something to focus on, to look forward to.

In a way, the distraction almost makes it feel like she's not alone.

CHAPTER 91

A large spider skittered up a tree trunk — a spindly thing, dark against the white bark of the birch. Its legs blurred so much that it looked like the creature just zipped along without moving them, sliding right up the tree like someone moving a piece over a game board.

There were more spiders here, both big and small, Darger had noted. More insect activity period. A bunch of them chirping and carrying on even now, their tiny throats droning endless tones.

The woods seemed thicker here, too. More undergrowth swaddling their ankles with each step. Maybe a little more humid, the air thick, heavy in her throat, unless that was only Darger's imagination. Then again, Alaska or not, this was technically a rain forest, she reminded herself. Humidity would be normal enough.

Feels like we've been walking for miles.

I mean... I guess we have.

She felt dumb for just a second. Something embarrassing about the dim cliché, even if she hadn't said it out loud.

Then she wondered how many miles they had actually walked. Five at most, if she figured the average hiking speed was two miles per hour. And with all the zigging and zagging they'd had to do, skirting around fallen trees, avoiding the steepest slopes, it probably wasn't a significant distance if you measured it by way of a crow's flight.

But none of it mattered. They weren't running a marathon or trying to break some sort of distance record, so she let it drop. Refocused on the land tilting up and down around her.

The mountain had grown closer than ever. It looked bigger through the trees, absolutely immense against the horizon now that they were closing on it. She had to crane her neck to get a glimpse of the peak.

She could see more of the detail now, too. The craggy angles in the rock face, angular like it'd been chiseled in the roughest spots, flat pieces cleaving off everywhere. Other areas looked softer, rumpled yet smooth like a papier-mâché sculpture, probably worn that way by the rain tumbling over the surface in sheets, slowly washing it down.

They trudged into a dense copse of hemlock, everything going dark around them, and the mountains vanished behind the curtain of needles again. Blotted out.

Darger pushed through the boughs. Felt the scratchy needles brush against all of her, like she was walking through a car wash that swept her with pine branches high and low. The crisp green scent blended with something sharp and earthy. Maybe that was the sap seeping out of the trunks like an acrid syrup. She wasn't sure.

They pushed through the last of the pines, and the land opened up again. Long pine needles carpeted the ground, even squishier than what they'd trudged through up by the cabin. It kept their footsteps quiet for the most part, and Darger was thankful for that.

Sadie pointed at the ground some ways ahead. A snake slithered there, a long striped thing disappearing into the brush almost as soon as Darger laid eyes on it. Darting. Fast to the point of being startling, but it apparently wanted nothing to do with them.

Well... wouldn't be a rainforest without snakes, would it?

The land leveled out into something like a plateau, and the

woods stretched out before them. More and more. Seemingly infinite variations of the same few ingredients. Endless and crushing.

Firs, spruces, and oaks formed the bars of their cell, their trunks making the vertical lines to cage them in here.

And then, along the ground, the low plants choked the ground, swallowed it in shades of green. Ferns. Vines. Moss. Brambles. It ate up all of the soil, covered it over like a lumpy blanket.

Darger strode on. Pushed into it. No matter how hopeless it might feel, no matter how the scenery showed her no mercy, convinced her there was no end.

She stared at the ground as she slogged forward, not really focusing her eyes. Watching the rug of bleary ground plants smear past. A shapeless stain tugging at her ankles.

The walk stretched out like that. Time holding still. Just her and the girl propelling forward into the thicket, plunging onward, beating a path like bowling balls rolling through it.

But then she lifted her head and something was different. Darger felt it, sensed it, before her conscious mind could understand it or explain it.

She squinted. Tried to concentrate.

Light.

Brighter light shimmered between the trees up there. Somehow, someway.

Darger felt excitement lurch to life in her middle. Electric snakes whirling, flopping, flinging themselves up the walls of her stomach. Leaping for her throat and snapping.

She pressed toward the light. Heard something crisp in her own footfalls. Choppy steps beating at the foliage.

Quickness. Urgency. Hope.

The brightness between the trees seemed to zoom toward

her. Closer, closer. Those shafts of light sucking her that way like tiny tractor beams. Pulling her along.

Holy shit.

She reached the light. Stepped through the last of the trees. Heart hammering in her chest.

The land opened up before her. Yawning emptiness.

No more woods. Just a nearly naked expanse of scrubby growth between her and the big peak.

A chill trembled up the length of her spine. Scraped slowly up her neck like a cold nail.

She let her eyes drift to that rocky growth in the distance. Gaze crawling up the peak.

The big mountain looked close. Its bottom half visible for the first time.

There.

Right there.

Just a stretch of flatlands between her and the slopes. Perhaps just a few hundred yards.

Open. Empty. Space.

But then she let her gaze shift lower. Closer.

She examined that open land between her and the peak. Looked. Really looked.

And she realized a big patch of swamp lay between them and the mountains. A few hundred yards not of clear land but stagnant water. Muck. Lily pads and scum floating on top of it, pale green.

She swallowed. Let the idea percolate. Let it settle.

A bog. They couldn't walk through that. They'd get wet. Muddy.

Could run into deep water.

Could find more snakes or other predators.

Could slip in the muck. Break an ankle.

She looked off to the right. Saw the tree line arc around the swamp.

They'd probably be better off going around the wetlands that way, which would cost them time.

She held still for another few seconds. A weird mix of excitement and defeat roiling inside of her. It made her breathe funny, frustrated puffs stuttering out of her nostrils. Eyes stinging, itching, blinking fast. Almost like she might cry.

Then it started to sprinkle.

CHAPTER 92

The dogs fire off into the woods one by one. Legs bounding. So many balls of fur shooting through the scrub like torpedoes.

Hounds and German shepherds make up most of the pack with a couple of labs and even one beagle thrown in, for good measure.

The small search teams are well spaced for the moment, positioned up and down the edge of the woods as per the plan, though the scent may lead to some close encounters between the teams sooner than later. That's the nature of a scent search, Rex Morton supposes — all roads invariably lead to one point, the source.

He stands and watches another handler release his beast. Watches the hound fly through the weeds and into the woods, his human search-mate falling in behind.

The dogs weave out into the thicket, headed in different directions depending on whether they're part of the manhunt, the rescue effort, or the search for human remains. It looks deceptively orderly for the moment.

The brush shakes as the canines rip through. Leaves jostling. Low branches wagging. The bear bells on the collars of the loose animals ringing out endless tunes devoid of melody.

The excitement is contagious, Rex thinks. He's been a handler for 17 years, and the thrill of this process has yet to wane. There's always an electricity in the atmosphere at the start of a hunt, the air crispy and bright with it.

He has his own dog, Jerry, on a short leash. Ready to let the German shepherd thunder out after the bad guy. Technically a search dog like Jer will look for any human he hasn't already smelled — i.e., anyone but the other search party members — meaning he could easily catch the scent of one of the missing people instead of the fugitive. But Rex has a good feeling about their assigned grid spot. It's nowhere near the last known location of the missing people, and his gut says Jerry will have no problem picking up the fugitive's scent.

Regardless, he doesn't mind letting some of the other search and rescue units go first. Better to give ol' Jerry the extra space to work on his own. If Rex knows his dog like he thinks he does, Jerry will storm past the others in any case — the beast is not just good with scents but clever about intuiting the trail. Quick to overcome backtracking and other such tricks employed by those being hunted. Not so much snuffling around as it is with most dogs. This one just has a knack for cutting right to the source, leaping right for the goddamn throat, figuratively. While some of the police dogs heading out now would have been trained to attack and take down perpetrators, the search and rescue dogs like Jerry are of a gentler nature, trained only to alert their handler of the person's location.

Rex has worked with dozens of dogs and witnessed hundreds of others on manhunts and rescue efforts like these. Jerry is the best he's ever seen.

He wades out into the weeds along the edge of the woods. Calf-high plants brushing at his pant legs. The dog bouncing a little at the end of the lead. Delighted to be here. Raring to go.

He checks his position on GPS. This is it — the marker for their search grid. They've created some space, at last, from the other searchers, which is a good thing.

Rex takes one last look around. Sees a few other dogs in the distance, still walking to their position, the ground tracking dogs pulling their handlers along on lengths of woven nylon. He hears the air scent trackers out in the woods already, their bells jangling out tiny sounds along with their steps — the bells serve, ideally, to scare off bears, but they also let the handler know where the loose search dog is, at least roughly.

Rex takes a breath. Speaks low to his dog.

"You ready, boy?"

The dog pants in response. Eyes bright. Locked on his with total focus.

Rex sprinkles a little baby powder in the air. Two shakes of the plastic bottle. He checks the wind direction as the white dust plummets, drifting back toward them as it catches the breeze.

He smiles. It's blowing right in their faces. That's perfect. They'll be downwind from the start.

The dog sees what his handler is doing and pulls on the leash immediately. Frantic. Knows it's go time. Ready to lurch to work, to find the human somewhere out there. Like *now*.

Rex leans close. Unclips the lead from the collar.

The dog jerks immediately. Bolts through the undergrowth. Bounds over a branch. Disappears into the shadowy woods.

Rex swallows. Feels his heart beat in his chest.

Jerry's bear bell rings out, a galloping wind chime sound rocking along with the dog's gait. Already the sound trails away. He's sprinting.

Already on the scent?

Maybe.

Rex hustles through the foliage. Gets just a glimpse of Jerry weaving up ahead in some ferns.

The dog snakes back and forth along the breeze to seek out — or keep on — the Butcher's scent. Snout lifting often to catch the wind. Then the dog ducks over a small hill out of sight again.

Rex picks up speed. Half-jogging through the wispy brush here.

He runs right past a couple of ground tracking hounds, one blood and one coon — these dogs use a scent bag containing a scrap of the Butcher's shirt and keep their nose to the dirt, sniffing along the trail of skin particles, following more than searching. He doubts they'll be of much use with the rain and the time lost on this case, though you never know what you might find when you give it a try. They must have found a starting point, at least — what would typically be a "last seen" point for the subject of the search, something this type of dog requires.

Of course, if the Butcher is living out here, running freely in these woods, stalking the forest day and night…

Rex snaps his head around. Eyes gliding over everything as though the wanted murderer might dive out of the thicket.

In any case, air scent trackers like Jerry typically excel given these conditions. A single air tracking dog could cover the area of fifty human searchers on a case like this. They didn't need a direct track to seek out a person, could search out the scent and get home to the source no matter how the hunted person got to where they were.

Rex's radio buzzes from his belt. Shakes him back to the moment.

He listens to a tangle of babble on the radio. Only sussing out after the fact what has been said.

One of the cadaver teams has stumbled upon human remains already. Their dogs lying down near a bear den, wagging their tails, waiting for their handlers to come see what they've turned up. Bones found nearby.

Damn. That was quick.

This could be over fast.

Rex tramples over the hill. Scans the forest ahead. Spots Jerry again.

The dog serpentines still. Nose tilted up. Following the breeze. Hard to tell if he has a scent just yet or if he's still searching for it.

Rex takes a deep breath. Wipes the thin film of sweat gathering at his brow. Keeps plowing ahead.

It smells like rain. The storm will hit sooner than later, supposedly, though Rex is hopeful it will come on slow. Sprinkle a while before the heavy stuff hits.

It's no problem for the dog, the rain. A properly trained search dog like Jerry can work in any weather conditions shy of the middle of a tornado, and he can work into the night if need be. Of course, the beast will need breaks and rest just like a person would, should the search drag on.

Rex gazes up through the branches above at that thought. Realizes how dark the encroaching storm has made it, black clouds blotting out most of the sky. He can't believe how fast the day is draining on them.

The dog keeps going, and so does he. His dream of the hunt ending quickly doesn't bear out.

Time passes. Rain falls. He keeps up with the German shepherd the best he can. The dog darting out of view off and on, and the handler bumbling along behind, breath going a little heavy as he does.

The next thing Rex knows, it's been two hours. Time draining like pus from a lanced boil. Oozing past all at once.

He knows now that Jerry doesn't have a scent. He's still searching for it. Except, he usually wouldn't keep on such a relatively straight line if that were the case. He'd widen his forward progress into a sweeping motion, search more of the breeze until it brought him something.

Rex feels his brow furrow. For just a second, he begins to question what's going on here, but he stops himself.

It's Jerry.

I trust him.

The two of them run into the darkening woods.

CHAPTER 93

The orange bucket is there. Tucked down in the weeds just where he left it, covered over with enough branches that no one could have found it unless they knew it was there.

The Butcher squats over the thing, loosens the catches around the edge of the lid. Then he pops the circular top free, pries it up like a manhole cover.

The reek of gasoline wafts out of the bucket. A bright smell. Clean, to him.

And what could be more cleansing than fire?

Little sniffs of laughter vent through his nostrils. Hissing in rapid pulses.

Electricity still lurches through his veins. The thrill of squeezing the trigger. Watching the chopper plucked from the sky like a swatted fly.

Falling.

Bursting into flame.

Into rubble.

Bye-e.

He feels fucking invincible now. Hell, he's starting to think that maybe he *is*.

He thinks of one of the lame poems they had to read, back in school. Can only remember the one line.

Look on my works, ye mighty, and despair!

Yes. It's exactly like that, this feeling he has right now.

He stands and lifts the bucket by the curved metal handle. Feels it swing at the end of his arm. Sees a flash of the faded lettering on the sidewall of the thing, the white hardware store logo mostly scratched away by all the walks through the brush.

He runs into the thicket. Leaves whapping at his arms, skinny branches clawing at his face.

Needs to be quick now. The next bit will happen fast.

This is where it was always headed. He can see that now.

The police swarming in. A whole convoy of them snaking out on the logging roads. Truck after truck after truck.

Cops outfitted like soldiers piling out. Armed to the fucking teeth.

Him making a stand against them. A final stand.

His blaze of fucking glory.

But if he's quick, if he's clever, he can hold them off, at least for a night.

He grins at the thought.

And if he doesn't? He'll do a lot of damage in the meantime. Take out a bunch more pigs just like he did the shitheels in the chopper.

He leans down next to the first woodpile — a substantial teepee-shaped mass of sticks and boughs about four feet high, some thicker logs wedged underneath.

He fishes one of the gas-soaked rags out of the bucket. Shoves it into the middle of the woodpile, near the bottom.

Then he flicks open his Zippo. Rasps the wheel with his thumb. Hovers the little orange triangle close to the cone-shaped pile.

The flame leaps when it touches the rag. Heaves out one violent breath as it jumps.

Then the fire draws back. Steadies. Grows. Glowing bright. Licking over all those sticks surrounding it.

That grin curves his lips harder. Bends itself toward a rictus.

Won't be here for a long time, but I will for damn sure have a good time.

He runs on. Gleeful.

Soon three big bonfires are raging.

He ditches the bucket. Then he picks his way up a sheer ridge. Uses his hands, fingers finding edges and handholds, to climb the last little bit where the cliff runs straight up.

He runs along the rim of the cliff. From here he can see two of the fires plainly. Stretched far apart just shy of the cliff face.

He hurls himself to his knees. Starts clawing at the dirt with his fingers.

There he has an old Coleman cooler buried in the ground. A huge behemoth of a thing.

He digs out some camo gear and pulls two pieces over his head. Long-sleeved shirt and a mask.

At the bottom of the cooler is the better scope for his rifle. He screws it on.

Then he lies down on his belly, worms right up to the edge of the ridge, all covered in ferns and creeper.

And he waits for the pigs to show.

CHAPTER 94

The rain drizzled steadily. Not pouring yet, but it didn't matter.

They were wet. Hair plastered to their heads. Clothes hanging funny from the weight of the moisture.

Darger had taken off her jacket and given it to the kid since she didn't have one. It quickly became apparent that it was a pointless endeavor. The fabric slowly wicked up rainwater. The jacket draped Sadie in fabric, so big on her that it reached down to her knees.

Darger's own shirt clung to her shoulders. Draped funny against her lower back. Felt like a wet rag wagging there, a soggy flap brushing at her skin.

Still, they walked along the line where the woods and swamp meshed. Feet slapping and sucking on the sloppy stuff. Sometimes the water crept past the tree line, ankle-deep bog trailing right up into the forest. The image somehow made Darger think of a high tide climbing higher on the beach. In those spots they had to retreat deeper into the woods, arc around the muck and maneuver through the foliage again.

For the most part, however, they could walk in the clearing just next to the woods. Faster going than most of their journey. The problem was the fact that they were walking parallel to the mountain instead of toward it. That and the rain slowly waterlogging the both of them.

The wind blew cold. Icy air hurling itself at them. Sent fresh chills rippling through Darger every time it picked up.

Even with the coat on, Sadie shivered. Teeth chattering.

"Are we almost there?" the girl asked, her voice fluttery and small.

"Just a little farther," Darger said and then gazed up into the dark clouds and scowled. They needed to get out of this shit.

They held hands now. The kid's clammy fingers clenched in Darger's hand. It felt, at times, like she was yanking the girl along, but if that was what it took…

Darkness encroached. Fell on them slow and steady. Not the darkness of night yet. Just the storm moving in. Squatting its black clouds over them, blotting out the daylight more and more as it did.

They still curled their way around the swamp. Moving, chewing up ground, and seemingly not making any real progress, the mountain staying out of reach.

Now that the rain had saturated them pretty good, Darger thought about just charging through the wetlands to get to the mountain ASAP. Both of them picking up their feet and running like that, high-stepping through the slop, splashing swamp water every which way.

She wondered how long it would take, knowing the distance was probably deceptive and the terrain would slow them. Twenty minutes, maybe? Thirty?

They'd come out of it scummed up to their necks, but it might be worth it.

She eyeballed it again. Tried to find some reference point to help her scale the distance. Mind working at all the angles of this possible route.

But then she pictured the snake she'd seen back in the woods, a fat green and black tube slithering into the thicket, and that stopped her figuring all at once.

She had no idea what other kinds of snakes were native to the area — which ones, if any, were venomous — and she didn't want to find out. Better to stay patient. Take the slow and steady route.

Low risk. Low reward.

The darkness descended fully now. Crept toward shades of night around them even though sunset was a ways off yet. The storm seemed to fall down out of the sky all at once, pulling down its black veil as it did.

Lightning flashed somewhere up on the mountain. Big and bright and close.

And then the thunder rumbled. Deep and loud. Pealing and shuddering. Echoing off the rock wall of the canyon before them.

Darger kept her head down and plunged forward.

CHAPTER 95

Shepard creeps into a copse of spruces, Kira ducking behind him. Both of them pressing their faces straight into the thicket.

The boughs smear over them. Firm, short needles. Tightly cropped. Wet and prickly like a bunch of toilet brushes.

Their feet scrape over a bed of pine needles the color of rust. Dried-out things now being rehydrated by the rain. Reminds him of ramen noodles somehow — those crispy crinkles slowly turning flexible in the hot water.

They press deeper into the pines. Leave black gouges in the ruddy carpet wherever the toes of their shoes touch. Deep black soil exposed in slashes.

And then they stop. Wait.

Shepard listens. Turns his head back and forth. Aiming his ears in all directions.

Nothing there.

They're alone.

He feels some of the tension release from his neck, his back, his chest, though he knows they're hardly any better off now.

So maybe they're clear of an imminent crossbow bolt to the throat or sniper bullet to the head. But they're wet with the cold moving in. Not good.

He takes one more easy breath, and then he pushes himself onward again. Makes sure Kira is there, just behind him.

He takes three steps forward, and it's there. At his feet… something.

What the hell is it?

A wad of withered plants covers a bulge on the ground.

Green tendrils shrouding the bulk, though its shape is obvious enough, especially now that the plants have slowly dried from their original lush green to sinewy husks. Dry and brown and fibrous and ropey.

Shepard stares at it for more than a few seconds. Thinking.

Something hidden here? Deep in the guts of this cluster of pine trees?

And it's been here for a while. At least from the way the plants look.

He kneels. Starts picking the plants off the top, one by one. Careful, like the humped spot might explode if he's too hasty, if he pulls the wrong wire.

The axe handle comes clear first. Curved wood.

He plucks a few more weeds out of the way. Tosses the strands to the side.

The head of the axe comes into view. A little rust visible there, the corrosion almost looking like ruddy fungus growing on the metal.

A weapons cache?

It's his.

It has to be.

Who else?

He keeps digging. There's more here.

A plastic bag lies beneath the axe. He brushes clods of black earth away from the glossy sheet. Finds it to be a Ziploc freezer bag, though he can't tell what it holds.

His fingertips pinch the smooth sleeve. He pries the bag out of the hole. Holds it up.

The plastic dangles from the end of his arm. Held up to about eye height. The weight of its payload pulling the bag taut.

There's a handgun inside.

CHAPTER 96

Jerry tears into the dark forest, and Rex follows.

Rain drizzles off the branches, a steady patter of white noise all around them.

Rex barrels through the damp woods. Not really affected by the rain at first. Focused on following his dog, seeing where this long trail leads.

The precipitation builds to a steady downpour so methodically that Rex doesn't notice until it's been that way for a while. The water pelts the dome of his ball cap. Drizzles off the cupped brim. Seeps into his clothes.

The cold feels kind of good for now. Bracing yet refreshing against his body heat.

The radio had gone distorted and dim some time ago. Now it remains silent. Probably out of range. It was inevitable out in these rolling hills, thick with trees.

He realizes he doesn't hear any other bear bells anymore, either. Just Jerry's. Part of him is pleased by that fact, proud that Jer has separated himself from the pack yet again.

Another part of him finds the toll of the lone bell eerie. Stark in the quiet. Something forlorn in the tone as it rings out over the undergrowth.

No more crunch of distant footsteps. No more soft babble of voices.

Just that singular bell, tinkling on Jerry's neck somewhere in the tangle of foliage. It makes a chill grip Rex's belly.

Cold and lonely in a dark, dark wood.

He would feel better, less lonesome, he thinks, if he could

just see the damn dog a little more often. Get a quick peek of the beast doing his thing, a glimpse through the weeds.

But Jerry has pulled away from him, energized and picking up speed while the handler gradually loses stamina. The tinkle of the bell is the only thing giving Rex faith that he's not so far behind.

The search pulls his mind into that trance again. Something like a runner's high overtaking his being, clearing his mind of thoughts.

He watches the ground. Sees the twisted green shoots of the creeper blur past, leaves jutting up from the mess.

He is emptied. Blank. And yet somehow present.

Just watching the forest floor smear past.

Time passes again. Seems to speed up. The sky darkening steadily.

The first crack of thunder shakes him out of the trance some. The ache of exertion resurfaces in his thighs and lungs, that fevered heat retaking his face.

He wonders how much longer the search will go on. Knows it could be hours yet. He needs to pace himself better.

Something crunches ahead. A loud sound. Heavy.

All Rex can picture is someone dropping an anvil or a manhole cover. Some heavy slab of metal crushing sticks and leaves.

A dog yelps. A single wounded sound.

And the bell's chime cuts out all at once. Silence.

Jerry.

Rex sprints toward the noise. All pain forgotten in an instant.

He pushes through a thick tangle of saplings. Bony things thumping at his chest as he fights through them.

He hits a clearing. Stops himself dead all at once.

Stares down at…

It takes him a second to process what he's seeing.

The ground opens before his feet.

A gaping pit. Six or eight feet deep.

A trap.

But it isn't empty.

Spikes rise from the earthen floor. Curved branches sharpened to points. A mouth full of needle-like teeth.

A German shepherd rests there in the middle of the death pit. Spiky bits protruding from the animal. Skewered.

And there's a man next to the dog. Wooden stakes punching through his chest, through his face turned to the side.

Rex feels his tongue click against the roof of his mouth. A cavernous feeling overtaking his body, icy pinpricks roiling from the middle out.

Christ.

Jesus.

He shuffles back from the horror. Tongue clacking against his palate again. Meaningless noise in his mouth.

But part of him knows. Awful as it is, part of him knows.

His voice comes out raspy. Shaky. Loud.

"Jerry! Come."

The bell jingles once more in the distance. His dog comes bounding. Slows as it draws near. Wearing that smile again, tongue lolling out of his mouth like a floppy piece of lunch meat.

Rex kneels. Wobbles. Feels like his legs are frozen cords of beef somehow holding him up.

He pets the dog. Strokes the fine fur atop the skull. Reattaches the leash to his collar. Fingers so numb he accomplishes it out of habit more than by feel.

"You're a good boy. Aren't you?"

But the dog gets that focused look again. Eyes beaming into his.

He's found something.

"Show me," Rex says, just above a whisper.

The dog pulls him along. Walks a line roughly parallel to the trap where the dog and handler have died.

And Rex sees it just a few feet before they arrive.

Another pit.

Another trap.

Another dog and master dead. Facedown in the spikes. Pinned in place.

Jerry must have come upon this one first. Wanted me to find him there.

But no. The dog keeps pulling. Keeps yanking. Insistent.

Rex staggers on. Not wanting to let the dog get too far ahead. Not wanting to fall into another one of the traps.

And still somehow unable to turn back. Like he has to see what Jerry wants him to see before he gets out of here.

They only go another thirty yards into the brush.

The dog stops. Sits. Smiling again. He's done his job.

But Rex doesn't see it. He tells the dog to stay. Stumbles into the ferns.

Nearly trips over the wounded man there.

The dog handler crawls through the weeds. Semi-upright on his side. Holes punched through him where the skewers must have gotten him. Bits of his guts visible like thick worms bulging out of his punctured middle.

Those cold prickles ripple over Rex's skin again. A ghostly chill. Heart pounding in his ears. Breath heavy in his throat.

Holy shit.

He must have pried himself off the stakes. Crawled out of the pit.

Somehow. Someway.

How the hell is this guy still breathing?

Before Rex can speak, the man tilts his head up. Locks eyes with Rex.

Fierce eye contact. Intense. Gives Rex another chill.

"He got 'im," he whispers, shiny blood visible on his teeth.

"What?" Rex says.

"The Butcher. He got my dog. Got my boy. Kilt 'im dead."

CHAPTER 97

The storm raged. Fierce winds and rain clubbing the trees, drumming at the land. Thunder crashing and echoing off the cliff face before them.

The day had gone dark as night around Darger and Sadie. Left them cold and wet. Shivering as they pressed deeper into the gloom.

The swamp smell intensified as the water drizzled down. Something pungent to it.

Darger finally rounded the stretch of swamp and staggered across the final straightaway to the mountain. Craned her neck to see the spiky silhouette of the peak against the black clouds. She felt like a tiny speck up against a mass of rock some three thousand feet high.

The land went craggy then. Jagged boulders facing off everywhere around them, great chunks that had cleaved away from the bluff and slid down the near-vertical wall.

The grade tilted underfoot, gently sloping upward now. The shadows were darker here near the mountain, the black of the storm combining with the natural gloom of the stark rock wall to block out the sun. It rendered everything in grayscale. Dreary.

When they reached the place where the land rose sharply upward, they turned and walked along the wall. The wind and rain seemed to die back some, and Darger realized the mountain itself was blocking the full brunt of the storm.

She took her phone out. Turned the flashlight on. A circular shaft of glow slicing through the murk. She swept it out in front of her.

The cliff glistened. Runnels of water drained down the chiseled face, cascading over dips and jutting bits of stone.

The rivulets glittered when the light touched them. Shimmered in a million bright shards, the dancing glow somehow looking as smooth as glass despite the many refractions.

Where is it?

She turned the light off quickly. Wanted to save the battery. Dark as it was now, they would be out here at night. All night, probably. A prospect that made her feel colder all at once.

They walked on. Darger swept her light overhead every few yards, searching.

Shaky arm lifting again now. Hand flexing. Thumbing the button.

Watched the shadows shrink as the light neared them and grow again as it moved away.

Still nothing.

The light clicked off.

After another ten feet or so, Darger tried it again.

The shaft of light climbed the wall. Brushed to the left and then the right.

Darger could see them now. Her heart rose. Hovered higher in her chest.

Indentations pitting the stone. Blemishing the cliff face like acne scars. Holes. Dark openings that trailed into the wall and out of sight.

But they were small. Most not much bigger than a dinner plate, if that. A couple might be barely big enough to squeeze into, perhaps, but she wasn't wriggling into a coffin-sized opening. Nope. No way.

They were higher than she'd like, too. Some fifty feet off the ground. She didn't think it was wise to climb that high, especially with the wet and dark working against them.

No. They would find something big enough and low enough for both of them to enter comfortably. Or they would huddle among the rocks all night and try not to freeze to death. At least here they were largely out of the wind.

She clicked off the light again. Let her eyes soak in the gloom a while. Pitch black nothing streamed into her pupils. Blind and blinking.

She shuffled onward. Sadie just behind her.

Darger let the fingers of her left hand graze along the wall as she took careful step after careful step. Kicking her foot forward before stepping down, trying to make sure she didn't trip on anything.

She made herself wait longer before she tried the light again. They walked a little farther. Needed to be patient now.

The wind changed angles. An icy gale rushing into the canyon. Moaning against the angular walls.

Its frigid touch ripped right through Darger's wet shirt. Saturated her skin. Made the bones in her arms and legs ache, the chill penetrating right through the meat and sinew.

Cold.

Wet.

Darger and Sadie stood still for a moment. Wind battering both of their faces. Freezing. Shivering against each other.

Darger wanted only to flee. To run and hide. To get out of this cold. Overwhelmed.

But she held there and endured it. Teeth chattering. Tried to tuck Sadie into her side, though she doubted it helped with both of them being so damn wet.

The wind adjusted angles again. Died around them all at once. Felt somehow like a sodden blanket being peeled away from her body, Darger thought, a heaviness fleeing along with the chill.

They pushed forward again. Feet clopping over wet stone.

Darger flicked her light up the wall again. Swept it up high and didn't see much. Brought it lower. Lower.

Gasped. Muscles jarring and jerking, shaking the light around.

It was there. Only about fifteen or twenty feet up. A hollow place in the stony barrier, a hole where the shadows swallowed up the glow of the beam, showed only black nothing even as the light speared it directly.

The mouth of a cave.

CHAPTER 98

The Butcher sprawls on his belly at the edge of the bluff. Camo ski mask shrouding his face. Rifle snugged into the hollow of his shoulder.

Waiting.

He watches the woods. Eyes endlessly scanning the terrain at the bottom of the ridge. Shallow breaths rolling in and out of his lips like waves on a placid sea.

The forest holds still. Motionless. Eerie.

It's raining somewhere in the distance. Storming pretty good based on the thunder he hears and the dark he can see off to the west, but for now it's still dry along his little ridge. He's glad for it.

Sweat leaks from his head and slowly seeps into the mask. Growing soggy against the dome of his skull.

His tongue tastes like metal. Copper, maybe. He's not sure.

The noise arrives all at once.

A cacophony of footsteps crunching through the foliage. Stabbing at the undergrowth with snaps and pops. Echoing in the open space.

He licks his lips. Adjusts the rifle against his shoulder.

The first dark figure appears between the trees. An officer outfitted in black tactical gear. Bulky Kevlar. Cargo pants. Assault rifle.

The officer slows. Body drawing a little upright. He approaches one of the bonfires, head swiveling everywhere.

Hold now. Let them walk into the trap.

The metal taste in his mouth intensifies. Some additional

mineral note in the flavor now. Like he's sucking on a buckwheat penny covered in that green scum.

More black-clad cops drift into view. Popping up one by one. Gliding toward the ridge. Quick and quiet. Like a bunch of spiders creeping out of the woods.

He stares through the scope. Sees the blown-up version of the first officer there.

Fleshy face. Tan. Chin cordoned off with a goatee shaved into thin lines. Reminds him of pubic hair.

He licks his lips again. Feels a silent giggle whisper over his teeth, over his lips.

Wait.

Wait.

Just a little longer.

Get more of them in the open.

The fire builds in his skull. Surges there until it stings in his eyes, in his teeth.

He fights the urge for as long as he can.

Then he squeezes the trigger.

That fleshy face in the scope jerks forward in a sneeze motion. The back of the head bursts. A dropped watermelon.

The cop plants facedown in the dead leaves and holds still.

He wheels to another head. Racks the bolt. Squeezes again.

Another skull pops in the scope. Bullet entering just above and behind the ear. Brain vented through the eye socket and part of the cheekbone on the opposite side.

He pivots again. Racks the bolt again.

The soldier in the scope ducks down. Rolls behind a thick tree trunk.

He waits. Lets another of those shallow breaths roll out. Holds it.

Empty.

Alert.

Alive.

The scope stays centered on the tree. But nothing moves there.

Seconds tick past. Seem to take days.

Finally the officer behind the tree moves. Shoulder appearing beyond the edge of the trunk first.

He pokes his head out. Peers around.

The Butcher fires.

Gets him in the jaw. Shatters the crook of bone beneath the left ear.

Not a clean kill.

Blood spurts from the gaping place where the bone had been. The remaining molars on the top palate exposed, set now in tattered flaps of cheek.

The cop grips a gloved hand at the broken place. Pats at it dumbly. Then he shuffles back in a crab walk.

The Butcher lines up another kill shot. But he holds off.

Fuck it.

Fuck him.

Let him bleed out.

Another officer rushes into the open to try to help his fallen comrade.

He trains the shot along with the helper's movement.

Squeezes.

Drops him in a heap a few feet shy of the bleeder. Limp body flopping into the ferns.

Yeah.

Yeah.

You know what that means, motherfucker?

It means: mine.

Mine.

He pivots the gun across the open land. Looks for any movement. Ready to fire again.

And again.

And again.

All of this. All that you see.

Mine.

CHAPTER 99

Darger reached up. Brushed the tips of her fingers along moist rock. Skimming. Feeling around the crag, hand bobbing for a while like a hound's nose picking out a scent. Patient.

Her fingernail caught on it first. A lip jutting out of the bluff. She tested it. Sturdy. This would work.

She gripped the mini-ledge. Pulled herself up enough to swing her other arm up.

Her legs dangled in the open a moment as she ascended. She kicked out to her right. Grazed her foot along the wall. Found a toehold and dug in.

Then she held still. Hugged the cliff. Leaned her weight against the cold rock and breathed.

The wall was slightly inclined here. Not completely vertical. It let her use gravity just a little to her advantage.

The rain was still coming down, but the sky had brightened a touch. Going from almost black to a dark gray, like the wispy edge of a charcoal smear. Darger was thankful for that.

She scaled up another few feet. Monkeying her way to the next handhold, the next crack or protrusion in the stone that she could grip. Working her way up at an angle.

A jutting vein of rock tilted up alongside her, running along a crevice. Perfect for digging in fingers and toes. She didn't think she'd have any real problem getting up to the cave mouth from here, even if it took her some time and left her exhausted.

She let herself look down. Eyes flicking to the little girl.

Sadie smiled up at her, though she was still shivering. Darger's wet jacket drooped off of her like the saggy sides of a basset hound's mouth.

Shit.

Darger had done a bit of climbing before. Years ago, back when she was a teenager. Growing up in the Rockies, it was somewhat of a rite of passage. So she wasn't worried about making the climb herself. The problem, of course, would be getting the girl up the wall. Darger had been too nervous to even let herself think about it until now.

Could she take off her clothes once she reached the cave? Tie them together to make a rope? Like all those movies where people made a sheet rope to sneak out of a window?

Probably not. She doubted her sodden shirt could withstand the weight.

The girl would have to climb. It was the only way.

Darger's mouth felt bone-dry all of a sudden. She swallowed.

"You think you can climb?" she asked, trying to keep her voice neutral.

She half expected the girl to be too scared to even try. It'd be understandable. A little kid like that. Shot at. Separated from her grandparents, from her sister. In the wet and the relative dark. A murderer prowling somewhere out here even now.

Instead, Sadie bobbed her head. Smiled harder.

The kid took a running start and vaulted herself up the wall. Lurched upward. Feet and fingers both finding holds easily.

She rushed right up the cliff in fast motion. Stopping only because Darger was in her way.

The agent shook her head.

Of course the kid can climb like a damn spider monkey.

"OK, but let me go up first. Just in case…"

She turned and looked up at the cave mouth again, thunder rumbling in the distance as she did.

And now the nerves attacked from a different angle.

She imagined actually reaching the cave. Poking her head up over the threshold. Pistoning her legs to hurl herself into the dark opening.

What if there was something in there?

She remembered sticking her head in the bear den. The soil smell intertwining with that of rotten meat. The dirt walls carved out by bear claws. The human foot rotting inside the earthen chamber.

The memory already seemed distant. Impossible that it'd been only yesterday. Still, it brought a sour taste creeping up her throat to perch at the back of her tongue.

She looked down between her feet. She knew bears were expert climbers when it came to trees, but what about sheer rock walls?

For all she knew, a bear could walk right up this wall and den out in the cave.

She let her eyes crawl upward, lingering on the clefts and crags she'd used on the way up. She tried to picture a big black ball of fur coming up the bluff. If a bear really wanted to do it, it probably could.

Hell, the kid had practically sprinted up the rock face. If a nine-year-old could do it, a bear could do it. Right?

Only one way to find out.

She got back to it. Dug her fingers and toes into that fissure in the stone. Worked her way up on the diagonal, Sadie just behind her.

The climb went slower toward the top, that crack going thinner and shallower, but it wasn't too bad. She just had to take more care with securing her grip before she let it hold her weight.

Finally she was there. The cave mouth just above her,

within reach.

She wiped the sweat from her brow. Took a deep breath.

Her hands patted at the lip forming the bottom of the cave. She clutched that stone, fingers curled like claws. Pulled herself up and wormed her top half into the opening.

She bent at the waist, her legs dangling over the breach. Then she squirmed forward, wriggled until her hips and thighs were over the line. She laid there a second. Cold stone frigid against her wet form, already leaching body heat out of her.

She sat up in the dark. Heart thudding.

The maw of rock opened wide. The tunnel tall enough for her to stand up in if she stooped. The dim light outside revealed only a couple of feet of the cavern. From there, it trailed off into the dark.

She crawled back to the cliff, leaned over the edge. Found Sadie waiting there, attached to the wall.

"You OK staying put for a minute?"

Sadie bobbed her head.

"Yep."

"Good. Let me take a quick look before you come up."

She dug out her phone. Shined her light into the dark. Plunging it down into the guts of the cave.

The shadows seemed to swallow the shine, smother it in gloom so she could still only see a few feet ahead.

She took a deep breath. Picked herself up. Walked into the tunnel.

The beam swept over dry rock. Craggy. Almost powdery-looking compared to the glossy wet stone outside.

She took a few steps into the shaft. Rounded a slight corner. She could feel how the rock wall had kept hold of some of the heat from earlier just inside the cave, but that warmth gave way to a deep cool as she took another few steps. Musty-smelling.

Almost dank like a basement.

Some part of her sensed the tunnel cinching tighter around her, the darkness growing deeper as the curve closed her away from the cave mouth. She looked back over her shoulder and swallowed again.

Then she turned back. Pressed deeper. Swung her beam of light around like a cutlass.

Shear wall stared back about ten feet ahead. The bluntness surprising her.

The cave ended there. Just a few feet deep overall. More of a curving chamber than a true cave.

She turned around and around. Brushed the light over the cave floor one more time. Just to be sure.

It was empty.

This would work.

CHAPTER 100

The rain pours. The sky darkens.

Rhodes meanders in the false night. The woods all look the same to her, especially in the dark. Trees. And trees. And more trees. Scrubby stuff strewn across the ground between them, texture there in the shadows more than anything of substance, like sprigs of parsley garnishing a steak house plate.

The helicopter was a sign. A rescue team is out here somewhere. She just has to find their base camp.

It's a prospect that sounds easy enough, but she could be going the wrong way entirely. Or maybe she has already walked right past it, like a rocket ship a few degrees off, zipping past the moon and darting out into the vast nothing of space.

She trudges on. Crests a hill. Tries to force her eyes to recognize some landmark, some touchstone, anything to orient herself.

But the woods hold onto their secrets too tightly. An endless repeat of the same few images. Indecipherable forest choking the land.

She starts down the hill. Little shivers creep up her back. Gather strength in her shoulders.

Unforgiving. That's what these woods are.

Harsh and unforgiving.

Not mean. Not spiteful. Not vindictive or nefarious.

Indifferent. Deeply, profoundly indifferent. Like a sociopath.

Nature doesn't feel sorry for her or anyone. Doesn't invest in her story. Doesn't consider the idea of fairness. It only deals in what is.

Rhodes prods at the pack of cigarettes in her inside jacket pocket. Still dry for now, or so she thinks.

She aches to smoke another one, but she dare not fish them out here in the rain and chance losing the whole pack to the wet. It feels too good to have them, to possess them. She won't risk it.

Her boots skid in the mud. She waves her arms to keep her balance. Rights herself. Keeps going.

She wonders if she'll just hold onto the cigarettes until her jacket soaks through. Lose them that way. Wait until it's too late.

Trying to hold onto something so hard she guarantees it will be squandered.

Too scared to ever spend what she has. Too scared to do anything.

And maybe, she thinks, there's some kind of lesson in that.

Something grunts to her left. A grumble coming out with a breath.

Not human.

And Rhodes finds herself ducked into the weeds. Surprised again. Not choosing the action. Just there, neck-deep in the plants.

She listens. Trains her ears past the sweeping drizzle that patters in all directions.

All holds quiet for several seconds. And then it's there again.

A breath and a rumble. Like a contented dog sound but bigger, deeper.

And then there's a wet sound. Different from the rain. Like lips smacking.

Slowly she turns herself. Squares her shoulders toward

where the sound is coming from.

She waits. Stares into the wall of weeds shrouding her view of… whatever it is.

She sees nothing in the gaps between the plants. Neither shape nor color nor movement.

Finally she straightens her legs in slow motion. Watches that veil of plants slide out of the way as she stands.

Black fur slouches in the distance. Leans over something on the ground.

The bear grunts again. Slurps and chaws and guzzles. Dips its head back toward that shape on the ground.

Wishnowsky lies there. Legs akimbo. Bear snout deep in his abdominal cavity.

The big animal tilts its head back all at once. Sniffs twice. Turns its head.

It smells me.

And Rhodes panics. Bolts into the woods. Running. Weaving. Hurtling. Finds that she's drawn her gun, realizing only after it's there in her pumping arm.

Knows that this is not what you're supposed to do. Run.

If you act like prey, the bears will treat you like prey.

Too late now.

She keeps running. Runs until her heart slams. Runs until her side pangs. Runs until her vision goes smeared along the edges like Crisco on a glass bowl. Keeps running.

Can only picture the hulking animal galloping somewhere behind her. Like a small car crushing through the foliage, blazing a wide trail.

Finally she can run no longer. Falls down onto her hands and knees. Gulps for breaths that somehow don't satisfy.

Face hot. Sweat shellacking her skin, mingling with the rain.

She rolls onto her back. Points the gun at the gap in the plants behind her, the way she came.

Waits for the bear to come ripping through. Glock shaking there. Ready to at least slow the animal down, though she doubts it will stop the thing.

But there's nothing there. No bear. No chase.

Still, she breathes. Gasping. Watches the path for a long time.

As soon as she gets her breath back, she reaches into her coat, pulls out a cigarette, and lights it.

CHAPTER 101

Darger leaned her back against the cave wall, the damp sheet of skin pressing into the cool rock, shoulder blades twitching as she settled in. She'd stripped down to her underwear, shed her wet clothes and laid them out on the smooth stone floor.

She took a big breath. It felt good to get the heavy wetness off her. To get off her feet and just sit for a minute. Every other worry could wait for later.

The cave kept them out of the rain, out of the wind. But they were still soaked like wet dogs. She'd try to do something about that soon, but for now, she relished the feeling of looseness in her lower back, the strain of all that walking finally giving way, a strange lightness radiating there instead.

Rest. Relaxation. She'd forgotten, somehow, how good they can feel when you really need them.

Sadie squatted on the other side of the cave. She, too, had gotten her wet shirt and jeans off, but she still had the soggy jacket draped over her frail form. She nibbled at another Pop-Tart — no frosting this time, though she wasn't complaining.

Darger ate the rest of her protein bar. Let her head loll against the craggy wall as she chewed.

The cardboard taste had grown on her somehow — richer flavors blooming in the last of the chocolate-covered composite. It almost had the depth of particleboard or even cork now. Woody, something oat-like to it, and a little sweet.

Not bad.

Maybe she was just really hungry, her sense of taste heightened by the lack of calories and the high-speed burn of their hike and climb. She didn't know. Or care much, for that matter.

Her incisors sank into the bar again. Tore away a sticky chunk and chewed.

A pile of sticks sat next to her. They'd gathered the wood before they'd settled in. Making a few trips up and down the wall. Bundling small bits of firewood in Darger's jacket and toting the loads up the crag.

They'd lucked into some dry pine needles deep under a big spruce, the boughs sheltering the ground in a great circle. Each of them had loaded every pocket with the stuff on every trip. A little got damp from their clothes, but Darger thought they had enough kindling that they could get a fire going anyway. The cave itself was as dry as that femur they found sticking out of the bear den, which would help.

On the last trip, she'd schlepped a pretty good sized branch up the wall — about as thick as a fire hydrant on the fat end. She'd handed it up to Sadie, who'd managed to pin it there in the cave mouth until Darger could get up to help.

Then the two of them had hoisted it up, sat on the lip of the cave mouth, and peeled the wet bark off the thing. Fingers prying and scrabbling and pinching and tearing until they got down to bare wood.

She pulled her back away from the wall. Felt how her wet skin had adhered itself there, sticking a little as she moved away.

Then she went to work getting the fire going. No more waiting. Better to just go for it.

She gathered a bunch of small sticks and made a tepee out of them, surrounding a wadded-up handful of the crispy pine needles.

Then she went to Sadie. Dug into the breast pocket of her

jacket. Found the smooth plastic tube there.

Darger had carried a BIC lighter in her coat pocket since she was a high school kid. Back then, it seemed like she was constantly handing the thing out to smokers in need. Made her feel a touch rebellious even if she hadn't actually smoked herself. These days, years went by without her using it or even thinking of it, but the old habit persisted nevertheless. The things were just so damn useful.

She shuffled back to her little cone of firewood toward the back of the cave. Knelt next to it. The skin of her legs shocked to be touching the chillier stone here.

Then she flicked the lighter to life. Brought the wavering flame down to the bundle of kindling.

The fire consumed a couple of the pine needles right away. Dispatched them as bright orange lines that immediately faded to ash.

The kindling crackled a couple of times. Shrill sounds. Sharp.

Then the fire whispered. Gave off a sound as slight as a breath.

Sparks jumped. An arc of pine needles turned black, a dark circle puddling outward from the point where the lighter had touched down.

The first flame among the kindling started small. One bright spot that grew. Blossomed upward and outward.

Darger beamed. Felt the tiny blast of heat on her cheeks, so small it might have been her imagination.

The fire licked at the sticks. Fluttered.

She added some more pine needles. Fed the fire slowly, carefully.

The flame built. Started eating at the sticks, too, slowly but surely.

The heat roiling off left no doubt now. This wasn't her imagination.

She sat back. Watched the fire take off on its own. Surging upward and outward.

And some glorious feeling washed over her at last. A mix of pride and relief. Jitters thrumming through her belly when she realized they'd found shelter and warmth for the night, that they'd really done it.

Sadie was there at her side all at once. Smiling. Still nibbling at that Pop-Tart.

Darger let her eyes dance over the flames. Deeply pleased to stare into the thrashing orange. Calmed to her core. She'd heard this feeling went back to the time of cavemen, that the peace humans get from staring into a fire is primordial, bred into us for thousands of years.

She tossed another few twigs into the blaze. Watched the brightness surround the fresh black silhouettes.

"Can I put the big stick on now?" Sadie asked.

"Not yet," Darger said. "We have to be patient. Let it grow."

Sadie nodded, her mouth forming an *O* shape.

Darger continued staring into the flames and then looked back down the tunnel. Saw the curving rock blocking out the cave mouth from her vantage point.

She didn't think a small fire would be visible from outside the cave, not with the rocks blocking the way. But they wouldn't let it burn deep into the night, in any case. They didn't have enough wood for that, and she didn't see herself going back out into the wet for more.

Maybe she'd take one more trip down once the real dark of night hit. Try to see how visible it was from afar. Just in case.

She imagined what it might look like from outside. A shimmering spot in the mountainside — not like the glow of a lit window so much as a stray flicker now and then, like light catching on the glass of a watch at just the right angle and refracting.

Maybe. Or maybe it'd be nothing at all.

That was another worry for later, though.

For now, they would get dry. Rig up some way of draping their clothes over the coals. Propping the coat up on sticks would be a good start, if she could figure out a way to keep it upright — that would probably take the longest to dry.

She smiled again. Another wave of excitement shuddering through her. If they were dry, the night wouldn't be so bad.

She held her hands up to the flames. Felt the heat seep into her skin, the wetness slowly receding.

CHAPTER 102

Shadows lurch everywhere. Silhouettes jerking among the trees, among the brush. The dark falling fast.

Officer Dale Simmons steps carefully. AR-15 held across his chest. Eyes scanning everywhere.

He falls back as he was ordered to. Too dark, they said. Too dangerous with the lightning and the wind and — oh yeah, the goddamn murdering bastard sniping and drawing the men into booby traps.

He walks under a dead tree. A spindly thing, maybe just thick enough to be a widow-maker should the wind catch it just right. Runnels of water drain down from the bare lower branches. Thick streams of cold pelting his head, sluicing down his face and the back of his neck.

He keeps moving. What the fuck difference did it make now? A man can only get so wet. After that, it's only more of the same, isn't it?

The plan, he suspects, is to rest and regroup. Head out again in the morning. He's heard the dogs work best in the early morning, something about downdrafts of wind or something.

If there are any dogs left, that is.

He winces at the thought. From what he'd picked up on the radio, the search and rescue effort had largely gone the way of a doggie bloodbath. Pit traps lined with sharpened sticks. There was something deeply wrong about it. Upsetting on another level.

Men had died today, too, of course. Cut down by the

coward's rifle fire or falling down in the traps alongside the dogs.

But the human loss is almost too big for Simmons to wrap his head around. A man's death is ultimately too complex to fathom. He's somehow a little numb to that part of today's toll.

The dogs, though? They are simple creatures. Innocent. Easy to understand and easier to like. And something about them dying out here for nothing… He shakes his head and spits on the ground. It rips his guts out just to think about it.

He turns sideways and shimmies between some bushes. Gets wet leaves smeared all up and down his person.

Or did I smear my wet self on the leaves? To be wet or to do the wetting. That is the question.

Upon stepping out of the shrubbery, he feels exposed. His paranoia renewed.

Because the Butcher is still out there. Probably close.

He'd change tactics now that we're falling back, wouldn't he? Stalk up behind us. Make that turn from the hunted to the hunter.

He stops. Points the rifle in front of himself. Sweeps it all the way around in a full circle.

Nothing there.

Good.

He plods on, slow and steady. Choosing quiet over speed.

He has to stay sharp. Vigilant. He's almost out of here now, and he's sure as shit not getting taken out at the last minute.

He climbs a hill. Feet swishing through mud. Thinks he's close to the road now. Another few hundred yards or so.

From there, it's maybe ten minutes until he's back at the trucks. Back to dry and warmth and food.

Ten stupid minutes. Nothing. But it'll feel like forever, he knows that.

He suspects he'll be sleeping out here tonight — there had already been talk earlier about commandeering the bunkhouses at the lumber camp — but that's OK. Just give him a sandwich and some coffee and point him in the direction of a cot.

He steps out onto the road, almost surprised to just land on it like that. No warning. No sense that it was imminent beyond that vague notion back on the muddy hill.

He shakes his head again. Puffs something like a laugh out of his nostrils.

Then he picks up into a jog. Might be able to cut those ten minutes down to five, if he pushes it.

Something cracks out in the woods. The splintery sound of sticks breaking, leaves crunching.

Heavy footsteps.

Coming from behind him.

His heart leaps up like it's trying to flee through his mouth.

He staggers back. Squats on the other side of the road.

The gun lifts before him. Trembles even as he sets the stock against his shoulder.

I knew it.

I knew it.

The hunter becomes the hunted.

The hunter becomes the hunted.

He tracks the sound. Lets instincts point the gun that way. Just a little to his right.

Waits.

This can't be happening.

Not to me.

Other people die. They do it all the time. Every day in every horrible way. Cancer. Heart attack. Car crash.

But not me.

I don't die.

He tastes acid. Knows the words in his head are nonsense. Trying to reason his way out of danger by presenting him with the evidence that he has never died before, as though this is some magical order of the universe that will hold out indefinitely. But he can't stop the flow of words pounding in his skull.

I knew it.

I knew he was stalking me.

But not me. You won't get me. You know why? 'Cause my goddamn gun says otherwise.

The footsteps draw closer.

He grits his teeth. Floats a finger out in front of the trigger.

The dark figure bursts through the edge of the woods.

Simmons squeezes. Feels the gun buck against him.

Again.

Again.

Pop. Pop. Pop.

The figure falls like a ragdoll. Face perforated. Back of his head coming apart. Limp before he hits the ground.

He sprawls. Lands facedown in the muck. Slides a few inches on his belly and then stops.

Motionless.

Holy shit.

Simmons stands. Legs electric with pins and needles. Face flushed. Throat tight. Hard to breathe.

He takes a step toward the slain villain. Feet slapping down in the muck.

But it's not the Butcher.

It's not him.

It's one of the other men.

Friendly fire.

Mooney. He'd just shot Officer Willard Mooney in the face.

CHAPTER 103

Darger snuggled against the cave floor, the rock still warm though the fire had died some time ago.

She opened her eyes. Stared into the total darkness around her. Reached out a hand and found the small bundle nearby — Sadie was still there, of course, even if the agent couldn't see her in the dark.

Darger closed her eyes. Tried to will herself to stop thinking, to rest, to find her way back to the sleep world.

She'd slept off and on. Sheer exhaustion had pulled her under quickly once she was dry but jagged nerves kept bobbing her back to the surface.

Fractured dreams about the woods had populated her sleep. Images of zooming through the endless forest sprawl. And she kept shaking herself awake, convinced that she'd heard something outside, something close. Listening for a long time before she could calm back down.

At some point, she'd felt around for her clothes in the dark. Dry. She'd gotten dressed. Wanted the extra warmth. The memory of this seemed distant now. Dreamlike in its own way.

She rolled over. Found a warmer bit of rock and curled into the fetal position atop it.

The rain poured outside. Thunder and lightning rumbled and flashed respectively now and again. Probably what had woken her, at least a few of the times.

The stone floor made for an uncomfortable bed. Smooth enough — nothing jabbing into her spine, at least — but it was far too hard. Darger was OK with a firm mattress now and again, but this was ridiculous.

She pictured a pillow top adhered to the cave floor. Those egg carton dips upholstered to the stone.

'Tis but a dream.

She sniffled something like a laugh. Realized that some of that jubilant feeling she'd found upon starting the fire still clung to her, a touch of glee stuck to her brain like a starfish.

While she was fantasizing, she might as well throw in a comforter. Goose down, if you please. A couple of fluffy pillows. And last, but not least, one Owen Baxter, snoring softly and radiating body heat.

She wondered if Owen knew she was missing. He must by now. Loshak would have called him once they'd figured it out. And now he was out there somewhere, worrying. She imagined him pacing the house, phone in hand, waiting for an update.

She considered their positions and decided his was the worse of the two. He was likely warm and dry, sure. But Darger knew where she stood. It was her against the Butcher. Her against the rain and the cold. If she could beat them, she'd live. Owen, on the other hand, had to contend with the vast array of terrible possibilities. The abyss of not knowing.

She drifted. Woke again when the thunder roared, her right shoulder shivering against the crag.

There was something familiar about this pattern of drifting and shuddering awake — the kind of fitful sleep that reminded her of being a frightened kid, scared of the shadows peeking out of the closet.

But they were dry in here. Safe and relatively warm. That was all that mattered.

She reached out a hand again. Touched Sadie's shoulder lightly. Just to be sure.

A sigh seeped out of her. A little of the tension draining

again, loosening muscles up and down her spine.

Something cracked outside. The sound of a branch snapping and echoing not so far off. Audible even over the pounding rain.

Darger opened her eyes. Stared into nothing.

Listened.

Maybe he was coming for them. It was all she could imagine.

She sat up. Looked at the area of blackness where the fire had been. The coals gone dark.

He wouldn't have seen the fire. Maybe an hour or two ago, but not anytime recently.

She moved in a low squat, the cave floor going chilly underfoot as she moved away from the residual warmth. Breath shallow. Heart punching.

She shuffled to the edge of the cave. Faintly aware of the line where the tunnel ended and the night began. Peered out into the dark.

The clouds above looked like cotton stuffing drifting in the dark. Stringy in some places. Balled into tufts in others. All of it scudding past in fast motion.

The lightning flashed, and all those gnarled birch branches and spiky pine trees were suddenly lit in sharp relief. Every detail clear for a fraction of a second and then gone in the dark.

She waited. Tried to see everything in the next lightning flash. Tried to pull her focus back to see the full panorama, take it all in, looking for any anomaly in the big picture.

The dark held for a few heartbeats. Black seas of nothing as far as she could see.

Rain sizzled down the rock wall just beyond the cave mouth. Sprayed her cheeks with the lightest dappling of cold where it dripped and exploded at her feet.

431

Finally, lightning flashed over everything again.

And the leaves thrashed everywhere. Looked like stop-motion animation in the flickering light from the sky.

Light glittered from the top of the wetlands off to her right. The swamp shimmering in the night.

She took in the woods as a whole. All of the trees and all of the spaces in between. Eyes seeing the broad perspective, everything at once in vivid detail, like a hawk looking down on a field and somehow picking out the tiny mouse.

But there was nothing there. No dark figure stalking closer. Just the night and storm. The empty forest. Gone quiet for now.

She sat there for what felt like a long time. Breathing the cool night air. Feeling that spritz of the drizzle on her cheeks. Looking out into the dark, dark woods.

Her breath settled down. Finding that trance-like rhythm of sleepiness. Something circular to the in-and-out pattern. Her body sending the clear message: ready to get back to bed.

When the lightning flashed again, she saw his dark figure at the bottom of the cliff.

CHAPTER 104

Loshak hobbled across the bustling camp. His cane shoving down into the soft earth between the cabins, pushing him along. His knee pulsed out a steady throb — still a dull ache for the moment. When it got back to that spiky pain, sharp enough to make him suck his teeth, he'd take another pill, but not until then.

Light spilled out of the open door of one of the cabins. Left glowing wedges on the ground, panels of illumination surrounded by the dark.

The faint glow allowed him a glimpse of one of the armed guards tasked with patrolling the perimeter of the camp. It made him feel a little better about being out here at night with the Butcher still on the prowl. But only a little.

Darger was out there somewhere. In the dark and the rain.

The chopper had flown over the Tongass Lumber logging site, where all the cabins lay still. No sign of life there.

Not far from the cabin, Whipple had pointed out a golf cart halfway down a ravine, lying on its side. Totaled, but empty. Something about it had looked deliberate. They'd spotted Bohanon's trashed Bronco just a few minutes after that. All four tires slashed, the hood hanging open.

It was clear to Loshak that all of it had been the work of the Butcher. Not a doubt in his mind.

Given that fact, they'd discussed looking for a place to land, but the lightning had started up then, bolts of brightness splitting the sky just a few hundred yards from their position, and they'd had to turn back to safety.

433

Loshak pressed toward the brighter light emanating from a large canvas tent now — that's where the new HQ would be set up.

Bodies funneled in and out of the cabins off to his right. Some of the men and women carried paper plates of food, looked like they were mingling at a family reunion instead of a major law enforcement operation.

Peering inside, he spied more people milling around a bunch of bunks, smoking cigarettes, and drinking coffee from paper cups. In the next cabin, a congregation of officers stood drinking coffee out of another one of those big stainless steel urns, thick brew glugging into paper cups. Everyone seemed tense. Unsmiling faces. Rigid body language.

Loshak supposed that made sense. The operation had been a disaster so far. They'd accomplished little and lost much, and now they'd fallen back until the following morning. They'd wait here all night, in the dark, knowing that the Butcher was out there somewhere.

Each of the little scenes playing out in the cabins cut out as he walked past. Somehow left him feeling like he was missing out.

So many people. Each of them off on their own little adventure in a way.

And me just walking through. Passing it all by. An observer. An outsider. Always an outsider.

He stepped through the threshold into the command tent. The acrid stench of burnt coffee hit his nostrils as soon as he did.

The leaders of the task force huddled around a map pinned up on one of the canvas walls. One of them tapped it with a telescoping stick that Loshak thought looked like a car antenna.

"He set the fires here, here, and here." He tapped the map

each time. Then he dragged the pointer along a diagonal stretch of map. "He drew us to this ridge, which he defended with aplomb. Used the high ground. First sniping a few of our officers with a hunting rifle. Then, when we maybe had the numbers built up to overrun him, he suppressed our approach with machine-gun fire, held us down enough that he could fall back."

"He's a piece of shit, but he's crafty as hell. Gotta give him that."

"Oh, it was smart. This whole deal. Well thought out. And the traps were something else. Those spiked pits. I mean, Jesus Christ. How long has he been out here setting up for this?"

They fell quiet for a second.

Loshak spoke up from the back of the tent.

"No one ever got eyes on him. Is that right?"

All heads turned to face the agent. The one with the pointer nodded.

"The men on the frontlines — the ones who lived, anyway — reported that he seemed to be changing positions throughout the firefight, but no one reported visual contact."

Whipple leaned forward, propping his arms on the table before him.

"Bottom line: this whole thing was rougher than any of us could have imagined, and I don't see it getting easier tomorrow. All of our advantages are pretty well offset by his guerrilla tactics. It's a shitty deal. We'll get him in time, that seems certain enough, but we'll pay a hefty goddamn price to do it."

Whipple sighed and shook his head.

"Anyway, there's not shit we can do about any of it until tomorrow morning, eh?"

Loshak knew Whipple was right. For now, there was

nothing they could do.

CHAPTER 105

Darger's breath caught in her throat. Choking. She cupped a hand over her mouth as though it might help keep her silent. Maybe it would.

She stared down at his dark figure. A wet shadow striding along the cliff wall. Hulking. Something aggressive in his gait.

The lightning cut out. The sky gone black all at once. That one-second vignette of him cleaving off in a cliffhanger.

No explanation. Nothing.

For a second her mind lay blank. Shocked into some oblivion. As hollow as the darkness that lay before her.

She stared hard at nothing. Consciousness drifting.

Then the voices inside arrived all at once. Panicked. Tangling over each other. Asking the same questions over and over.

Did he see me?

Sense me?

Feel me?

Smell me?

Is he coming for us now?

She didn't know.

She didn't know anything save for that he was here. Down there in the dark. Close.

Here and now.

Vast nothingness reached outward from the cave mouth. The ground down there somewhere. The Butcher down there somewhere. All of it veiled in impenetrable black.

After a second's delay, the thunder split the sky and

rumbled through the canyon. The deep boom going tinny as it echoed off the rock walls. Ringing and shrill on the reflection.

Darger shuffled back from the edge of the cave mouth. Careful. Light on her feet.

She snugged her hand around the grip of her Glock. The polymer body still warm from being pressed close to her. Cozy compared to the chilly night air. She felt better touching it.

And still she stared into the black below. Eyes flicking around. Seeing nothing.

She waited.

The dark stretched out. The sky exhaled the last grumble of the thunder, and then it went empty.

The sizzle of the rain rose to fill the void. Babbling and splattering as it tumbled down the rock wall.

She could still see him in her head. The lightning's afterimage glowing pale blue over everything, seared into the screens of her eyelids.

The dark shape lumbering among the bright flash of the bolt. Broad shoulders draping a shadow over the ground. Movement flickering along with the light like a stop-motion animation. Then all of it swallowed up by the dark.

She blinked. Twice. Eyes full up with gloom, open or closed.

She tried to anticipate the next round of lightning. Seemed like it was taking too long.

Was he climbing up the wall even now? Reaching through the shadow. Hand over foot. Navigating the cliff in the murk.

She tightened her grip on the Glock and used her free hand to pat her pocket, making sure the FlexiCuffs were still there.

If he did come up here, she'd be ready for him.

She brought her hand back to her mouth. Breathed just a little through the cage of fingers over her lips. The wind feeling feathery on her hands. Tickling streams of air.

The lightning flashed again.

And he was there.

Not on the wall.

Walking away. Weaving through the boulders on the ground below.

Head down. Shadow drifting along with him like a companion.

He hadn't seen her.

When the lightning gave way to darkness again, she crept forward until she was at the lip of the cave.

She waited again.

Staring into gaping nothingness. Feeling that cold spray on her cheeks — just a misting.

Listening to her heartbeat in her ears. A pattering rhythm like a horse's gallop. Something strong in it now.

The fear giving way. Something else taking its place.

After the next flash of lightning, she lowered herself into the gloom beyond the cave mouth. Draped her legs into the nothingness.

Her hands held tight to the lip of the cave floor. Arms shaking as she eased herself down.

Her legs kicked outward. The tips of her boots scraping over the wall. Finding toeholds and digging in, one and then the other.

She started climbing down the cliff.

CHAPTER 106

Darger looped a leg down. Foot arcing into empty space. Extending. Straining. Flailing.

Then her boot struck something. Skidded just the toe over wet rock, as far as she could reach. Flat. Substantial. Barely touching it but able to sense how vast this plane was, even in the dark.

A breath sniffed out of her. Not a laugh but something close to that.

She inched down the wall a little more. Fingers adjusting. Forearms twitching. She kicked out for that slab again.

Got a better piece of it this time. Able to plant her foot on it. Put her weight into it.

There. That confirmed it.

She found the solid ground beneath her. A concept that almost felt wrong in the dark. Alien. Like something she couldn't quite trust even after just a few minutes of climbing.

She lowered herself that last bit. Both feet touching down. Then both hands. Wet rock smooth against her palms.

She stayed there a second in a crouch as though testing it. The ground held her. She could trust it.

She drew her gun then. Waited and listened.

Heard only the rain. Pattering into the trees in the distance and hissing against the stony places.

The lightning flashed. Flickered a wash of blue light over the land. Exposed her and all around her.

She couldn't see him now. Just boulders dotting the way ahead. Woods way off to her left.

For a second, that empty path before her sent a twinge of fear through her. But she knew that it made sense. It had taken several minutes to get down the cliff.

He'd pulled away from her in that time, slowly but surely. He'd been plodding along, at least when she'd seen him. The dark and wet would slow anyone. She thought she could catch up if she were crafty about it.

During the next flash of lightning, she measured out the route she'd take. Drew a map in her head. A zigzagging way to avoid the boulders and pitted places.

Then she darted into the black. Dared to run full out for now. Trusting the thunder and rain would cover her footsteps.

Her boots scrabbled beneath her. Sliding around in the wet.

But she fought through it. Leaned her head forward. Pumped her legs as hard as she could. The forward momentum won out.

She ducked behind the one snaggly bush that managed to take root in this rocky terrain. Breathed. Waited for the next round of lightning to chart the next leg of her journey.

Then she ran again. Into the dark. Into the thick of it. Thunder so loud it shuddered through her chest, vibrated into the meat of her limbs.

This time she ducked behind a boulder just about the size of a La-Z-Boy. Forced breaths. Wet in her throat.

The lightning flashed.

He was there. His back to her in the distance. Still lumbering along. Slow and steady.

Two more lightning strikes, and I can be close enough to take a high percentage shot. Maybe three. But I need to be quiet now.

She picked her way forward. Not pressing it as hard this time. Ducking behind another boulder.

The lightning flared. Bolts of brightness reaching down

441

from the clouds to touch the earth.

He was closer now. Bigger.

The details of his clothing grew sharp. A camouflage jacket draped over his shoulders, water beading on the surface. Wet pants clinging to his calves. Somehow this only served to make it all the clearer how big he was. Quads like tree trunks. Shoulders about a man and a half wide.

The glow cut out.

She pressed forward once more. Wove around some puddles to avoid the extra splashing sounds. Ducked into the few ferns here. Got low in the bed.

The dark still veiled the both of them for the moment, but she thought she was close enough now.

This is it.

This is it.

She raised her weapon. Pointed it into the dark where he had been. Waited for the lightning to flare and lay him bare.

Waited.

It seemed to take a long time. She chewed the inside of her cheek. Felt how sodden her clothes had gotten in just a few minutes out here. All that hard-earned dryness sacrificed quickly. But it was about to be worth it.

She shivered a little. Shoulders shimmying.

The lightning forked through the sky. Strange tendrils of light shining everywhere.

The rocky landscape glowed. Flickered to life. Juddered funny in the choppy light.

She brought her finger to the trigger. Clenched her jaw.

But he wasn't there.

CHAPTER 107

He stops. Stands. Realizes all at once that there's someone near, someone getting closer.

Doesn't hear it exactly. Not consciously, anyway.

He feels it. A cold touch. A prickle tickling at the hairs on the backs of his arms.

He stands still. Lets the feeling take hold. Rain pelting his neck and shoulders. Cold droplets bursting against his form.

He listens. Hears nothing. But that doesn't mean anything.

He's experienced it before. Felt the presence of an *other* like a wave in the air, its frequency somehow tuned into his skin, beamed into the fine hairs on his body. Hunting. Both animals and humans have triggered the response, helped him close in for the kill.

When you stay out here long enough, your body starts to acclimate to the forest. Muscles. Nerves. Pores. Follicles. They all learn nature's rhythms, its vibrations. Sharpening day by day until bodily intuition takes over entirely. Until no thinking is necessary.

His skin roils harder. All the hairs pricking up. That tickle intensifying.

Yes. It's happening.

He obeys the sensation now. Surrenders to his instincts. They've yet to fail him.

He cuts hard to the left. Turns sideways to squeeze between a pair of ankle-high rocks he can feel more than see. Picks up into a jog.

Hurtles himself into the darkness.

Leaning. Running.

His hip grazes one of the bigger boulders. He skims off the rock. Bounces to his right like a pinball. Keeps going.

The thunder thrums through the craggy ground. Reaches its throb up into his ankles, into his calves. Quaking and then receding.

The dark gapes before him, a featureless void, and he runs into it face first. Unperturbed by the abyss.

Then he hits the woods, and the world turns solid again. The tree trunks just that little bit darker than the night. Stringing up columns around him. Markers. He runs a couple of feet into the forest.

Then he takes another sharp left. Runs back the way he'd been walking, weaving through the mess of foliage on a parallel line. Instincts alone keeping him on his feet here.

He needs to double back. Circle around whoever might be back there.

Another wave. Another frequency.

If someone is following him, they'll be in for a big surprise. And soon.

He feels a smile slit his lips at the thought. Teeth wet in the opening. Lips curling at the corners.

He loves surprises.

CHAPTER 108

Darger gaped at the blank space where he'd been, where he should be. Blinked as though he might reappear in the vacancy.

Nothing.

Just a mess of rocks jutting up from the ground. A scrubby bush here and there, plants taking root in the shallow soil built up in dipped spaces in the rocky terrain. Scraggly and withered, like a mangy dog.

All of the silhouettes flickered in the blue glow. A shimmering, fluttering piece of land. An Alaskan landscape painted in the lightning's glow. Empty of life.

The lightning sheared off to black. Left her staring into nothing.

She swallowed. Throat feeling sandy. Dry despite her skin and hair being soaked.

The rain kept pouring. The thunder roared and then grumbled.

She swallowed again. Some empty feeling expanding in her gut. Quivering there.

Then she scrambled forward all at once. Either instinct or desperation twitching the muscles in her legs. Thrusting her over the ground.

Maybe he's hiding behind one of the rocks up there. Maybe.

She could still picture a bigger rock there. One of the better hiding spaces he would have had.

She ran for it. Or for where she thought it was.

The dark once again stretched out. The lightning seeming to delay its next appearance for dramatic effect.

445

She slowed a little when she felt she was getting close. Pointed the gun in front of her. The Glock made the faintest ripple in the blackness before her. Its matte polymer blacker than black.

She staggered onward. Feet stabbing into the rocky ground. Legs feeling almost numb.

The lightning flared just as she came upon the big boulder. The column of electricity sizzling as it angled to the earth.

She did a jump stop just past the boulder. Swept her gun into the place behind the rock.

Empty.

Nothing.

She swiveled back around. Pointed the gun behind her.

But the light was already gone.

The shadow closed around her like a fist. Thick night air encroaching. Constricting.

Dark.

Dark all around.

She backpedaled. Swiveled the gun back and forth in front of her. Pointed it at nothing. Uncertain now. Untethered from the reality of her situation, which had seemed so solid until just now.

Where the fuck is he?

She stepped into a puddle. Heard the plunk and splash. Then felt the cold fluid envelope her foot a beat later.

Shit.

The lightning flared again. She looked down at her soggy boot. Lifted it. Watched water sluice out of the eyelets housing the laces.

Then she heard a flutter of footsteps. Loud clapping against the wet stone. A rapid beating like bat wings but deeper, thicker.

The pitter-patter echoed off the canyon walls. Seemed to be coming from all angles. Everywhere at once.

She spun. Lifted her gun. Whirled it in front of her. Looking for any movement in that stop-motion flicker all around her.

The light cut out.

Dark.

Nothing.

Darger gasped in a breath. Lips bucking and lurching. Felt like a fish trying to breathe in the open air.

She stared into the gloom. Squinted. Willed herself to be able to see through it.

Something solid reached out of the murk and struck her. Center mass. Took her from the back. A bony knob colliding with her spine, accelerating into her with a loud pop. Pain exploding outward from her vertebrae.

The force ripped her off her feet. Flung her into the emptiness.

She floated. Laid out like Superman. Drifting. Felt gravity ripping.

She could still feel that bone driving into her back. Then his arms cinching around her middle.

The word *tackle* occurred to her. Two distinct syllables among the gibbering noise inside.

Then she crashed to the ground. Bright light bursting inside her skull. Teeth clacking shut hard.

Pain.

She skidded over wet stone. Belly down. Slushy sounds all around her.

His weight came down on top of her. Crushed out her breath.

Pain.

Thunder roared around them. Sent a fresh shudder through the rock. A cold vibration convulsing through the earth.

Their bodies tangled in the dark. Limbs intertwining. Hands and legs scrabbling over each other. Confused.

Darger managed to squirt out from under his bulk. Wriggled onto her back. Swung the gun in front of her.

And then he slammed down on her again. What must have been his elbow lancing into her solar plexus.

Pain.

She fired the gun. Twice. Felt the Glock buck in her hand. Heard the twin barks.

His torso flashed there in the orangey muzzle flare. Dark and huge. All above and below the torso left in shadow, left in the void.

And then the light was gone.

She'd missed.

Fired off into the canyon.

He pinned her shooting arm down to the wet slab of stone beneath them. Folded it there like a chicken wing. Trussed meat trapped beneath his knee.

Darger struck out with her free hand. Swung hooks with no leverage. Pattering at that bulky torso. Trying to at least keep him off balance.

But his weight came down. Settled. Squeezed. The hard muscles of his thighs crushing her.

An immense slab of a human writhing atop her. Rough hands sliding over her. Confused, too. Searching her.

It felt like she was fighting the darkness itself. Endless shadow crushing, constricting, snuffing her out.

She jabbed the heel of her hand upward. Thrusting straight instead of hooking. Slammed him. A solid connection for once. Maybe in the chest. Shifted him back perhaps an inch.

She kept the arm there. A lever wedged between them, his weight pressing down again.

He jostled. His wet fingers gripping at her arm and slipping away.

She slid the hand higher. Brought her fingers up over his face. Felt the stubble bristling over an angular jaw, the hair cutting off abruptly at the rim of his mouth.

She jammed an index finger into his lip. Wormed it along the sides of his teeth. Yanked his cheek out to the side like she might rip it off.

The flap of skin drew taut against her finger. Flexed. Popped.

He squirmed and jerked back.

Hurt him.

She could feel it in his body language. Like a wave rolling off of him.

Good.

The lightning flashed, and she saw him finally. His snarling face rising up over her. Dead eyes like black pits over a set of chiseled features.

His back arched. His shadow creeping higher on her, splitting her.

Then the light was gone.

Something leaped in the dark and thumped her on the side of her head.

Twice.

A meaty fist that connected like the head of a sledgehammer.

Motes burst across her field of vision. Little smudges of brightness that spread like a starburst and illuminated nothing.

And then the darkness got bigger.

CHAPTER 109

He rocks forward on his knees. Leans over her.

She's out. Mostly. Wiggling a little now and then. Like a troubled sleeper. Like a bad dream.

He takes her gun. Pries it out of her fingers and tucks it into his belt. Pats her down to make sure there are no other surprises.

Nothing. She's clean.

Finally he sits back and breathes. Two big cold lungfuls of wet air entering him. Filling him. Then blowing away.

He feels the pain flaring where the bitch fishhooked him. Cheek feels ripped at the seams. Hanging there but loosely. Bright agony emitting from the cheekbone and along the jaw.

He tongues the teeth on that side. Tastes blood in his mouth. Salty.

Fucking bitch.

The pain throbs in time with his anger. A sped-up beat. Aggressive.

He sticks out his hands in front of himself. Splays his fingers in the dark. Slowly curling them like claws. Feels some kind of power in all those flexing muscles.

He still has control. Still runs the show out here. And it'll be that way for a while yet, he suspects.

Good e-goddamn-nough.

He shakes his head. Takes another couple breaths. The hood of his jacket has fallen down and cool rain mists the back of his neck. That feels kind of good, at least. Even with the wetness seeping into his clothes, the cool feels good.

His hair hangs in wet tendrils in front of his eyes. Looks like a bunch of noodles there. He slicks it back. More droplets draining down the back of his head and neck.

He wonders a second what morning will bring. Then laughs a little at himself for asking the obvious.

More cops, armed to the fuckin' teeth. That's what the morning will bring.

More dogs. More helicopters. Maybe they'll bring in real troops to finish it off. National Guard or some shit.

Morning probably brings the end for him, the end of his story. Death by cop. That seems plain.

They will overrun him. Outnumber him to the point that they make their victory inevitable, even if he takes out a slew before it's done.

So this is the last night.

Well so fucking what? Everyone reaches their last night. From the day we're born, we're just counting down the days, winding down the clock. And out of all those thousands of nights, one of them has to be the last one for each and every one of us.

I just get to do it on my own terms. Write the end of my own story. Go out how I want, when I want.

Gotta make it count.

Then he looks over to the dark spot where she lies. Can only really see her when the lightning flashes.

Her brow furrowed. Lips pursed into some subtle scowl. One of those serious-looking sleepers. A lot of fight in this one.

But what to do with her?

Seems like he should come up with something special, no? It'll serve as a grand finale of sorts, whether he wants that or not.

The rain whispers against the rocks as his imagination starts whirring. The runoff babbling that endless hiss.

He needs to make an example.

CHAPTER 110

Darger woke to being dragged by the ankle. Shoulder blades skidding over the slab of wet stone. Head lolling back and forth on a limp neck.

Pain throbbed inside her skull. Piercing twinges like the stab of an ice pick. The hurt somehow lined up with her heartbeat. Rhythmic brain punctures pounding along.

Her eyelids fluttered. Opened.

She stared into a roiling mess. The dark clouds above like tendrils of black smoke curling around each other. The open sky over the canyon.

Then the wall of the cliff formed in her field of vision. A darkness looming over her right shoulder. Blocking out all the light that way.

The night was brighter now. Just a touch. Silvery moonlight poking through the clouds. Offering shimmering contours in the darkness, even if some of the shapes were still too dark to be understood.

The cold had bloomed, it seemed. Iciness saturating her flesh from head to toe. A wintry touch creeping into the night air fully. She could kind of see it in her breath, little plumes faintly visibly against the glinting moonlight.

Lightning skittered across the sky. A forked bolt of brightness. Flashing and waning.

And his silhouette was there before her. Broad shoulders swaying as he moved. Body tilted back toward her.

His grip felt metallic on her ankle. Steel cylinders digging into her flesh. His strength pulling her over the ground with little apparent effort.

She stared at the back of his head. Or the darkened shape of it. Didn't break her gaze from it. Didn't blink.

The gun was gone. She knew that before her fingers even fished down into the empty holster on her hip, the flap cold and wet.

Emotions flooded her, arriving after some delay. Soft things. Fearful things. But she tamped them down, hard and fast.

No fear now. Only fight.

She resisted the urge to sit up. Resisted the urge to tense herself and struggle.

Her body held limp instead. A sack of potatoes with arms and legs being tugged over the vast wetness.

He was oblivious to her state for the moment. She needed to press that advantage. It was the only one she had.

She licked her lips. Let her eyes dance around her, the rocky terrain sprawling in all directions, the scattered bits of undergrowth here and there, all of it cast in murky silhouettes.

Then she extended her right arm. Fingertips skimming over the craggy ground.

Watched his head to see if he'd turn back. Notice the change in his payload.

He didn't. His head kept facing outward.

She patted around. A sheet of wet stone sliding by. Felt like there was about a quarter inch of water laid out over everything. Fingertips dipping into the endless puddle.

Then she found it. Wrist butting against something hard. Angular. Hand clutching it quickly before it was gone, pulling it close to get a look.

A rock.

A rock about the size of a grapefruit.

Again she resisted the urge to act, to fling the stone at his head, to bring on the final confrontation here and now.

Better to wait. To catch him off guard.

She tucked her hand down in the folds of her wadded-up jacket. Concealed the rock there.

And she waited.

CHAPTER 111

Claudia Rhodes staggers toward the light on legs gone numb. Something divine shimmers in the road ahead. Something that adds solemn weight to her chest.

She shivers from the cold, from the religious feelings stirring inside, from that crooked glow waiting at the end of the logging road. She almost can't bear to look.

Her gaze won't seem to lock on the camp some few hundred yards ahead, eyes flitting of their own accord, turning away from the tents, the squat buildings, the spotlights angling down on it all.

Some superstitious part of her expects it to all go away. A mirage folding up into nothing before her eyes. More dark woods rising to blot out the encampment.

Pessimism coos dark words in her head.

There's no salvation. Not here.

Still, she presses on. Persists. Moves for the camp even if she can't bring herself to look at it directly.

Her feet scrape at the dirt road. Sink into the mud. The wet sand clumping funny around the soles of her shoes. Deep footprints.

And the lights grow closer, grow bigger. Soon she can see movement there.

Silhouettes framed in bright doorways. The blur of foot traffic scuttling everywhere on the grounds. Bees buzzing around the hive.

The land tilts underfoot. Sets her on an incline. And the final climb toward the light feels real all at once. Concrete.

When Darkness Falls

She lifts her head. Moisture weeps down her back. Gathers in her eyebrows and drips down over her cheekbones.

One of the spotlights points down into the road before her. Slices a shaft out of the darkness.

She steps into the glowing circle. Watches the details of her limbs come into stark focus, the wet clothes swaddling them. Somehow feels the light on her skin — a throbbing prickle. Icy.

And then there are people around. Sentries rushing for her. Gibbering. Faces blazing with excitement and concern. Bright eyes and wet teeth.

Her mind pulls her away from the moment. Retracts deeper into her skull like a tortoise head. Overwhelmed.

More faces gather near her. Flutter about her like jack-o'-lanterns. Lips flapping. A silent movie.

Still, she moves for the camp. More brightness. More pins and needles pricking all over.

They take her there. Rush her into a med tent set up along the edge of things. Sit her down on a cot there.

She blinks. Stares down at the hem of her pants. Watches droplets drip down from there.

When she looks up again, Agent Loshak is there. Kneeling in front of her. Eyes wide to try to connect with hers.

He speaks slowly. Carefully. And she hears him.

"Are the others OK?"

Rhodes blinks again. Feels a rush of emotion flood her skull. Scalding fluid lurching into her cheeks.

She bursts into tears.

CHAPTER 112

They stopped all at once. That strange momentum of being dragged over the wet stone cutting out. Leaving Darger feeling strange, vulnerable, cold, and alone as inertia settled over her.

He released her ankle. Let her foot drop to the rocky ground. It splatted into the wet and lay still.

She closed her eyes most of the way. Watched him through slitted lashes.

His bulky silhouette lumbered into the deeper shadows. Footsteps scuffing away from her.

Gone.

Empty.

Quiet.

Then he dug at something nearby. Sounded like pine boughs swishing over the soft earth. Whispering and scraping.

All went quiet again for a second. Darger listened to her pulse in her ears. Gripped the rock tighter. Told herself to wait, to wait, to wait.

His footsteps shuffled back toward her. Slapping at the sheet of wetness laid over the rock. Kicking wet burbles everywhere.

When he came back into view, he had a stick balanced in front of himself. A long rod with a familiar curve to it. A heavier-looking metal wedge on one end.

The reality came to Darger all at once.

An axe.

He has an axe.

He dropped the weapon to one hand. Leaned a palm on the

handle with the head stabbed into the ground like a cane.

"Wake up," he said.

Darger didn't move. Didn't breathe.

He raised his voice. Something raspy in it.

"Hey!"

He leaned the axe handle against his hip and clapped his hands a couple of times. Wet slaps echoing everywhere.

"Come on, now. Rise and shine, sweetheart. I think you're going to want to be up for this. You're part of something here. Something important."

He waited half a second.

"You wouldn't be fakin', would ya?"

He stepped closer. Bent at the waist. Leaned in real close.

Closer.

Closer still.

His face hovered just beyond hers. She could feel his breath flutter over the bridge of her nose, could smell something sour in it.

Darger kicked. Twisted her hips. Brought her leg around to hammer at the back of his knee.

She felt the top of her foot catch the curved place where the thigh and calf meshed.

Felt the joint buckle.

Something in his leg popped.

He toppled forward. Off-balance. Planted his free hand on the rock floor just next to Darger's head.

Darger spun. Catapulted herself around. Swung her arm along with the uncoiling of her body.

Banged the rock down on his flattened hand.

She threw all of herself into it. The force of her torquing hips unloading. Expelling.

His hand crumpled beneath the stone. Collapsed.

Bones crushed.

Shattered.

Splintered.

He screamed. Scrabbled back. Flailed.

Ended up on hands and knees. Trying still to back away.

Eyes and mouth wide open. Lips chittering out wordless sounds.

Darger dove after him.

She brought the rock up and down again. Bashed the bad hand like she was wielding a hammerhead the size of a grapefruit. Hit so hard she felt the impact recoil up into her shoulder.

He screamed again. Shrill. Raspy falsetto.

He brought the bad paw up. Hugged it into his chest.

A twisted-looking thing. A smashed spider at the end of his arm.

The lightning flared. Revealed some toddler look etched into the folds of his face. A cartoon grimace.

Darger brought the rock up over her shoulder. Bent at the waist as she heaved it down with both hands.

Crushed his good hand. More tiny bones splintering. The crunch audible this time. Shredded wheat.

The prop of his arm skittered out from under him. Planted him facedown in that endless puddle.

And then she was on him. Turning around. Riding the bronco. Thighs clenched around his waist like a cello.

He bucked. Hard. Whole body thrusting backward in a burst, flinging her bodyweight about.

But she held on. Gripped him by the meaty shoulders.

Then she shifted. Drove one pointy knee into his spine.

He moaned. Squirmed.

Her elbow meshed with his brain stem. She shoved his face

460

down into the muck.

He fought still. Jerked and lurched. Tried to throw her off.

But she kept her grip. Grabbed on tighter while he really thrashed.

And then she picked her spot to jam his face into the puddle and grind. Felt his skull grating at the craggy stuff. Lips still gibbering, blowing bubbles in the sheet of wetness.

It felt like trying to wrestle a pit bull. All hard slabs of muscle underneath her. Bulky and bulging.

He ripped his head out of the water. Bucked and lurched again.

She waited this time. Let him thrash around longer. Let him spend himself.

Then she timed up her elbow drop. Got his nose straight into the rock. Heard it crack like a small-caliber gunshot, followed by a gristly pop as the cartilage splintered against the shard of bone.

Broken.

For sure.

When he picked up his head, the blood drained out of his nostrils. A gushing red waterfall tumbling over his lips, over his chin.

He didn't fight as hard after that. The strength draining from him all at once. Still moving beneath her, but there was no energy to it.

Even the biggest bully in the world goes as soft as high-thread-count sheets once you shatter his fucking nose. Note to self.

Still, she had to wrestle with him a while to get either of his arms behind his back. Losing her grip a few times before she got hold. His busted hands already swelling like balls of rising dough.

She wrenched his left arm. Pinned it under her knee. Got the first side of the cuffs secured.

He seemed to struggle harder when he heard the *zzziiiip* of the tiny plastic teeth locking into place, felt the zip tie pinch into the soft flesh of his wrist.

He threw himself back again, and Darger held on. Grabbed one shoulder and one handful of hair. Gritted her teeth while he flailed.

She wriggled up higher on his back. Ground her forearm into the back of his skull again. Shoved his broken nose into the rock and swished it back and forth over the craggy surface like she was trying to grate what was left of his snout into shredded cheese.

He screamed into the shallow water. Gurgling and spitting. Kicked both his legs, arched his back again, like he was trying to swim away from her.

Then he let up. Deflated. Gasped for breath.

And she wrangled his second arm behind him. Wrested those thick cords of muscle under her command. Got the other side of the cuff snugged up tight.

She leaned back and breathed. Icy night air rolling into her. Feeling strange against her fiery throat and lungs. Stinging. Painful.

The rain beat down. Dappled at her forehead, at her brow. And the thunder boomed and rolled over the land, farther away now.

He just lay there on his belly. Arms pinned behind his back. Fighting just to keep his head out of the water. Face plopping down every few seconds and bobbing back up.

And all at once it was over.

CHAPTER 113

When Darger finally caught her breath, she squatted down beside the Butcher. She fumbled at the jacket and finally found her Glock tucked into his waistband. It felt good to have the weapon in her hand again.

Then she kept searching and found another gun — a Baretta — tucked near the small of his back. She took that, too.

"What's your name?"

He laid there, silent and unmoving. But she knew he was awake. The faint silver light of the moon reflected off of the whites of his eyes, and every few seconds, those glimmering orbs disappeared when he blinked.

"OK, listen carefully," Darger said. "I'm going to help you to your feet. You're going to walk slowly in front of me and do exactly what I say."

She tried to come up with a plan. Get him up. Get moving. Head back to the cave. Back to Sadie. She'd thought that far ahead, but then what? Even if she uncuffed him, he wouldn't be able to climb with two busted hands.

I'll figure it out when we get there.

"This next part is important," she went on. "If you try to run, I'm going to shoot you in the foot. Do you understand me? I won't kill you. I'll just make it hurt more than it already does."

Darger had done the math. Her gut told her that this guy would try for the old suicide-by-cop routine if he had the chance. Would rather go down here and now than allow himself to be trapped in a cell somewhere.

When he didn't respond, she nudged him with the gun.

"Nod if you understand."

A second passed. And then another.

Finally, she saw the slightest downward movement of his chin.

"Good."

She kept the gun on him. Leaned over and took hold of his upper arm, poised to pull him up.

There was a sudden crash in the foliage off to the left. Something big. And it was coming straight for them.

Darger's mind flashed on the bear den they'd seen the day before, and ice water shot through her veins.

She brought the Glock up. Trained it on a break between two scraggly bushes. Tried to keep her breath from coming out in terrified gasps.

She caught a glimpse of it. Something large and solid staggering through the brush.

Darger moved her finger to the trigger. Waited. She'd have to be smart about taking this shot. Had to make sure she got it in the head. The lightning wasn't coming as frequently now. She'd probably have to take her shot in the dark.

Her heart thrashed in her chest like a fish in open air. The pulse in her neck spasming.

It was maybe twenty feet out now. Then ten. Five.

The beast took a step forward and rose up on two legs.

Darger gasped. Finger twitching against the trigger. Her mind taking a few beats to catch up with her eyes.

She lowered the gun.

"Shepard?"

The man stepped closer.

"Agent Darger? Holy Jesus, am I glad to see you."

His eyes flicked down to where Darger had one foot planted on the Butcher's back. She hadn't wanted him getting any ideas while she was distracted with the bear-that-turned-out-to-not-be-a-bear.

"Is that—?"

And without waiting for an answer, Shepard strode forward, pulling a gun from his waistband.

Darger grasped the old man by the arm.

"Shepard, no."

Hatred burned in his eyes as she stared down at the Butcher.

"Do you have any idea what he's done?"

"Yes. I do. But we have to do this the right way." She tightened her grip on his arm. "OK?"

The old man's nostrils flared. And then he nodded.

"What's the plan?"

"We get him up. If he tries anything, shoot him in the leg or the foot. It's important that we keep him alive."

"Alright. Then what?" Shepard asked.

"There's a cave not far from here. Sadie's there."

All at once the man's face softened.

"You have Sadie? Is she OK?"

"She's fine. You've got one tough granddaughter."

Shepard smiled at that.

"Make that two tough granddaughters."

"Kira's with you?"

In lieu of an answer, Shepard turned. Gave a single whistle. A moment later, a tiny silhouette appeared, taking the same path Shepard had to the clearing. She went to her grandfather and clung to him, as if suddenly shy to be around other people again.

Shepard locked eyes with Darger.

"Ready when you are."

☾

A fire roiled in the middle of the craggy cavern, and the thrashing light gleamed against the wet rock near the cave mouth. Shone like orange glass.

The cave Shepard and Kira had holed up in was about a half-mile from the one Darger and Sadie had found. It was smaller, too, but lower to the ground, accessible to even the Butcher's crushed hands. He'd been able to scrabble in with his wrists bound behind his back, Darger and Shepard each clutching an arm to keep him upright.

The reunited sisters huddled near the flames, both wearing some of the oversized shirts from Shepard's pack — far too big, but dry. Sadie rubbed her hands together and then held her fingertips up to the fire.

The Butcher sat in the shadows at the back of the cave, staring at the ground. Gummy blood caked around his mouth from where his broken nose had drained. A listless look pulled his face down, something almost saggy in the cheeks and brow where all that fierceness had been.

"I'll take first watch," Shepard said, eying the killer.

Darger stared at the man huddled in the shadows. Part of her still didn't trust the Butcher, wanted to keep one eye on him at all times. But she could see the fight had gone from him, utterly and completely.

"OK," Darger said. "Though I don't know if I'll actually be able to sleep."

"You should try. We're going to have a long hike out tomorrow."

Darger nodded and watched steam rise from her shoes where she placed them near the fire.

They were silent for some time before Shepard spoke again.

"Did you happen to see any of the others?"

Darger shook her head.

"It's just been me and Sadie the whole time," she said. "I heard gunshots at one point. After we ran from camp."

The furrows on Shepard's face deepened when he frowned.

"That was Wishnowsky. He didn't make it."

The silence swelled. Stretched out. Shepard went on.

"The bastard got Haywood, too. Not sure about Chief Rhodes... or Marilyn... but I'm not optimistic."

Darger felt a flash of anger and hatred. Reconsidered her insistence that the Butcher be handed over to the proper authorities. But it fizzled quickly.

Death was what he wanted, she was certain. For that reason alone, it was worth it to keep him alive.

CHAPTER 114

Rex glances up at the sky. He and Jerry had set out that morning at the first weak glimmer of twilight. The first team to restart the search. And even now, two hours later, the sun continues its battle against the dark clouds hanging over the island like a woolen blanket.

The anemic light renders the landscape in grayscale. A monochromatic backdrop in charcoal and silver.

Rex doesn't mind. Doesn't even mind the fact that it's still raining. He's wearing a poncho, and the exertion of the hike and the desire to complete the mission keep a fire burning in his core.

His mind flashes on what he'd seen the day before. The mangled dogs in the pit. The dying man crawling through the brush.

It had shaken him. As he'd huddled in one of the logging cabins at base camp, shoveling spoonfuls of tasteless stew into his maw, he'd felt his resolve wavering. Search and rescue wasn't without risks, but this? Well, this was something else entirely. That man with his guts torn out could have been him. One of those dogs could have been Jerry.

And yet, as much as Rex had felt an almost primordial urge to flee, he'd resisted it. Decided he'd sleep on it. And lo and behold, after a halfway decent night's sleep and a warm breakfast, the fear he'd felt the night before had evaporated.

Even more than that, he feels a new sense of purpose now. He will not run from the Butcher. He will not let that scum win.

Rex Morton is a lot of things, but he isn't a quitter.

Up ahead, Jerry hurdles a fallen tree. A few moments later, it's Rex's turn to clamber over.

He's keeping the dog closer today. Wary of the possibility of more traps.

They continue on for another half hour or so. Picking their way around small boulders and scrubby undergrowth.

Jerry disappears over the crest of a small hill, and Rex follows. It's only when he reaches the apex that he realizes the dog is no longer in sight.

Worse, he doesn't hear the bell either.

Rex freezes. Scans the scenery from left to right and back again. Ears straining to hear over the faint patter of the rain.

But there is nothing.

He opens his mouth, about to call the dog back, when he hears it.

A single bark.

CHAPTER 115

Darger paced back and forth near the mouth of the cave, still feeling a palpable sense of relief at the fact that it was morning. As if part of her had believed it might not come. That they'd be stuck in some sort of permanent midnight.

Outside, the rain continued, alternating between sprinkling and pouring. Now that they were sheltered and dry, Darger was almost glad for the rain. Shepard had rigged up a small tarp just outside the cave, which had allowed them to collect more than enough water to keep them all moderately hydrated.

Well, except for the Butcher. Darger had offered him water three times now, and each time he refused. Still battling for some shred of control. The fool.

Darger's stomach grumbled. She tried to remain grateful that they weren't thirsty *and* hungry, but all she'd eaten in the past 36 hours were a few Pop-Tarts and some protein bars, and now that the adrenaline from the previous day had faded, she was starving. The empty feeling in her gut seemed to intensify every hour, throbbing along with her heartbeat.

A faint scrape sounded behind her. She turned and saw Shepard uncoiling from his position on the floor. He rose to his feet and came to peer outside.

"Still coming down, eh?"

"Yep."

He stretched and something popped in his back.

"You still think hiking out is the way to go?"

Darger nodded.

"If we knew for certain they were going to use the

470

helicopter again, I'd say we might as well stay put and figure out a way to signal that we're here. But with the storm, who knows? I'd rather be proactive."

Shepard crossed his arms.

"Can't say I fancy the idea of waiting around. So I'm with you." He cocked his head toward the sleeping girls. "Guess I'll get the kids up, then. No reason to dally."

There were grumbles from both girls at being awoken, which was followed by further grumbling about the lack of food.

"I wish we had more Pop-Tarts," Sadie said.

"Me too," Darger agreed.

Kira rubbed her eyes.

"I have to pee."

"Sadie, take your sister to go pee." Shepard pointed at his pack. "There's TP and hand sanitizer in the front pocket."

While the two girls loped off into the trees to answer nature's call, Darger and Shepard began packing up their meager supplies, filling water bottles, and making sure the fire was out.

"How long do you think it'll take to get back down to the road?" Darger asked.

Shepard stooped over the tarp, folding it into a rectangle and then rolling it into a tight cylinder.

"A few hours. The good news is that it's mostly downhill. The bad news is that we have to go around that damn swamp. But I think if we keep to the—"

"Grampa! Guess what?"

The girls scurried back into sight, their faces flushed with excitement.

Shepard scowled.

"Hold on a minute, Sadie. You're interrupting." He blinked

at Darger. "Now what was I saying?"

"The swamp."

"Oh right." He stuck his arm out. "I think if we keep on this side of it, that'll be the quickest way around. It'll add almost an hour to the hike, but there's nothing to be done."

He finished stowing the last few items in his pack and slung it over his shoulder.

"OK, girls—" He frowned, eyes moving from side to side, scanning the area. "What the hell…"

Darger followed his gaze.

Sadie and Kira had disappeared.

Darger whirled around, certain she'd find the Butcher gone, certain he was responsible. But he was still in the same place. A dark, inanimate lump toward the back of the cave.

Shepard stalked a few paces into the woods and brought his hands to his mouth.

"Sadie! Kira!"

Darger heard something then. A faint tinkling sound and then… a voice? No. Not human.

Shepard started to shout again, and she put a hand on his arm.

"Wait."

He turned, panic in his eyes. Darger held up a finger.

"Listen."

The sound came again. This time Darger knew exactly what it was.

The barking of a dog.

And then she spotted them. Sadie and Kira, running alongside a German shepherd.

They led the dog right up to the mouth of the cave, eyes gleaming with delight.

"Grampa, see what we found?"

When Darkness Falls

"I think maybe it's the other way around," Shepard said, chuckling. "I think he found us."

EPILOGUE

Darger stood outside an interview room at the Ketchikan Correctional Center, bundled into a wool sweater she'd bought at one of the gift shops and clutching a giant cup of hot cocoa. It had been approximately 24 hours since their rescue — she'd taken several near-scalding showers and guzzled about a gallon of hot beverages, but she still couldn't seem to drive that last bit of chill from her bones.

Loshak was inside, taking his turn at interrogating Walton Banks. So far no one had gotten a word out of him. But he hadn't asked for a lawyer, either, so they kept trying.

The door at the end of the hall opened, and Chief Rhodes stepped into the corridor. Her face was pale and drawn.

"You OK?"

"No," Rhodes said, coming to a stop and leaning against the cinderblock wall. "Whipple and I just did the family notifications."

"All of them?"

Rhodes nodded.

"Bohanon's mother, Haywood's father and stepmother, and Wishnowsky's ex-wife. I guess she's technically still his wife, but… whatever."

Darger had only witnessed one of the death notifications — Shephard finding out about Marilyn when they reached the temporary base camp. Once was enough.

"Couldn't Whipple do it by himself?"

"Sure. But I volunteered," Rhodes said. "I had some idea that it'd make it easier on the loved ones. If I was there to… I don't know… explain things. But how do you explain something like this?"

Darger pictured Bohanon's head on a spike again, and Rhodes scrubbed her face, as if trying to rid herself of the same image. She angled her head toward the interview room door.

"He said anything yet?"

"Nope."

"Think he will?"

Darger considered it.

"Somehow I doubt it." She shrugged. "It happens. They get arrested, and they clam up. Refuse to talk. On TV, the villain is always dying to tell their story. To let us in on their depraved plan. Some of these guys never say a word."

"Other than to insist that they're innocent," Rhodes said.

"Right. I think for some of them, all that superiority they felt at getting away with it vanishes. So a new game begins with the goal of seeing how much information they can withhold. Guess it's all they have left."

Rhodes shook her head.

"You know, when word first went around base camp that he was in custody, I overheard some of the search and rescue guys talking about trying to get in the transport helicopter with him so they could toss him out at altitude. Upset about the men and dogs they'd lost, obviously. And I was sitting there thinking, 'Yeah right, motherfuckers. You have to get in line behind me first.' But then I got a look at what you did to him." Rhodes let out a bitter laugh. "And I thought, 'Christ, it looks like he got his nose caught in a meat grinder.'"

She sighed.

"Anyway, I don't care whether the little shit talks or not. There's a whole island of evidence against him. If he wants to rot away in prison with his little fucking secrets keeping him company, let him. The sooner, the better.”

☾

Banks still hadn’t talked by the time Darger and Loshak flew back to Quantico. Darger had slept for much of the flight, and now, on the car ride home from the airport, Loshak seemed to want to catch up for the lost time.

“I’ve been thinking about Walton Banks and where he fits on the dismemberment spectrum. From what I observed at the scene, I suspect the initial decapitation of his friend, Taylor Higgins, was a classic aggressive dismemberment. Done in a blind rage, and aside from dumping him in the cellar, no real effort to conceal the crime. From there, the subsequent crimes showed the hallmarks of a ritual. An homage to the original murder.”

“Aggressive to necromanic, then,” Darger said, nodding. “I had that thought once I saw the body parts near the bear den. I mean, it’s really not cannibalism, but it almost felt close to it. A lot of killers who eat the flesh of their victims make it out to be an almost ceremonial thing. And there’s something about Banks feeding the body parts of his victims to a predator that feels like he was making some sort of… offering.”

“In any case, I figure he’ll make an interesting addition to our course materials,” Loshak said.

Reverting to profiler mode somehow calmed Darger. The academic language etched an order into things, an order she hadn’t felt out in the woods.

When they reached her house, Darger bid Loshak farewell and climbed out of the car. She pulled her suitcase from the trunk, the wheels *bump-bump-bump*ing over the seams in the sidewalk leading up to the house.

Owen must have heard her coming, because the door opened before she'd reached the front steps.

He scrambled down to meet her.

"You're limping. Why are you limping? You said you weren't hurt—"

"I'm not. Unless you count the fifteen blisters on my feet."

He wrapped his arms around her and pulled her close.

"You can't do that."

"Do what?"

"You can't go off into the woods and disappear. That's not allowed."

"I promise to never do it again."

Owen squeezed her once more.

"Good." He stepped back and plucked the suitcase from her hand, pulling her inside. "What do you need? Food? Sleep? A hot bath? Your wish is my command."

Darger already knew her answer.

"I want to lie in bed with every blanket we own, and eat a big bowl of soup."

Owen laughed.

"OK. That is way more specific than I thought it'd be."

"I had a lot of time to consider this."

"I don't suppose you have a particular soup in mind?"

"One quart of every kind they have at Park Street Deli."

Owen laughed harder.

"They serve like six soups a day."

"Yeah."

"That's over a gallon of soup."

"Good point. It might not be enough. Better make it two quarts of the chicken noodle."

COME PARTY WITH US

We're loners. Rebels. But much to our surprise, the most kickass part of writing has been connecting with our readers. From time to time, we send out newsletters with giveaways, special offers, and juicy details on new releases.

Sign up for our mailing list at:
http://ltvargus.com/mailing-list

SPREAD THE WORD

Thank you for reading! We'd be very grateful if you could take a few minutes to review it on Amazon.com.

How grateful? Eternally. Even when we are old and dead and have turned into ghosts, we will be thinking fondly of you and your kind words. The most powerful way to bring our books to the attention of other people is through the honest reviews from readers like you.

ABOUT THE AUTHORS

Tim McBain writes because life is short, and he wants to make something awesome before he dies. Additionally, he likes to move it, move it.

You can connect with Tim via email at tim@timmcbain.com.

L.T. Vargus grew up in Hell, Michigan, which is a lot smaller, quieter, and less fiery than one might imagine. When not click-clacking away at the keyboard, she can be found sewing, fantasizing about food, and rotting her brain in front of the TV.

If you want to wax poetic about pizza or cats, you can contact L.T. (the L is for Lex) at ltvargus9@gmail.com or on Twitter @ltvargus.

LTVargus.com

CPSIA information can be obtained
at www.ICGtesting.com
Printed in the USA
LVHW110252201122
733282LV00024B/434/J